The Enemy Called "They"

Randall C. Hale

PublishAmerica
Baltimore

© 2003 by Randall C. Hale.
All rights reserved. No part of this book may be reproduced, stored in a retrieval system or transmitted in any form or by any means without the prior written permission of the publishers, except by a reviewer who may quote brief passages in a review to be printed in a newspaper, magazine or journal.

First printing

Copyright Permission
Scripture taken from the NEW AMERICAN STANDARD BIBLE®, Copyright © 1960, 1962, 1963, 1968, 1971, 1972, 1973, 1975, 1977, 1995 by the Lockman Foundation. Used by permission.

Associated press article written by Tom Hays Reprinted with permission of the Associated Press.

ISBN: 1-59286-027-3
PUBLISHED BY PUBLISHAMERICA, LLLP
www.publishamerica.com
Baltimore

Printed in the United States of America

This book is dedicated to all those who have served, sacrificed, and dedicated their lives and fortunes to freedom and overcoming tyranny throughout the world. Although they are few, scattered throughout the world, and do not personally know each other, a Band of Brothers and Sisters still carries on for that cause.

ACKNOWLEDGMENTS

Special thanks to Rick Hake for his time, interest, encouragement and support while this book was in progress.

Thank you Chris Bogden for your faith and confidence that I could accomplish writing a book while it was still a dream.

Thank you Joe and Joan (the J's), Don, and Caroline for your encouragement and support.

And I cannot forget Robert and Maxine Hale (Mom and Dad). You both were there for me from beginning to end even when you disagreed. I love you both.

May God bless you all for being there when I needed you most.

I feel compelled to give acknowledgment to the those local, state, and federal officials allegedly elected and chosen to govern, without whose actions this book would not have been inspired and written. I do pray for them and although it is sometimes difficult, still love them as human beings.

CONTENTS

Introduction		9
Chapter 1	The Bill of Rights and What It Means to Me	13
Chapter 2	Evil's Methodology for Enslavement	28
Chapter 3	Methodology Tools	37
Chapter 4	The Hate and Prejudice Template (Divide and Conquer)	74
Chapter 5	Shock, Humiliation, and Intimidation Template	80
Chapter 6	The Global Template Called the Programming and Control Template, Better Known as the Politics Game	93
Chapter 7	Actual Oral Arguments in the Court Case	106
Chapter 8	I Was the Plaintiff and So Were You	119
Chapter 9	The Corrupted Operating System	139
Chapter 10	A Few Lies Exposed	162
Chapter 11	For Your Safety and Security	188
Chapter 12	The "Partisan System" Exposed	215
Chapter 13	The Revealing! Christian, Do You Really Believe?	229
Chapter 14	The Truth	241
Chapter 15	Freedom from the Clique	258
Epilogue		273

INTRODUCTION

The statement, "None are more hopelessly enslaved than those who falsely believe they are free" is attributed to Goethe over 200 years ago. I interpret that to mean, those who mistakenly believe they are free are hopelessly enslaved.

What is revealed in this book is not for the *faint hearted* and if you are an individual that cannot cope with the truth, then proceed no further, put the book down and walk away right now.

This book is created due to recent personal experiences, observations, and lessons learned in Jackson County, Oregon. You will see the City of Medford, Jackson County, and Oregon referred to many times. I am positive that many reading this book will be able to relate the occurrences revealed in this book to occurrences happening where they live.

Copyright law requires that a person obtain written permission to quote material someone else writes, even if the author provides the credit to the individual that wrote the material. I was taught that the basis for copyright law is to keep a person from *plagiarizing* someone else's work and passing it off as his or her own work. If a person gives the credit to those that wrote or published material that is used as a reference in a book, then that person is not claiming the material as his or her own. The true purpose in copyright law is to prevent someone from *selling* another person's material as his or her own and can be considered a greedy purpose.

So, if credit is provided the individual that wrote the material, there is no purpose in having to obtain written permission to use that material other than greed. Or is there?

Did you know that copyright laws are derived from the old British feudal system and that these copyright laws started approximately three centuries ago? Am I mistaken, or do we have a huge celebration and holiday on July 4th each year celebrating our Independence from that British feudal system? Why then, and for what purposes then, are we still under that system's law? Isn't that hypocrisy?

There is not one thought that human beings possess that has not already been thought by the Creator and given to us by that same Creator to share, thus, knowledge is not ours to own and hoard for greed and profit. God gave us knowledge, and the wisdom and ability to interpret that knowledge in order to put it to good use, to SHARE with each other, not for personal and financial gain, but for spiritual gain and not to put under a copyright to prevent others from sharing that knowledge. This nation's founding fathers knew this to be true because they were exceptionally wise and intelligent men. An 8th grade education in their day exceeds a 12th grade education and is equivalent to a college education by today's standards.

Isn't it amazing, that in a supposedly free nation, with supposedly free speech and freedom of the press, a person is required to obtain written permission to "quote" definitions from a legal reference, a standard dictionary, or quote from a newspaper? Although I did request permission, I did not receive that permission from West Group to quote legal definitions from *Black's Law Dictionary* because my request *exceeds what West Group considers a reasonable amount*. Having been refused permission to quote definitions from their law dictionary, I did not attempt to obtain permission to quote from another work published by West Group called *American Jurisprudence*. I did receive permission from *Webster's* who agreed to let me use 10- or 12-word definitions. I decided to use definitions, *as I understood the definitions meanings presented in all the works*, so the definitions for words provided in this book are not direct quotes but are definitions as I understand them and many are composites. News articles are not exact quotes, except one, and are presented, as I understood them. I did gain permission to quote an Associated Press article for a fee. To its credit, The Lockman Foundation included a "permission to quote" statement in *The Bible* it published.

Could it be the real reason for copyright is that THEY want to screen and censor what one may or may not use or write because THEY are hiding something? Yes, THEY are hiding something and THEY use greed as a tool to help keep the secret. What THEY are hiding and who THEY are will be revealed in this book.

A good *investment an individual can make* to discover how their God-given Constitutionally guaranteed freedom is denied is to invest in 6th and 7th edition law dictionaries (such as *Black's Law Dictionaries*), or earlier editions if possible, a standard dictionary such as *Webster's*, and a good thesaurus. All these can be purchased at your local Barnes and Noble bookstore.

Research word definitions and look up synonyms for words that you may not understand that are used in the Constitution, especially the Bill of Rights. Compare the "legal" definitions with the standard dictionary definitions, and especially compare the legal definitions from earlier edition law dictionaries with the newer edition law dictionaries. A *Bible* is another good investment one can make to learn what is going to happen and who is behind what is happening today. If you do not mind spending the time, it is not necessary to purchase the dictionaries. Go to the local library or county legal library and do the research. I found it advantageous to do the word definition research at home so I purchased the legal dictionaries.

Definitions in this book will be explained as I interpreted and understood the meanings read in Black's Law Dictionaries *and* Webster's Dictionary *unless otherwise indicated. I want to make it perfectly clear I do not consider myself to be, nor do I pretend to be an expert at anything, including languages and word uses. I only reveal what I have learned through research, observation and personal experience.*

This book will be focused around Jackson County, Oregon, because that is my home and that is where much has been revealed to me about the methodology, the system, i.e., the conspiracy to keep human beings enslaved.

This book is not about religion. I am not a religious person. I am a Christian, an American, and a human being. I believe that Christianity is a way for human beings to live life, not a religion. Believe me when I tell you I have a long way to go in accomplishing that goal.

This book is not science fiction, has nothing to do with sex, color, gender, ethnic background, religious background, or any other prejudice being used to divide human beings. This book is not for entertainment. It is about life and the truth as it has been revealed to me. As little as three years ago I would not have believed and would have labeled the person insane that told me what is revealed in this book.

This book is about God-given rights that have been constitutionally guaranteed and the *methodology being used to deny those rights.* It is about freedom and slavery. It is about race. It is about the human race and another race that has human beings enslaved and the methodology being used for that purpose. *This book is about the real enemy and what THEY truly represent.*

Mankind is enslaved and there is a scheme, a plan, a system, a methodology, i.e., a conspiracy to keep mankind in that condition and through its simplicity has grown more powerful than human beings can ever imagine. Who or what is behind that methodology will be exposed.

If you want perfection in grammar, spelling, punctuation, and want to look for fault with what is written here, I am sure you can find those things because I do not claim to be perfect. I will not point fingers at individuals because *all human beings are manipulated through deception* and play a part in the methodology. I will present information, as I understand that information. I will question, I will challenge, and I will attempt to stimulate your own sense about right and wrong. I will not judge others, their religions, their beliefs, their cultures, etc. I will make every attempt to avoid playing the finger pointing blame game, although I will present evidence that demonstrates how "We the People" are being *manipulated through deception* into doing the things that we do and the atrocities we commit against each other.

I reveal these things so they can be exposed to the public eye, so the people can make a wise decision, so the people may truly become free. God frees us all and saves us all if only we ask. Christ tried to tell the people, and the people did not listen. He was crucified on a cross for our wrongdoing (misconduct, bad behavior, criminal offenses, unlawful activity, or sin if you prefer) that He was sent to expose. He suffered due to what "We the People" are doing to ourselves, and He suffers because "We the People" continue on the same path. His message is, wake up before it is too late, the deadline is near. Many who read this book will not believe. If that is your choice, so be it. Your only choice is between good and evil, right and wrong, freedom and slavery. That choice is yours to make.

CHAPTER 1

THE U.S. BILL OF RIGHTS AND WHAT IT MEANS TO ME!

Lincoln said, "Study the Constitution!" "Let it be preached from the pulpit, proclaimed in legislatures, and enforced in courts of justice."
A SLAVE is any person being detained by someone else as a possession to provide service or work. A person that has lost or surrendered controls over himself/herself and is dominated by something or someone else is a slave. Anyone working for another is a slave. A few synonyms for slave are bondservant, chattel, toiler, victim, and worker.

SLAVERY is surrendering to another's control or power and letting another dictate what you do, say, think, work, learn, etc.

CHATTEL are possessions such as personal property (car, boat, furniture, SLAVE, etc.). Chattel does not include real estate. So, real estate is not considered a possession or personal property.

BONDSMAN is a person who takes on the responsibility for a debt secured by a bond (slave). In essence a *bondsman is also a slave and is called a bondman.* A bondman although a slave is the head slave and takes responsibility for another slave and/or the debt owed by that slave.

BOND is to transfer something or someone into a debt. A security such as a car, boat, house or SLAVE, or put another way, a person, place or thing that has been put up as security for a debt owed or a loan.

BONDAGE is the period or time required, *by law*, that a slave serves to pay back a debt or loan owed.

BILL OF RIGHTS and what it means to me:
Amendment 1
Congress shall make no law respecting an establishment of religion, or prohibiting the free exercise thereof, or abridging the freedom of speech, or of the press, or the right of the people peaceably to assemble, and to petition the Government for a redress of grievances.
Prohibits Congress from making any laws in regards to organizing a

religion, founding religion or authority over religion, and *prohibits Congress* from passing any laws that forbid people from practicing religious beliefs that the people may choose. *Prohibits Congress* making any laws that restricts the people from verbally expressing ones thoughts or opinions, or from publishing those thoughts and opinions, or other material. *Prohibits Congress* making any laws that restricts the people to *peaceably assemble* anywhere and time they want, in any number they want. *Prohibits Congress* making any laws that restricts the people petitioning the government such as a formal petition or writing letters, or lobbying to set right those complaints and injustices people may have about its government. Government cannot restrict or put limits on these things. *All laws are a restriction, restraint, and/or limit.*

So what are all these hate speech laws being passed? They are unconstitutional. Politically correct speech laws are unconstitutional. Copyright laws are unconstitutional. Laws putting restrictions, such as requiring a permit, on the right to peaceably assemble are unconstitutional. Laws putting restrictions on the petitioning process are unconstitutional. Laws against setting up a church in certain locations are unconstitutional. Laws restricting these things in any way are unconstitutional.

Abridge means to deprive. A few synonyms for abridge are limit, restrict, reduce, and diminish. Recently, in Oregon, laws have been passed abridging the Constitutionally guaranteed right to petition. No longer are the people permitted to petition outside supermarkets, in or around malls, or other public places. Only registered voters are allowed to sign a petition. County clerks now remove those who have not voted in the past 5 years from the active voter list and put them on an inactive list. This means one must re-register to vote. This reduced eligible petition signers in Oregon by a considerable number. In fact, it was reported that there was more than a 50 percent jump in rejected petition signatures due to this one action. Today, in Oregon, one third (33%) of all petition signatures are rejected. This is a travesty. *The Constitutions guarantee the people's right to petition, not just registered voters.* Slowly, through the years, the people that do not vote have surrendered all rights to those that do vote. Even the Constitutional amendments passed in the Oregon Constitution for the past 40 or 50 years favor the registered voters. So, now, in Oregon, if a person is not a registered voter, that person appears to have no rights. It also appears the voters themselves are also being denied their rights.

Petitions allow issues to be placed on the ballot. Voters still get to vote on these issues. According to what I read in newspapers, voters in Oregon are tired due to all the initiatives placed on the ballot. Yet, it is the voters that are putting these issues on the ballot. The voters are concerned as to what the reasons are behind all these initiatives having to be placed on the ballot by the people in the first place. If those chosen to govern were upholding the Constitutions, all these initiatives would not be necessary. In reality, it is those allegedly chosen to govern that have become tired concerning all these initiatives and the petitioning process. These officials would rather have voters vote on measures and constitutional amendments denying the people their rights than face all these issues each election. The election officials claim it is too time consuming for THEM and too much for the *average person* to deal with.

All the laws passed in the county and state abridging the people from petitioning are unconstitutional. State, County and City governments are bound by the same U.S. Constitution as the Federal Government. Although those allegedly elected and chosen to govern in local government are not members in the U.S. Congress, that does not give them the authority, nor have they been provided that authority, to violate the U.S. Constitution's Bill of Rights. But, the voters in Oregon have been and are being *manipulated through deception* into allowing the Oregon Constitution to be rewritten by those now in authority. In fact, I can show at least one instance where the Oregon Constitution has been rewritten in one article to blatantly contradict itself in another article.

I find it deplorable and very sad that the local Oregon newspaper editors are in agreement with the state and local governments in abridging the people's 1st Amendment rights to petition. One would think that the supposedly free press would be the first to speak out against such atrocities. One would think that a supposedly free press would be most concerned about a 1st amendment violation. One would think that these editors would be screaming their heads off in defense for the people's 1st amendment right.

What do the editors advocate? These editors support the right to petition in principle. But, they claim, that principle is groups of thoughtful, involved, citizens asking voters to enact laws the legislature won't or can't, or to repeal laws the legislature shouldn't have enacted. But, what do Oregonians get according to the editors? Oregonians get cynical interest groups bent on dismantling government. Oregonians get paid signature-gathers that don't care about the issues they promote.

As I interpret what the editors claim, they are against the petitioning process for everyone but those willing do it their way. Their way is the marketing way. Their way is to have petitioners go door to door gathering signatures, or at an advertised place where one may sign a petition. Considering most people work, it has now been manipulated that the only time for petitioners to gather signatures is in the evenings and on weekends. This means that petitioners disturb people at home during their dinner, or while getting the children ready for bed, or expect these busy people to come to you to sign the petition. What will the newspaper editors do when the state and local governments abridge the newspaper 1st Amendment right? Or, perhaps that is already being done and the government is dictating what the newspaper can print. Considering what the newspaper editors advocate, it sure makes one wonder!

The primary purpose for the 1st 10 amendments to the Constitution called the Bill of Rights was to *protect the people from each other*. The Bill of Rights was to prevent a "clique" from taking control in government and oppressing other people. The nation's founding fathers knew that humans are *manipulated through deception* into committing atrocities against each other. The Bill of Rights protects the individual or the few from the majority (tyrants). A majority can be as big a tyrant as a king can. The Bill of Rights protects the majority from the few or the individual (tyrant). The nation's founding fathers were very intelligent men with common sense. They knew from first hand experience the tyranny *any* government can impose on the people.

Every house has a foundation and a footing, and whether or not that house stands is based entirely on the foundation and its footing. If termites, carpenter ants, or other insect parasites eat at the foundation, the foundation is weakened or destroyed and the house crumbles. If a small animal such as moles undermines the foundation's footing, the house may collapse. If too much water gathers under the house, it may rot the foundation and undermine the footing. Protecting the foundation and the footing is the most important aspect to keeping the house strong. Preventing termites, carpenter ants and other parasites from destroying the foundation is most important. Preventing moles from undermining the foundations footing is most important. Pumping the water from under the house is important. Protecting the other parts in the house structure against these same threats is also important.

It is the same with our national house. This nation's foundation was built on the Constitution and its Bill or Rights. This nation's foundation for the law is a Constitution. The footing for the Nation's foundation is Christian teachings and values. Today the nation's foundation is being attacked by parasites. The Christian values, which are the footing for the nation's foundation, are under constant attack by those that are eating at its foundation and will eventually result in causing the nations collapse. The nation's laws are changed so they no longer stand on the Constitutional foundation. The parasites have infiltrated our nation and are eating away at the foundation. Moles have been placed within the nation to undermine the nation's government and its Christian teachings and values.

Personally, there are many organizations within government I would like to see dismantled because those organizations have proven to be harmful for the nation and stand against the Constitutional foundation. These organizations are parasites and moles within the nation's government and are slowly eating away at and undermining the nation's foundation and footing.

The holes created in government by these parasites and moles are causing the nation's lifeblood to drain away and now the foundation is rotting. If action is not taken real soon, it will be too late to save the foundation and the house is going to collapse.

I keep hearing about the "Separation of Church and State." Prayer in school was eliminated because a Supreme Court decision in the 1960s determined the First Amendment to the U.S. Constitution advocated the Separation of Church and State. The First Amendment states: *Congress shall make no law respecting an establishment of religion, or prohibiting the free exercise thereof; or abridging the freedom of speech, or of the press; or the right of the People peaceably to assemble, and to petition the Government for a redress of grievances.*

How this was interpreted to mean a Separation of Church and State is beyond me. *It says Congress shall make no law respecting an establishment of religion*, which I interpret to mean they will pass no law relating to any religion or stating a specific religion is the "national" religion. Our country was founded on Christianity, i.e. the Christian way to live life and *not* the Christian religion. There is a huge difference. Congress could pass no law in regards to an association with religion (belief). This has nothing to do with separation of Church and State, but LAW cannot be made giving any faith preference over another. The Supreme Court decision in the 1960s did that exact thing. It MADE LAW respecting an establishment of a *religion called Atheism*. Is this not a *belief* that there is no GOD, or put another way, a belief in non-belief of a GOD. Is this not in itself a religion in non-belief and that LAWS have been made and passed respecting this "belief or adherence in non-belief of a GOD" which in effect is respecting an establishment of religion. Not only does the first amendment state "Congress shall make no law respecting an establishment of religion," it goes on to state "or prohibiting the free exercise thereof." Since the Supreme Court decision concerning the Separation of Church and State, Congress has MADE several LAWS prohibiting freely exercising one's religion, not only the Christian religion, but all other religions as well (prayer in school, at graduations, etc), hence, respecting (giving preference to) the Atheist religion. How was that for twisting and distorting your First Amendment Right to exercise your religious belief?

I remember many years ago I took karate on a little island called Okinawa. The instructor was from Okinawa and was a Buddhist. After each lesson, he insisted we all get on our knees and pray. He prayed to Buddha, I prayed to the Father, Son and Holy Ghost. I prayed to my GOD. That is why I have had a difficult time understanding why people belonging to different religious beliefs get upset when a prayer is said in school or at any public event. What is to prevent anyone from making the prayer to the GOD in whom they believe? Personally, I believe there is only one God, and all human beings are praying to that same God, just calling Him by a different name, *because our languages are different.*

If a person is an Atheist, that person can ignore the prayer. What is the big deal? When someone says a prayer in school or at a public gathering, they are exercising their God-given religious right guaranteed under the U.S. Constitution. It does not mean Congress has made a law respecting an establishment of religion. If the person saying the prayer is Muslim, Buddhist, Christian, Jewish, whatever, while they are praying I pray. Doesn't anyone recognize what is happening? This "Separation of Church and State" is nothing more than another way to distort and twist our Constitution and its Bill of Rights by using *manipulation through deception* in order to deny you your freedom to believe in GOD, and at the same time, keep "We the People" divided. Was this not what the government did in the former Communist Soviet Union, made Atheism the national religion (belief) and the State the supreme power?

Very Basic Religious Comparisons

Christianity—teaches that the secret to life is brotherly love. Teaches and holds greed to be the cause for the world's woes and the secret to life is love. Teaches to fear, yet love God. Teaches that God loves all His creatures.

Teaches that one must accept Jesus as Savior. Teaches to love your enemy. Teaches to treat others the way you want to be treated and to love your neighbor, as you love yourself. Teaches that the God they worship is the God that Abraham, Isaac and Moses worshipped. Teaches that they are not to have any other gods before their God. Teaches that Jesus Christ is God's spirit manifest in the flesh.

Buddhism—teaches that the secret to life is brotherly love. Teaches selfishness causes the world's woes. Teaches the secret to life is love. Teaches loving one's enemies is the greatest achievement in this life. Teaches hatred cannot be stopped until it is under love's power.

Islam—teaches that Christ is the Word and the Spirit of God. Teaches that Abraham, Moses, and all the prophets of God taught essentially the same thing. Teaches to completely submit body and soul to the will of God (Allah). Teaches obedience to God (Allah), results in brotherhood, righteousness and peace. Teaches thou shall have no other Gods before God.

Amendment II
A well regulated Militia, being necessary to the security of a free State, the right of the people to keep and bear Arms, shall not be infringed.
   Well—Means healthy, fighting fit.
   Regulated—Means coordinated or synchronized in the same rules, goals, purposes, and/or equipment.
   Militia—Citizen soldiers that includes every healthy male citizen in a nation, and is organized as a part in that nation's armed forces to be called to serve in an emergency.
   Infringe—Means to invade or intrude by *attacking* and taking something owned by another, such as a possession or right and is accomplished by small progressions or steps.
   Keep—Means for an individual to store or hang on to in their possession.
   Bear—Means for an individual to possess and carry, hold, or transport in their possession.
   Encroachment—Means to slowly intrude/invade by taking another's possessions or rights (infringement), and is accomplished by small progressions or steps.
   Trespass—Means to intrude or invade on someone's property, territory, possessions or rights without just cause.
   The Second Amendment *prohibits government* from passing *any laws that infringe* on your right to keep and bear arms. The men involved in writing

the Constitution's Bill of Rights knew from *first hand experience* the importance in the people's right to "keep and bear" arms. The founders recognized the dangers included in the Constitution's framework that could result in the same oppressive government's shackles being implemented that they had just fought a revolution to break in order to be free. They wanted to ensure that future American generations would always have the means to do the same; hence, the first ten amendments to the Constitution (Bill of Rights) guaranteeing certain God-given rights from *any* government control. The second Amendment to the Constitution of the United States had nothing to do with hunting or the NRA as you are led to believe. This Amendment stands against a clique, an elite, that *Evil One*, from gaining total control and power over the American people by utilizing *manipulation through deception*.

Since the Civil War ended, the Second Amendment has been *constantly attacked*. It started with the sheriff requiring the guns to be turned in and picked up at the sheriff's office when the cowboys rode into town. Then came laws requiring people to obtain a permit to carry a concealed gun. Then came laws requiring people to attend a concealed weapons class in order to obtain the permit. Then came laws *prohibiting* the "Saturday night Special" (whatever that is). Then came laws *prohibiting* "assault weapons" sales (any weapon including a ball bat can be used for an assault). Then came laws requiring stricter registration, background checks and waiting periods. Then came laws requiring trigger locks, laws requiring guns to be stored at home in a certain fashion. Then came laws allowing the gun manufacturers to be sued if a gun they manufactured is used in a crime. Then came laws on gun sales at flea markets, and further restrictions on private buyers and sellers at gun shows.

If the above paragraph does not fit the definition for encroachment, I have no idea what does. Infringement, by definition, is encroachment. Every time a new law is passed "controlling" gun sales or ownership, that is another encroachment (infringement) on your right as a citizen to "keep and bear arms." That right gives the people the power to oust a corrupt, oppressive government.

Each encroachment is another step toward that right being completely deprived. I have already heard numerous American citizens say they believe guns should no longer be allowed to be owned by private citizens. If the American people do not recognize the dangers involved in surrendering even one God-given right protected in the Constitution, they do not deserve what so many have died trying to protect, that being their FREEDOM.

Article X (Roman numeral for 10) in the Oregon Constitution plainly states that the Legislative Assembly shall provide by law for the organization, maintenance, and discipline of *a state militia for the defense and protection of the state*. The National Guard is not a state militia as "We the People" are *manipulated through deception* to believe. That is proven in the fact that the Federal Government has deployed the National Guard overseas to fight.

Article V, Section 9 in the Oregon Constitution states that *the Governor is the Commander-in-Chief over the state military and naval forces and may call out such forces to execute the laws to suppress insurrection or to repel invasion*. That means the Federal government is to have no involvement in the State Militia. The National Guard is a federally sanctioned, trained, equipped, and regulated militia, and is not a state militia.

Amendment III
No Soldier shall, in time of peace, be quartered in any house, without the consent of the owner, nor in time of war, but in manner to be prescribed by law.

Prohibits government from forcing persons into allowing military personnel to be housed in their homes in peacetime, unless the owners provide permission. In war time military personnel can only be housed in a home in accordance with the prescribed law. A home can be considered a society as well as an individual residence. America is our home. It is with "We the People's" consent that a military has been created, established, and housed in our home (America). This has been allowed as a preventive measure from outside forces for "We the People's" common national *defense* in peace and our survival in the event that a war is started against this nation. For the past one-half century, our military has been used for every purpose other than what its creation was intended. It has been used for a financial "elite's" greed. There are those that are now using that military against "We the People." What happened at Waco IS the evidence, i.e., proof.

Amendment IV
The right of the people to be secure in their persons, houses, papers, and effects, against unreasonable searches and seizures, shall not be violated, and no Warrants shall issue, but upon probable cause, supported by Oath or affirmation, and particularly describing the place to be searched, and persons or things to be seized.

Prohibits government officials from searching you, your papers, your belonging, your home, and confiscating anything belonging to you unless those officials have reason, supported by evidence, which leads one to believe that reason is truthful. The officials are permitted to search only after having *obtained a sworn guarantee* by the officials that they will not and are not violating the person's God-given Constitutionally protected rights and that the *things to be searched and/or seized are connected to a specific crime.* The officials must specifically explain what they will search and will be looking for. The official doing the searching and seizure must have taken the Oath of Affirmation that he/she will uphold the Constitution and their actions will not breach or transgress the person being searched and/or seized God-given Constitutionally guaranteed rights.

Amendment V

No person shall be held to answer for a capital, or otherwise infamous crime, unless on a presentment or indictment of a Grand Jury, except in cases arising in the land or naval forces, or in the Militia, when in actual service in time of War or public danger; nor shall any person be subject for the same offense to be twice put in jeopardy of life or limb; nor shall be compelled in any criminal case to be witness against himself, nor be deprived of life, liberty or property, without due process of law, nor shall private property be taken for public use, without just compensation.

Prohibits the government from holding a person in custody for a capital or infamous crime unless a formal written accusation is initiated by a grand jury that is made up from the citizens. The grand jury was originated in English Common Law to protect the citizens. Our founders did not intend for grand juries to be under government control, i.e., the county prosecutor or legal counsel, and was intended to conduct independent investigations and determine from the evidence gathered that enough evidence exists that charges be brought against the individual. This is to cover any facts that the independent grand jury investigation may discover and should those facts constitute a crime. Further, the U.S. Constitution does not stipulate that the grand juries are to be kept secret. The purpose for the grand jury is that it *prohibits the government* from convicting people and sending them to prison or administering capital punishment (the death penalty) on its own accord. This amendment requires a grand-jury indictment for the prosecution in capital (death penalty) or infamous crimes, *which includes all federal felony offenses.* Infamous crimes are crimes that are so monstrous that they could only be committed by a demon-possessed individual. In federal court, felonies are offenses punishable by death or by imprisonment for more than one year at hard labor. This means that states cannot declare minor offenses or misdemeanors as felony offenses, which is exactly what many states are doing.

Exceptions to this are in such cases in the military, Naval, and Militia forces and happen while serving in wartime or national crisis. *Prohibits the government* from bringing charges against a person twice for the same crime that puts his/her life or limb in jeopardy. A way or manner in which one chooses and is accustomed to living life is also considered life in my opinion. This also means that the three strikes and you are out laws are unconstitutional because, in reality, the person is being punished for the same crimes more than once. *Prohibits the government* from making a person testify against himself/herself and admitting to a crime they did not commit. Prohibits the government from depriving people life, liberty or property without due process from the law. *Prohibits the government* from taking a person's private property for public use without paying the person a fair market value or other equitable compensation agreed upon by both parties for that property.

Amendment VI

In all criminal prosecutions, the accused shall enjoy the right to a speedy and public trial, by an impartial jury of the State and district wherein the crime shall have been committed, which district shall have been previously ascertained by law, and to be informed of the nature and cause of the accusation; to be confronted with the witnesses against him; to have compulsory process for obtaining witnesses in his favor, and to have the Assistance of Counsel for his defense.

Prohibits the government from denying an accused person a jury trial open to the public and from deliberately delaying and publicizing the trial in order to influence potential jurors decisions before the accused can present evidence in their defense. *Guarantees* the accused that an unbiased jury will be selected from within the district where the crime was committed. *Prohibits the government* from bringing charges against an individual without informing the individual about the crimes for which they are accused and providing the accused the opportunity to confront the witnesses to the crime. Makes it mandatory that the accused be allowed to produce witnesses in his/her favor. *Prohibits the government* from convicting an accused in a crime without legal Counsel for the accused defense. *Basically, prohibits* government from railroading people into prison for crimes they did not commit.

Amendment VII
In suits at common law, where the value in controversy shall exceed twenty dollars, the right of trial by jury shall be preserved, and no fact tried by a jury, shall be otherwise reexamined in any Court of the United States, than according to the rules of the common law.

Common law cases are generally civil cases and do not entail crimes or require criminal proceeding. The decisions made by previous judges in such cases and not based on the constitution are called common law or case law, or judge-made law. *Prohibits the government* from denying a jury trial in such cases involving more than twenty dollars. *Prohibits the judge* from overturning the jury's decision in such cases. Yet, every day, judges overturn jury decisions and people are denied a jury trial. In fact, in most cases, a person is being required to take such cases to small claims with no jury trial and the only decision is the judge's decision and is exactly the same as the old English common law.

Amendment VIII
Excessive bail shall not be required, nor excessive fines imposed, nor cruel and unusual punishments inflicted.

Prohibits the government from imposing unreasonable bail, fees, fines or vindictive punishments. The court system is supposed to be about justice and not revenge. The punishment or fine is to be reasonable and to fit the crime. Reasonable standards are to be set and followed. If the people decide the bails, fines and punishments are excessive, the government is to change these things. Excessive is extreme, unwarranted, disproportionate, etc. Cruel is unkind, harsh, nasty, mean, vindictive, etc. Unusual is strange, uncommon. All these words describe the punishments and fines forced on the people in Jackson County and Oregon. In recent years, traffic fines were tripled. The fines are then doubled in construction zones.

Depending on who commits the crime, I have heard in the news bails being set for the same offense from $100,000 to $1,000,000. That seems unreasonable and unfair. For the same offense the bail is to be the same for everyone.

Sometime between April 2 and April 7, 1996, a man in the Jackson County Jail allegedly beat himself to death while strapped to a restraint chair for approximately 10 hours in a room at the county jail. Say what? Doesn't that seem cruel and unusual? The man was restrained because he was an alcoholic and had gone into the DTs.

How does a man beat himself to death strapped in a chair? For what purpose is a man left for 10 plus hours strapped in a chair? How does one beat one's self with their hands and feet restrained, especially with deputies supposedly present? Doesn't that seem unusual? For what purpose was this done? Doesn't this whole thing seem unusual? *Police instructors claim the deputies were in accordance with methods taught in training.* For what purpose did a county deputy place a call to a doctor that was a medical witness in this case and ask why the doctor did not like police officer? Intimidation perhaps? That is also tampering with a witness. Something stinks in Jackson County.

Amendment IX

The enumeration in the Constitution, of certain rights, shall not be construed to deny or disparage others retained by the people

Rights provided by our Creator, guaranteed and protected by the U.S. Constitution, and State Constitutions, are not all the God-given rights retained or held by the people. These rights are too numerous to list in detail and the founders knew this. We all know within ourselves our God-given rights. *Prohibits the government* from denying other God-given rights not listed in the Constitution, and *prohibits the government* from abusing or depriving those other rights. *Prohibits the government* from abusing all human beings in this nation.

Amendment X

The powers not delegated to the United States by the Constitution, nor prohibited by it to the States, are reserved to the States respectively, or to the people

The Constitution specifically states what powers have been granted to the Federal Government and the restrictions imposed on the government by the people. The powers that have been granted to the federal government in the U.S. Constitution have been surrendered by the states to that government. The restrictions imposed on the federal government by the U.S. Constitutions are also imposed on the state and local governments. The states have to honor the Constitution with the Bill of Rights, and the states are under the same restrictions listed in the U.S. Constitution. Any powers not granted to the

Federal Government in the U.S. Constitution are reserved for the States, i.e., the people in the state.

That is the way I interpret and understand the Bill of Rights. That is the way most people I know interpret and understand the Bill of Rights. "We the People" *must be wrong* because according to the courts, the authorities, the lawyers, i.e., those running things, "We the People" are *told* that we are wrong. THEY tell "We the People" that THEY interpret the Bill of Rights differently. THEY dictate to "We the People" that THEIR legal definitions are evidence and prove that "We the People" are wrong, that "We the People" are morons and do not know what we are talking about.

There are those who wish to exercise controlling others and to do that they must give the impression, the illusion, that they provide human beings their God-given rights and privileges and that they can take human being rights/ privileges at their whim.

Article 1 in the Oregon Constitution is its Bill of Rights, which includes the same *restrictions on the State* that are put on the federal government, plus additional *restrictions imposed by the people*. There are forty-five sections in the Oregon Constitution's Bill of Rights. I would recommend people in Oregon read them and people from their respective states read their state constitutions. It will shock people to learn the people's *God-given Constitutionally guaranteed rights* and the restrictions put on the local and state governments that are being *deliberately ignored/denied* by the local and state authorities. The Constitutions with the respective Bill of Rights *restricts the government* in what it can do and the laws it can institute. It tells government officials God-given rights belongs to the people and that the government officials are not to infringe on or deny these rights in any way through laws that the government officials impose. The Constitutions are intended to protect the people and their God-given rights from government and those that would be tyrants.

The authorities within the local, state, and federal governments are ignoring the restrictions imposed by the Constitution's Bill of Rights and it is being done deliberately. The people are deliberately being denied (deprived) their God-given and Constitutional guaranteed rights. Those allegedly elected and chosen to govern are in office to UPHOLD THE CONSTITUTIONS, not to ignore the Constitutions. For what purposes do so many in the local, state, and federal governments insist on ignoring the Constitutions? The allegedly elected representatives are *manipulated through deception* into helping keep "We the People" enslaved. *Those allegedly elected and chosen to govern are manipulated through deception into considering themselves special and then are further manipulated into imposing the will of those doing the manipulating on all human beings. Those actually doing the manipulating are called THEY and it is THEY that are keeping all human beings enslaved.*

Human beings are being used as a bond (security) for money owed (debt) by governments to a financial elite. That financial elite is controlling and keeping human beings enslaved throughout the world. This is done by dividing human beings, creating war between these divided human beings, loaning the human being governments money to fight the war, then loaning these same governments money to rebuild after the war. Once in debt, the government taxes (security) the people to pay the debt. Due to the high interest on this debt governments are unable to pay the debt to the financiers. Soon, the interest on the debt is so high the taxes (securities) on the debt can no longer cover the interest being added. Taxes (securities) are raised against the people, but the interest is now to a point that the taxes cannot even keep up with the interest being added. Public lands are sold off, pensions and retirement funds depleted to help pay the debt. Eventually these governments allow the populace to be put into bondage (slavery) through LAWS that favor the financiers (bondsmen) for the debt owed.

CHAPTER 2

EVIL'S METHODOLOGY FOR ENSLAVEMENT

For what reason do human beings commit atrocities against each other? The answer to that question is, a methodology (synonyms: plan, plot, scheme, system, conspiracy) is being used to program, teach (educate, indoctrinate) human beings to hate, fight and kill each other. Most have heard the aphorism "divide and conquer." A methodology and templates have been developed to accomplish that very thing in order to allow a clique, an elite, i.e. an "evil one" to enslave human beings. This methodology divides, isolates, and allows human beings to be conquered, to be enslaved. How that is accomplished is through templates. This methodology is called *Manipulation through deception*. There are three basic templates being used by the Clique, the Elite, this "evil one" and they are:

THE HATE AND PREJUDICE (DIVIDE AND CONQUER) TEMPLATE:
Used to manipulate human beings to give up God-given inalienable (FREE WILL) constitutionally guaranteed rights by denying other human beings their rights (FREE WILL).

THE SHOCK, HUMILIATION, AND INTIMIDATION TEMPLATE:
Used to justify denying human beings God-given rights, jobs, transfers, promotions, political office, etc., by taking those things through distorting the truth and destroying individuals' self-confidence, character, and value system, and making them feel inferior by insulting, humiliating and embarrassing them. It takes a person's dignity. Most people either quit, or totally relent to those in authority and do the authority's bidding to keep jobs, positions, etc.

THE PROGRAMMING AND CONTROL TEMPLATE:
Used for programming, enslavement and total control over human beings. Identifies resistance in the early stages in child development and identifies individuals that are a threat to the methodology and/or system. Identifies those who are willing to follow and those that aren't. Is used for training and practice for those who will be someday be in authority. It includes variations in the other two templates.

The Elite, the Clique, i.e. the *Evil One* use all three templates to gain and maintain control over human beings. We are being attacked from three sides with these three templates. There may be more templates, I am not sure. I have seen and personally experienced these three templates or variations being used against human beings. All one has to do is look around, open their eyes, and they will recognize what is happening. It is happening to your friends, coworkers, it is happening to your relatives, it is happening to you. It is happening to our nation. It is happening throughout the world.

The methodology is so subtle most human beings are totally unaware it is taking place. Once the three-sided template methodologies have been used against an individual personally, and they succumb to the *Evil One* who use it, it is too late. Their lives will be virtually destroyed because they will have fallen into the trap and those other beings will have the individual enslaved and own their soul. Human beings are being manipulated and pitted against other human beings, lives destroyed, and souls lost with this three-sided template methodology.

It is a triangle, much like a pyramid scheme, except the stakes are much higher. The stakes are human beings' freedom, their souls. Truth is the only way out. Our nation's founding fathers knew this and attempted to free themselves and their future generations from this methodology and the templates. They provided us with different templates, i.e. the Constitution with the Bill of Rights, the Declaration of Independence, and they schooled children in *The Bible* and a belief in God, the creator.

It is important to read this whole document, for if you do not, it will be even more difficult to understand and you may not recognize the templates. I hope you can understand and become willing to tell others.

Together, we all have the channel to do so, and it is called spreading the word. To say the least, I was shocked, bewildered, and could not believe, but the evidence is all around us and is overwhelming. All one has to do is open their eyes and their ears. Let those who have ears hear, let those who have eyes see. Many are going to call me crazy, a nut case, a conspiracy theorist, etc. Those people who think so have fallen into the trap and have become a partner in the methodology being used to get human beings to discredit the unbelievable, that which we cannot see, that which we cannot understand. Only by recognizing the trap, the methodology, can we be free from its bonds.

ISOLATION SHOCK METHODOLOGY

The suffix -*ism* is a distinct doctrine, cause or theory used to manipulate people into an adherence to such a doctrine, cause or theory. *Ism* is actually a methodology called Isolation Shock Methodology and is used to divide people into large groups before *ist* (Isolation Shock Therapy) is used to further fragment people into smaller groups. Below are some methods used to fragment people into large groups, which can then be fragmented further by Isolation Shock Therapy. The methodology is proven and templates developed that have been in use for several thousand years to divide and conquer human beings. The semantics change but the results are the same. *Divided*, *confused*, *fearful*, and *conquered* human beings that have surrendered to the Clique, the Elite, the "Evil One."

The Isolation Shock Methodology and *ist* Isolation Shock Therapy are administered through templates used to promote fear, petty jealousies, greed, and hate among human beings so they can easily be *manipulated through deception*. Following are just a few *ism* words used to divide human beings into large groups. There are additional words that have been used in the past and more are developed as time progresses and the need arises. Definitions are mine based on how I believe they apply as to what I observe happening in the world today:

Nationalism is the doctrine that advocates the greatest ethnic group or nation on earth.

Patriotism is the doctrine that advocates my Country, right or wrong.

Communism is the doctrine that advocates the state above all else. The state decides your needs.

Capitalism is the doctrine that advocates the business profits above all else. The business decides your needs.

Fascism is the doctrine that the state needs to outweigh individual needs and one individual decides everyone's needs.

Satanism is the doctrine that advocates worshipping and loving the "evil one," greed before all things humane, and hate for God above all else.

Feudalism is the doctrine that advocates the Clique (Elite) above all other human beings.

Militarism is the doctrine that advocates one nation's human beings killing other nation's human beings believing they are fighting evil.

Terrorism is the doctrine that advocates human beings killing human beings for the purpose of using coercion/intimidation as a means for tyrannical political gain.

Naturalism is the doctrine that advocates natural desires must be satisfied at any cost to human beings, i.e., if it feels good, do it.

Environmentalism is the doctrine that advocates protecting other animal species in the surrounding environment take precedence over protecting human beings in the same environments.

Fanaticism is the doctrine that advocates human beings within a religious group killing humans in another religious group.

Racism is the doctrine that advocates human beings with a particular skin pigmentation being superior or inferior to human beings with a different skin pigmentation.

Extremism is the doctrine that advocates human beings utilizing extreme political measures, such as violence, against other human beings (radicalism).

Elitism is the doctrine that advocates nations, states, societies, organizations, etc. into believing that they are superior to other nations, states, societies, organizations, etc., and are the only ones qualified to be rulers or leaders in the world. Best of the best. Cream of the crop. Top 10%.

Criticism is the doctrine that advocates judging other human beings.

Aphorism is the doctrine that utilizes quotations to influence human beings' thinking.

ISOLATION SHOCK THERAPY

IST is an acronym for insulin shock therapy. Insulin is a word derived from the Latin word insula (island). Insulate is derived from the same Latin word insula (island). Isolate is a synonym for insulate. Substitute the synonym isolate for insulate, IST now is Isolation Shock Therapy.

Therapy is treatment designed to bring about a certain social adjustment. A template is a pattern or a mold used as a guide to produce a specified thing, usually in mass quantities. In essence both definitions are the same since therapy is designed to produce a specified thing in mass quantity called social adjustment. Isolation shock therapy is designed to produce a human being that adheres to or advocates a specified doctrine, system, or behavior code. Isolation Shock Therapy is being used *against* human beings in order to produce an unresisting, obedient robot type slave for the *Evil One*.

The methodology used to brainwash a prisoner of war in order to make them talk, turn them against the other prisoners, to make them submissive or to convert them over to the other side is to first isolate that prisoner. Then shock and humiliate that prisoner, hurt the prisoner, instill hate and fear into that prisoner, then coerce that prisoner.

These same tactics are being applied to the human race, only in a very subtle manner. With a POW, time is short, information is needed in a hurry, and the methodology is hurried. What is done with the POW is to make them strip naked. This humiliates the prisoner. The prisoner may be shocked with cold water or an electrical shock can be used. Lies are told to the prisoners about the other prisoners in attempts to turn prisoners against each other. Lies and distortions are used to tell what is happening with the war, their family, country, etc. Then beatings and torture occur. Food, water, and sleep depravation are also used.

Once the prisoner is left without hope, a carrot is provided to the prisoner, such as kindness, food, water, sleep, and medical care for injuries, etc. Many succumb to the procedure to keep from going through the horrors, the process again. They obey their captors and give them whatever they want. The prisoner has succumbed to the tyranny perpetrated against him/her.

With a large populace and when there is no need to be hurried, the same tactics can be applied over a longer period without being easily recognized. If you will notice, these same type of tactics are being used against all Americans, all human beings, today, only in a very subtle manner.

The 9-11 twin towers was the shock and humiliation treatment. America was shocked that such an atrocity could occur in this nation. Some Americans are humiliated that those committing the attack could have access to the nation and circumvent the airline security measures so easily. Many Americans were afraid to get on aircraft for fear the aircraft would be hijacked and flown into another building. A hate fervor was built up against those who supposedly committed the 9-11 acts. Many Americans wanted to "go over there and wipe them out."

Some airports and airlines were shut down for weeks depriving people air travel. Then, the government started taking people's God-given Constitutionally-guaranteed rights for "safety and security," making the people appreciative of the government for protecting them against these "terrorists." Airports were allowed to open and airlines began offering good deals for flying. How many people have you heard about that have been stripped searched at the airports the last 6 months? Airport strip searches are now becoming a normal procedure. This is nothing more than the shock and humiliation treatment starting over again, but now on an individual basis, and it is being done "for your own safety." Now think about Waco, Ruby Ridge, Oklahoma City, etc. Now think about the prisoner in the POW camp.

Sleep depravation is accomplished for the masses via daylight savings time. Twice a year the time is adjusted by first moving it up an hour and six months later back an hour. This affects human beings' sleep patterns, and we never really fully adjust, mentally or physically.

Mental torture is more effective than physical torture. Human beings are tortured mentally by being subjected to mental stresses. Financial stress is one means to do this. Job stress is another. Taking a person's job and livelihood is another way to promote mental stress. The stock market is used to cause stress. Inflation is another means to create mental stress. Selling devices that do not work properly cause mental stress. Creating heavy traffic patterns and unnecessary rules that a person must remember and obey is another cause for mental stress. Heavy class load required for students in the schools and colleges cause mental stress. The hurried lifestyles that people are being *manipulated through deception* into living causes mental stress. Mental stress is nothing more than mental torture. Human beings are being subjected to these tortures. Lump several little stress factors together and a person can be driven to a nervous breakdown, and can be put into an institution where more intense measures can be used to make the person "come around to THEIR way of thinking."

There is, and has been, a movement to profile human beings such as criminals, the politically incorrect, religious fundamentalists, environmentalists, extremists, racists, feminists, terrorists, sexists, nationalists, abortionists, and any other IST (Isolation Shock Therapy) that can be used to divide and conquer human beings. I mentioned there are templates used for this purpose and I am going to demonstrate those templates to you later in this book.

I like to call those behind all the world atrocities "tyrants." My definition for a tyrant is: 1. One who *manipulates others through deception* into performing the world's tyranny and evil; 2. One who *manipulates others through deception* into worshipping money as God; 3. One *who manipulates others through deception* into greed as a way to live life and doctrine; 4. One *who manipulates others through deception* into using terror as a tool for the tyrant's political gain; 5. One that *manipulates through deception human beings* into committing tyrannical acts against other human beings.

Following is a condensed word list developed by the *Evil One* for its use in *IST* (Isolation Shock Therapy). There are many other words that have been used in the past and others are developed as time progresses and the need arises. The definitions are mine as I have observed them applied in everyday life:

Racists are human beings *manipulated through deception* into believing the claim that their race is the most oppressed race but superior to all other races.

Sexists are human beings *manipulated through deception* into believing that men or women are only sex objects.

Cultists are human beings *manipulated through deception* into believing that their cult is superior to all other cults.

Terrorists are human beings *manipulated through deception* into believing it is justified to kill other human beings on a smaller scale for doing evil, while in actuality committing atrocities for the tyrants' political gain.

Rightists are human beings *manipulated through deception* into believing that truths are lies and lies are truths while human beings know in their own hearts the real truth.

Leftists are human beings *manipulated through deception* into believing that right is wrong and wrong is right, while human beings know in their own hearts what is right.

Feminists are human beings *manipulated through deception* into believing that men are the enemy.

Individualists are human beings *manipulated through deception* into believing things other human beings do not like.

Communists are human beings *manipulated through deception* into believing and following Communism and its doctrine.

Fascists are human beings *manipulated through deception* into believing and following Fascism and its doctrine.

Nationalists are human beings manipulated through deception into believing that their nation is above all other nations.

Capitalists are human beings *manipulated through deception* using their own greed as the driving force. The more they have, the more they want and will use whatever means necessary to acquire more.

Environmentalists are human beings *manipulated through deception* into believing that other animal and plant species in the environment take precedence over human beings in the same environment.

Satanists are human beings *manipulated through deception* into worshipping Satan and believing his lies.

Militarists are human beings *manipulated through deception* into believing it is justified to kill other human beings on a large scale for doing evil.

Elitists are human beings belonging to a powerful minority group *manipulated through deception* into believing that those within his/her group is superior to all other human beings and are the only ones qualified to be a ruler or leader.

Semanticists are human beings *manipulated through deception* into believing they are specialists in semantics (language/word use).

You will notice most human beings fall into one or more IST (Isolation Shock Therapy) previously mentioned.

Take as an example the *word* nigger. That particular *word* has been used to convince human beings with a dark skin pigmentation to hate human beings that are a lighter skin pigmentation if that word is even spoken. It is okay for human beings with dark skin pigmentation to use the word, but no other human being with a lighter skin pigmentation is permitted to use the word without violence or a law suit from the human beings with a dark skin pigmentation. Human beings have been taught that the word is so bad that the politically correct now call it the "N" word because to even utter or mention the word means one is a *racist*. Considering we all belong to the human race, how can that be? Wouldn't it be more appropriate to say that individual was a pigmentist and not a racist. It is unbelievable that some humans have become so fearful that a single word frightens them.

I remember as a child when I heard the word nigger, I was curious as to its meaning. I looked it up in a dictionary and I remember it was defined as pertaining to a thief or a lazy, lowly person. Years later, I again looked the word up in a later version dictionary, and the meaning had been changed to mean a derogatory word pertaining to those in the Negro race. So, at one time when the word was used to describe a particular individual, it meant that individual was a thief or a lazy lowly person. It did not matter about the individual's skin pigmentation. Today it is a derogatory term against those people with a dark skin pigmentation. How did this happen? Who or what decided that particular word was to be derogatory against human beings with dark skin pigmentation? Who and for what purpose? The purpose is to perpetuate hate. Who THEY actually are will be revealed in a later chapter.

Another word example is the word *gay*. When I was a child, the word gay meant happy and carefree. Now it has an entirely different meaning. Today gay is a person that has a sexual preference for the same gender. Frankly, I do not care what a person's sexual preference may be. That is their choice. Do not attempt to force that choice on me or expect me to accept your choices. I will make my own choice, thank you. I believe the homosexual lifestyle to be repulsive and unnatural, and my choice is to refuse to accept it as a lifestyle for myself. Each person has the God-given right to choose. I do not answer to the Creator for anyone but myself, and I have enough baggage (logs) that I already have to answer for and do not need others baggage. I haven't the need to know a person's sexual preference, and if a person prefers the homosexual lifestyle, I wish for them to keep it to themselves. I can accept a person as they are but their sex life is not something I need to know about.

I have heard people say, "sticks and stones may break my bones, but names will never hurt me." Words can hurt, and hurt deeply, *only if one allows them to hurt and humans are being programmed to allow that to happen.* The sole purpose is to perpetuate hate.

Another example is the word "napkin." In America a napkin is a sanitary device for wiping ones mouth. In England, the word napkin can be offensive because it is a sanitary device used by women during their cycle. Both are sanitary devices, but depending on who hears the word, it may be or may not be offensive.

I recall when I passed through Christ Church, New Zealand on my way to Antarctica, many people would start laughing when I was introduced to them. I found out that my first name, Randy (short for Randall), meant horny to the English, New Zealanders, and Australians. I could have taken offense at those laughing at me, but instead, I laughed with them. I thought it amusing.

CHAPTER 3

METHODOLOGY TOOLS

Before discussing and demonstrating the templates, I would like to reveal and discuss a few tools used within or in conjunction with the templates:
HYPOCRISY IS the greatest critic and a great tool.

One that uses and practices criticism cannot be a called criticist because there is no such word. Critics are those beings that judge and live off human beings and their misery much like a tick. A tick is a blood-sucking parasite. Those that practice hypocrisy are hypocrites and are those that say one thing while practicing another. Training people to be critical is accomplished in many formal education classes within the education system. Public speaking and debate classes are prime examples. Students are taught to look for and criticize perceived faults in the way the other students present their subject matter, in their body language, and manner. Criticism is actually judging people by standards that have been developed by some unknown force as being the right way to do something.

Speaking is a natural ability that most people possess but "fear" prevents many people from speaking before a group, because they fear people will laugh at them, mock them, shun them, i.e., "criticize" them in some way. And they are right, because human beings are taught to criticize what others say or do.

I say, speak from the heart and have no fear. Many great leaders and speakers never attended a public speaking class in their life. Let people think what they may because nothing you say or do is going to change the way people think about you if you are truly honest. No matter what you do, you are not going to satisfy everyone. People claim to want honesty and the truth, but many actually fear honesty and the truth because human beings are taught that being honest can be hurtful. Young children have not yet learned the game and many times blurt things out that most people fear can hurt others. People are trained from birth to let truth and honesty hurt them, and to fear honesty and the truth.

A true friend will not tell you what you want to hear, but will most likely tell you what you don't want to hear, that being the truth. Answering honestly is not being judgmental. If a person is a caught stealing, has the object stolen in their possession, and is then called a thief, that is honesty and is not passing judgement. If a person lies, is caught in the lie, and is then called a liar, that is honesty. We all make mistakes and do things that are wrong. An individual that is judgmental or condemns others for wrongdoings that the individual themselves have committed is hypocritical. Being hypocritical is passing judgement, and as Christ said, "judge not least you be judged." Christ does not tolerate hypocrisy.

The greatest, and in my opinion, most severe hypocrisy today is abortion. I personally believe everyone has a right to choose and along with those choices come responsibilities. A woman has a right to choose by saying no to sex. She has a right to choose a contraceptive if she decides to engage in the sexual act. She has the right to choose to tell or not tell the man to wear a condom before engaging in the sexual act. She may or may not choose to participate in the sexual act. Once she has made the choice to participate in the sexual act she knows that a life might be created. After engaging in the sexual act and life has been created and started in her womb, the woman and the man who chose to engage in the sexual act that created life still have a choice. They can choose to accept the *responsibility to the life they created* or they can choose to *murder* the life they created. I include the man in this because he has the same choices as the woman and bears the same responsibilities. They may also choose not to accept the responsibility to raise the life they created and put the child up for adoption.

The courts have decided to make it *legal* to "murder the baby in the womb and/or as the baby is being born." I do not agree with the courts. Abortion, at any stage, is murder. In my opinion, Roe vs. Wade and the laws passed since Roe vs. Wade concerning abortion are unconstitutional. I totally disagree with the Supreme Court on this issue (as well as other issues). The 5th amendment to our U.S. Constitution states "No Person shall be...*nor deprived of life, liberty, or property, without due process of law.*" The preamble to this same Constitution states, "We the people of the United States, in Order to form a more perfect Union, establish Justice, insure domestic Tranquility, provide for the common defense, promote the general Welfare, and secure the Blessings of Liberty to ourselves and *our Posterity*, do ordain and establish this Constitution for the United States of America."

THE ENEMY CALLED "THEY"

Posterity means "all upcoming future generations."

Abortion is denying "life" to some in the future generations. To kill something means that it has been *deprived its life*. A synonym for kill is murder. When a *human being is murdered* that means the human being was *killed unlawfully and with premeditated malice*, i.e. was slaughtered gratuitously and was put to an end. We have passed laws making it unlawful to "kill" fish, plants, insects, rodents, and eagles, etc., yet have passed laws making it lawful to kill human "babies."

How can we as a nation permit slaughtering babies? Do any really think that as a nation, such depravity will go unpunished? What has caused this nation to reach a point that we hold and revere life *except "human life"*? What caused human mothers to become the only species that will even consider killing their own young before they are born? What caused this disregard and irreverence for human life? What caused this nation to grow so cold hearted? There is more respect for bugs, rodents or plants life than for a human baby's life. What caused this? What has *manipulated human beings through deception* into committing such acts?

I have heard people say the woman has a right to do what she wants with her body. I agree. If she chooses to murder an unborn baby the creator has blessed her with, to care for, nurture and love, that is her choice. That choice has always been available since the beginning. Killing the baby was always considered illegal both in God's law and man's law. Human beings have always had the choice to choose between what is legal and illegal, between good and evil, between what is right and wrong in God's eyes.

Just recently, man's law made it legal to murder the baby in the mother's womb or as the baby is being born, i.e. partial birth abortion, but *in God's law, it is still illegal*. HE is the one this nation and its people will answer to sometime in the future. For those mothers that chose to murder their babies I say that although man's law has made it legal, that is not the authority you will answer to in the end. God's law is that law to which everyone will eventually answer, and in His law murdering babies is illegal. When making your choice, make sure it is the right choice. For those who are "pro abortion" I ask this question: *"What if you were the one your mother had chosen to abort?"*

More than 43 million babies have been slaughtered as an "option," as a choice, in this nation. This will not be forgotten. Every nation has had to answer for breaking our Creator's laws, and in time every nation has paid. None have created the debt this nation has accumulated in innocent lives sacrificed in order to have a good time to gratify ourselves sexually. For that, GOD will bring a wrath on this nation like none has ever seen.

I am pro-life and I am also pro-choice. I believe every human being has the GOD-given right to life once that life has started in the womb. GOD may take that life at anytime, for the Creator gives life and the Creator takes life, but man does not give life and does man have the right to take life? God told human beings that in His commandments. I also believe people have the GOD-given right to choose. GOD will hold us responsible for the choices we make.

A person can *choose* to do anything they want, murder, rape, theft, sodomy, child abuse, lying, cheating, adultery, homosexuality, etc., etc., etc., or choose to obey God's laws. In some instances, man's law will hold the person responsible and accountable for certain actions. God's law will hold the person responsible and accountable for "all" actions, good and evil. Man changes his law to suit his needs, wants, desires. God does not change his laws and has stated clearly what acts violate HIS law.

The Supreme Court has taken it upon itself to contradict and violate God's laws and the Constitution our founding father instituted. Human beings that substitute the word "choice" for "responsibility" may not accept the "responsibility" and be held "accountable" for the choices made at this time, but they will be held "responsible" and "accountable" for those "choices" at some point in time. When that time comes at least have the *GRAVITAS* to say to the CREATOR, "I chose not to believe in You or Your laws, so I did not obey Your laws, I chose to obey man's laws." *"GOOD LUCK!"*

Another great hypocrisy that amazes me is that one religious group "labels" another religious group a cult. All religious groups are a cult by definition. Any formal religious worship is a cult.

Cult = religious group = sect = faction = group = faction = sect = religious group = cult.

If you do not believe me, look up the definition and synonyms for the word cult.

Most religious groups consider other religious groups a cult. Most take offense at being called a cult. Most Christian religions teach about the same God, the same Christ, the same love, yet each considers the other wrong. Each considers the other evil. Either one believes in God, the Christ, the Spirit, the love, or one doesn't. Those that believe the opposite believe in a totally different religion. In truth, there are only two religions, each with many different groups. There is the good religion, those that believe in and worship

God, Christ, and the Spirit with love as the foundation, and there is the evil religion that believes in and worships Satan, Lucifer, and the evil spirit with hate as the foundation. In other words, there is Good and there is Evil. Those are the only two real choices. Which denomination one chooses within the two religions is an individual choice. The denominations are broken down into even smaller groups. The Evil One is using human beings religious differences to divide and conquer.

Christianity is not a religion, but a way to live life the way Jesus Christ taught human beings. Those that follow Christ's teachings do not lie, cheat, steal, rob, con, swindle, murder, rape, commit adultery, abort children, or do anything else to harm other human beings. That is not a religion, but is a way to live life. That is what Christ taught. That is a way to be free. Pointing fingers and telling others their religion is a cult, to those I say, perhaps a mirror check is in order. For Christ said in Matthew 7: 1-5: *"Do not judge so that you will not be judged. For in the way you judge, you will be judged; and by your standard of measure, it will be measured to you. Why do you look at the speck that is in your brother's eye, but do not notice the log that is in your own eye? Or how can you say to your brother, 'Let me take the speck out of your eye' and behold the log is in your own eye? You hypocrite, first take the log out of your own eye, and then you will see clearly to take the speck out of your brother's eye."*

I can picture the Jewish Pharisees, Sadducees, and the Roman hierarchy during the period that the Christian church was being formed. I picture them behind closed doors in a panic about this new religious cult being formed around the man Jesus that they had recently crucified and the threat this new cult presented to the religious and political structure. I can picture them saying how this cult met in the catacombs beneath the cities and made all these devious plans to overthrow the religious and political order in that day and that something drastic must be done to stop that cult from spreading its religious hate. I can picture these Pharisees, Sadducees and Roman aristocrats making plans to have atrocities committed against the people in order to blame it on this Christian cult. Once done, the people would turn away from this Christian cult and then Rome could take appropriate action such as feeding this Christian cult to the lions and bringing it to an end. Today, I now see those within the Christian religion being *manipulated through deception* in the same manner only against other religions. More hypocrisy that Christ deplores.

I have learned that many churches professing to be Christian cannot handle the truth. My first significant lesson was when I was a high school Sunday school teacher and the teacher for the Junior Church in the church I attended from 1971 to 1977. I learned the truth was not acceptable in the church. I learned that through an Easter Sunday experience in 1977. I was asked to teach a kindergarten Sunday school class. I used puppets to tell the Easter story and what Easter was truly about. The truth about the Easter bunny was revealed. That truth caused some parents in the church to be upset with me and I was no longer permitted to teach Sunday school and within a few weeks, I was no longer allowed to teach Junior Church. That is when I learned the truth is not acceptable within the Christian religions.

Many will say it was not my place to tell the children there is no Easter Bunny. Excuse me, what is the church to teach if not the truth? Is the church to teach and perpetuate a lie or lies? From what occurred, it was obvious the children were not being taught the truth, even at home, or in other Sunday school classes. For what purposes does one go to church? It is to feel good about one's self or to learn the truth? If you want to feel good about yourself, then learn the truth, live the truth, and do what you know is right. Do not let others tell you that there is no right or wrong, good or evil. These things do exist and you have the free will to choose between the two.

Looking at Christ's life during the three years it was recorded He tried teaching the truth to the Jewish people, and the Jewish religious leaders turned on him. He tried explaining the laws as to its truth and application in everyday life. He tried explaining the Spirit in the law. THEY killed Christ for that.

I do believe that if Christ came today in the same capacity as he came 2000 years ago, the Church that professes to follow Him and His teaching would be the first to put him right back on that cross. The reason I say this is the hypocrisy I see from those religions that claim to be His church. I will say it again, Christianity in not a religion, it is a way to live life, and by no means am I judging the Christian religion, I am just saying, think about what you are doing. Anything that perpetuates hate is not from God; it is not Christ like and is not Christian. Any church that professes to be Christian and will not teach the truth is teaching lies. That is not Christ's church. It is hypocrisy. It is evil.

What lesson do children learn if they are taught a lie for seven to nine years, such as Santa Claus or the Easter Bunny, and then it is revealed to the child that Santa and the Easter Bunny never existed? After 7-9 years it is revealed these things only existed in the child's mind because they were lied to so that the child would believe they existed and these things were really a myth. The child realizes that for 7-9 years their parents, the schools, the churches, businesses, the authorities, etc., were lying. What does that do to the child's trust factor? Then the church tells the child to believe in God who is in heaven and Jesus his son who died 2000 years in the past. Do you think that child is going to believe? That child is going to have serious doubts. That child is going to think he/she is being lied to again. Think!

Another hypocrisy I find interesting is within the homosexual community. Some people within the heterosexual community allege that homosexuality is unnatural and a choice, a sexual preference. Within the homosexual (gay) community people allege that homosexuality is an act of nature, that homosexuals have no choice and are born that way, that sex with the same gender is a natural act and plays a part in the natural laws and scheme of things. The homosexual community asks the heterosexual community, "who are they to argue with nature?"

There is much discussion today from both sides concerning the issue that homosexuals be allowed to adopt children. Heterosexuals allege homosexuality is unnatural, is a choice, and argue that raising children in such an environment is detrimental to the children, will adversely influence the children and turn the children into homosexuals. Homosexuals allege that homosexuals make good parents and that a homosexual relationship will have no influence on the children as to sexual preference since homosexuals are born that way.

If what the homosexual community alleges is true, then using the homosexual community's own reasoning and argument that homosexuality is not a choice, that nature made them that way, then it can further be determined that nature did not intended for homosexuals to conceive or raise children. If nature had intended for homosexuals to conceive and raise children, then those individuals who are homosexuals would have been able to conceive children naturally within the same gender, yet it cannot be done naturally. That being the case, then it can further be established that it is a contradiction and a violation against nature and the natural laws for homosexuals to raise children.

In order to perpetuate the human species, Nature has determined that it takes the male sperm and the female egg to conceive children. Although a woman can conceive a child through artificial insemination using male sperm, conceiving children is generally accomplished through a natural sexual act between a man and a woman. Since nature has determined that it takes a male sperm and a female egg to conceive a child, then it is obvious that nature intended for a man and a woman to be a child's father and mother. It can therefore be established that nature intended that a child be raised by a father and a mother.

Assuming homosexuality is natural as argued by those within the homosexual community, then it is hypocrisy within the homosexual community to insist on adopting and raising children. So, nature determined that reproduction and raising children is not a part in the homosexual process. "Who are the homosexuals to argue with nature?"

If it is not to cause dissension, for what purpose is the homosexual community wanting to go against nature and the natural laws on this issue since nature is the one that made the determination that homosexuals cannot have children?

Looking at it from the heterosexual side and assuming homosexuality is a choice, then the homosexual community made a choice not to reproduce by choosing to have sexual relations within their own gender, voluntarily making the choice not to have children. Thus, a homosexual claiming to want to adopt and raise children is a contradiction because homosexuals made the choice not to have children when choosing the homosexual lifestyle.

Using the homosexual community's reasoning that homosexuals were born that way, then what is the purpose behind all the arguments, tension, and strife since nature and the natural laws have already made the determination that homosexuals are not to raise children? Is it to create hate using *manipulation through deception*?

Again, using the homosexual community's reasoning, rapists, murderers, pedophiles, arsonists, kidnappers, robbers, etc., could argue that they were born that way, thus nature made them that way, they do not have a choice in what they do and should not be held accountable for their actions.

Everything human beings do in life is a choice, and that choice is between good and evil. Human beings are *manipulated through deception* into believing in and choosing evil, but that does not release those human beings from being responsible for the choices they make. The sole purpose behind the hypocrisy is to perpetuate hate between human beings. It is working very well isn't it?

FEAR IS the source root for *hate*.

Human beings are taught to fear, and then that very fear is used to control them. For it is fear that leads people to hate things that are not understood. Understanding other humans appears to be the most difficult thing to do, yet almost every human being wants basically the same things in life. It does not matter what country, culture, or even the language spoken, most human beings want a comfortable, secure life for themselves and their loved ones. But as human beings go through life, we are taught about our differences and then to hate those differences. Many differences are natural and cannot be changed. Some changes may be made in our differences, but does it really matter in the grand scheme? Is it necessary for people to change and fit into a mold that others say they should fit into? I think not. Christ did not attempt to change anyone. He told them the truth and let them decide for themselves.

Skin pigmentation is a difference no one has any control over. Nature gave human beings the skin pigmentation they have and people cannot change that. It is unreasonable, ridiculous, and serves no useful purpose for humans to hate humans with a different skin pigmentation. It makes absolutely no sense. We are all human beings. Yet human beings are taught to hate and fear people with a skin pigmentation different than their own. For what purpose is this taught? To divide, conquer and control!

Human beings are taught to fear and hate human beings that speak a different language, those that cannot be understood. Human beings are taught to fear and hate human beings from different religions, ethnic groups, cultures, etc., etc., etc. The sole purpose is to divide, conquer and control!

I have told many people that the Arabs think differently than Americans, and that is a fact. That is due to their culture. The Islamic faithful are taught to hate infidels, and so are those in the Christian faith. The way I understand the definition, an infidel is someone that is unbelieving and unfaithful, and can be one who opposes Christianity, or is an unbeliever in any specific religion and is an atheist. Christians consider Islamics evil and the Islamics consider the Christians evil. Who is right and who is wrong in this case? Neither is right, so both must be wrong. Both religions believe in the God of Abraham, Isaac, and Jacob, yet both believe the other to be infidels. Both religions have hate mongers in their mists. The Islamic have the Taliban, *al-Qaida*, and numerous other groups belonging to other Islamic organizations. The Christians have the Neo-Nazi, KKK, and numerous other Christian organizations. In every major religion, there are small factions causing hate. Each religion has been infiltrated by the Evil One to perpetuate hate against each other. Think!

Matthew 7: 13-14: *"Enter through the narrow gate; for the gate is wide and the way is broad that leads to destruction, and there are many who enter through it. For the gate is small and the way is narrow that leads to life and there are few who find it."*

SEMANTICS IS word games, i.e., THE SYNONYM GAME.

The American people are allowing Semantics or the Synonym Game, as I like to call it, to be used against them to control their lives and deny their freedom. How many times have you heard people say they do not want to get involved in Semantics, i.e., the Word Game? I have said it myself. Like it or not, we are all involved in the semantics game. Since we are already involved in a game in which we have no choice, it will help to learn what the game is about and how it is used against us.

Basically, Semantics ARE word games used to deceive and trick people to enable blood-sucking parasites to feed off them. Semantics is a major tool used by the *Evil One*.

THE SYNONYM GAME:

A synonym is a word or phrase, that in essence, has the same or near the same meaning as several other words or phrases in the same language. Following are some synonyms that might interest most people:

PARADIGM = example = instance = CASE IN POINT= instance = example = PARADIGM

Paradigm is a clear or representative case in point or prime example.

It is my desire to provide you with meaningful paradigms in this message.

APHORISM = saying = PROVERB = saying = APHORISM

An aphorism is a brief statement about a belief. A paradigm that is an aphorism is "Perception is the Truth." Do you believe that proverb?

OPPRESSION = domination = power = control = MANAGE

Oppression is wielding authority or power unfairly and/or harshly. Normally it is called abusing authority. Do you know any in management or supervisory positions that are a paradigm and fit the definition and abuse authority?

TAX = toll = charge = FEE

A tax is money charged against the people and the people's property, which is forcibly collected for unrestricted use by those in power. A fee is in reality a tax. It is called a fee because most people do not think about a fee as a tax. Taxes are called fees in order to justify double, even triple taxation. The American people are paying "fees" for services that they already pay for through taxes.

PREJUDICE = bias = favoritism = preference =FIRST CHOICE

Prejudice is a view or leaning opposing something without adequate information. If you make a first choice about anything, you can be considered

THE ENEMY CALLED "THEY"

PREJUDICED.

HATE = disgust = aversion = dislike = FIND OBJECTIONABLE.

Hate is extreme hostility and dislike usually resulting from fear, anger, or a sense of injury, such as hypocrisy. The root cause for hate is fear. So anything you may find objectionable can now be considered a HATE crime.

BIGOT = extremist = radical = militant = ACTIVIST.

A bigot is a person that is so devoted to his/her own church, party, belief or opinion, that they can be construed as stubborn or intolerant. Every person I have met is opinionated and is devoted to either a church, party, belief, something. By definition, everyone is a bigot. So, when labeling someone a bigot or by any other label, perhaps it would help to look in the mirror. All activists can also be considered bigots.

THE OTHER SIDE IN THE SYNONYM GAME:

OPPRESSION = domination = power = control = MANAGE = control = power = domination = OPPRESSION

Manage really means to transform others through manipulation and with absolute authority in order to accomplish one's goal to produce. No one likes to be made into something they're not, and that's exactly what is being done to people today. Most managers *are manipulated through deception* into attempting to make employees into mindless robots that will obey without question. What some companies call team building, I call brainwashing. I cannot become a part of any team that advocates deceiving the customer and the employees.

Yet, many big corporations do that very thing. One such national company where I was a manager in training for a new store that was opening likes to gather all employees together in the morning before opening to sing childish, mindless songs and have, in effect, rah, rah cheering sessions pertaining to the company. This is supposed to build "team spirit." From what I experienced, it was just plain brainwashing.

The company advertises that it always has low prices, buys U.S. products to sell whenever possible, and that it treats its employees fairly. This same national company likes to sell their products at a low price after first opening, driving competition out while getting a good customer base. Within a few months, the company raises prices to a point just as high, if not higher, as the competitor they destroyed. Three out of four items I checked in the store had "Made in China" stamped on them. I saw price increases day after day once the store was open for about 2 weeks. Some items' prices were increased two or three times in a week. Employees' hours were cut so that most employees were unable to receive medical benefits and other benefits promised. Everything the store preached was a lie.

I left the company after a few months because my value system was in conflict with the company's value system. The company's value system was based on greed and my value system was based on honesty and was causing me internal conflict. I felt as though my values were being oppressed and I would be expected to do the same to the employees I would be supervising. Managers, employees and customers are all being *manipulated through deception*.

TAX = toll = charge = FEE = charge = toll = TAX

A fee is a toll, such as property taxes, charged against your land for *your* service and homage to the local government. It can also be a fixed cost or charge for professional services that may be provided. If you do not pay this fee on your land, the government will take it. If you do not pay service to the government, it will take your property. "We the people" pay additional fees to the government for their professional services that our taxes have already paid for. Fee/taxes: same thing.

PREJUDICE = bias = favoritism = preference = FIRST CHOICE =preference =favoritism = bias = PREJUDICE

First choice means "coming before another in time, space, or importance." We make choices in our everyday lives concerning people, places and things. Every choice we make in most cases is without sufficient knowledge. Buy a car and what do you really know about that car? Did you watch it being manufactured, all the parts that go into it being manufactured, and watch it being put together? You only have the information provided to you by others interested in selling you the car. You only have the information provided by reports that "tested" the vehicle for a very short time. You still do not have all the information necessary to make an unbiased opinion. You never will. If you ever owned a lemon in one model, you may never buy that model again.

It is the same with most things. We base our opinions on what we know, think we know, have heard, etc., and not necessarily all the "correct" information. We have to make decisions based on what we can find out, and sometimes, that information may not be correct. Sometimes, that can lead us to make the wrong decisions. Even when we know all the correct information, we can still make the wrong decision. Many times we go on gut instinct. That has proven to be the most correct. In the political word game, we are all prejudice because we all make first choices and we all have preferences.

HATE = disgust = aversion = dislike = FIND OBJECTIONABLE = dislike = aversion = disgust = HATE

Objectionable generally means something or someone is offensive. We all find many things offensive. I find many smells offensive. We all do, say, think, and practice things that are offensive to others. Do we make everything that is offensive to others a hate crime? I think not. If we did, then soon, there will be nothing anyone can do because everything done, spoken, or practiced offends someone in some way. How many times have you heard it said, "there ought to be a law against this or that"? Well, that is exactly what is happening today. EVERYTHING IS becoming against the law.

Everything IS becoming a hate crime. I find many things people say objectionable. Do I think a law should be passed against it? No! The First Amendment to the U.S. Constitution guarantees that right and no law shall be passed abridging that right. Free speech is a God-given right. Very soon, things like smoking and wearing perfumes will be hate crimes. Anyone want to put money on it? For what purposes do those in government institute laws against things people find objectionable about other people and make those things a "hate crime"? Control!

BIGOT = extremist = radical = militant = ACTIVIST = militant = radical = extremist = BIGOT

An activist is a person that is devoted to a dogma or tradition that puts emphasis on direct forceful action (as a mass demonstration or riot) in support or opposition to one side in a controversial issue. Compare it to the bigot that is a person that is so devoted to his/her own church, party, belief or opinion, that they can be construed as stubborn or intolerant.

Today, it is okay to be an "activist" in supporting or opposing certain issues, but it is not okay to be a bigot supporting or opposing the same issues, yet bigot and activists are virtually identical in essence, or if you prefer, spirit. According to those who claim to be activists, it is not okay to be a bigot, and those who are said to be bigots, deny being bigots and will not try to understand the opposing side. Both sides are dedicated to their own side and opposed to the other's side and each label the other side, yet cannot recognize that the labels are one in the same. Is this not hypocrisy at its peak?

As a paradigm, I will use racism. Put simply, we are led to believe by *manipulation through deception* that RACISM is the belief that one group is superior to another group due to skin pigmentation. But that is not actually racism. How can it be racism if we all belong to the human race? Racism is actually one race that believes itself superior to another race. Since human beings belong to the human race, what other race can consider itself superior or inferior to the human race? That will be revealed later in the book.

Black activists claimed that most white people are racist and claim that white people believe they are superior to other races. White bigots claimed the same thing about the black activist. The black activists claimed that most white people are bigots, and that these white bigots were doing everything they could to keep the "black" person down. You notice, I said to "keep the black person down" because at that time these activists were not concerned for other groups with a different skin pigmentation than their own. These activists wanted the white bigots to not only stop what they were doing to keep the black person down, but to institute special laws giving black people special rights over all other people in order to "compensate" the black people.

Therein lies the problem. It is not good enough for the activists to "stop" the one group from committing the atrocities against everyone else because they believe they are superior. Those same activists want special laws that will now provide their group superiority and special privileges over all others. They want special laws allowing them to commit the same atrocities against all other people and become what they fought against.

It is in the Constitution that no laws are to be passed providing privileges or immunities to one group or class that shall not belong to all citizens. In other words, no citizen is supposed to have any privileges (rights) or immunities that cannot belong to all citizens. Yet, every day our federal, state and local representatives pass laws providing privileges and immunities to one group or another that are not provided to other individuals or groups.

The election process is another prime example (paradigm). Laws have been instituted providing two "major" parties privileges and immunities that do not belong to other groups or individuals. There are laws providing the "major" parties a special election that no one other than party members are allowed to participate. There are laws providing the two "major" parties privileges that are not extended to other groups or individuals.

These two parties do not have to gather signatures for an election, all the two "major" parties need to do is "guarantee" the signatures. Other parties or individuals are forced to petition for the signatures to have their name placed on the ballot. There are different rules and different forms that have to be filled out by the other candidates. Different information is required from the other candidates. The whole process is different for the candidates not belonging to the two "major" parties. These two parties are identified as the MAJOR parties and other parties as MINOR parties and individuals as INDEPENDENT. The very word MAJOR puts the two "major" party candidates at a distinct advantage. Those truly posing a threat to the "major" party candidates are not permitted on the ballot, are not invited to debates, and are not allowed to participate. This is free and equal?

Would you want to compete in a 1000-meter foot race where the other individuals had a 200- or 300-meter head start? I think not. These two "major" parties control and have made the rules favorable to THEIR first choices. The two parties, what I call the Clique, believe other's choices to be inferior to their choices and have instituted laws that ensure only major party choices are elected. Considering the Clique controls the vote count, when necessary to ensure their first choices are elected, I perceive the vote count is fixed.

And considering that all human beings are being manipulated to some degree, it doesn't seem to matter who is elected because those elected actually perpetrate those things they claim to oppose. Most everyone is on one side in the equations or the other, and the equation is the same on both sides, just reversed. It is like looking in a mirror and pointing a finger at one's self.

Human beings are offensive to other human beings because they let themselves be manipulated through deception by the Evil One using semantics as a means to take what rightfully belongs to all human beings. When any human being is *manipulated through deception* by the *Evil One* into having a law passed to take another human beings' God-given rights, *that right is denied all human beings. That law is usually written in such a manner that it can be distorted and interpreted to exclude the ones initiating the law.* Some founding fathers knew this to be true and attempted to guarantee those God-given rights. That guarantee is the Constitution with its Bill of Rights. The problem with any guarantee is it is only as good as those willing to support it.

Presently we have government resulting from those allegedly elected and chosen to govern being *manipulated through deception* refusing to support that guarantee. They take what is believed to be the easy way out and pass more laws that do nothing but deny rights and oppress the people.

An APHORISM IS basically a saying, an opinion, or perception, used to influence the way human beings think.

Take for example the aphorism, "the mind is a terrible thing to waste."

This aphorism is used throughout the education system. Have you really thought about what it is saying, literally? You are *manipulated through deception* by those that wish you to believe that what's being said is that it is a terrible thing to let a mind go to waste. But that is not what the aphorism is saying. The aphorism is saying, "the mind is a terrible thing," "to waste."

Normally, what do people do with terrible things? They throw them away, give them away, and/or send them to the waste dump. What is the present education system doing with the children's minds? Are the children being educated? Not from the complaints I have been hearing from people.

How many times have you heard that the education system is *dumbing down* the kids? Have you ever encountered or read about a high school or college graduate that cannot read, write, or do simple math? I have. Is this what you want your tax dollars paying for? I think not. *Dedicated teachers are actually being coerced into quitting or excuses found to fire them for challenging students, making them do homework, making them think for themselves.* Those in authority are *manipulated through deception* into believing the mind is a terrible thing and that people are incapable of thinking for themselves. That is why those in authority make every attempt to ensure children's minds are wasted through the present public education system. They believe that they can make the decisions that are best for everyone. That is why they want you and your children's minds to go "to waste." The public education system is doing a good job accomplishing this, don't you think?

Presently, the systems favorite aphorism is "perception is the truth." If anyone perceives something a certain way, that makes it the truth. I was actually told that very thing by a supervisor in a city government. Say something to an individual, and that individual can take what you say, twist and distort it to give it whatever meaning they want, and because that individual perceives it that way, it makes it the truth. Perception is someone's opinion. That does not make it the truth.

Another aphorism is "your vote counts." You are led to believe everyone's vote is counted and that the individual or measure getting the most votes win. Taken literally is this really saying that your vote is actually counted (added up) to decide who is elected or if a measure gets passed? Or is it actually saying your vote is considered, or viewed? "Your vote counts" does not mean that your vote was actually used in the final decision, the final selection process. The vote is nothing more than you being permitted to voice your opinion. Those in authority are actually making the final decisions as to the individuals "appointed" to office and what measures go into effect. Those in authority have been *manipulated through deception* into taking it upon themselves to only take into consideration the people's vote. They have used the authority provided to them by the people, and secretly circumvented the constitutional election process. They did it in secret because they abused their authority and are afraid to take the responsibility for what was done in the past and continue to do it the "way it has always been done."

Here is a favorite aphorism used by most people: "Do as I say and not as I do." What this is saying is, "do what I tell you to do, not what you see me do. I cannot practice what I preach, but you must." This is a great hypocrisy teaching tool for parents. I will bet almost every parent, including myself, has used that one. What message do the children receive from this? My parents are hypocrites.

The system does the same thing. Laws are passed telling you not to do certain things, and you are punished if you do those things, yet those within the system do those very things without receiving any punishment and the people think those in authority are hypocrites. "Do as I say and not as I do" is nothing but blatant hypocrisy.

An aphorism human beings are *manipulated through deception* into believing is *there is no right or wrong*. If there is no right or wrong, then for what purpose did our founding fathers institute a *Bill of Rights* into the Constitution? If there is no right or wrong, then what is the purpose for being told is it wrong to use certain words? If there is no right or wrong, for what purposes are laws written forbidding murder, rape, arson, kidnapping, robbery, prostitution, etc.? If there is no right or wrong, for what purpose are any laws actually instituted and shouldn't human beings be able to do as they please, do what they want when they want, and be allowed to murder, kill, rape, steal, cheat, rob, etc., if that is what they want? If there is no right or wrong, for what purpose are the tobacco companies sued for the wrongs their products have done to the people who used their product? If there is no right or wrong, for what purpose do people sue for being wronged? If there is no right or wrong, for what purpose have special laws been passed protecting special groups from being wronged by other groups? If there is no right or wrong, for what purpose are police departments financed? I could go on, but do you hear what I am saying? There is a right, and there is a wrong. It is time human beings woke up and admitted that fact.

Another favorite aphorism those *manipulating through deception* want human beings to believe is, "do not take things so literally, read between the lines."

Do take everything you read literally and pay attention to what is being said because while you are trying to read what is between the lines and decipher what you think THEY might be saying, THEY are doing exactly as they are literally saying. And in the process, THEY are taking everything you have and believe in, including God, home, country and the U.S. Constitution.

For example, the "Rule of Law" is exactly that, it is a "Rule of Law." According to the U.S. Constitution and what I have always been taught, this is a nation that has a "Rule of Constitutional law." All laws are to be within the Constitution's boundaries. Notice how conveniently the word Constitutional has been removed from the "Rule of Law" aphorism. *The "Rule of Law" is totally different than "Rule of Constitutional Law." "Rule of Constitutional Law" restricts and prohibits the laws that can be instituted by those in authority and protects the people's God-given rights. "Rule of Law" allows those in authority to institute any laws they want, without restriction. "Rule of Law" permits those in authority to deny God-given rights at THEIR whim.*

PROFILING IS a basic outline and developed standards that represent something and/or someone and puts that someone into a certain category.

The problem with profiling is, a single profile can usually be made to fit just about anyone. Profiling has become the latest tool in the enslavement methodology.

ARE YOU A TERRORIST?

According to what I interpreted and understood from an Associated Press article written by Tom Hays titled "Suicide Hijackers Lived by the Book" and published in the *Rocky Mountains News*, Saturday, September 22, 2001, *WE are all terrorists or terrorists in disguise.* Although the article was in all probability not intended as a *profile* by the author, I believe that IS exactly *what the authorities* who provided the information for the article *intended to accomplish.* By utilizing *manipulation through deception*, the authorities that provided the information for the article actually profiled those that are considered to be terrorists. According to the profile (outline) all human beings are terrorists. According to the 180-page terrorist manual that the experts claim was allegedly found, and the excerpts provided from that manual providing an outline (profile) to the 9-11 terrorist/hijackers, we are all terrorists or terrorists in disguise. The profile in accordance with what was reported in the article as being in the terrorist manual is provided. The *underlined italicized portions are excerpts from the article and the alleged*

THE ENEMY CALLED "THEY"

180-page terrorist manual experts claimed they had found. The manual allegedly instructs the terrorists in how they are to conduct themselves to keep from being identified as terrorists, i.e. *terrorists in disguise.* My personal comments follow the underlined excerpts from the article. The article is reprinted with permission of The Associated Press:

No beards or other Islamic characteristics. If you wear a beard you are Islamic and a terrorist. If you do not wear a beard, you are a terrorist in disguise. Also, if you are Islamic, you are a terrorist. If you aren't Islamic, you are a terrorist in disguise. Everyone have that straight? Good.

Do not speak loudly or otherwise draw attention to yourself. So, I guess that if you speak loudly or otherwise draw attention yourself, you are a terrorist. If you do not, you are a terrorist in disguise. So everyone, keep your mouth shut, that way you do not draw attention to yourself that you are a terrorist. If you do talk loudly or draw attention to yourself, you are no longer in disguise and now have exposed yourself as being a terrorist. Everyone have that straight? Good.

Rent apartments in newly developed areas where neighbors do not know each other. If you are renting an apartment, and do not know your neighbors, you are a terrorist in disguise. If you go around introducing yourself to all the people in an apartment complex and get to know your neighbors, you are a terrorist. Everyone have that straight? Good.

Do not address others with traditional Islamic greetings in which Allah's name is invoked. Allah is the name for GOD in the Islamic religion. If you greet others with the expression "God be with you" or "go with the grace of God," etc., you are a terrorist. If you pray to GOD you are a terrorist. If you do not do those things, then you are a terrorist in disguise. Everyone have that straight? Good.

Do not cause trouble in your neighborhood. Do not park in no-parking zones. If you cause trouble in your neighborhood, or if you park in a no-parking zone, you are a terrorist and have exposed yourself. If you do not do these things, then you are a terrorist in disguise. Everyone have that straight? Good.

Do not live near police stations. So, if you do live near a police station, you are a terrorist, because only terrorists live near police stations. If you do not live near a police station, you are a terrorist in disguise. Everyone have that straight? Good.

Do not appear to be overly inquisitive. If you are curious and ask too many questions you are a terrorist. If you are not curious and you do not ask questions, you are a terrorist in disguise. Everyone have that straight? Good.

Burn letters immediately after reading them and get rid of the ashes too. If you do not burn letters immediately after reading them and do not get rid of the ashes, you are a terrorist. If you burn letters immediately after reading them and get rid of the ashes too, you are a terrorist in disguise. Everyone have that straight? Good.

Use codes when talking on the phone. If you do not use codes when talking on the phone, you are a terrorist. If you do use code when talking on the phone, you are a terrorist in disguise. Everyone have that straight? Good.

Other interesting statements from the article are underlined and italicized below. My personal comments follow the underlined and italicized portions from the article:

Television images depicting the men thought to have been aboard the airliners show most without beards. People who encountered them said they wore Western clothes. Having been in many Arab countries, most Arabs do not have beards. Some do, some don't. Many Arabs also wear Western or European clothing. Some Americans have beards, some don't. Most men aboard the aircraft were westerners, i.e., Americans. So, are all those without beards and that wear Western clothing terrorists in disguise? Those with beards and that do not wear western clothing, are they all terrorist? According to the new airport security measures implemented, I think so.

Neighbors of some of the men in California, Florida and Maryland said they lived in suburbs where they did not stand out. In Florida, they moved frequently, staying in motels and apartments around the state. If you live in the California, Florida and Maryland suburbs, and you do not stand out, you are a terrorist in disguise. If you do not live in the suburbs and you do stand out, you are a terrorist. If you live in Florida, move frequently, stay in motels and apartments around the state, you are a terrorist. If you do not move frequently, nor stay in motels and apartments around Florida, you are a terrorist in disguise. Everyone have that straight? Good.

They also joined gyms. If you join a gym, you are a terrorist in disguise. If you do not join a gym, you are a terrorist. Everyone have that straight? Good.

One made small talk with a neighbor about sports. If you make small talk with a neighbor about sports, you are a terrorist in disguise. If you do not make small talk with a neighbor about sports, you are a terrorist. Everyone have that straight. Good.

Another posted a personal ad on the Internet. If you post a personal ad on the Internet, you are a terrorist in disguise. If you do not post a personal ad on the Internet, you are a terrorist. Everyone have that straight? Good.

People who came into contact with them described them as quiet, friendly and sometimes timid men who gave few, if any, hints that they harbored deep resentment against the United States. So, if you are quiet, friendly and sometimes timid and do not display any hints that you harbor deep resentment against the United States, you are a terrorist in disguise. If you are not quieting, friendly and sometimes timid and you do display hints that you harbor resentment against the United States, you are a terrorist. Everyone have that straight? Good.

Nawaq Ashamzi, a suspected hijacker aboard the jet that crashed into the Pentagon, lived last fall in a new 175-unit San Diego apartment building where so many people came and went that he was barely noticed. He always paid the rent on time. So, if you live in a new 175-unit San Diego apartment building where so many people come and go that you are barely noticed, you are a terrorist in disguise. If you pay your rent on time, you are a terrorist in disguise. If you do not live in a new 175-unit San Diego apartment where so many people come and go that you are barely noticed, you are a terrorist. If you do not pay your rent on time, you are a terrorist. Everyone have that straight? Good.

Some of the hijackers appeared to bend a rule in the manual stating that "there is nothing that permits drinking wine or fornicating." So, I guess terrorist/hijackers are not permitted to drink wine or fornicate. If you do these things, you are a terrorist. If you do not do these things, you are a terrorist in disguise. Everyone have that straight? Good.

Days before the World Trade Center attack, Mohamed Atta and Marwan Al Shehhi were seen drinking at a sports bar in Hollywood, Fla. Majed Moqued was spotted perusing adult videos in two Laurel, Md., stores. He did not buy anything. If you are seen drinking in a sports bar in Hollywood, Fla., you are a terrorist in disguise. If you are spotted perusing (reading, checking, examining) adult videos in two Laurel, Md., stores, and do not buy anything, you are a terrorist in disguise. If you do not do these things, you are a terrorist (see above). Everyone have that straight? Good!

I ask again, are you a terrorist or a terrorist in disguise?

According to the article, *"The suicide hijackers in last week's attack apparently practiced terrorism 'by the book,' a 180-page manual for Muslim operatives living undercover among their enemies in the worlds godless areas.*

"The manual, Military Studies in the Jihad Against the Tyrants, *was*

discovered last year during an investigation of Osama bin Laden. It gives terrorists precise instructions on how to act while they await their orders to strike.

Investigators have not said whether the 19 hijackers read the manual. But glimpses of their lives suggest they conducted themselves according to its instructions during the months they spent in the United States.

Experts say the manual illustrates the inner workings of bin Laden's al-Qaida organization, the prime suspect in the attacks. It also foreshadows the suicide highjackings themselves, in which the terrorists used box cutters and knives.

For example, the manual's assassinations section gives precise instructions on how to use weapons with blades, saying the "enemy must be struck in one of these lethal spots: Anywhere in the rib cage, both or one eye, the back of the head, the end of the spinal column."

The hijackers seem to have followed the manual as closely as they could...making sure no one knew the whole picture, said (name omitted) a former deputy head of anti-terrorism for the FBI's New York City office.

Now let me get this straight. The hijackers who committed the attacks against the World Trade Center and the Pentagon went by the book. The hijackers/terrorists may not have read the manual, but seem to have followed the manual as closely as they could, making sure no one knew the whole picture. They may not have read the manual, but followed its instructions closely, yet drank and did things that the manual said they were not supposed to do, and bent some rules. The manual gave precise instructions on where to strike with the blade. Let me see, the rib cage, both or one eye, the back of the head, the end of the spinal column. I guess the WTC terrorists read the wrong manual, they cut throats. Experts say the manual illustrates the inner workings of bin Laden's al-Qaida organization. It also foreshadows (predicts, warns of) the suicide highjackings themselves, in which the terrorists used box cutters and knives. So, the experts knew it was going to happen, were forewarned about how it was going to happen and the weapons that were going to be used. What did the experts do to prevent this from happening when they knew it was going to happen? They did absolutely nothing! For what purpose did they do nothing? Could it be they played a part in this atrocity?

Do you notice how easily the profile can be made to apply to *anyone*, especially if it is twisted and distorted by someone such as me? From your own personal experience with government, at any level, aren't many in our government proficient at doing the very same thing that I did with the article? Do you also see the dangers in this profiling methodology that human beings are being *manipulated through deception* into accepting as the way to catch criminals, i.e. terrorists?

A profile can be presented in such a manner it can apply to just about anyone accused or arrested, and is a prosecutor's dream come true. No need to find those that actually commit the crimes. *The profile can be made to apply to the person on trial perfectly, so the person must be guilty.* The only problem is that the profile can be made to apply to all human beings. And who are the real masters at twisting and distorting the truth? The *Evil One*, that's who. The sole purpose for profiling is get human beings to look upon each other with suspicion, divide and conquer.

COMPETITIVENESS IS instilled in every creature including human beings.

Human beings are born with a competitive nature. Healthy competition is good for everyone.

The key word is healthy. Too many times human beings are taught to be competitive outside their natural competitiveness. A person can be competitive and continually strive to make himself/herself better at a sport, job, game, etc. A person can compete against a clock, another person, even themselves, etc. As long as the rules are fair and applied equitably, competition against another person is healthy, although it can be fierce. When a person gives their best effort and still loses in a fair contest, that person can hold their head high because they gave it everything they had. They can be comfortable in knowing that the other person's effort was more than they could personally produce. The greatest satisfaction a person can have is in knowing that they have won fair and square. The next greatest satisfaction is in knowing that even if you lost, you did your absolute best. The opponent just flat outperformed you. Most human beings can accept that.

When an opponent cheats, changes the rules, or a judge uses favoritism to decide, then the competition is no longer healthy. It causes strife and jealousies. The person losing feels cheated. They know that the other person is not really the winner. Real winners do not resort to cheating. Real winners do not change the rules as the competition is in progress. Real winners do not need the judges to play favorites.

Today, human beings are taught to "win at all costs," or "the only thing that matters is winning," or "second best means you are a loser," or "in winning, the end justifies the means," etc., etc. These aphorisms change the competitive nature into a jealous nature and are unhealthy teaching tools. These aphorisms get human beings hurt because the only thing that matters is winning and not how one performs.

Even the different military services within our own nation are taught to compete against each other, when it would seem necessary that they work together as a team. A team is people with different skills and backgrounds working together for a common goal.

From what I have observed the past 20 or 30 years in America, a team player is someone willing to suck up to the boss and not question what the boss says, right or wrong. That is not a team player and that definitely is not teamwork. Each person on a team has unique skills and abilities, something they are best at doing because they enjoy doing it. Everyone has the ability to do anything they put their minds to, and most can do well in almost any job. No one is irreplaceable. But individuals excel at things they love to do because their hearts, their spirits are in it. In order to reach a common goal it is necessary to let the people on the team ask questions and provide input, and whenever possible, place individuals in positions where they can excel because they love the work. In the end, the final decision rests with those *chosen as the leaders, the ones with the responsibility* to make the final decision where to place individuals on the team. Too many times, individuals are selected that are not best suited for a position or job. The individual dislikes the work he/she is forced to do so vehemently, they perform poorly or their work is shoddy. When a person is found who enjoys their work and does a good job, one usually likes to keep them in that position on the team and will do everything within reason to keep them there.

Problems arise when there are different rules for different people on the team. One person is considered to be worth more than another person and is paid more for their work. Or some are the bosses' friends and/or favorites and are granted special privileges that others are not allowed. People on the team are prevented from providing input and forced to keep their mouth shut. People are allowed to do their own thing, allowed to do it their own way because the one responsible for the team does not want to make the hard decisions.

If one person on the team makes all the decisions all the time, without allowing for any discussion or input, that is not a team effort. If the one responsible for the decisions that affect the team plays favorites, does not enforce the rules equitably, and is harder on some than others, that is not a team. If the one responsible for making the decisions does not accept that responsibility and is not held accountable, that is not a team. That is a group secretly pulling in different directions. That is a team divided. When the boss is not around, everyone thinks they are the one in charge and that results in arguing, bickering, and chaos. "When the boss is away, the mice do play." When the boss returns he/she usually finds people ready to kill each other.

A team or a nation divided is easy to conquer and then control because they have no direction. They are isolated groups doing their own thing causing confusion and chaos. It is necessary to have order for a team to function properly. That is why there is a team structure, a chain of command if you wish. Each person in the chain knows who is next in the chain and in charge if something should happen. That way there is far less conflict and division. It is necessary for human beings to have a direction. Human beings divided are easy to conquer and then control.

If the team leader has performed his/her job properly, when the leader is gone, that leader will not be missed and the individual team members will perform the same as if he/she were still there. In other words, a good team leader will not be missed.

I used to tell individuals in the military, "You only have as much responsibility as you are willing to accept, and you only have as much authority as you are willing to enforce and the stripes/crow on your sleeve gives you all the authority you need."

The team leader is responsible for each member on his/her team and their actions. Too many times, team leaders are not accepting responsibility for their own actions, let alone the team's actions. Eventually, hate abounds on the team. Today, in America, throughout the world, we have leaders that do not take responsibility for their actions. These leaders hang team members out to dry in the public eye to save their own necks and hate abounds on the human being's team today. The purpose is to perpetuate hate, divide and conquer.

SAFETY/SECURITY IS a tool that has been used for several decades to undermine God-given constitutionally guaranteed rights.

"They that can give up essential liberty to obtain a little temporary safety deserve neither liberty nor safety" is attributed to Benjamin Franklin.

From the preceding statement attributed to Ben Franklin, safety/security was being used over 220 years ago for the same purpose.

Do not get me wrong, I think that safety/security is an important aspect in life. I also believe that most people have a built-in warning system that lets them know when something is unsafe. The problem is that we are taught to ignore that warning system through various aphorisms. How many times have you heard that life is a gamble? Or if you do not take a chance in life you will never succeed at anything, you will never get anywhere and you will never be rich? How about the aphorism about nothing ventured, nothing gained? In the system practiced, some that gamble do get ahead, but most end up with nothing and a slave to those that created the system. Many gamble with their lives, and most that do end up in an early grave. We are taught to ignore our built-in warning system and take a chance. Those that do take a chance usually end up gambling away their fortunes and/or lives.

Have you noticed that most states now have lotteries and other gambling methods such as video poker and blackjack machines? Have you noticed the big push to entice people into going to Las Vegas, Reno, Atlantic City and other gambling spots? I have been in those cities and have felt the evil that permeates those places. Most leave these places broke or near broke. People are told not to lose more than they can afford. Most people cannot afford to lose anything because they are already in debt up to their ears and are hoping to leave these places rich. People *are manipulated through deception* into ignoring their built-in safety warning device with the glitter, sounds, free drinks, and other "perks" offered by the casinos. Alcohol diminishes a person's judgement and safety warning system. THEY know this and THEY rely on this. The slot machines make sounds to mesmerize a person. THEY do not call slot machines one-armed bandits for no reason. A slot machine is designed to take your money. For every winner, hundreds lose. Welcome to the gambling pyramid. The odds always favor the house no matter what the game because THEY control the game and program the machine and are designed to rob your financial security. Think!

Have you noticed that since OSHA was formed, that the only thing it has really accomplished is that certain big businesses that sell safety products make huge profits while virtually destroying small businesses and forcing individuals such as doctors from practicing? Medical doctors are quitting their practices in droves due to OSHA or insurance costs? Do people really need an agency such as OSHA dictating their safety needs? I think not. All that is necessary is for people to listen to their built-in safety warning system. On the job, we all know when we commit a dangerous act. If people are properly trained in a trade, safety practices are taught. Anything that produces flying chips or particles is a danger to the eyes, and wearing goggles is common sense. Yet people have been taught to ignore their warning system and "take a chance." I have done it myself. Many have lost their eyesight in one or both eyes and then blame and sue the company and refuse to accept responsibility for their own actions. When we ignore our built-in warning system, that is usually when we get into trouble. We are responsible for our actions, but want others to be held accountable for what we do to ourselves. People give up their God-given constitutionally guaranteed rights for the government to keep them safe.

My safety warning system is screaming that all the security measures being put into place by our government due to 9-11 is nothing more than a ploy to deny more God-given Constitutionally guaranteed rights. My warning system is screaming that THEY are *manipulating the people through deception* into accepting these "tighter measures" claiming it is for our own safety/security. Does anyone truly think the government is concerned for your safety? Having worked in government, and from what I have experienced, observed, and seen in actual practice, THEY have no concern for your safety or security. It is a pretense and it is being used to deny you what is rightfully yours and it is done for greed.

Have you noticed that government costs have increased due to OSHA requirements and environmental requirements? THEY created OSHA and the EPA and are the ones responsible for the increases resulting in tax increases for the people. Could this be to confiscate more money through taxes? I think so.

The government creates agencies that create and administer ridiculous safety and environmental laws and practices that are extremely costly, then tell you that your taxes have to increase to administer these things within government. Catch 22, anyone?

I remember going through an OSHA safety inspection at the auto hobby shop I once managed at Norfolk Naval Facility in Norfolk, Virginia. I was very strict on shop safety and the naval personnel that used the hobby shop were expected to adhere to all shop safety practices. During an OSHA inspection, the OSHA inspector walked right by the only customer in the shop who was violating shop safety procedures. The young man had his car jacked up supported solely with the hydraulic jack. He was underneath the car working. I told the young man to either use the shop supplied jack stands to support the vehicle or leave the shop immediately. The OSHA inspector appeared completely oblivious to what I was talking about and was more concerned with cracked electrical plug outlet covers than a shop safety infraction that was actually endangering a human life.

If the pretense for safety/security is not for greed, then what is the purpose? There is no other purpose. It is a beast that never has enough and will eventually have to turn on and eat those within its own system to keep from starving. The signs are already there from observing what THEY are now doing with the government employee pension funds and the Social Security pension funds. Those funds are being "robbed" by the very government that put those systems into place. But remember it is for your financial safety and security that these systems were put into place. THEY want to ensure that the financial safety and security you rely upon being available is no longer there for your elderly years.

GREED IS the one tool that touches almost every human being.

In Matthew 6:24 Jesus Christ said, *"No one can serve two masters; for either he will hate the one and love the other, or he will be devoted to one and despise the other. You cannot serve God and wealth."* 1st Timothy 6:10 says, *"For the love of money is a root of all sorts of evil, and some by longing for it have wandered away from the faith and pierced themselves with many griefs."* From personal experiences and observations that is an undisputed fact. Almost every atrocity human beings commit against each other has its roots in greed.

There is no need for the government to make laws censoring what is published. All that was necessary was to put copyright laws into place and let greed do the rest. Most newspaper editors and publishers would be infuriated if the government instituted laws censoring what was published. Yet the newspaper editors and publishers themselves censor what is published and it is perfectly acceptable. Is this not hypocrisy. Nonsense, most newspaper editors and publishers will say. We do not censor the news or what is published.

Censorship is exactly what they do. It is called editing. It is called controlling what will be published and what won't be published, what will be heard and what won't be heard. How many letters to the editor aren't published for one reason or another? That is censorship. It is said that for every book that gets published, there are nine hundred and ninety-nine that the publishers rejects. Put another way, 1/10 of 1% is heard, 99.99% are silenced. That is censorship. If an author cannot get his/her book published, that author has been silenced. That author has been censored and it is all for *greed.*

Everyone involved in the publishing process from the writer, to the literary agent, to the editor, to the publisher, to the publicist is involved in censorship. They decide what is or is not adequate for publishing based solely on one thing and that is greed. Writers get a copyright because the publisher demands it or they do not want their written material to be sold by others. Editors edit out what they do not deem appropriate or because they do not like the way the author presents the material, and fear that it may offend someone or prevent someone from buying the book. Publishers only want books they "know" will sell. Will the book sell and what audience does it appeal too, i.e., is the market big enough that a huge profit can be made? Publicists charge a huge salary to market the product. Many great literary works have been turned away by these "experts" in the field, only to be best sellers by those few willing to publish not for profit, but for principle. These best sellers made huge profits for those publishers with principle. Using greed as the foundation, human beings have been *manipulated through deception* into administering censorship, *and it is administered by the very human beings that profess the loudest that they detest censorship.* Hypocrisy resulting from greed.

I also believe that the stock market is nothing more than one big gamble and is a government sanctioned LEGAL yet elaborate pyramid scheme THEY created and is solely based on greed. Few people truly get rich dealing in the stock market. The few that really get rich are the ones running and manipulating the market. On July 12, 2002, a stock market analyst made a comment to the effect that the stock market decline was due to a market struggle between fear and greed, and he was sorry to say that fear was winning out over greed. Do you really believe that two evils are combating each other over which one will rule the market?

It is not fear that is struggling with greed in the stock market. It is people's safety warning system that something is amiss in the market. It is a little late, but at least the people are starting to listen to their warning system. It is good that the people aren't letting greed overshadow their natural warning system. Greed is the problem in the stock market. People in major companies have been *manipulated through deception* into reporting false numbers and profits in order to make the stocks appear more valuable than they are actually worth. That deception is now being exposed and the people are being careful and they are looking out for their own financial safety. Yet the analyst thinks this is bad. It may be bad for the market, but is sure healthy for those that have been taking a gamble on the market and have lost their shirts. At least those people are now starting to think.

STRESS/FRUSTRATION are two very effective tools used in the templates to influence people to do moronic things.

Most everyone is familiar with and has experienced stress and the resulting frustration. It is also a fact that stress can lead to poor health, heart attacks, and other serious medical problems. If there are any among you reading this who has not experienced stress and frustration, I say more power to you. Personally, I have yet to meet an individual that has not experienced and been affected by these tools. They walk hand in hand. One comes with the other. I find it ironic that government and major organizations spend millions each year on teaching supervisors and employees what they call "job-related stress management." It seems logical to me that if jobs are structured such that those jobs cause excessive mental and physical stress on individuals, all possible avenues would be taken to restructure jobs in order to remove that stress. It makes no sense to pay millions each year teaching job-related stress management when it would be less costly and more effective to remove or help alleviate those things causing the stress. In most cases, the stress is caused by the person having too many functions to perform in the allotted time or too many senseless rules to follow. The person then becomes stressed, and soon burnout is reached. Burnout is basically a nervous breakdown. Rather than find ways to help relieve the stress factor, companies and the government spend millions on stress management classes that do absolutely nothing to relieve the stress. The reason is, THEY do not really want the stress removed. THEY just want to provide the illusion THEY are concerned for people's health and welfare related to stress and send people to a class that does nothing more than teach simple exercises. The job related stress is not relieved because it is still built into the job. People still have to cope with the stress and related frustration.

Those people that work in a post office are a good example. Work in a post office for a short time and you will quickly learn. Postal workers are put under tremendous stress, and that stress is created from within the postal organization with the nonsensical rules and procedures governing the employees and management's cold heartedness. Postal workers are only allowed so many seconds to case each piece of mail. They are only allowed so many seconds at each post box on the route. Supervisors will secretly follow and time them on the route. They are not allowed to talk while casing mail. Anything you say and do is held against you. Postal workers are expected to be and act like robots.

A postal worker was stopped at a mail box and putting mail in the box when her postal vehicle was struck from behind. Upper management said the accident was driver negligence. Management claimed the driver should have been aware of everything going on around her, and should have been able to move her vehicle in time to avoid the accident. Say what? For what purpose was this done? The Postal Service considers all driving accidents preventable, and the last person that can prevent the accident is the one responsible. The postal driver is the last person that can prevent an accident while driving a postal vehicle. Ridiculous, you bet it is. Luckily, even the Postmaster at the post office where she worked could not agree with the decision. Yet, think about the stress factor that young lady was put under while waiting for the decision if she was going to be disciplined or allowed to keep her job.

Postal workers are held responsible for things they have absolutely no control over. When a customer complains they did not receive an advertisement from a store that sends out *addressed* flyers to "preferred" customers, it is the postal worker's fault even though no advertisement was actually addressed to the customer complaining. That complaint goes on the postal workers record and counts against the postal worker as a customer complaint come evaluation time. A postal worker delivers mail to an individual at a certain address for weeks. One day a complaint is filed against the postal worker stating that mail for that particular individual is no longer to be delivered at that address, but to forward the mail to another address. Several weeks later, another complaint is filed against the postal worker for not delivering the mail to the address as before. Seems a guy and his girl friend broke up, and several weeks later, got back together. The one customer found it easier to call in a complaint than fill out a change of address card. The results are that two customer complaints go against the postal worker that will reflect on the postal worker's evaluation. Is that ridiculous? I think so. Does it happen? Yes it does. Does it cause stress and frustration? What do you think? Multiply this by many other nonsensical rules and procedures and what do you think the ultimate results will be? Those that need the job cannot cope with the stress and frustration related to the ridiculous policies and end up going POSTAL. This is just one example in one profession in this nation.

Highly trained and the safest drivers on the road are truck drivers. Or are they? Truck drivers go through an extensive 4-8 week course and spend up to $5,000 to obtain a CDL. The drivers are provided a federal regulation book they are supposed to follow that is the size of *The Bible*. The company for which they work provides a rules manual on company policies and expects those rules to be followed. They have to remember the "essential" federal safety rules to keep from getting in serious trouble. Some fines for a truck driver, such as missing and driving by a weigh station, can cost the driver up to a thousand dollars, on the spot.

Truck drivers are trained that they are supposed to drive legal and their logs are to reflect their actual driving times and that they are to stay within the federal regulations. The companies for which drivers work demand that the logs the drivers turn in be legal. You notice, I said the logs turned into the company are to be legal. The companies then put the drivers in situations where it is impossible to drive legal and stay within the regulations. Drivers are forced to log hours as being in the sleeping birth when they are actually on the road looking for pallets, dropping off pallets, getting repairs, etc. A driver is to log 15 minutes in the on-duty not driving status on the log for reasons such as fueling, pre-trip and post-trip inspections, loading and unloading. If they take longer than 15 minutes, they are to log that extra time as sleeper birth time. At some busy truck stops, a driver may have to take an hour doing such things as fueling and weighing the rig. The driver's sleep time is eaten up little by little by functions that are supposed to be logged in either driving status or on-duty not driving status. But those times generally go against sleeper birth time. The company wants that driver to drive the full allotted driving time and sacrifice sleep time. Do they tell the driver this? Absolutely not! Drivers are told to log legal and that the log should reflect what the driver is actually doing. But the company will put the drivers in situations that the driver has to drive outside the log or log time in the sleeper birth when the driver is actually driving in order to get the load to its destination on time. Sleep depravation combined with nonsensical rules and the frustration factor skyrockets. When drivers use their logs to gather evidence to take that evidence to the authorities to "blow the whistle" in order to show what the company is doing, the authorities hammer the driver. It is the drivers that are ultimately held responsible. It is the driver's responsibility to drive legal and log legal. A truck driver has three choices. Quit and "try" to find an honest trucking organization (good luck), stay with the organization and take their chances they won't be caught by authorities, or change professions. Blow the whistle, no one will listen, the driver will be hammered, and most likely will never see another truck driving job.

The companies pay the drivers by the mile and use the driver's need for a job and money to support his/her family in order to *manipulate the drivers through deception* into "breaking the law" and driving outside their logs. Some drivers maintain two logs. I have no idea how this is accomplished, but I do know these drivers cannot be getting much sleep.

THE ENEMY CALLED "THEY"

Most drivers, when logging seventy hours' driving in eight consecutive days according to regulations, are most likely putting in 100 plus actual working hours in that eight-day time. There are 192 hours in 8 days. You can imagine how tired a driver is working 100 plus hours in 8 days. You do the math for someone maintaining two logs. Imagine now you have an extremely tired, stressed-out, frustrated truck driver driving down the highway at 65-70 MPH in an 80,000-pound rig that takes the length of 3 football fields to stop. Due to the stress and frustration, some drivers end up using drugs to stay awake to do the job. Now you have a stressed-out, frustrated, sleepy driver on drugs driving down the highway at 65-70 mph with an 80,000-pound rig that takes 3 football fields to get stopped. Do you really think THEY are concerned for public safety? Do you really think the regulations are put into place to protect the general public and the drivers? I don't think so. The regulations are put into place to put people under stress in order to frustrate people into committing moronic acts in order to get the job done.

Now think about this, the driver is paid by the mile. If that driver drives according to regulations, and does nothing more than spend 70 hours driving in 8 days and is paid $.31 a mile, how much is that driver getting per hour? Saying that a driver can average 62.5 miles per hour for those 70 hours driving that equals 4375 miles in 8 days. Multiply 4375 times $.31 per mile, that equates to $1356.25 for eight days' work. Divide that by 70, that equals $19.38 per hour. That is a nice wage right? But, the driver is actually working 100 hours in that 8-day period. In reality, that driver is making $13.56 per hours. Plus, that driver is spending weeks, even months, away from home, family and loved ones. That driver is sleeping in a cubby hole in a truck when he/she can get some sleep, is under tremendous stress, all for the same wage as a 40-hour-a-week job staying at home. Reality is, it is difficult to maintain a 62.5 miles per hour over a 70-hour driving period. 50-55 mph is the norm unless speed laws are broken. Most drivers start at a lower per mile rate at approximately $.21 or $.22 cents per mile, and it takes several years to work one's way up to the "good money." In fact most drivers make approximately $8.50 and hour. It only seems like good money because it is not being spent and they are working a double shift. Drivers can also make a little extra money by padding the paperwork turned in for what they pay to laborers to load and unload for companies that provide such labor cost.

To actually make a decent paying wage, the driver is manipulated into breaking speed laws, Federal regulations, and skimming money through unethical practices. The more THEY can manipulate the people into doing these things, the more control THEY have over those people. Why, because THEY know exactly what that driver is doing at all times. Everything and every move that driver makes, THEY know. And the drivers know THEY know. That also increases the stress and frustration factor, especially for those trying to make a living following the rules. And those that speak out against these practices end up losing their jobs. Is it right? I don't think so.

I have absolutely no proof, but I believe some states may be accepting payoffs from the trucking companies to let those company drivers skate through the weigh stations while hammering the independent truckers and other companies that don't pay. The only evidence is that it appears some major trucking company drivers have little if any problems getting through the weigh stations, and their drivers aren't subjected to the same standards as other drivers by the authorities in many states. But that is just my "perception."

Imagine the stress and frustration factor that a school bus driver goes through driving a bus loaded with children. Now add to that the stress and frustration the harassment management will deliberately put on the school bus driver. What is the purpose? To gain, maintain and keep control over the driver. Personally, I enjoyed the job with the kids while doing it, and tried to maintain a firm yet friendly rapport with the children. Upper management and upper management's policies were my downfall in that job, and in reality, in many jobs that I have left. Most immediate supervisors are pretty decent individuals, but trying to administer upper management's policies causes many immediate supervisors some real stress and frustration problems.

But, keep in mind, THEY want the employees, including most management personnel, stressed and frustrated in order to maintain control.

School bus drivers receive much adverse publicity whenever there is an incident involving children aboard school buses. I believe it is time tell the other side in that story. The safety rules aboard the school bus are not only about safety, but are also about maintaining control aboard that bus. *Safety is about maintaining control. All rules and regulations are about maintaining control.*

There has to be some control in this world, or there would be anarchy. A school bus is a perfect example. I have experienced anarchy on a school bus. Many new drivers experience anarchy aboard a school bus. Even experienced school bus drivers switched to a new route can experience anarchy aboard a school bus. The children want to know their limitations from a new driver and those children will immediately put that driver to the test. If the driver allows a few to break the rules, within a short time all the children are doing as they please. And many things the children do endanger themselves and everyone aboard the bus.

It is baffling that parents are willing to immediately believe their children can do no wrong. I have three children and although they were taught to respect all individuals, they weren't perfect and had to be corrected. I have had elementary through high school children scream, "I will get you fired," or "My parents will sue you." One 4th grade girl told me, "You piss me off." Another child stated, "My mother said I don't have to listen to you." I saw children hitting each other in the head with lunch pails, punching each other, and tripping each other while loading and unloading. I saw children climbing across seats, standing in seats, bigger children refusing to let smaller children sit down, children sticking their hands, arms and heads out of the windows while the buses were driving down the road. I saw wanton destruction to the bus seats by children cutting or poking the upholstery with sharp objects. Several drivers have had students shout profanity at people in cars and on the street and make provoking gestures with the middle finger. Children have caused car accidents throwing objects out school bus windows. I did not tolerate such actions and these things were corrected and stopped immediately on buses I drove. That made me a mean school bus driver. So, I guess most school bus drivers are mean school bus drivers because they do not tolerate such actions either. Other drivers have been hit in the head with flashlight batteries, and one driver was threatened with a knife. School bus drivers have had to ask other drivers to come to their assistance because they couldn't get some children calm enough to continue the routes. In my opinion the children who behave in these manners have little or no discipline and have no respect for anything or anyone including themselves.

The only disciplinary tools available to drivers are an informal warning slip or a citation. The citation goes to the school principal who may or may not take action. Usually, if the parents protest loud enough, the principal will nullify the citation, leaving the children with the impression they can do as they please. This happens at many schools. Some local principals believe drivers enforcing the rules are violating the children's Constitutional rights. What about the students' Constitutional rights who do behave and want a safe ride home? What about the driver's Constitutional rights? When the children learn to respect each other and each other's God-given rights, and to treat others aboard the bus the way they want to be treated, then the bus becomes a pleasure to drive.

Calls to schools' transportation departments concerning overly strict drivers are commonplace and the overly strict accusations are usually from children's parents whose child has been issued a warning slip or citation by the "mean" school bus driver. The belief is that it is the driver who makes up all these "dumb" rules the children are supposed to follow and that the driver has poor or no children management skills, and obviously does not like children.

In reality, these are the rules and regulations governing students' conduct aboard the bus as set forth by the Federal Government, State Department of Education and any additional rules as set forth by the Local School District and were established for the SAFETY of the children. These are the rules the allegedly elected representatives have allowed to be put in place. Some school districts have parents sign a form at the beginning of the school year agreeing that they have read and explained these rules to their children and their children will comply.

The number one priority aboard any school bus for the drivers is the children's safety and most drivers are not permissive when it comes to enforcing the rules governing the children's safety. Most drivers have children and/or grandchildren and their concern for your children is reflected in the rules' fair enforcement. The accusations about not liking children are unfounded, hurt the drivers deeply, and are really irrelevant to doing the job properly. People who do not like children usually do not take jobs where they have to deal with children. I perceive that most school bus drivers are more concerned for the children's safety than school district upper management and even some parents. Several parents have called demanding that drivers be fired or removed from routes for enforcing these safety rules. Be thankful the School Transportation Division's immediate supervisors normally refuse to remove or fire a driver who is doing the job right, and be thankful for the many drivers who care enough to take the effort to enforce the rules fairly so the children arrive at their destinations unhurt and safe.

Permissiveness aboard a school bus is dangerous and the distractions that are caused by an unruly child endanger not only that child, but also all the children aboard the bus. The individual responsible in an incident or accident is the "*driver*," not the child whose unruly behavior may result in an incident or accident. During the 30-40 minutes the drivers have to safely transport the children to their destinations, drivers haven't the time to interact with the children the same way a teacher does in the classroom, or you as a parent does in the home. The driver is controlling a 26,000-36,000-pound, 40-foot long moving vehicle, while remembering to obey all traffic laws, stop at each child's stop, and keep your child's safety in mind at all times. Because the driver has his/her back to the children they try to maintain control looking in a rear view mirror. I believe that is more than enough responsibility, stress and frustration for a school bus driver making $6.35 to $9.00 an hour. Add to that stress and frustration, that which management dumps on the drivers, and then insert unruly, undisciplined children into the equation, and the stress and frustration become unmanageable. That is when drivers end up doing moronic things such as yelling at a child, stalling a bus on railroad tracks, and some drivers have been known to strike a child. Of course, that driver is immediately disciplined and in some cases fired. Yet, it is the system THEY have created that is the real problem, and no one wants to address the real problem. It is easier to treat the symptoms such as firing the driver, or writing children citations, or suspending children from school for misconduct aboard the school bus than addressing the real problem, i.e. the system THEY have manipulated human beings into creating.

Parents, the next time your children complain about the "mean" school bus driver, tell them it is "their" responsibility to practice "their" skills in obeying the rules and regulations designed for "their" safety aboard the school bus. No child's rights are being violated by the school bus safety rules, if the driver is administering them properly and fairly. Along with rights there are responsibilities. The school bus is not a place for games. Save the games for the playground and home.

Hopefully most people will now be able to recognize the tools discussed, i.e., hypocrisy, fear, semantics, aphorisms, profiling, competitiveness, safety, greed, stress and frustration when being subjected to the templates used against human beings. There are probably other tools being used. I only brought to light those that are most obvious.

Now that the methodology and a few basic tools used within that methodology have been explained, the next several chapters will examine the actual templates and their practical uses.

CHAPTER 4

THE HATE AND PREJUDICE TEMPLATE (DIVIDE AND CONQUER)

The following is an example on how *ist* (Isolation Shock Therapy) is used to turn human being against human being. The template demonstrated below is what I call the Hate and Prejudice template and is used to divide and conquer.

This is an extremely dangerous template. I do not advocate its use. I expose it to you so you will be aware it is being used to manipulate human beings. I attempted to expose it by having it printed in the form below, and my garage door was painted with fascist pig in big black letters and a cigarette butts were piled in my drive way. I do not think the person read past the first paragraph. So, it exists, it is effective, and it works. Be real careful with this one, I do believe it can get a person physically hurt. Hopefully, you will recognize the pattern being used to turn us against each other, divide us, alienate us, rule us.

Remember the old saying, "divide and conquer." Well, this is the template used. I use smokers, perfume users, and bicycle rider as examples. The first two have something in common through smell. The latter has nothing in common with the first two, but you will be able to see how the template can be used to fit any group you want to attack. One can substitute black, white, Republican, Democrat, Hispanic, Christian, Jew, Catholic, police, teacher, man, woman, heterosexual, bisexual, homosexual, fat, skinny, environmental wacko, etc. Just change the words to match the group or individuals one wants to attack. One will get results. Just distort the truth about the group or person and relate what they are doing as being harmful to other's health and safety. Works great if one doesn't mind people being badly hurt, possibly killed.

THE HATE AND PREJUDICE (DIVIDE AND CONQUER) TEMPLATE:

Smokers, Take Note. Your cigarette smoke is a danger to everyone. Cigarette smoking is one of the most gross, filthy and disgusting habits ever encountered. The non-smokers outnumber you, and for the welfare of the community are going to do whatever it takes to keep you from smoking on the streets, in the restaurants, bars, and eventually, in your homes. The non-smokers will do whatever it takes to make you smokers quit and become a non-smoker. The non-smokers will eventually stop you. You retail store, restaurant and bar owners also take note, either you "stop" permitting these smokers to smoke on your premises and property, or the non-smokers are going to ensure you are put out of business and run out of town. The non-smokers have rights and do not care what has to be done to ensure those rights are not violated. "The rights of the individual smokers cannot be considered over the rights of the majority." Once the restaurant and bar owners become either part of the non-smokers agenda or otherwise eliminated, the people who make, sell, and distribute those filthy, dangerous, gross, disgusting cigarettes will be next. The non-smokers will not be denied their rights. The non-smokers who want "clean air" will prevail. Non-smokers unite, it is time to stomp out those gross, filthy, disgusting smokers of dangerous cigarettes!

Users of Cologne, Perfumes, Aftershaves, Etc. take note. The non-users outnumber you, and for the welfare of the community are going to do whatever it takes to keep you from using those products on the streets, in the restaurants, bars, and eventually, in your homes. The fragrance of some of that stuff gags and chokes those who choose not to wear it is and a danger to everyone. Many have breathing conditions such as asthma and find those smells quite offensive. The use of colognes, perfumes, and after-shave lotions is one of the most gross, filthy and disgusting habits ever encountered. Either people who use these kinds of products stop, or those who choose not to use them will stop you. You retail store, restaurant and bar owners also take note, either you "stop" allowing these users of colognes, perfumes, after-shave lotions, etc from using these products on your premises and property, or the non-users are going to ensure you are put out of business and run out of town. The non-users have rights and do not care what has to be done to ensure those rights are not violated. "The rights of the individual users of these products cannot be considered over the rights of the majority." Once the restaurant and bar owners either become part of the non-users agenda or otherwise eliminated, the people who make, sell, and distribute those filthy, dangerous, gross, disgusting colognes, perfumes and after-shave lotions will be next. The non-users will not be denied their rights. The non-users who want "clean air" will prevail. Non-users unite, it is time to stomp out those gross, filthy, disgusting users of dangerous colognes, perfumes, and after-shave lotions!

Bicyclists take note. The car drivers outnumber you, and for the welfare of the community are going to do whatever it takes to keep you from riding bicycles on the streets, on sidewalks, and on the sides of the road. The slow riding bicyclist gags and chokes traffic and impedes those who choose to drive and is a danger to everyone. Many car drivers are in a hurry and find those slow bicycles quite offensive. The use of bicycles is one of the most gross, filthy, disgusting, dangerous sports ever encountered. Have you seen those disgusting tight fitting outfits the riders wear? Either people who ride bicycles stop, or those who choose to drive cars will stop you. You retail store, restaurant and bar owners also take note, either you "stop" allowing these cyclists from parking their bicycles on your premises and property, or the car owners are going to boycott your establishments. The car-owners have rights and do not care what has to be done to ensure those rights are not violated. "The rights of the individual bicyclist cannot be considered over the rights of the majority." Once the retail store, restaurant and bar owners either become part of the car-owner agenda or otherwise eliminated, the people who make, sell, and distribute those slow moving, gross, disgusting, dangerous bicycles will be next. The car owners will not be denied their rights. The car-owners want safe roads and will prevail. Car-owners unite, it is time to stomp out those disgusting bicyclists, and their dangerous bicycles!

Democrats take note, Republicans take note, Blacks take note, Gun owners take note, Christians take note, Property owners take note, Everyone take note! As the rights are denied the individual, so go the rights of the majority for don't we all constitute the majority?

Did anyone recognize the methodology, the template, i.e., the pattern? At what point do we wake up, stop the insanity, consider each other and *"In everything therefore, treat people the same way you want them to treat you, for this is the Law and the Prophets."* Jesus Christ, The Bible, Matthew 7:12.

I watched a program on TV one evening that put the template into perspective. The program addressed law enforcement in Michigan enforcing a law that forbids fighting dogs for profit. The dogs involved were mostly pit bulls. When taken to Animal Control, these dogs that have been used for fighting are usually euthanized for people's safety and other animals' safety.

THE ENEMY CALLED "THEY"

One animal control officer made the following comments concerning a dog she was showing:

"Look at this. See the puncture wound here, something got a hold on him. Look at the scars here, here and here. This dog has been in a lot of fights. He has been trained to fight and kill and is a winner. But he will have to be euthanized. It is a shame. They come in here friendly and wagging their tails but what else can we do." Another Animal Control officer commented that the dogs were trained by the time they were 18 months old and some people bet as much as $60,000 on one single dogfight. These dogs are trained to fight and kill for entertainment and for profit.

Human beings are also being trained to fight and kill for entertainment and profit. Again, you are probably saying to yourself, this guy is a lunatic. Am I? Think about this. What is the purpose for professional boxing, football, hockey, etc? Young people, from a very early age, are taught to stand and fight against the other guy, the opponent, those made out to be the bad guys, competitors. If the other person is your competitor, that person is the "bad guy," the "enemy." This is unhealthy competition.

We have developed organizations that teach the young a few military and survival skills as they are growing up. These organizations are the boy and girl scouts, religious organizations, youth military academies, etc. These organizations teach children about good morals, values and principles.

These same organizations then turn around and teach children it is okay to fight and kill other human beings over those same morals, value and principles. The children are taught to distrust, even hate other people that look, speak, or act differently than they do. They are taught to blindly follow morals, values and principles that do not exist within the system that IS teaching them. These things are an illusion in the system doing the teaching. The children are taught that other human beings have different morals, values and principles and are a threat to *their* morals, values and principles. They are taught *their* morals, values and principles are far superior to other human beings' morals, value and principles.

Every human being is born with God-given morals, values, and principles, and knows the difference between right and wrong. *Human beings are taught hate*. Reality is, the entire system is the same throughout the world, and those behind that system *manipulate human beings through deception* for THEIR entertainment and profit. It is done with the templates about which I am writing and attempting to expose.

The U.S. military services are recruiting children in grade schools and entering them in cadet programs. By the time they are *18 years old*, many enter the military service to defend their country. The only problem is, they are not defending their country. They are fighting and killing an "enemy" that has been created in their minds by those doing the *manipulating through deception*. The first things that are taught in Army and Marine Corps boot camps are to obey without question, fight, and kill.

This same scenario is going on in other nations as well. Wars are created and these young people are pitted against young people from other nations. (Dogfight anyone, or if you prefer, Gladiator fight anyone.) The strongest become the winners and survive. Many come out with wounds and scars, much like the dogs mentioned previously. If the person survives the wars or they are no longer needed or useful for entertainment and profit, they are turned loose in society, and more young are trained while a new "dogfight" called WAR is being set up for entertainment and profit. If you do not think it is for profit, look at the $250 billion dollar defense budget in this nation alone. As a carrot, retirement and medical benefits are promised those that stay for 20 or more years. Only, after 20 years, the medical benefits are not there. The retirement is a pittance and the individual cannot survive on what is provided. The promise was an illusion.

I accepted a job opportunity in Russia in 1990. I had served in our military for twenty years, defending what I believed were ideals, principles, morals, values and freedom unique only to my nation. I learned differently in Russia. I learned the Russian people were frightened into believing that the United States was going to attack and invade their nation. Does this sound familiar? The things I was taught about my country, I learned the same things were taught to the Soviet soldiers about their country. The things I was taught about my supposedly enemy, the Soviet soldier, those same things were taught to the Soviet soldiers about their enemy, me. (Dogfight, anyone?) Keeping human beings fighting for entertainment and profit is a big business for those doing the manipulating and in control.

In Oregon, by law, "voluntary" euthanasia is allowed for the sick people desiring to use that method. *I PREDICT THAT WITHIN A DECADE, EUTHANASIA WILL BE REQUIRED FOR THOSE OVER A CERTAIN AGE, OR CAN NO LONGER "CONTRIBUTE," CAN NO LONGER "PERFORM," OR CAN NO LONGER "FIGHT."* This could even be accomplished by a remote controlled implant containing a poison placed under a person's skin. Next in line for your computer implant chip step forward please.

Those in control have human beings euthanize dogs. What makes anyone think those in control won't do the same to human beings? Remember that soldiers are referred to as the "Dogs of War."

For those in control, human beings are nothing more than another animal species to be experimented with, manipulated, controlled, and used for entertainment and profit.

Today, athletes are bought and sold like animals, yet we are *manipulated through deception* into believing that slavery ended in this country. People will say, but it is voluntary, athletes make the choice to do what they do, it is the profession they chose. That is true, to a point. Many are manipulated into becoming an athlete. They are unaware that they are actually going to be sold on the market like a slave. They go to the highest bidder. It is called the *Draft*. Almost every professional team sport has a draft. Even after being *bought* by a team, they can be *sold* to another team. They can be uprooted from a home they love by being "traded" (a synonym for trade is sold) to another team. The way athletes are treated is nothing more than slavery in a very subtle, yet different form. And color has nothing to do with it.

Was this the reason our founding fathers tried to end conscription and tried to end slavery? Although the Civil War was fought mainly about State rights, Abraham Lincoln still wanted to end slavery in this nation. Could it be he was killed because by doing so it would have ended enormous profits and created control problems for "those in control"? Instead, those in control just made it appear slavery ended in this nation, when in fact it has just been transformed into a different illusion, and color, nationality, culture, etc., has nothing to do with it. It is about enslaving human beings.

In the present system, any person working for another person is in reality a slave to the person or company for whom they work and subject to that person's or company's bidding. You may be told what to wear, how to cut your hair, what you can or cannot say, when to come to work, when you can go home, when you can eat, when you can rest, and coming soon, what you can think, etc. In the present system, the only real choice human beings have is to choose the job in which we want to be enslaved. Those choices are being limited, and soon, those choices will come to an end and everyone will be *told* in which field or profession they will work. No one will have a choice. Those refusing to succumb to the system will be eliminated, i.e., euthanized with the remote controlled computer chip implanted under the skin.

CHAPTER 5

SHOCK, HUMILIATION, AND INTIMIDATION TEMPLATE

How many times have you applied for a job or a promotion and know deep down in your gut that you should have been selected for that job or promotion, but for some unknown reason, you were not? You later find out the individual selected allegedly had a qualification that put that individual heads above all the other candidates yet was not a qualification necessary for the job. Or there is a hint that age, race, gender, or some other unconstitutional discrimination criteria was used for the selection, or an influential person's relative or friend was selected, etc.

Most times, people ignore it, accept the rejection, and either go about doing their job, or decide to seek better employment elsewhere. Those that question the process are told different stories about why they were not chosen, are then labeled a troublemaker, disgruntled employee, or worse yet, have their character impugned and eventually are intimidated into quitting or reasons found by management to fire the individual.

I have seen it happening to others, I have heard about it happening to others, I am certain it has probably happened or will happen to you, and it has certainly happened to someone you know. Many people end up resigning although feeling less confident but taking comfort in the fact they had stood by their principles and that "they will not stay where they are not wanted." This whole process entails a template designed for that purpose.

An actual incident in how the shock, humiliation, and intimidation template is used:

Names in the following incident have been changed to protect the people involved. This is an actual application in which the shock and humiliation template was used against an individual who "questioned" the selection process for a government related job. Put another way, he questioned the "system."

THE ENEMY CALLED "THEY"

I would like to tell you about this real person's experience and what was discovered from that experience. Many will probably think I am writing about them because this or a similar incident has most likely happened to them. If the template fits your experience tell people about this template being used against them.

A fellow I will call "Joe" worked for a school district and applied for another advertised position within that same school district. It was a job most people can do and really does not require any special skills or ability that Joe did not already posses. In fact, when Joe first went to work in that particular district three years previous to this incident, another school bus driver who could no longer drive due to an injury was placed in a similar parking lot security position while waiting for disposition on her injury claim. The desirable qualifications stated in the application for the parking lot security position Joe applied for were:

Knowledge of: basic first aid

Ability to: communicate positively with high school students; to be assertive yet maintain composure and objectivity in potentially hostile circumstances: to maintain a harmonious working relationship with other employees: to write legibly with proper paragraphing and sentence structure.

Education/Experience: equivalent to the completion of the twelfth grade. This provision may be waived by the school district.

During the previous 4 years Joe had been a school bus route driver and had been trained in and had utilized all the qualifications required in the position advertised. Those same qualifications basically apply to a school bus route driver. Joe had previously given up several school bus routes he was offered. He had requested they be given to other individuals who indicated they needed the routes more than Joe did. He made the decision to apply for the parking lot security position at the high school even though it was at a lower hourly wage.

Although his hourly wage would be lower, his monthly take home would have been considerably higher due to more hours worked, plus the position had medical benefits. Joe was not selected for the position and he was somewhat disappointed. He thought he had done well during the interview. He had been honest with the board, and the board members appeared to have been pleased with his answers.

Joe asked why he was not selected and was told that although everyone was equally qualified the individual selected had EMT training *(first aid was required for the job, which Joe had*). Joe was told it was felt this individual could be a great asset in emergencies, at games, and could give shots. Joe was then told this individual was nearer to the age group he would be supervising and would be more in tune with the kids. If Joe had known EMT training was going to be used as selection criteria, he would not have applied for the position. Joe had been dealing with kids in all age groups for the past 4 years as a school bus route driver, and the reasoning for the selection sounded bogus and appeared to be age discrimination.

Joe felt insulted and thought about resigning, but instead decided if they wanted the particular individual selected that was fine. Yet it appeared age discrimination was involved, and if so, that needed to be corrected and stopped in the selection process in the future. Age discrimination is against the law and costly lawsuits that the district cannot afford could result. Joe followed established procedures and requested the reasons for his not being selected be put in writing. Joe had his doubts they would actually put what was discussed with him in writing, but thought it was worth the attempt. Joe did receive the letter although it was somewhat different than what had been discussed.

According to the letter, Joe was no longer equally qualified as he had been told and his answers to three questions were now rated lower than the other candidate's answers. What had been discussed was stated in the last paragraph in the letter but the story had been changed. No longer was Joe equally qualified. This started to raise further questions in Joe's mind about the process. Why had he been informed all the candidates were equally qualified then later told he had scored lower on answers to three questions? According to established procedure, Joe showed the letter to his union representative who said it appeared to be age discrimination and to contact the union field representative. Joe contacted the union field representative who set up an *informal meeting* with management so the selection process could be discussed and if age had been a factor in the selection process. Joe made it clear to the union field representative the job was irrelevant at this point, that the process needed to be changed if age was being used as a factor in the selection process. The union field representative agreed.

Joe and the Union Field Representative attended a meeting with management on February 14th 2000. Joe was introduced to everyone, and sat down. Joe was then handed a sheet with all the candidate "scores." The numbers were meaningless for there was no explanation as to the grading criteria used, although the five interview questions asked were provided. The numbers next to his name were lower than the other candidate numbers. He was *shocked* to see he now rated lower in all the categories. *He had gone from being equally qualified, to being rated lower in three categories to being rated lower in all the categories.* It was then stated by a member in management, *"the reasons you were not selected for the parking lot security position are when you were asked why you wanted the position you stated it was for financial reasons."* Joe replied that is correct. *Management then went on to say "your answer should have been you wanted to work with kids. The district is looking for the best people it can find; not people like you who just want a paycheck. Your answers to the other questions indicate you are "too" authoritarian and that you display "a lack of empathy" toward the kids. These remarks do not apply to you as a school bus driver, only for this position."*

Joe was totally *shocked and humiliated* by the statements, and could not believe he was viewed this way by upper management. He could not understand how these statements did not apply to him as a school bus driver as well. Joe started to turn in his resignation right then and there but something inside said don't. Joe does not remember much about what happened after that in the meeting or what was said. He was in shock and agreeing to everything that was said. He does remember being "told" that age discrimination was not a factor in the selection process. He also remembers being "told" to check with his immediate supervisor and get her assistance in "updating" his resume and provide her a copy for any future job openings.

During the next 4 days Joe kept thinking about the remarks that had been made by management. These remarks were burned into his memory. On the Saturday following the meeting, Joe decided to turn in his resignation come the following Monday. He did not want to stay where he was viewed this way by management.

Joe was typing his resignation on his home computer when he noticed something. Everything said was true, *to a point*. He does want a paycheck, doesn't everyone? *Isn't everyone's true purpose for working is to get a paycheck in order to survive? Joe did display a lack of empathy toward the kids and is authoritarian because these attributes were required in the job as school bus driver. He was trained during his school bus driver training to be authoritarian and control the children aboard the school bus.* Anyone who has children knows it is necessary to be authoritarian or chaos will prevail. Sometimes Joe could have cried due to the stories some kids told about their home life and he wanted to hold and comfort them, but Joe was trained not to do display his emotions or personal feelings toward the children because it would give the *"wrong impression."*

Only, these attributes in which he had been trained had been twisted and distorted to provide the appearance they were wrongful or negative to justify the school district breaking the law in order to deny Joe the job.

Joe had started out trying to bring what appeared to be a discrepancy in the hiring process to the districts attention, and in doing so had been lied to, his character had been questioned, his dignity stripped, and he had been embarrassed and humiliated. For what purpose was this being done? Joe now knew something was definitely wrong. He changed his letter and wrote a 2 page memo stating the matter was not settled. Joe decided it was time to make a stand. Something was wrong, He recognized this same process had been used in the past, not only to him, he had seen it done to others that he knew, and not only where he was presently working. He realized he had seen this same methodology used in other government organizations as well. He sent the memo to his union field representative and to district management. The union field representative was not happy with Joe. The district was not happy with Joe. The district refused to cooperate and provide requested information the union alleged it had requested.

The union started dragging its feet and appeared more concerned for management rights than Joe's rights. Joe was now asking himself, if there is not a problem with the process, for what purpose have they gone to the measures they have? For what purpose was the truth distorted to make it appear something negative? Was something being hidden? For what purpose is a person penalized in the job selection process for wanting to improve their financial situation, plus gain benefits? For what purpose is a person penalized in the selection process for following existing rules and policies and enforcing existing rules and policies, and *doing the job the way one was trained*?

Further, it made no sense that an individual that was already working with kids for the past 4 years, would state that they wanted to work with kids when asked why they wanted the job during the selection interview? Wouldn't that seem pointless and redundant? Why had Joe gone from being equally qualified to suddenly being rated lower than the other applicants were rated once he started questioning the process? For what purpose did the district refuse to provide the information the union representative allegedly requested concerning what went on in the selection process? Did the union representative actually request the information? All management would say is they followed the procedures. What Joe was trying to ascertain were the procedures within the law?

Joe had stumbled across a template being used in these situations to justify discrimination in the job selection process. It is also used to attack an individual's character and is designed to embarrass, confuse, and humiliate them in order to put the individual on the defensive and to gain control in any situation. The quickest way to gain control over an individual in most situations is to embarrass and humiliate that person when others are present.

On the day Joe and the union representative had met with management Joe was *told* what he should have said during the job interview, his character was attacked, and he was virtually *told* there was no issue. Nothing was *discussed* concerning age discrimination. It was *dictated* there was no age discrimination. Management told Joe the issue was settled to which Joe had agreed because Joe was too embarrassed, humiliated, and shocked from the character attack to respond or to realize what was happening until four days later. Several weeks after the incident, Joe discovered the real reasons behind his not being selected. It seems nepotism was rampant within the organization and other people were also being denied promotions, transfers, etc. One day a district school board member told Joe the district did not like to hire prior military as supervisors because they were too strict.

When Joe had first tried to explain to the union field representative what management had done during the meeting, the union field representative called him a liar. He told Joe he was in the same meeting and those things did not happen, that the things Joe claimed were stated were not what was said. What could Joe possibly gain by lying? He already knew he was not going to get the job. He knew that by pressing the issue, things were going to get worse for him. But principle was involved. The worst part was, this is not a private firm, but a government entity that did this to Joe. A government entity is supposed to abide by the law. *Do as I say and not as I do.*

Joe decided to turn the tables to demonstrate the template to the union field representative and show him how it worked. Maybe he would then believe what Joe was telling him. Joe arranged another meeting with the union field representative. He asked a friend to be a witness. His friend knew shorthand and he wanted her to record everything in writing. She explained her shorthand was rusty. Before going into the meeting, Joe tried the template on his friend, and quickly explained what he had done. His friend was shocked and almost told him what he could do and where he could go until Joe explained the template, what he had done, and that he just wanted to verify its effectiveness.

During the meeting with the union field representative, Joe taped the conversation and later typed all that was said from the tape, using the shorthand notes to verify everything.

At the meetings beginning Joe stated to the union field representative what had been said to him, but with a variation. Joe substituted the union field representative name for his own, and reworded it a bit to fit the field union representatives situation with Joe.

After making the statement to the Union Field Representative, Joe told him what he had done and tried to explain the template. The Union Rep was upset for almost 45 minutes and was very defensive throughout the meeting, even after Joe had explained what he had done. To this day the union field representative does not believe that Joe was demonstrating the template.

Following is that template and what was said to Joe at the meeting with management. Names in this article have been changed to protect those involved. Joe's story is used as an example to show how the template works and how it is used. Many in lower and middle management are unaware that it even exists. It is taught subtly in upper management classes. This template is exposed so you can be aware this is happening. This template was used against Joe when he tried to explain to management within the school district in which he worked that using age as criteria to deny anyone a job is against the law. This template is designed to shock, humiliate, embarrass, frustrate, and distract the individual from the real issue and as justification for denying a job, promotion, or lateral transfer within an organization. In essence, it attacks one's character and strips one's dignity.

Using this template is dangerous. It can cause deep emotional scars to people and I do not recommend its use. Some people use it to keep a public office, public jobs, and/or power for themselves, their families, and friends. It can also be used to destroy a persons moral values and principles. It is exposed so you will know the way we are all being *manipulated through deception*. Only those who have had it used against them will probably recognize it for what it is. Others will recognize it as it is happening to others. Some may say hogwash this guy is nuts. I personally have nothing to gain, or nothing to lose. I am exposing you to the truth. Do with that truth what you wish. I guarantee this template is used on most people in some variation or in some way throughout their lives.

WHAT WAS SAID TO JOE IN THE MEETING WITH MANAGEMENT.

Joe, we decided to hire David. He is nearer the age of the kids and is in tune with the kid's needs more clearly. Further, he is EMT trained and can handle the situation in an emergency. The reasons for this are: During the job interview when asked why you wanted the job, you said it was strictly a financial decision and the answer to the question should have been you wanted to work with kids. The District wants only the best people it can find, not people like you who just wants a paycheck, Your other replies indicated you were too authoritarian, and you displayed a lack of empathy toward the kids. I am not saying this applies to you as a school bus driver, just in this particular job. I suggest you update your resume and give it to Sue. She can advise you in the future about any other jobs that may arise. As you can see, age was not a factor in the selection process.

Following is what Joe said to the Union Field Representative which made the union field representative upset throughout the meeting even after being told that Joe was only using the template as a demonstration as to what had happened to Joe. He has a witness and secretly tape-recorded the entire conversation and meeting with Frank, the union field representative:

Frank, I have decided to hire Hank, he is nearer the age of the elderly and relates to the needs of the elderly more clearly. Further, he is a trained lawyer, and can handle the situation if it should escalate. The reasons are: When I spoke with you the other day, the reply to my letter should have been that you think management is wrong. The union wants only the best people it can find; not people like you who just wants to work with management. Your reply indicated you were too succinct. You displayed a lack of interest toward the members. I am not saying this applies to you as a Union Representative, just to this particular case. I suggest you take the paper work, up date it, and give to you boss. He can advise you in the future on any other cases that may arise.

Sample Template

WHAT WAS SAID TO THE UNION REPRESENTATIVE IS BOLDED
WHAT WAS SAID TO JOE IN THE MEETING WITH MANAGEMENT IS IN ITALICS AND BOLDED

Frank, I have decided to hire **Hank**. He is nearer the age of the **elderly** and **relates to** the needs of the **elderly** more clearly.

Joe, we have decided to hire ***David***. He is nearer the age of the ***Kids,*** and is ***in tune with*** the needs of the ***kids*** more clearly.

Further, he is **a trained lawyer** and can handle the situation **if it should escalate**.

Further, he is ***EMT trained*** and can handle the situation ***in an emergency***.

The reasons for this are:

When I spoke with you the other day, the **reply to my letter should have been that you think management is wrong**.

When I spoke with you the other day, the ***answer to the question should have been I want to work with kids***.

The **union** wants only the best people it can find; not people like you who just wants to work **with management**.

The ***District*** wants only the best people it can find; not people like you who just wants to work *for a* **paycheck**.

Your **reply** indicated you were too **succinct**
Your ***answers*** indicated you were too ***authoritarian***

You displayed a lack of **interest** toward the **members**. I am not saying this applies to you as a **Union field Representative**, just to this particular **case**.

You displayed a lack of *empathy* toward the ***kids***. I am not saying this applies to you as a ***School bus driver***, just to this particular *job*.

I suggest you take **the paper work**, up date it, and give it to **your boss**. **He** can advise you in the future on any other **cases** that may arise.

I suggest you take *your resume*, up date it, and give it to *Sue*. *She* can advise you in the future on any other *jobs* that may arise.

The Union Field Representative to this day does not believe it is a template and did nothing to help Joe after Joe demonstrated the template to him. Even after Joe immediately told Frank he hadn't hired a lawyer, and he was only demonstrating the templates effectiveness, throughout the entire meeting, Frank kept referring back to Joe's lawyer and other comments Joe had made in the statement. This template's effectiveness is amazing. It puts the individual to which it is aimed at a distinct disadvantage in any debate or complaint, and the individual from that point will agree with just about anything you say, or become totally incoherent, or be too humiliated to say anything. It humiliates and then puts the individual in shock. Even if a person is aware it is happening, *it can still have some effect on the person.*

Joe eventually did resign. His extra curricular hours were cut and he was only working 15 hours a week. For a job providing him 15 hours a week, he decided it was not worth the hassle. Further, Joe had decided to put himself forth as a candidate for public office to try and change things and believed it improper to hold a government job while being a candidate for public office. Plus, he had discovered that he and other drivers had been manipulated into driving school buses with unsafe tires and believed because he had allowed himself to be duped, he had put the children's safety at risk. In his own mind, he did not deserve to drive the kids any longer. Although what Joe did was done unknowingly, what those in authority did was deliberate. He had done nothing wrong intentionally, but he had the gut instinct he was getting set up for a fall and decided the job was not worth it. Joe turned in his verbal resignation stating it would be his last school year with the organization. His supervisor asked for it in writing.

The following day Joe turned in his written resignation stating he was leaving at the school years end. That afternoon, Joe was informed a parent complaint against him was being investigated because, in essence, *Joe told an eighth grade girl to think about what she was doing*. He was also informed that he might be terminated if the investigation warranted such action. Several days later, during what was called an investigation interview concerning the girl, Joe underwent an inquisition, which is recorded on tape. Joe told the truth, but when he refused to agree that he would not exercise his God-given Constitutionally guaranteed right to free speech he was told the incident needed further investigation. Now he was convinced he was being "set up" so Joe just made his resignation effective six weeks earlier than planned, and quit on the spot. He left the room, remembered he had forgotten something, and went back into the room. A member in upper management was laughing and commenting to the others on the investigation committee, "did you see the look on his face when I," and at that point he saw Joe and did not proceed with his comment. To this day, Joe wonders what he was going to say. Another employee commented to Joe that the whole thing was management just wanting to get it licks in on Joe before he departed the organization.

All Joe wanted was to gain a little financial stability and medical benefits. Because the organization for which he worked did not want that for Joe, he was temporarily shocked, humiliated and intimidated by those within the system. When he stood against them, they made things worse for Joe. When he decided to try and change things within the system by running for a public office, Joe was eventually coerced into quitting earlier than planned. This incident occurred in Jackson County, Oregon, and Joe has now been unemployed for over two years, cannot even get a job interview in the county and has decided to no longer waste his time, effort or money trying.

This is a first for Joe in his 58 years. He never had difficulty in finding a job before this happened. Joe thinks his problems truly began about 4 or 5 months previous to the above incident when he declined to take a field trip that involved driving a school bus loaded with children across a wooden bridge that did not have posted load limits. His supervisor did not know the bridge load limits, so as the driver responsible if anything happened, Joe decided to call the county engineers department. They could not tell Joe the load limits on the bridge and he was referred to the County Parks department. No one in the County Parks department could provide the information. Joe's supervisor and management were not happy with his decision to check on the bridge's safe load limits before the trip and his decision to decline the trip because he did not believe the bridge safe to cross for school buses loaded with children.

Up to that point, Joe had been utilized regularly on field trips involving sports and other activities in the local area, but after this incident, Joe remembers that for over a month he was not given a single field trip. It was as if it was a subtle way to punish Joe for bringing up a "safety related matter." The situation was further aggravated when Joe decided to resign and run for a political office to ensure the system treated everyone fairly. That is when things really got exciting for Joe and that story is revealed through a Jackson County Court case oral arguments in chapter 7. This is a government organization that did this to Joe, the very government that is supposed to protect your rights, your children's safety, and ensure things are fair and equitable for everyone.

The following scenario will explain how this same methodology with the shock, humiliation, and intimidation template is used on a larger scale. I am sure many will recognize it as having been used before and quite extensively since NAFTA was put into effect:

A major U.S. company is having difficulty with the widget branch employees. The employees are demanding higher wages and want better medical benefits. Management's Union representatives are no longer able to control the employees. Management does not want to negotiate with the employees or meet their demands. Management decides to use the widget branch employees as an example to other branch employees in other locations. Either accept what we want to give you, or we will move the entire company to new locations where the people want the work and will be appreciative. It is put to all the employees in the company in this manner:

Management would like to take this opportunity to address all company employees. The owners have decided to move the "widget" branch to China. The raw materials needed for production are readily available, close to where the company widget branch will relocate, are less costly, and more nearly relate to company needs. Further, the people are more adept at unskilled labor positions, can be easily trained, and we are confident they will be able to produce more product at less cost, thus passing on the saving to the consumer. The reasons company management made this decision is: management has been unsuccessful in attempts to hold talks with labor and labor demands to management were not in the companies best interest. Labor refused to compromise in their demands and were unyielding. Labor displayed a lack of interest toward management and the stockholders. The company, in order to survive, needs the cheapest labor and raw material it can find, and that is not being found here. Management is not saying the people in the widget division are not a good work force, just that they are no longer adequate for this companies particular needs. Management wants to help ease the transition and is providing everyone six weeks before closing the widget branch doors and moving. This should provide everyone in labor enough time to seek other avenues in employment. Management is here to advise and assist everyone in anyway possible.

DID YOU RECOGNIZE THE TEMPLATE?

The company owners want larger profits and actually want to cut employees and encourage the other company employees to work harder and increase productivity. In other words, management wants the employees to work at 100% maximum capacity 100% of the time. Realistically, we all know that no machine can work at 100% maximum capacity all the time without breaking down. Neither can human beings. In fact, for a human being to work at 80% maximum capacity for more than a few hours a day is extremely difficult. Human beings are not machines. But, management and the owners do not care. They want more and more while providing less and less. In this case, management wants slave labor at slave wages.

SYNONYM GAME:
 EMPLOYEE = WORKER = TOILER = SLAVE = TOILER = WORKER = EMPLOYEE

CHAPTER 6

THE GLOBAL TEMPLATE CALLED THE PROGRAMMING AND CONTROL TEMPLATE, BETTER KNOWN AS THE POLITICS GAME

The Programming and Control Template is the "Global Template." The other two templates are used in conjunction with this template against human beings from birth. Initial programming for the template begins at home through family, friends, and relatives who have previously and successfully been subjected to all three templates. The most intense programming is encountered in the public education system. That is where I will start the template. Most human beings involved are completely unaware they are being manipulated in this manner.

GAME: POLITICS GAME
The way the game is played:
Bullies control the schoolyard and equipment the school provides the children to play with at recess. (This template is used from Kindergarten through College, at different levels of complexity, difficulty and intensity).
THE OBJECT OF THE GAME:
The bullies must not lose control over the kids in the schoolyard
WINNING THE GAME:
Like monopoly, the winners end up with everything including the other kids property and money. The winners follow the same type kids through life picking up new ones along the way. The kids throughout their lives support these winners. Unlike monopoly the winner ends up with complete control (enslavement) over the people and the people's souls.
THE RULES:
The bullies are provided an advantage from the beginning. They are allowed to do "anything" to keep from losing that advantage or control over

the schoolyard and the kids. The bullies are allowed to make the rules as they play the game. Nothing ethical or moral is allowed. Lying, cheating, stealing, intimidation, threats, coercing, beatings, fighting, etc., are allowed as long as the bullies are not caught or revealed by the kids and the control is maintained.

LOSING THE GAME:

The bullies lose control over the kids and the schoolyard and the kids gain their freedom and independence from the bullies. Different bullies take charge and start the game over with new kids. Or the kids that gain their freedom take control, refuse to be bullies, their souls are saved and they end the game forever.

LET US PLAY.

The school policy says the kids are to share the equipment so everyone has an opportunity to play with or on the equipment. The bullies' classes are released early and the bullies control the equipment every day. They hold a first vote among themselves and their friends to choose which bullies they want to be captains before the other classes let out for recess. The kids in the classes that are let out a few minutes later for recess and were "left out" in the first vote are not allowed to put their choices for captain up for the second vote. The bullies and their friends are the only ones who ever seem to be able to be chosen for captains. The bullies always choose the best equipment and the kids they want to let play on that equipment. Some kids complain about the choices for captains, that the choices are not the kids they prefer. The bullies tell all the kids they can't let too many kids try to be captains, it would just confuse things, and it best for all the kids to let the bullies choose who should be captains. Most kids say no, we just want some other choices outside your groups. The bullies say no that those are the rules.

The "left out kids" are never chosen to be captains or get to play on the best equipment or in the games. Every day it is the same kids who are "left out." The bullies always choose their friends. The "left out" kids are afraid to tell the teachers the bullies will not share the equipment or let them play in the games for fear the bullies will beat them up. The bullies even charge them a "toll" to use the equipment the bullies don't want to use or make special rules so only a few so-so friends can use it. Some kids buy their own toys and bring them to the schoolyard to play with, but the bullies take the toys and claim the toys are needed for play by some kids who are the bullies friends. It does no good to complain to the bullies, they just say that is the way it is. Those who make the rules, rule. If you don't like it, go tattle to a teacher.

THE ENEMY CALLED "THEY"

Schoolyard Rule # 1 one says, "don't tattle, if you do, you will get the stuffing beat out of you, because no one likes a tattle tale." Rule #1 is usually enough to discourage most kids from going to the teacher. A few kids do try telling the teachers what the bullies are doing is not fair and is wrong but those who do end up being terrorized by the bullies. They are then ignored by their friends and others because the bullies and their friends put the kid down, call them tattle tale, make things up, tell the other kids lies about them, and sometimes beat them up. All the kids fear the same thing will happen to them. Some kids become even more afraid or discouraged, and go off by themselves to be alone. The "left out kids" complain among their friends and ask, why doesn't somebody do something, but no one hears, or seems to care because the bullies terrify most kids. Then one day a new kid gathers up enough courage to stand up to the bullies and tries to reason with them. Someone has to stand for the weaker and smaller kids in the schoolyard against the bullies. He tells the bullies he wants to put himself up for the vote to see if he can be chosen as a captain to make sure everyone has the same chance to play on the equipment and in the games. The bullies tell the new kid the rules in their captains manual they made up says he has to beg the kids in school to sign giving him their permission for him to be in the second vote to be a captain. They tell him he will have to fill out 4 forms. Plus, he can't get the signatures without the bullies' permission so a bully will have to sign the paper so all the kids will know the bullies gave their permission for him to try and be voted a captain. Further the bullies like the headings on the paper with the signatures typed. He is told he cannot beg for the signatures until after the bullies have chosen who they want to be voted for captains. He is told if he gets enough signatures, he will not have to pay the bullies his lunch money to be a part in the vote for the captains.

The new kid asks the bullies why they don't have to follow those rules or why can't he go through the same rules they do to try and get voted as a captain. He explains to the bullies what they are doing is unfair, that all they to do is say they want to be captains for the main vote but the bullies won't listen. The bullies say, because our rules say you have to do it this way. The new kid says he should be able to claim he wants to be a captain and be in the main vote for captain the same as the bullies. He tries to explain to the bullies that it is school equipment for all the kids and not just the bullies. The "left out kids" have as much right to become captains and play on the equipment as the bullies. The bullies say no, our rule ORS 249.002(7) says it is school Bully equipment. The new kid says no, it is not, it is school equipment for all the kids, not just the bullies, and what they are doing is unfair. It goes against school policy. The bullies say, it is in our schoolyard rules, if you don't like it, go tattle (remember schoolyard rule #1).

But if that is not enough, the bullies appear to have an ace in the hole. They brag to all the kids in the schoolyard about how the teachers are on their side, they are the teacher's favorites, and if you tell a teacher, she will turn you over to the bullies to do as they please. They make the rules in the schoolyard and not the teachers. Their parents can get the teachers fired or their parents are the teacher's friends. The other kids pass this on to the new kid who is standing up and speaking out. He is told horror stories about what happened to their friends and others when they went to a teacher. A few tell how they went to a teacher and got in trouble because the teacher couldn't be bothered with their whining. Another said the teacher said there wasn't enough equipment for all the kids to participate, and who ever gets it first makes the rules. Another teacher punished one kid by taking away his recess for a week and he had to stay in the classroom for being a "tattle tale." Another teacher said that if teacher XYZ said that is the way it is then drop it. Another teacher stated recess was over, the time was up, so it did not matter. Another teacher said the rules the bullies made up seemed fair to her, she knew the bullies well and spent time with them in the classroom, ate lunch with them, and they were smart and always did well.

The "left out kids" are now afraid to go to teachers. They believe the teachers are against them and are for the bullies, and now fear all the teachers. The bullies frighten them. The bullies make the rules and enforce the rules. The bullies rule in the schoolyard. No one can stand against the bullies, not even the teachers. The "left out kids" now believe they are destined to just stand and watch, wishing they could play on the equipment and be in the games.

But the new kid is determined and goes to the teachers. One teacher tells the new kid "that is the way it has always been, and that is the way it will always be." Another teacher said he is too busy to be bothered. Another teacher said she doubted very seriously that the bullies were being unfair. The new kid still cannot believe what is happening, it is not fair or right. Disregarding the horror stories he heard and the experiences with the teachers, The new kid tries to get a teacher to take him to see the principal. He can't find a teacher that will represent him with the principal.

The other "left out" kids tell him to forget it, the principal used to be a teacher and will agree with what the teachers said. The new kid believes there

THE ENEMY CALLED "THEY"

has to be one fair and honest person in the school. Aren't the teachers and principal supposed to be fair and be there to help all the kids and teach them and help them resolve the problems in school? Aren't the teachers and principal supposed to listen to "all" the kids and not just the bullies? Aren't the teachers and principle supposed to be honest? Aren't the teachers and principals supposed to make sure everyone follows the school policy? Sure, he is afraid the bullies will beat him up but there is something in this new kid that says fair is fair, and right is right. He won't be bullied.

The new kid goes to the school office and asks to see the principal to tell his story. The people working in the office give him a hard time and tell him that is what teachers are for. The new kid insists on seeing the principal and asks if a few "left out kids" can be there too. He is told he will have to file a complaint, but it is complicated and he will need a teacher to make out the complaint, that is what teachers are for, and he will have to get permission to see the principle. He also must get a teacher's aide to talk to the bullies so the bullies are provided an opportunity to give the aide their side in the story before he sees the principal. The new kid cannot believe it. Even the office workers are bullies. He cannot find a teacher willing to help him with the complaint, so he does his best to make out the complaint himself. He takes the complaint to the office and asks permission to see the principal. He also requests permission for some left out kids to be there to listen and tell that they also believe the bullies' schoolyard rules are unfair. The office bullies rules say they will have to speak with the bullies before he can see the principle to get their side in the story.

But instead of answering the new kid's complaint, the schoolyard bullies tell the office bullies that the new kid is lying, that he is just jealous. They say they will tell the principal that what the schoolyard bullies are doing is okay and fair. That they do share, and that they do not forcibly take lunch money from the other kids. They also make an appointment to see the principal. Once informed about the situation, the principal asks to see the new kid and the bullies, but the other children are not allowed in the meeting, only the new kid and the bullies against which the new kid raised the complaint.

The new kid hears more horror stories from other kids about what is going to happen to him when he talks to the principal. The principal is going to eat him alive, lock him in a closet and throw away the key. They tell the new kid he must remember the principal used to be a teacher, and is one of them. He is the head bully. They tell the new kid to drop it they will suffer through, that they don't want to see him punished for something he didn't do. The new kid is scared, but he doesn't like what is happening to the "left out" kids. He has his doubts because he has only been to see a principal once, and that was a long time ago for something he did not do, but the principal punished him anyway. Now he is beginning to have doubts that anyone in the school will listen and make a fair and honest decision. He remembers the teachers and the other adults telling the kids, "life is not fair." Surely, there is one fair person in the bunch who will listen and make a fair and honest decision.

The principal listens to the bullies and their opinions. The bullies tell the principal she should not listen to this new kid and not to ask the "left out kids" if the rules are fair. They tell the principal the rules are fair. They tell the principal she should forget the whole matter, the rules are on their side, their class teachers said so. They state the new kid doesn't know what he is talking about, he is a troublemaker, he doesn't understand or follow their rules, their rules are fair, and he is not one of them. The bullies tell the principal the new kid is stupid and doesn't know anything, he can't even read the rules and understand them. Besides, the recess period he is complaining about has been over for a long time and why should he be allowed to complain now.

The new kid explains to the principal that the bullies' rules have not changed on the schoolyard, that they still don't allow any "left out" kids a chance to be voted for captains in the second vote and choose who gets to play on the equipment. The new kid explains to the principal the school policy says the school equipment is provided for all the kids to play, and not just the bullies. The new kid tells the principal, if you don't believe me, "ASK THE LEFT OUT KIDS, ASK THE LEFT OUT KIDS IF THE RULES ARE FAIR." The new kid explains that if the bullies are allowed to get away with what they are doing, that means the school policy is a lie, that what the school policy says means nothing. He asks the principal, if that is true, then tell me so that I can tell the "left out" kids and others that the school policy is a lie, it means nothing, and the bullies can do what they want and there is nothing we can do about it. Tell me the bullies have your permission to terrorize all the kids on the schoolyard. Tell me the bullies are your favorites so I can tell the other kids. Tell me you give them your permission to take our lunch money as they please, take our toys as they please, do with us as they please. Tell me so I can tell all the other kids.

The principal recognizes the new kid is upset and has heard whispers about discontent among the other children. She has already noticed increased violence on the playground and is afraid the discontent could lead to more violence. Maybe the new kid is right. Does she want to involve the "left out kids" and provide them an opportunity to speak and ask them if they think the bullies' rules are fair or unfair? If she listens to the bullies and does as they wish, she is giving them permission to further terrorize the "left out" kids in the schoolyard. The principal knows that will lead to more violence. Further, why don't the bullies want her to ask the "left out" kids if the rules are fair? Are the bullies hiding something? Are the elections they hold for choosing captains and who gets to play on the equipment fair to the other kids? Should she go against the bullies and help this new kid and the other "left out" kids. If what the new kid says is true, how should she punish the bullies? Now the principal has a decision to make.

Do the bullies lose control or are the kids enslaved? You be the principal. What would you do? You can select more than one choice or write in what you would do. Remember that your decision will be how you are judged in history and by God:

    Change the game rules
    Change the school policy
    Make the rules apply to everyone and enforce those rules (no
          double standards)
    Hang the bullies
    Hang the new kid
    Find for the bullies and let them terrorize the other kids
    Stop the bullies and make them start a new game
    Destroy the game
    Find other alternatives to this game
    Tell the kids to share and knock off the nonsense
    Tell all the kids none of them are allowed to play with the
          equipment because of what the bullies have done
    Tell the kids to treat others the way they want to be treated and
          to be polite, courteous, and share.
    Stop the bullies and tell them their rules are not the school
          policy
    Other (write in what you would do)

Now, go to the word substitutions below and play the game again, with different words. Try it and see how it goes, see if you can recognize how it is being used around you, against you, against the world. Substitute as needed. It is okay to add new words as needed and to change definitions as needed.

That is the way the game is played. Make the rules as you go along. Remember, those who make the rules, "rule."

A FEW SUBSTITUTION WORDS:

School—Government (City, County, State, Federal, or WORLD)

Bullies—The Elite, Clique, Republican Party, Democratic Party, Groups, classes, teams, popular kids, athletes, stars, special kids, etc.

Play—Participate, partake, be included, join in, etc.

School policy—U.S. Constitution, State Constitution, Church Constitution, Company policy, etc.

Rules—Laws, ordinances, procedures, ways of doing things, regulations, convention, system

Parents—Bully members who have children in the school ("left out kids" parents, do not count)

Teacher—Lawyer (usually adults), attorneys, highly educated, expert, educator, instructor, representatives, leaders, middle manager, deacons

Principal—Judge (usually adults), boss, CEO, manager, pastor

School equipment—Public offices, school offices, play ground equipment, jobs, church offices, etc.

Captains—Representatives, leaders, senators, congressmen, commissioner, mayor, class president, treasurer (captains and teachers and their substitutions are interchangeable entities in the game)

Captain's Manual—Candidate's manuals, qualifications manuals, job descriptions, etc.

Choices—Candidates, participants, applicants

Choose—vote, elections, select, hire, etc.

School Bully equipment—Partisan public office, partisan office, public partisan office, imminent domain, personal property

First Vote—Primary election, screening selection process (used for jobs)

Second Vote—General election, final selection process (used for jobs)

Friends—Children of elite parents, constituents, party member, aides, etc.

Office bullies—Bureaucrats (usually adults). People hired by the parties, companies, etc. and coerced by money, job etc to unknowingly do dirty work of the Elite. These include civil servants, police, firemen, military, security, human resources, labors, employees, workers, etc., etc., etc.

Kids—General public, public, people, human beings

"Left out Kids"—General public not allowed to participate, poor white trash, Blacks, Hispanics, Native American, homeless, unemployed, poor, renters, home owners, property owners, third world countries.

New Kid—Independent, minor party, individual, outcast, loner, etc.

Tattle—Sue, complaint, whining, griping, sniveling, argumentative

Tattle-tale—Whistle blower, disgruntled employee, troublemaker, malcontent, plaintiff, defendant.

Share—equal, equality, belonging to everyone.

Schoolyard—District, City, County, State, Nation, World

Opinion—Verdict, judgement, perception.

Fair—Constitutional, right

Lunch money—Taxes, fee, toll, etc.

Permission—Endorsement, approval, authorization, consent, sanction, allowed, permitted, certification, etc.

Beg—Petition, ask for, plead, pray, solicit, seek, request

Say—declare, speak, claim, etc.

NOW ASK YOURSELF, WHO ARE THE WINNERS, WHO ARE THE LOSERS IN THIS GAME?

The preceding template was derived from oral arguments given in an actual court case, but was modified to demonstrate how the template is taught and practiced. In the actual oral arguments, the plaintiff *attempted* to use all three templates against the system itself. The plaintiff had filed a motion demanding a trial by jury within a week the original pleading was filed and several months previous to appearing before the judge. That motion was never addressed. The Circuit Court judge dismissed the case. The case was then filed in the State appellate court, and was dismissed by the Appellate court on a "catch 22."

By the time a person graduates from high school, all three templates have been used over and over, in slightly different forms, to program human beings. If the person attends college, the templates are "fined tuned" for the individual to either instruct or lead others into becoming programmed slaves, i.e. sheep to sheer and be led to slaughter. The system in place is designed to shock, humiliate, intimidate, ignore and exclude all those who may pose a threat to the system. As a last resort, those individuals that refuse to succumb, or be intimidated or ignored, eventually a way is found to eliminate those individuals.

The templates demonstrated are the "basic" templates. They can be adapted as necessary for real life situations.

The templates practical uses are in our everyday lives. These templates also allow the Elite, the Clique, i.e., the viper's brood, the *Evil One*, to identify those who may pose a danger to their race's control and power. The templates are being used by those who rule to help prepare selected offspring for Government, Politics, CEO's etc. Most human beings involved are unaware they are being used and manipulated in this manner. For proof, just look around you. And it is said there is no conspiracy.

Once everyone has been manipulated through these templates and succumb to the process, most are now an *ize* (Isolated Zombie Enslaved).

The suffix *ize* is to engage in a specific activity to cause something to become, conform to, or resemble, a specific thing. (Such as treating and/or infusing DNA and combining it with other DNA to produce something else). This same principle can also be done with human beings behavior patterns using teaching methods in order to produce human being into becoming productive slaves.

A Zombie is a voodoo *snake* god in some societies today. According to voodoo, a supernatural power may enter into and reanimate a dead body. What is created is a will-less, speechless human capable only of automatic movement, and is sometimes referred to as the walking dead. Some think a zombie is a person markedly strange in appearance and/or behavior that have been drugged into comatose hours before the burial.

A few synonyms for zombie are *automaton*, *robot*, & *android*.

Those in control want to know if you have become an ized (Isolated Zombie Enslaved Demon):

Nationalized are human beings that believe theirs is greatest ethnic group or nation on earth. The Country (state, fatherland, motherland, kingdom, etc.) right or wrong.

Communized are human beings that believe the state above all else. The state needs outweigh individual needs and the state decides your needs.

Capitalized are human beings that believe the business organization is above all else. The business decides your needs.

Institutionalized are human beings that believe the establishment (tradition) above all else. Worship and love the Evil One, Satan. Hate God. Loving money is everything.

Militarized are human beings that believe by killing another nation's human beings they are fighting the Evil One.

Terrorized are terrified human beings killing other human beings believing they are killing the Evil One

Criticized are human beings that meekly subject themselves to other human beings that are judging them so that the other human beings can make themselves look good.

THE ENEMY CALLED "THEY"

Plagiarized are human beings that have meekly allowed their ideas to be used for personal gain by someone else.

Naturalized are human beings that allow their natural desires to be satisfied at any cost to other human beings, if it feel good, do it.

Compartmentalized are human beings that have allowed other beings to put them in a certain place, in their niche in life, in the right slot or hole, and separated from other human beings.

Earlier I mentioned that insolate was a synonym for insulate. Now that the person has become an Isolated Zombie Enslaved Demon that means the person has successfully been *insulated from the truth*. So now that person is considered an Insulated Zombie Enslaved Demon. Every day life in their system is the final test to find out if one has become an *ized* (Insulated Zombie Enslaved Demon). The human beings that have not successfully been compartmentalized (separated, isolated, or divided) and have not willingly succumbed to their system, their conspiracy, are the human beings that stand against their tyranny. Those that do not succumb to the templates eventually end up as the "criminals," "outcasts," "outsiders," troublemakers, malcontents, religious fanatics, etc. These human beings are unacceptable, are no longer allowed to participate in their system, and must either be silenced and/or eventually destroyed. *The human beings that have not been or cannot be acceptably ized are eventually eliminated.*

Human beings are already being used to accomplish this through wars. Wars are becoming costly and cause too much damage, and war for the *Evil One's* purposes is coming to an end. Soon, wars will no longer be needed to destroy those who do not succumb. The numbers are growing smaller among human beings that are resisting. Human beings that have succumbed to their system are now being used to capture, incarcerate and/or kill those that will not succumb. THEY are eventually going to use human beings to "euthanize" or otherwise eliminate these other human beings, the same as THEY now have humans do with dogs.

Do you notice the three strikes and you are out laws being passed in various states? Under the three strike and you are out laws, three felony offenses gets a person incarcerated for life. The three strikes and you are out laws are unconstitutional. Previous crimes are being used to determine a persons prison sentence. That is cruel and unusual punishment. The person has already paid the penalty for the other crimes and according to the Constitution, a person is not to be tried twice for the same crime. Using previous crimes to increase a persons prison sentence is actually punishing that person for a crime more than once. A Felony at one time was considered the more serious crimes such as burglary rape, arson, murder and kidnapping in which a person was incarcerated for a year or more. Do you notice that more and more minor offenses are becoming felony offenses? Killing an eagle, a cougar, or a wolf has become a felony offense. A DUI (Driving under the influence of Alcohol) has become a felony offense in some states. Exercising your first amendment right and saying certain things about a "special group" or "special individual" has become a "hate crime" and a felony offense. Most illegal drug use or drug possession offenses are now felony offenses, regardless the amount in one's possession. Arguing with security personnel in an airport terminal is a felony offense. Mistreating an animal in any way has become a felony offense in some states. Notice all the petty and ridiculous laws being passed that are, or soon will be, "felony" offenses.

Do not get me wrong, I do not advocate drinking and driving, mistreating animals, or other people. At the same time, I do not advocate making everything we do a felony offense, i.e. a serious crime and then *mistreating human beings* due to felony offenses. Soon, even traffic violations will be a "felony offense." Minor offenses and Misdemeanor offenses are becoming old-fashioned. Read for yourself the Bill of Rights in the U.S. Constitution and your state Constitution and you will see for yourself the Constitutions guarantee *such laws are prohibited*.

Presently, anyone committing a felony crime within the "Rule of Law," is incarcerated and further intense methods with the *Isolation shock methodology* and *Isolation shock therapy* are used to convert the individual into an *Insulated zombie enslaved demon* by the mental and prison institutions. These intense methods are similar if not the same as those used in POW camps. The day will soon arrive when those efforts will no longer be necessary and those refusing to succumb will be *put to death because they have committed three felony offenses*. Euthanasia is derived from eu- (Greek for easy) and thanatos (death). Eventually, those that will not succumb to the system will be provided an "easy death" or euthanized. Human beings that have succumbed, that are easily manipulated and controlled, and have become *Insulated Zombies Enslaved Demons* are, and will continue to be used to destroy other human beings that cannot be controlled, that are no longer useful, or just to old.

Do you recognize the methodology, the templates, and the patterns? As the rights are denied the individual, so go the rights of the majority for don't we all constitute the majority? At what point do we wake up, stop the insanity, consider each other and *"In everything therefore, treat people the same way you want them to treat you, for this is the Law and the Prophets."* Jesus Christ, The Bible, Matthew 7:12

SYNONYM GAME:
LAW=COMMANDMENT=DIRECTIVE=DECREE=JUDGEMENT
PROPHETS=FORECASTER=INTERPRETER=JUDGE

"Do not judge so that you will not be judged, For in the way you judge, you will be judged; and by your standard of measure, it will be measured to you." Jesus Christ, The Bible, Matthew 7:1-2.

CHAPTER 7

ACTUAL ORAL ARGUMENTS
IN THE COURT CASE

Following is the actual oral arguments presented in the court case mentioned in the previous chapter. The plaintiff had filed a motion demanding a jury trial within the first week the initial pleading was filed. That motion was totally ignored and never addressed.

The two italicized underlined templates included with the global template were thrown back at the system in the plaintiff's oral arguments:

PLAINTIFF'S ORAL ARGUMENTS FOR DENYING DEFENDANTS MOTION TO DISMISS, OREGON JACKSON COUNTY CIRCUIT COURT CASE # 004001Z3
Your Honor,

Plaintiff is a Pro Se. I attempted to hire an attorney but was unable to find an attorney willing to take a case against the county and state, nor can I really afford an attorney, especially an attorney from another state. I have been advised that most attorneys would rather not involve themselves in litigation against the county and state for financial and political reasons.

As a pro se, I humbly ask for the courts understanding in that I am not an attorney. I ask for the court's indulgence for any errors I might make in form and procedure, and ask for the court's tolerance in that I lack the skills of a trained orator. This is a very passionate issue to me and ask the courts forgiveness if, at times, I appear overly passionate.

My most important values are GOD, home, country and the constitution with the bill of rights. I am a simple man, a Christian man, one of God's children. I am not highly educated. I served in the armed forces that guard this nation and its way of life and I am still prepared to give my life in its defense.

I prefer being any place in the world today than in this room, before this court, suing the government I served, for not only my constitutional rights, but in essence, the rights that are supposed to belong to every American. Suing the very government that, during my approximate 20 years in the U.S. Military, made me swear an oath to: "SUPPORT AND DEFEND THE CONSTITUTION OF THE UNITED STATES AGAINST ALL ENEMIES, FOREIGN AND DOMESTIC; THAT I WOULD BEAR TRUE FAITH AND ALLEGIANCE TO THE SAME."

That oath is why I am before this court today. The enemy is now in my back yard, my home, and my country, in the government I served. That enemy is tyranny.

I have been told repeatedly that I cannot win this case. I have been told that the county and state control the lawyers. I have been told the county and state control the courts and I am going to end up in jail on such charges as can be concocted by legal authorities for questioning the election laws, the bureaucrats, the status quo, the authorities. I have been told the court will not listen. I choose to believe that what I have been told is wrong and this court will listen, I will receive justice and fairness from this court, and that this is not a county or state controlled court and the court system has transcended corruption, intimidation, and treason. I believe so, I hope so, and I pray so.

I was raised in this valley. This is my home. I left to serve my country through military service. I eventually returned to the valley to live the American Dream. I wanted to find a job to supplement my military pension, and live that American dream. The defendants in this action do not choose to allow that to happen. From the time I returned home, to the time I filed this case, I observed injustices against the people in Jackson County perpetuated by the defendants. I listened to the people's cries and complaints about the injustices and oppressive actions by the defendants. I asked the people why they didn't choose leaders that will uphold the Constitution and its Bill of Rights, the documents the leaders have sworn to support, to put a stop to those officials that abuse their power.

The people said they have no voice, no choice. The people I spoke with complained that they did not have a legitimate choice. The candidates offered by the political parties were not who they wanted to represent them. The system prevented them from choosing fair and honest individuals who would actually serve them, represent them. I have read of increased tyranny by the defendants, but I still believe we have a system that can be corrected. As time progressed, I not only observed the oppressive actions and injustices against the people by the defendants, I personally started experiencing those actions. I questioned many of those in authority and asked why, sometimes not so politely. The more I questioned, the worse it became for me. Now I was one among the many wondering "why doesn't somebody do something?"

My frustration and astonishment grew at the actions against the people by the defendants. I kept wondering why somebody didn't step forward and do something. Why didn't someone step forward and say, I will stand and speak for you, I will try to correct the system. I will try to do what is right and just. I will try to be honest. I will support and defend the Constitution.

One day I finally determined that I had a moral obligation to try and serve my fellow citizens. I decided to offer myself as a choice to the people as a candidate. I was more than a little reluctant. But, I believe it is still my duty, my sworn oath, to stand against those elected and appointed individuals who are using the laws they make and the power granted them by the people, to abuse, obscure and violate the inalienable God-given and Constitutional rights owned by the people. To violate the very Constitutions they swore to support.

I attempted to get on the ballot and offer myself as a candidate for county commissioner. What progressed—or I should say regressed—from that point is what led to the case before this court today.

As stated before, I am a simple man and try to keep things in simple terms. So if the court will allow, I will state my arguments through a simple analogy that I believe everyone understands. I hope the analogy is not offensive to the court in its simplicity, for it is not intended in anyway to offend but to help clarify my arguments in a manner that is easily understood.

I liken this whole case to a bunch of bullies controlling the schoolyard and ball the school provides the children to play with at recess. The school policy says all the kids are to share the ball so everyone has an opportunity to play. Two classes (Bull and Lies) that shall be called the "bullies" are released early and they control the ball every day. They choose and vote among themselves who will be captains before the other classes let out for recess. The kids in the classes that are let out a few minutes later for recess are "left out" of that first vote and not allowed to put their choices up for captain in the second vote. The bullies and their friends are the only ones who ever seem to be able to be chosen for captains and the bullies always select their friends to play. Some of the kids complain about the choices for the final vote and that the choices are not who most of the kids prefer as captains. The bullies tell all the kids they can't let too many kids try to be captains, it would just confuse things, and it is best for all the kids to let the bullies choose who should be captains. Most of the kids say no, we want some other choices outside your classes. The bullies say no those are the rules. None of the "left out kids" are ever chosen to be captains or get to play. Every day it is the same kids who are "left out." The "left out" kids are afraid to tell the teachers the bullies will not share the ball or let them play for fear the bullies will beat them up. The bullies even charge them a "toll" to watch the bullies play. Some of the kids buy their own toys and bring them to the schoolyard to play with. But the bullies charge them a "toll" to play with the toys or take away the toys claiming the toys are needed for play by some of the other kids or sell the toys to their friends. It does no good to complain to the bullies, they just say that is the way it is. The bullies say this is the RULE OF LAW: "Those who make the rules, rule, those who rule, make the rules." The kids tells the bullies, "that isn't fair, it is not right." The bullies state, "if you don't like it, go tattle to a teacher." Schoolyard rule number one says, "don't tattle, if you do, you will get the stuffing beat out of you, because no one likes a tattle tale." Rule #1 is usually enough to discourage most kids from going to the teacher. A few of the kids try telling the teachers what the bullies are doing is not fair and is wrong but those who do go to a teacher end up being terrorized by the bullies. They are then ignored by their friends and others because the bullies put the kid down, call them tattle tale, start rumors and tell the other kids lies about them, and sometimes beat them up. All the kids fear the same thing will happen to them. Some kids become even more afraid or discouraged, and go off by themselves to sit and be alone. The "left out kids" complain among themselves and ask, "why doesn't somebody do something," but no one hears, or seems to care because most of the kids are terrified of the bullies.

Then one day a new kid gathers up enough courage to stand up to the bullies and tries to reason with them. Someone has to stand for the weaker and smaller kids in the schoolyard against the bullies. He tells the bullies he wants to put himself up for the vote to see if he can be chosen as a captain to make sure everyone has the same chance to play. The bullies tell the new kid the rules they made up says he has to get some of the kids in school to sign a paper giving their permission for him to be in the vote to be a captain. Plus, he can't get the signatures without the bullies' permission so one of the bullies will have to sign the paper so all the kids will know the bullies gave their permission for him to try and be voted a captain. Further the bullies like the papers typed. He is told he cannot get the signatures until after the bullies have chosen who they want to be voted on for captains. He is told if he gets enough signatures, he will not have to pay the bullies his lunch money to be a part of the vote for the captains. The new kid asks the bullies why they don't have to follow those rules or why can't he go through the same rules they do to try and get voted as a captain. He explains to the bullies what they are doing is unfair, that all they to do is say they want to be captains for the main vote but the bullies won't listen. The bullies say, because our rules say you have to do it this way. The new kid says he should be able to say he wants to be a captain and be in the main vote for captain the same as the bullies. He tries to explain to the bullies that it is a school ball for all the kids and not just the bullies. The "left out kids" have as much right to become captains and play as the bullies. The bullies say no, our rules say it is a Bully Class Ball. The new kid says no, it is not, it is a school ball for all the kids, not just the bullies, and what they are doing is unfair. It goes against school policy. The bullies say, it is in our schoolyard rules, if you don't like it, go tattle (remember schoolyard rule #1). But if that is not enough, the bullies appear to have an ace in the hole. They brag to all the kids in the schoolyard about how the teachers are on their side, they are the teacher's favorites, and if you tell a teacher, she will turn you over to the bullies to do as they please. They make the rules in the schoolyard and not the teachers. Their parents can get the teachers fired or their parents are the teacher's friends. The other kids pass this on to the new kid who is standing up and speaking out. He is told horror stories of what happened to their friends and others when they went to a teacher. A few tell how they went to a teacher and got in trouble because the teacher said she couldn't be bothered with their whining and had more important things to do than spend time settling kid squabbles. Another teacher said there wasn't enough balls for all the kids to play, and who ever gets it first makes the rules. Another teacher punished one kid by taking away his recess for a week and he had to stay in the classroom for being a "tattle tale." Another teacher said that if teacher XYZ said that is the way it is then drop it. Another teacher stated recess was over, the time was up, so it did not matter. Another teacher said the rules the bullies made up seemed fair to her, she knew the bullies well and spent a lot of time with them in the classroom, ate lunch with them, and they were smart and always did well. The "left out kids" are now afraid to go to any of the other teachers. They believe the teachers are against them and are for the bullies, and now fear all the teachers. The bullies frighten them. The bullies make the rules and enforce the rules. The bullies RULE in the schoolyard. No one can stand against the bullies, not even the teachers. The "left out kids" now believe they are destined to just stand and watch, wishing they could play ball. But the new kid is determined and goes to the teachers. One teacher tells the new kid "that is the way it has always been, and that is the way it will always be." Another teacher said, "I am too busy to be bothered." Another teacher said, "I doubt the bullies are being unfair." The new kid still cannot believe what is happening, it is not fair or right. Regardless of the horror stories he heard and the experiences with the teachers, the new kid tries to get a teacher to take him to see the principal. None of the teachers will take him to see the principal. The other "left out" kids tell him to forget it, the principal used to be a teacher and will agree with what the teachers say. The new kid believes there has to be one fair and honest person in the school. Aren't the teachers and principal supposed to be fair and be there to help all the kids and teach them and help them resolve some of the problems in school? Aren't the teachers and principal supposed to listen to "all" the kids and not just the bullies? Aren't the teachers and principle supposed to be honest? Aren't the teachers and principals supposed to make sure the school policies are followed by all of the kids, including the bullies? Sure, he is afraid of being beaten up by the bullies but there is something in this new kid that says fair is fair, and right is right. He won't be bullied. The new kid goes to the school office and asks to see the principal to tell his story. The people working in the school office give him a hard time and tell him that is what teachers are for. The new kid insists on seeing the principal and asks if some of the "left out kids" can be there too. He is told he will have to file a complaint, but it is complicated and he will need a teacher to make out the complaint, that is what teachers are for, and he will have to pay a toll to see the principle. He also must give the bullies a copy of his complaint so they can answer his complaint before he sees the principal. The kid cannot believe it, even the office workers are bullies. He cannot find a teacher willing to help him with the complaint, so he does his best to make out the complaint himself. The office bullies make him pay a toll for the instructions for filling out the complaint. He takes the complaint to the office and pays the toll to see the principal. He also fills out a form requesting some of the other kids be there to listen and express their opinion if the bullies' schoolyard rules are fair. The office bullies rules says he cannot just give the schoolyard bullies a copy of the complaint, he has to find someone else to give them a copy and fill out another form saying they did. The new kid ends up having to pay someone else to give the schoolyard bullies a copy. But instead of answering the new kids' complaint, the schoolyard bullies go to the office bullies and fill out a form asking the principal to forget the whole thing. The bullies say they will show this principal that principals in other schools said what the schoolyard bullies were doing was okay. They also made an appointment to see the principal. The new kid fills out another form and gives it to the office asking the principal not to forget it and to see him at the same time he sees the bullies. The office person again tells him that is what teachers are for. The office bullies collect more money from the new kid for someone to take notes. A time is set up for the bullies and the new kid to see the principal, but none of the "left out" kids are allowed in this meeting. The new kid is told more horror stories from the other kids about what is going to happen to him when he talks to the principal. He is told the bullies will tell the principal lies about him and the principal is going to eat him alive, lock him in a closet and throw away the key. They tell the new kid he must remember the principal used to be a teacher, and is one of them. He is one of the bullies. They tell the new kid to drop it, they will suffer through, that they don't want to see him punished for something he didn't do. The new kid is scared, but he doesn't like what is happening to the "left out" kids. Now he is beginning to have doubts that anyone in the school will listen and make a fair and honest decision. He remembers the teachers and the other adults telling the kids, "life is not fair." Surely, there is one fair person in the bunch who will listen and make a fair and honest decision. The kid is given an appointment to see the principal along with the bullies. The principal listens to the bullies and their opinion. The bullies tell the principal she must not listen to this new kid and it isn't necessary to ask the "left out kids" if the rules are fair. They tell the principal the rules are fair. They tell the principal she should forget the whole matter, the rules are on their side. Other principals in other schools said so. The bullies state the new kid doesn't know what he is talking about, he is stupid, a troublemaker, he doesn't understand or follow their rules, their rules are fair, and he is not one of them. Besides, the recess period he is complaining about has been over for a long time and why should he be allowed to complain now. The bullies further state their rules say that they can't be punished for what they do to the other kids. The new kid explains to the principal that the bullies' rules have not changed on the schoolyard, that they still don't let any of the "left out" kids choose who they want as captains to be in the final vote and choose who gets to play ball. The new kid explains to the principal the school policy says the school ball is provided for all the kids to play, and not just the bullies. The new kid tells the principal, if you don't believe me, "ASK THE LEFT OUT KIDS," ASK THE LEFT OUT KIDS IF THE RULES ARE FAIR." The new kid also asks "besides, who died and put the bullies in charge in the schoolyard?" Who gave them this power over the other kids? Who made the bullies God? Who gave the bullies the power to violate school policy? The new kid explains that if the bullies are allowed to get away with what they are doing, that means the school policy is a lie, that what the school policy says means nothing. He asks the principal, if that is true, then tell me so that I can tell the "left out" kids and others that the school policy is a lie, it means nothing, and the bullies have your permission to do as they please. Tell me the bullies have your permission to terrorize all the kids on the schoolyard. Tell me so I can tell all the other kids. The principal recognizes the new kid is upset and has heard whispers of the discontent among the other children. She has already noticed increased violence on the playground and is afraid the discontent could lead to more violence. Maybe the new kid is right. Does she want to involve the "left out kids" and provide them an opportunity to speak and ask them if they think the bullies' rules are fair or unfair? If she listens to the bullies and does as they wish, she is giving them permission to further terrorize the "left out" kids in the schoolyard. The principal knows that will lead to more violence. Further, why don't the bullies want her to ask the "left out" kids if the rules are fair? Are the bullies hiding something? Are the elections they hold for choosing captains and who gets to play ball fair to the other kids? Who did put the bullies in charge in the schoolyard? Are they violating school policy? If what the new kid says is true, how should she punish the bullies? Now the principal has a decision to make.

Your honor, those same bullies are in the courtroom today. That new kid standing up to the bullies is before you today. The bullies don't want you to ask the "left out" kid's for their opinion, if the rules are fair or unfair, constitutional or unconstitutional. They want you to again deny an American his Constitutional right to be heard and granted due process under the law, deny me the opportunity to present my case in front of a jury of my peers according to the Oregon Constitution Article 1 Section 17. They want you to deny the people a chance to voice their opinion in this case.

This is not about my being elected or the election, this is about the equal opportunity for the "left out peoples" right to choose candidates and for individuals to offer themselves, as candidates, to the people as a choice, not have the choices forced on them by the defendants. This concerns whether the Oregon election laws, as written by the defendants, are constitutional and I have asked for that to be decided by a jury of the people, my peers. Now those same "defendants" want to deny the peoples jury an opportunity to listen to both sides and decide if the election laws in question are Constitutional. The defendants are trying to tell this court what it should do. The defendants are telling the court to dismiss this case, forget the whole thing, because other courts, in other times, in other places, in other cases, under different circumstances stated what they are doing is constitutional. They are telling the court the time has run out, the election is over. The defendants are telling this court not to think for itself, do as the defendants' dictate. The rules are fair. Drop it.

My questions, why don't the defendants want this case to go before a jury, the people? Are they hiding something? If so what? I have had many people tell me they don't vote because they do not believe their vote is counted. Are the votes being properly counted or are the ballot counts being fabricated? Could this be true? Most important, why are the defendants afraid to ask the people, the electorate the defendants are supposed to be serving, if the election laws the defendants instituted are constitutional?

I was taught and understand that the U.S. and State Constitutions were put in place to protect the health, safety and welfare of the American people. I understand that GOD creates all people equal and allows governments to be instituted among men to control their actions and to keep them from harming each other. I understand laws are necessary or there will be anarchy. I try to obey the laws, rules, and regulations. I admit I am not perfect, make mistakes and apparently that violates some of those laws and rules, although for the most part, unknowingly and especially when the rules are confusing and convoluted. My problems begin when I see and experience some laws as being inequitable, some being applied inequitably and people being abused and oppressed by the laws deliberate inequitable application.

The people want the best individuals they can find as candidates to choose as leaders, as representative, as servants, not people like the defendants, who appear to be in it just for power, money, pride and self. The defendants have created a system that is tyrannical and presently that system displays a total lack of understanding for the people's health, safety and welfare, or the constitutions the defendants swore to support. The defendant's deliberately enact laws making it more difficult, and in some cases, virtually impossible for other candidates to challenge them in the elections, while granting themselves special privileges. The people are becoming increasingly cynical about the electoral system. Some people suspect their vote doesn't count when electing the leaders, and some suspect the vote is not being counted period. The people would not have felt a need for term limits if they could trust the present electoral system. Common sense dictates there would be no need for term limits if the present electoral process were fair and honest, yet it is for the reasons just stated the people enacted term limits. As everyone knows, the defendants are fighting the term limits the people recently enacted. Why are the defendants fighting those term limits?

Your honor, the arrogance thus far displayed by the defendants in this case is inexcusable. When I reached out to representatives elected by the defendants parties, I was told "that is the way it has always been and that is the way it will always be." I was told "I doubt very seriously that your constitutional rights are being violated" or "I am too busy to be bothered right now, I am running my own election." When I told the defendants what they were doing was unconstitutional, I was told "if you do not like it, sue." The fact so many people are claiming their CONSTITUTIONAL rights are being violated by the defendants abuses is an indication to me there is a problem somewhere within the County, States, and Federal government electoral systems. The very cases the defendant's use as precedence to dismiss further indicates to me there are problems with the present election process. It indicates there are others standing up to the bullies in other places in Oregon, in the country. That what the defendants are doing is unconstitutional under the equal protection clause of the U.S. Constitution and the Oregon Constitution.

The combined non-affiliated, independent, and minor party voters outnumber the individual parties, and the political parties know this. The laws the parties have passed to protect their status quo and positions in government is one of the most blatant disregards of the constitution and bill of rights ever encountered and borders on treason. For the welfare of the community, The non-major party people will take whatever legal or constitutional steps necessary to make the established political parties stop bullying the people. The rights of the political establishment cannot be considered over the rights of the majority of the people. It is necessary that EVERYONE'S rights be protected. What the major parties are doing is a danger to all and is causing violence. Do the defendants perpetuate even more violence? The rights of the individual cannot be ignored. As the rights of the individual are taken, so go the rights of the majority, which is something the Major Parties seem to forget. Our constitutions with their bill of rights were put in place to "protect" the rights of the individual, because our founders knew when the individual's rights were taken, so were the majorities rights.

I have been asked why I want to sue, what have I got to gain. I did not want to sue and have absolutely nothing to gain. Truth is, the whole process has cost me money from my savings I did not wish to spend and could not really afford. It has cost my job and any hopes of finding another job in this valley or in this state as long as the defendants are in control. It has caused a stressful situation with my friends and relatives. It has cost me an enormous amount of time. I do not believe anyone should have to sue for constitutional rights. THE DEFENDANTS TOLD ME TO SUE. Now the same defendants are trying to dictate to this court to dismiss the case. I wish I could be someplace else, but I have my life, liberty, and home at stake. Where do I run too? This is my home and this is not a school yard game. The lives of people are in the balance. Taking anyone's inalienable GOD given and constitutional rights is the same as denying life and liberty. It is my sworn duty to support and defend the constitution, and that is why I am before this court today. The defendants left me with no alternative, but to bring my complaint before the court.

GOD sets up governments among men and gives certain individuals the wisdom to judge man's actions and the law he creates. Those who have been given the gift of wisdom and the authority by GOD to judge man's actions as being right or wrong, just or unjust, fair or unfair will themselves be judged for the decisions they make by that same GOD.

I took an oath to support and defend the U.S. Constitution. The defendants took an oath to support that same document as well as the Oregon Constitution. Today this court can release me from my sworn oath. Today this court can dismiss this case as moved by the defendants. By doing so this court will be telling me and the majority of the non-represented citizens of this state, for all to read and hear, that the U.S. and Oregon constitutions are not worth the paper they are written on. That those documents are a lie, that I have no rights, that the "left out" people have no rights and the defendants have this courts permission to continue governing by tyranny, that the bullies are the RULING classes and will continue to RULE regardless of the Constitutions. Or, you can hold me to my sworn oath by telling the people of this state that the defendants do not rule, and that they are the representatives, the servants of the electorate and that they do have to abide by the U.S. and Oregon constitutions. That those constitutions are still in effect and let the people of Oregon, a jury of my peers, the electorate the defendants are supposed to represent and serve, decide if the defendants have violated those documents through their election laws and permit this case to proceed to a jury trial. I believe the essence of the decision made by this court today will be looked upon in history as the decision that either released total tyranny upon the populace, or stopped tyranny dead in its tracks. To paraphrase your honor, this new kid has brought this complaint before this principal to stop the tyranny displayed by the bullies in the schoolyard.

Plaintiff moves the court to deny Defendants State of Oregon, Secretary of State, Oregon Jackson County and Jackson County Clerk's motion to dismiss and permit this case to proceed to jury trial based on the points and authorities in the Plaintiff's Amended Complaint, Plaintiff's Motion to Deny, and the arguments presented here today. Plaintiff thanks the Court for its time and awaits the court decision.

End Oral Arguments.

The judge assigned in this case stopped the oral arguments before the plaintiff could finish, asked for a copy and promised he would read the argument and render a decision. He stated he understood what was being said. After 60 days, and in accordance with Oregon rules for civil procedure, the plaintiff sent the judge a letter informing the judge that 60 days had passed since he had taken the matter under consideration. Three days later, the Judge dismissed the case, ignoring the plaintiff's plea for a jury trial. The plaintiff filed an appeal with the Oregon appellate court and the entire process started again. The appeals court sent a letter to all the parties explaining that the appeals court could not take action because a "judgement" by the circuit court judge had not been rendered. Plaintiff believes dismissing the case was a judgement. The appellate court stated in the letter that the plaintiff needed to file an amended appeal once that "judgement" was rendered. The defendants filed for a summary judgement, which the judge refused to sign stating that the plaintiff had filed an appeal on his decision, stating the decision was appealable.

The plaintiff was now caught in a "catch 22." The appellate court would not consider the plaintiff's case until the circuit court judge rendered a judgement and the plaintiff filed an amended appeal. The circuit court judge would not render a judgement because the plaintiff had filed an appeal with the appellate court asking them to overturn the decision to dismiss. The plaintiff believed the judgement was the judge dismissing the case. The plaintiff could do nothing because both courts refused to act. After several months, the plaintiff received a letter from the State appellate court stating the case was dismissed for failure to prosecute by the plaintiff. Say what? *The appellate court did not award any costs to the defendants.*

At this point, the plaintiff knew that no matter what he did, this case was not going to be allowed before the people and a jury. The plaintiff realized he had wasted time, effort, and money against a fixed system in which his God-given, Constitutionally guaranteed rights would be denied no matter what approach he took. He was expecting a corrupt system to willingly expose and fix itself. Much like having the fox watch the hen house. So, plaintiff did not pursue the case any further within the system and decided to expose the system in other ways. He started informing the people about what he had discovered. *Several months later, plaintiff received a bill from the state for costs.* Plaintiff to date has refused to pay the state and the county for denying his God-given Constitutionally guaranteed rights.

Plaintiff suspects that within a few weeks or months, he will receive another bill from the state, except this time there will an attached Judgement signed by the Circuit court judge awarding costs to the county and state. It he does, it will be totally illegal because it would have to be backdated to reflect the decision was made before the plaintiff filed the appeal. If dated after the plaintiff filed the appeal, the court was required by Oregon rules of Civil Procedure to send him a copy, which was not done. With that judgement the plaintiff would not have been placed in a catch 22 and would have permitted the plaintiff to pursue the case in the appellate court.

That is the system in Oregon and that is the system that has been or is going to be adopted in all the states.

During this entire incident and while writing this book, the individual involved had several attacks against his computer. Individual documents underwent virus attacks. It was as if someone was in his computer selecting the documents they wanted destroyed. Documents the plaintiff was working on would suddenly start doing strange things, sentences would disappear and reappear in different locations, his computer would freeze up for no apparent reason, documents would start scrolling to the bottom, etc. One day, after running an anti virus program, he discovered he had 3 viruses and 1 Trojan horse. Having used the Internet for years and having never gotten a computer virus until he attempted getting involved in local politics, he is certain at least one or more attacks were deliberate. It was after plaintiff attempted to get involved in local politics that these problems started.

The analogy the plaintiff presented to the court is the third template, the "The Programming and Control" template, the actual "Global template." Did you recognize the template and have you experienced it or any variations in the template while attending school or in your life?

CHAPTER 8

I WAS THE PLAINTIFF AND SO WERE YOU

Joe's story is my story. The plaintiff in the court case in the previous chapter was myself so I know the incidents are true.

Knowing this, there will be some that will say, "this guy just has a bone to pick." My answer to that, you bet I do. And if you will think about it, so do you. Using the systems own aphorism, "experience is the best teacher," *then what better teacher is there than experience? What better way to learn than to experience the atrocities?* Others I know have been subjected to similar experiences within the system. And if you will think about it, you also have a bone to pick because the system in place and being practiced is not the system you are told is in place and being practiced. THEY are lying to you and you continue to accept the lies, the deceptions. For what purpose are you doing this to yourself?

Now think about this. THEY intimidate you into paying THEM taxes utilizing *manipulation through deception*. THEY deny your God-given constitutionally guaranteed rights utilizing *manipulation through deception* so you are paying THEM for the privilege to deny you those rights. If you do not succumb to THEIR *manipulation through deception*, THEY use whatever *force* necessary to take what is yours to sell to get the money for taxes THEY allege you owe THEM. THEY DENY the right for your vote to elect representatives and THEY appoint the representative THEY choose. That is TAXATION WITHOUT REPRESENTATION. Does that sound like school yard bullies that pick on and threaten the weaker kids to fork over their lunch money or anything else the bullies may want and then gang up on the weaker kids if they refuse to pay? It does to me. Wake up.

Our founding fathers did not sacrifice everything they had for the same system that they had fought against to be put back into place, and that is exactly what has happened. We are now back under the same feudal system, the same ruling class and the same "Rule of Law" that our founding fathers fought a revolution to free themselves and future generation from living under.

The three templates being used by the tyrants have been presented to you. The decision as to whether you believe or not believe is yours to make. Just remember that the choice is between two systems. The system the *Evil One (Clique)* created and the system Christ told us about. The *Evil One (Clique)* system is the one being practiced throughout the world today, and has been being practiced for several thousand years. The Christian constitutional government system is the system to come and the system that truly protects the individual. That is the system our founding fathers tried to set into place to protect human beings in this nation. Only the *Evil One (Clique)* persisted in attacking that system with illusions, distortions and lies. That attack was from within and so intense that the *Evil One, a Clique,* gained control over "We the People" and virtually destroyed that Christian Constitutional government before it could really even begin. Thomas Jefferson indicated as much before he died when he made a statement to the effect that everything they had done and sacrificed so much to gain was for nothing because their children had already turned the system back over to the tyrants.

To regain what has been lost, it is time to expose the *Evil One (Clique)*, its illusions, and the system is has created. NOW is the time for "We the People" to wake up and choose human citizen legislators willing to lead in the struggle for freedom and expose the tyrants and the tyranny within, not career politicians. NOW!

This system, this methodology that is being practiced in the world today is the antichrist and has been among human beings since the beginning. The antichrist is not to come, but is already here and has always been here. The antidote for an insulated zombie enslaved demon is the truth. Jesus Christ and His teachings are that truth.

Christ, is the *"One"* who said "judge not, least you be judged." If you will notice, the word Christ is also an *ist* but to the *Evil One (Clique)* is an unacceptable *ist*. It is Christ and only Christ who will be the one to judge human beings. It is He that is *truly the insulin and the cure*. It is He that is the true island against the world's insanity and the *ism and ist methodology* that has been created by the *Evil One* to hide the truth about Christ. It is Christ the *Evil One (Clique)* cannot control. It is Christ the *Evil One* wants to isolate from all human beings with the illusions the *Evil One (Clique)* creates by its *ism* and *ist* system called Isolation Shock Methodology and Therapy. *GOD SENT HIS SPIRIT IN HIS SON, JESUS CHRIST AS THE ANTIDOTE TO*

THE ENEMY CALLED "THEY"

HELP GOD'S CHILDREN.
The system being practiced loves acronyms. Following are a few acronyms I developed:

J	JEALOUSIES	J	JUSTICE	C	CONSTITUTIONS
E	ENSURE	E	ENTAILS	H	HELP
S	SLAVERY	S	SPECIAL	R	RESTRAIN
U	UNLESS	U	UNDERTAKING	I	ISOLATION
S	SOMEONE	S	SUPPORTING	S	SHOCK
				T	THERAPY
C	CONFRONTS	C	CHILDREN	I	IN
H	HORDE	H	HELPING	A	ALL
R	REGULATING	R	RESIST	N	NATIONS
I	ISOLATION	I	ISOLATION		
S	SHOCK	S	SHOCK		
T	THERAPY	T	THERAPY		

"The whole aim of practical politics is to keep the populace alarmed (and hence clamorous to be led to safety) by menacing it with an endless series of hobgoblins, all of them imaginary."—H.L. Mencken

"Every law is an infraction of liberty."—Jeremy Bentham.

"Perception is the truth."—An aphorism utilized throughout government and in the media.

In the war against the Clique, the *Evil One*, the Tyrants, the vipers brood, or whatever label one chooses, and the terrorism they perpetuate, human Christian Americans have surrendered, have allowed themselves to become:

APATHETIC
<u>A</u>ngry, <u>P</u>oor, <u>A</u>lienated, <u>T</u>ired, <u>H</u>elpless, <u>E</u>ntrapped, <u>T</u>errified, <u>I</u>ncredulous, <u>C</u>heated

COMPLACENT
<u>C</u>onned, <u>O</u>ppressed, <u>M</u>isled, <u>P</u>opulace <u>L</u>auding <u>A</u> <u>C</u>lique <u>E</u>nslaving <u>M</u>ankind <u>T</u>otally.

LOSERS
<u>L</u>ost, <u>O</u>ppressed, <u>S</u>hocked, <u>E</u>nslaved, <u>R</u>elinquished, <u>S</u>ouls

Many men that signed the Declaration of Independence and led the American Revolution for Independence sacrificed their fortunes, homes, families, friendships, and some sacrificed their lives. These men were labeled troublemakers, rabble rousers, malcontents, terrorists, and criminals by the English government and were "wanted dead or alive." These were the leaders that founded this nation. These men talked the talk and walked the walk. These men fought to REGAIN and keep their God-given FREEDOM that was being DENIED by an oppressive King and his underlings. These men stood against the schoolyard bully and his friends. These men stood up to "THEY." These men refused to become Insulated Zombie Enslaved Demons.

I heard a Democratic Congressional Representative from New Jersey, once state that the Second Amendment to the Constitution is antiquated and is no longer applicable, and that he was tired of hearing people say how they needed their guns for hunting and sports shooting. Well, I am tired of hearing people say the same thing.

The Second Amendment right to bear arms is needed today, as it was needed 230 years ago. Not for hunting or sports shooting as the manipulated through deception NRA leads people to believe. The Second Amendment provides human beings the means to defend themselves from the TYRANTS that would deprive human beings their God-given and Constitutionally guaranteed rights, which is the true purpose behind the founders putting the 2nd amendment into the Constitution's Bill of Rights in the second place.

Our nation's President has declared a "War on Terrorism." According to the Constitution, the President cannot declare war. Who is the war declared against? From what I am seeing and hearing in the news, it is not the terrorist accused in the attack against the WTC. So far our government has been bombing the people in Afghanistan, overthrowing the Taliban government in order that a government our government chooses can be instituted in Afghanistan and Americans have been whipped into a blind patriotic frenzy against another people's religion. And now, THEY want to attack Iraq.

He that would make his own liberty secure, must guard even his enemy for oppression; for if he violates this duty he establishes a precedent that will reach unto himself.-Thomas Paine

Laws contrary to the U.S. Constitution and that deprive American citizens their God-given Constitutionally guaranteed rights are being put into place in America today for "security" and "safety." *"They that can give up essential liberty to obtain a little temporary safety deserve neither liberty nor safety."*—Benjamin Franklin, Historical Review of Pennsylvania, 1759.

I ask again, who was this war on terrorism declared against? I perceive it is the American people. Who is behind it and what is their purpose? I perceive there are those that have infiltrated all levels in our government leadership through "election fixing," and are now using the power and authority stolen by *manipulation through deception* from the American people to overthrow our Constitutional Government and the American way of life from within.

Those that actually committed the atrocities at the WTC and the Pentagon were pawns for those behind the scenes in these acts of war. Those truly responsible will most likely never be apprehended and brought to Justice, although other higher ranking pawns (Bin Laden and his close associates) participating in the atrocities may be killed as scapegoats and/or perhaps offered world leadership positions later on to keep them quiet.

Consider the fact that in the 1970s Yassar Arafat was the most wanted terrorist leader worldwide. Interpol, the FBI, CIA, Israeli intelligence, etc. wanted him. Now I begin to wonder what was the real purpose behind his being "wanted"? Once he was "found," he became a renowned world leader perpetuating terrorism throughout the world. He was also awarded the Nobel Peace Prize. THEY are telling us, look at this, we awarded him the highest honor that can be bestowed on a person for his efforts toward peace. Terrorism = peace. I think not. Could this be *Manipulation through deception* at work? Hmm. I think so.

The 9-11 attack was well planned and from what we are being told, it would have been absolutely necessary to have people placed in key position within our nation's airlines and security to pull it off. It would have been necessary to have people within our own intelligence community keep information hidden that they now claim to have had previous knowledge about.

Look at the failed attempts at capturing Bin Laden. The news media has easy access to this man and can record him on video. Yet the greatest government, with the best intelligence, with the most advanced technology in the world today cannot even get close to this man. Say what? Americans are led to believe this man who supposedly has over a half-billion dollars is living in a cave in a desert in Afghanistan. I ask you, if you had a half-billion dollars, where would you be living? Isn't anyone questioning the information that is being told to the American public? Who has or will benefit financially from the atrocities? The Red Cross, the Airlines, Big Oil, the Civilian Military Industrial Complex, Big Bankers, who?

No one seems to question how coincidental it is that a camera or cameras were so conveniently set up to capture the planes hitting the World Trade Center. No one seems to question the news reports that went out minutes after the first attack that a "fourth plane *involved* is missing." How did anyone know how many or what planes were involved and especially that a plane involved was missing, or that any missing plane was involved?

No one is questioning the inconsistencies in the numbers reported killed in the WTC and Pentagon attacks months after the attacks occurred. No one is questioning the fact that most new restrictions being put on American Citizens at the airports have nothing to do with what happened in these attacks.

No one is questioning because the media and some government officials have whipped Americans into a blind, patriotic, frenzy and have turned the American people into frightened hate mongers against 800 million people who had nothing to do with the attacks. I am questioning because something stinks.

Tyrants using terror tactics are attacking our Constitutional Government and human Christian Americans have to wake up and stand against that attack. Wars on Poverty and Drugs have been declared against the American people in the past. We have been losing those wars for the past 20-30 years. Poverty and drug use in America has skyrocketed since these wars begin. Now a War on Terrorism has been declared against the American people, our Constitutional government, our way of life, but not from the direction people are being led to believe. Smoke screens, flanking movements, ploys, and every other deception is being used to convince American people the attacks are coming from other places, *while all the time, the major attack is from within.*

The news media *is manipulated through deception* into perpetuating this attack from within with the propaganda that they put out day after day, week after week, year after year, continually brainwashing the American populace with the *Evil One's* half truths, lies, and illusions. Next to the public education system, the news media is the greatest propaganda mechanism the *Evil One* controls with *manipulation through deception* as an on going brainwashing source for the *Evil One*. This media is in constant use, 24 hours a day, 7days a week, 365 days a year. This media includes radio, television, movies, Internet, telephone, newspapers, magazines, books, music, flyers, and Isolated Zombies Enslaved. For the past year, I have begun to question much about what is being reported.

The evidence indicates that these wars against Americans are being instigated from within our own borders. Has anyone noticed many government officials and people in the news media keep calling these a War *on* Poverty, a War *on* Drugs, and a War *on* Terrorism and not *against* these things. Wake up. We need to discover *those truly* behind these atrocities and bring THEM to justice.

The few human patriotic Americans trying to raise questions are being shouted down, intimidated, told to shut up, or told to move to Afghanistan. Are the individuals doing the shouting and telling human Christian patriotic Americans to shut up and move to Afghanistan involved with the conspirators and tyrants? I ask this question because shouting down people that disagree, using intimidation, and labeling people is the hate and prejudice template used by the tyrants which plays a big part in the overall Evil's template to gain and maintain control over human beings. The answer to the question is, these human Americans are being *manipulated through deception* with the hate and prejudice template and the "my country right or wrong aphorism."

Human Christian Patriotic Americans now is the time to wake up and stand against the tyrants and the terrorists that the Evil One has infiltrated and instilled within our government and are destroying America from within. Now!

The acid tests for determining if those who profess to be our elected and chosen leaders are truly for or against human beings, for or against America, and the Christian way of life is to ask, "are the decisions they make and the laws they advocate instituting Constitutional." And, "do they believe that Jesus Christ came in the flesh." It doesn't take a rocket scientist or a Supreme Court Justice in most cases to make that determination.

Our founders wrote the Constitution so that it could be literally interpreted by the people, i.e. human beings. There are no hidden secrets or code. Just read the Bill of Rights and if a word is confusing, consult a Dictionary and or Thesaurus. *Now, I ask all the Human Christian Patriotic Americans, when was the last time you read the Constitution's Bill of Rights and compared it with what is being said and done by our professed leaders/ representatives? When was the last time you read the Declaration of Independence and compared it with what is happening today?*

Claiming to be a human, a Christian, a patriotic American and waving the flag is one thing. Knowing what the flag truly represents and its meaning, and the sacrifices required for that flag to continue flying and for the principles, values, and the Constitutional government it represents to stand is entirely different. *Do you talk the talk, or do you walk the walk, or do you do both?*

Are you willing to make whatever sacrifices may be necessary to regain and keep the freedom that the U.S. flag represents in order to keep that flag flying over this nation? Are you willing to sacrifice your job, your home, your saving, your reputation, your family, your friends, and/or your life for that freedom? Are you willing to be labeled a troublemaker, mal content, disgruntled, unpatriotic, or worse? Are you willing to have criminal offenses fabricated and brought against you for exercising God-given freedoms and rights that the Constitution's Bill of Rights guarantees the government can't deprive?

That may be what it takes before this war is over brothers and sisters, my fellow human beings, because the final conflict is upon us. Now is the time for all human Christian Patriotic Americans willing to stand and fight against the tyrants and the tyranny to come forward and be put into harms way.

"So long as the people do not care to exercise their freedom, those who wish to tyrannize will do so; for tyrants are active and ardent, and will devote themselves in the name of any number of gods, religious and otherwise, to put shackles upon sleeping men." —Voltarine de Cleyre

Human beings in nations are being used as a bond for money owed by governments to a financial Elite. That financial Elite is controlling and enslaving the world. This is being done by dividing human beings, creating war between these divided human beings, loaning the human being governments money to fight the war, then loaning these same governments money to rebuild after the wars. Once in debt, the government taxes the people to pay the debt, but due to the high interest on this debt, the governments are unable to pay the debt to the financiers. Eventually these governments allow the populace to be put into bondage through LAWS (Legally Authorizing Worker Slaves) to the financiers for the debt owed.

Human beings are taught that if they do not know something, it cannot hurt them. That is pure garbage. Ignorance can be dangerous. At the same time, depending on the knowledge and in the wrong hands, knowledge can be just as dangerous. There are those who will use knowledge for all the wrong purposes such as to con human beings for greedy purposes and/or to enslave human beings. Knowledge can be used to accomplish good or evil. Knowledge can be used to better human beings condition on earth, or knowledge can be used to enslave human beings on earth. Today, knowledge is being used for the wrong purposes. Using greed as its foundation, evil has taken control. Anything goes to enslave human beings. The human Nation has been enslaved financially through WAR. *WAR = Wronging A Right.*

The word WAR is derived from the German word *werran (to confuse)*

which is derived from the Latin word *verrere (to sweep)*. Sweep means to destroy completely or remove from a surface with one single forceful action. War is basically an action resulting from RAW hate and is utilized to confuse and destroy human beings with force. My acronym for RAW is Righting A Wrong. Look at the word RAW in a mirror, it is WAR or Wronging A Right.

How can war be wronging a right you might ask? Wars are fought to right the wrongs one nation does to another you might say. Are they? Think again about *manipulation through deception*. There is an aphorism that goes "two wrongs don't make a right." Yet, I have actually heard people say that two wrongs do make a right. There is no way that two wrongs make a right. Actually, the aphorism goes "two wrongs do not a right make." That is totally different from "two wrongs do make a right."

"This war is unlike any war we ever have fought before." How many times have you heard this rhetoric, this aphorism? I have heard it used for WWII, Korea, Vietnam, Granada, Gulf, Cold War, War on Drugs, War on Terrorism, War or Poverty, etc. etc. etc.

WAR is armed hostile *competition* between nations, states, or opposing forces for a specific goal. War is man's inhumanity to man created by *manipulation through deception* for greedy purposes. I find it ironic, that in war, *all the participants believe they are in the right*. Truth is, in war no one is right because war is human beings killing human beings. Two W̲rongs make A̲ R̲ight. WAR is wronging a right. WAR is never right. It is one nation being manipulated to fight another nation that is being manipulated.

War is peace. Freedom is slavery. Ignorance is strength. –George Orwell

This is an example surrounding "word speak" in the George Orwell book 1984. Everything is supposedly opposite what it really says. Anyone that thinks peace is gained through war, or that freedom is being a slave to a cruel or kind master, and that ignorance is strength, believes that something can be created from nothing.

Daniel Webster once warned, "Human beings will generally exercise power when they can get it, and they will exercise it most undoubtedly in popular governments under pretense of public safety."

War is war. How one fights a war, the weapons used, and the human beings killed may not be the same, but the war is no different. Human beings are slaughtered and killed. War's essence is, human beings die. So, how does this War "on" Terrorism make it any different than any war we have ever fought? Human beings have fought in every war conceivable, and the end result is the same, human beings die. War is human beings killing other human beings. What makes any war special over another war?

In reality, nothing. In the Evil One's" Divide and Conquer Methodology, it is everything. In order to convince human beings that war is just, that war is right, that war needs fighting and that the ends justify the means, it has to be a *"war unlike any war we have ever fought before."* In all the wars this nation has fought, human beings have been killed. We have fought wars in ranks, in trenches, in jungles, on our own soil, in streets, on the sea, in the sea, on foreign soil, in the air, from the air, and used every weapon conceivable. So, I ask again, what makes this 'War "on' Terrorism' so special, unlike any war we have ever fought before. NOTHING!

The only difference is, over time the weapons that have been developed can be used to kill humans in larger masses. For example, for what purpose would a bomb be created that will kill all human life, yet leave everything that has been built in tact and unharmed? The Neutron bomb does that very thing.

What is the reason for such a bomb?

What if one race could manipulate another race into being its salves to do its bidding to build large cities and nice comfortable living quarters and to provide them comforts? Yet, the race that is enslaved is extremely costly to maintain as slaves because they have what is known as a freewill and continually seek freedom. What if the race doing the manipulating could clone the race that they enslaved and had the ability to program the clones to be without a freewill and still serve as slaves? Take enough blood from the original slave, store that blood by freezing it and that slave can be cloned and programmed to be a slave for an eternity. What if that race then manipulates the race they have enslaved into virtually destroying itself with a bomb such as the neutron bomb? The race that did the manipulating can walk in and take over everything built by the race that destroyed itself, clone and program more slaves without a freewill. Unbelievable you are probably saying. Science fiction you say. Is it? Think about it.

This 'War "on" Terrorism' is being fought for the same reason as all wars, that being an "Elite's" (Clique, *Evil One*) greed.

It is being fought with weapons, we are dropping bombs, and human beings are dying. The divide and conquer methodology is working well isn't it? The *other beings*, the Elite, the Clique, the vipers brood, the *Evil One*, are *manipulating human beings through deception* into slaughtering each other in "wars for peace." World War I is described as "the war to end all wars." How many wars has this nation fought since WWI? Answer: WWII, Korea, Vietnam, Gulf War, and now Afghanistan. To get around calling some wars a war, THEY label them a "police action." And some call me insane?

I wish someone would really explain to me how any war could be war human beings have never fought before! Wars play a big part in enslaving human beings. Wars go against God's commandment "thou shall not kill." *Human beings killing human beings* violate God's commandment. God did not say it was okay for human beings to kill human beings in WAR. *Human beings are manipulated though deception into believing it is okay to kill each other in war.*

Any government that adopts a previous enemy's methodologies has now become that same enemy to the people it serves. The people's rights are taken one individual at a time.

"In Germany they first came for the Communists and I didn't speak up because I wasn't a Communist.

Then they came for the Jews, and I didn't speak up because I wasn't a Jew.

Then they came for the trade unionists and I didn't speak up because I wasn't a trade unionist.

Then they came for the Catholics, and I didn't speak up because I was a Protestant.

Then they came for me by that time no one was left to speak up."—Pastor Martin Niemoller

Evil forces *manipulate* a nation's leadership *through deception* into believing that the nation is superior to other nations, is being threatened by other nations, and that it is necessary to start a war to defend the nation's interest. The nation's leadership then *manipulates* the people within the nation into believing the same things *using the same deceptions.*

The opposing nation's leadership is also being *manipulated through deception* by the same forces into participating in the war by defending against the aggressor nation. All the nations involved believe they are in the right. Both sides are *manipulated through deception* into believing that fighting and killing other human beings make the whole thing right. But it is wrong, and those doing *the manipulating through deception* know this. THEY created Wronging A Right. THEY created WAR. THEY are truly the enemy that we need to seek out, fight, and destroy. And I will say it again *THEY are not human beings.*

The shepherd drives the wolf from the sheep's throat, for which the sheep thanks the shepherd as his liberator, while the wolf denounces him for the same act as the destroyer of liberty. -Abraham Lincoln

SYNONYM GAME:
DECEPTION=DISHONESTY=LYING=DISHONESTY=DECEPTION

Although a person may be enslaved physically, as long as that person's mind is free, that person's spirit will never be enslaved. Yet, by physically enslaving an individual, it becomes easier to enslave the person's mind. Once a person's mind is enslaved, the person's spirit can be enslaved. Once the spirit is enslaved, the person's soul (being) belongs to the *Evil One*. Given enough time, every human being can be enslaved if they are not provided a way out.

A person may be *manipulated through deception* into believing he/she is free, while in reality he/she is truly a slave, therefore, one cannot be a slave and be free. That is the *Evil One's* system today. It *manipulates human beings through deception* into believing they are free, while enslaving them in their evil system. In order to be free, it is necessary that the lambs (human beings) be well armed against the wolves (*Evil One*). Today, the wolves (*Evil One*) are doing everything within their power to distract the shepherd (human leaders) and to disarm the lambs (human beings). The wolves (*Evil One*) have manipulated through deception the nation's Shepherds (human leaders) that THEY are concerned for the lamb's (human beings) safety and welfare, and the shepherds (human leaders) are leading the flock (human beings) to the wolves (*Evil One*). The wolves (*Evil One*) are now disarming the lambs (human beings) and soon will be at the lambs (human beings) throats. Human beings are being led to the slaughter for the *Evil One* to feed on. Human beings are provided a free will by their Creator. Human beings are born free. It is the *Evil One* that enslaves human beings, but only with the human beings permission. Our human leaders are presently providing that permission to the *Evil One*.

Strength comes from a fighting fit and armed populace. That may sound as if I am contradicting myself from what was previously written about WAR. I was talking about human beings killing human beings in wars created by the *Evil One* for the *Evil One's* benefit. The *Evil One* isn't human.

Human beings have the God-given right to defend themselves against those things that would harm them. Every human being possesses the will to survive, just as all creatures have the will to survive. The EVIL ONE once wanted human beings armed in order to create wars using the human will to survive to *manipulate human beings through deception* into fighting wars between each other. That has changed. Soon the *Evil One* is going to be exposed for what it is and does not want human beings to have the means to physically resist the *Evil One's* forces. The *Evil One* has been instituting laws that will allow the *Evil One* to eventually take human beings weapons before the *Evil One* is exposed to the light. *The Evil* one and its Insulated Zombie's Enslaved Demons will be the only ones allowed the weapons. The *Evil One is not human* and does not want the human populace to have the physical means to resist.

...there being nothing more evident than that creatures of the same species... should be equal amongst one another without subordination or subjection... -John Locke

Human beings are provided a free will by their Creator. Human beings are born free. It is the *Evil One* that enslaves human beings, but only with the human beings permission. *Strength not only comes from a fighting fit and armed populace, but the willingness by that populace to use those arms against the tyrants.*

"*Democracy is two wolves and a lamb voting on what to have for lunch. Liberty is a well armed lamb contesting the issue!*"—Benjamin Franklin 1759

As long as human beings allow themselves to be controlled by these other beings, this Clique, this *Evil One,* this vipers' brood, there will be hate, prejudice, wars, killing, injustices, etc., and that is how long truly Patriotic Christian human beings must stand and fight against the tyranny. Our founding fathers recognized this and provided human Christian Americans a free nation and a Constitution with which to combat this *Evil One*. Only, human Christian Americans have forgotten that and have allowed themselves to become apathetic and complacent. Human Christian Americans have allowed this Clique, this *Evil One*, the vipers' brood to take control in America and throughout the world.

DO YOU TALK THE TALK OR WALK THE WALK?

I am a Christian, but do not belong to the Christian religion. I have become convinced that *religions* are being *manipulated though deception* by the *Evil One* to divide and conquer human beings. Being a Christian is about faith in GOD. Being a Christian is living life the way Christ taught. Being a Christian is having free will and letting human beings make their own choices. Being Christian is a way to live life.

Being a Christian does not mean you have to like or accept the others choices as your own, but providing the information to the other person and letting them choose for themselves the path they wish to walk, the path that either leads to heaven or hell, freedom or slavery. No where in Christ's teachings did he try to coerce or force anyone to do anything. At no time did he speak about harming another human being. The only ones he spoke against were *the vipers' brood* i.e., *the Evil One*. The *vipers' brood* is not human and it is the *Evil One,* ruled by Satan in his world.

I hear many Christian people say they worship another GOD, are not of this world, and don't want to get involved in politics. Christians state Christ didn't get involved in politics and He was not of this world. Christians then claim that throughout *The Bible*, GOD put in place Kings and established their Kingdoms. I ask you, if that is the case, is that not politics? Is that not also contradictory? Is that not hypocrisy?

GOD put in place Kings and established their Kingdoms. I ask you again if that is the case, is that not politics? Yet Christians state they are not to get involved in politics. Christ was a Carpenter. Does that mean every Christian must become a Carpenter. It amazes me the excuses Christians make trying "not to get involved in politics," yet set up political structures within Christian denominations.

It is proper for Christians to hold down jobs in every profession known to man, but not be involved in politics. If it is proper for Christians to be involved in every other aspect in this world, why not politics? Christ was not a newsperson in his day, yet he reported all He knew to the people. Christ was not a journalist in his day, yet HIS story is the greatest story ever told. Christ was not in education, yet He was the greatest teacher ever known. Christ was not a "religious leader" in his day, yet thousands followed him, listened to Him speak, and established religions around Him and His teachings.

Although Christ did not "run" for or try to get elected to any "political" office, he was greatly involved in politics. HE was so involved that He upset the religious and political order in his day. HE was a threat to the "system." Threatening the system is getting involved. He was not of this world, but he was in this world and so are Christian people today. We are in this world to make a difference and be involved. There is a difference between being involved in what goes on in this world and being "of this world." Each individual is to get involved in the way Christ leads them.

I believe many Christian people are being "called" and led into politics, but are ignoring that call and "doing their own thing." Like it or not, Christian people "are" involved in politics, the game, the system. We are involved in politics because *we are born into the politics game* and there is no way around being involved in politics whether it be in church politics, on the job politics, or politics on the city, county, state, or federal level. If you vote (even though evidence indicates that vote isn't counted), you are involved in politics. If you work you are involved in politics. If you are a church member, you are involved in politics. If you go to PTA meetings you are involved in politics. If you eat, sleep and breathe, you are involved in politics. No matter what we do in life, we are somehow involved in politics, *in the game*. Human beings are born into the game.

Christians are being *manipulated through deception* into believing they *should not* get involved in politics. Politics is at Satan's heart. Politics is his domain on this earth. Politics is Satan's evil foundation on this earth. By controlling what goes on politically, Satan controls the economy, education, and religions, etc. Christians saying they do not want to get involved in politics is disturbing to me. Christians are already involved, yet prefer to stay on the fringes and let Satan's viper's *brood manipulate through deception* and control what goes on in the world. Human Christian Americans have an opportunity to strike at Satan's heart, his evil foundation, his system, yet act afraid. I do not understand why Human Christian Americans are reluctant to take an opportunity to strike at Satan's heart, his evil foundation, his system and fight him on his own ground, at his own game. Human Christian Americans surrender (give up) before the game is even played. They do not want to compete. Human Christians 0, Evil One 10.

I hear many Human Christian Americans say, we are in a spiritual battle, I cannot concern myself with what goes on in this world. As Human Christian Americans we are in a battle. This battle is not a battle about wronging a right for the *Evil One. We are in a battle for survival against another race.* We are living in a physical world with physical bodies and physical limitations. We are put here for a purpose, and I believe that purpose is to make a difference, set the example, and stand against Satan on this physical ground. On this earth, Satan uses a methodology to ensnare souls. We have the means to change that methodology, that system here on earth.

As Human Christian Americans we are involved in not only a spiritual battle, but a physical battle as well. Like it or not, we are involved in this world, in the game, and the Human Christian Americans have let the *Evil One* take over the politics game, and run this world THEIR way. How can Human Christian Americans be combatants in a spiritual battle against the Evil One if they cannot be relied upon to be combatants in a physical battle against that same evil? It is time for all GOD loving human beings, Christian, Islamic, Hindu, Muslim, etc. to band together and seek out, and fight the *Evil One*, that very same *Evil One* that has gained control and is running the world today. Human Christian Americans keep saying, "God is in control. Satan can only do what God allows him to do." *Have any ever thought that maybe God is waiting for Human Christians to take a stand before he steps in and intercedes. I keep hearing Christians repeat the aphorism that "God helps those who help themselves."*

    I liken the whole situations to a son who is afraid that the bully will "beat him up." His father wants his son to stand up to the bully, and will intercede only if the bully is more powerful and his son can be seriously hurt. The father tells his son not to start any trouble, but to stand up to the bully the next time the bully confronts him and to do his best. The father shows the son a "few pointers." The bully confronts the son and ends up defeating the son. The father again tells the son to stand up to the bully the next time he is confronted by the bully. The son begins to notice that each time he stands up to the bully's advances, the bully seem less confident. Finally, one day, the son defeats the bully and is no longer bothered by the bully. In fact, the bully now avoids the son. That is the way I believe it is with God, our father, he wants us to stand up to the bully, the tyrant, the *Evil One* and do our best. He tells us that he will not let anything seriously hurt us, that he will intercede before that happens. Just have faith and believe in that. But he wants us to stand against the bully alone to show us what a real coward the bully truly IS, so that when the bully truly shows himself for the coward he IS, human beings will not be afraid when the final fight comes. In the final fight between the Son and the Evil One, The bully (Evil One) is going to bring all its "friends" (Insulated Zombie Enslaved Demons) and its dad (Satan). The son (Jesus) will bring all his friends (Christian human beings) and will also bring his dad (God). God came as the Son, showed human beings how to defeat the enemy, departed, and promised to return. I believe He will return as the Son leading the battle when human beings stand against that enemy in the enemy's own back yard. That backyard is the political arena and the battle is the manipulation game that is being played on human beings here on earth.

    Human beings know there is only one GOD, and we all worship that same GOD. Sure, we call him by different names, but that is because our languages are different. The *Evil One* worships Satan. *This is not a war between Christian and Islamic and Muslim and Jew, etc. as human beings are manipulated through deception into believing by the Evil One. This is a war between good and evil and human beings are losing that war.* The *Evil One* is *manipulating human beings through deception* into committing atrocities against each other such as terrorism, wars, ludicrous laws, greed, adultery, murder, lying, robbery, arson, etc.

Every human Christian is looking forward to the day that Christ returns and makes everything right. In the meantime, many human Christians are ignoring Christ's teachings, are playing "ostrich" and hiding their heads in the sand, not wanting to "get involved" in worldly things. JESUS told His people to obey the laws of the land. HE told His people to render unto Caesar what is Caesars.

HE did not tell His people to do nothing. By doing nothing human Christians are playing into the Evil One's plan. The *Evil One* knows human Christians are not of this world, but are in this world to make a difference. By doing nothing and by not getting involved, human Christians make it easier for *the Evil One* to enslave human beings and ensnare many souls that will end up staying in the *Evil One's* world forever. In Matthew 5:5 Christ said, "*Blessed are the gentle for they shall inherit the earth.*" Personally, I do not want to remain here on earth. I want to be in heaven with the father. When Christ spoke the Sermon on the Mount and taught these things, he was talking about the way human beings are to treat other human beings. In Matthew 5:16-20, Jesus told us "*Let your light shine before men in such a way that they may see your good works, and glorify your Father who is in heaven. Do not think that I came to abolish the Law or the Prophets; I did not come to abolish but to fulfill. For truly I say to you, until heaven and earth pass away, not the smallest letter or stroke shall pass from the Law until all is accomplished. Whoever then annuls one of the least of these commandments, and teaches others to do the same, shall be called least in the kingdom of heaven; but whoever keeps and teaches them, he shall be called great in the kingdom of heaven. For I say to you that unless your righteousness surpasses that of the scribes and Pharisees, you will not enter the kingdom of heaven.*"

Christ was saying that the commandments were still in place, and that he came to put into practice what they truly meant and they would not be done away with until everyone was proficient in their practice. He came to show us how to live what is called the Christian life. He told us to let our passion for *Righteousness* (goodness, integrity, honesty, morality, uprightness, justice, and/or decency) stand out. He did not tell us to do nothing.

The *Evil One* tricks human Christians into believing they can do nothing, convinces human Christians they cannot make a difference and they should hide in fear and just wait for Christ's return. That way, the *Evil One* can run up the score on enslaving human beings with little resistance. Human

Christians are standing by and watching while human souls in the millions are enslaved through greed, lust, homosexuality, war, hate, pretending to be GOD, etc. By doing nothing human Christians believe they will ensure Christ's speedy return, but at what cost in human souls enslaved by the *Evil One*?

We do not know when Christ is returning, but HE has left human being Christians as caretakers in this world and we are to make a difference in this world. Whatever human being Christians do in life it is to glorify HIS name. Not everyone can be involved as clergy, missionaries, etc., but each and every human Christian can "witness" to people. The best way to witness is by setting an "example."

When people see Christian people getting involved and trying to correct the injustices against their fellow human beings, that will be a witness to others. When Christians set up a business and run that business so the customer and the employee are dealt with honestly and fairly without being cheated, that will be a witness to others? When people see Christians get involved in government and make a positive difference in that government, that will be a witness to others. To change men's hearts, Christians can "set the example" by getting "involved in human affairs on this earth.

The worst witness is to "claim" to be Christian, talk about being Christian, and then sit back and let the *Evil One* practice its will without doing anything to counter the evil or stand in the *Evil One's* way. How many famous Christian TV ministers have been involved in wrong doings that have been made public? I believe those are very poor examples to be setting. How many human souls were forever enslaved to the *Evil One* due to those poor examples, the hypocrisy? Those ministers talked the talk, but they did not walk the walk. Which witness do most people remember, the talk or the walk?

Many Christian people today want to "shout" from the rooftops about Christ and the Christian faith and that is fine, but the best witness is by setting the example, and the greatest witness is to do both?

Do you notice that parents tell their children one thing while the parents do another? If you don't believe me, ask your own children. Children generally follow the examples set by the adults, not what they are told by the adults? Why is that? Could GOD be using this as an example to the adults? Could it be HE wants us to recognize our own hypocrisies? Children readily recognize the hypocrisies and that is probably the greatest cause in what is happening with the children in our world today. As parents, we lead by example. The best leaders lead by example. The best athletes lead by example. The best Christian witness is by example?

Christ taught us how to live the Christian life and that was to *love GOD, love our neighbor as ourselves, and treat others the way we want to be treated.* He taught us to *love our enemies* and pray for those who persecute us. He was talking about our fellow human beings.

He did not tell us to exterminate human beings that do not believe or think the same as we do. *Not getting involved in what is going on around us, keeping our mouths shut to injustices and wrong doings, and letting wrong doings permeate the land without taking action is the poorest examples I believe, as Christians, we can set.* As the old maxim states, "talk is cheap." Many Christians can talk the talk. How many Christians really walk the walk?

I ask you, as a Christian, do you talk the talk or do you walk the walk? Do you walk in Christ's footsteps by taking a stand against the *Evil One*? Or do your hide your head in the sand, talk the talk, and let the *Evil One* have its way in intimidating, coercing, humiliating, bulling, cheating, robbing, conning, mistreating, even murdering human beings and enslaving their souls with its system?

I ask all who profess to be *Human Christian Americans, for what purpose have Christians surrendered to the Evil One the system that was inherited from our founding fathers and allowed that Evil One to institute a system that oppresses the people and denies God?* I say it is time to *FREE THE PEOPLE.*

I have learned from experience that the system being practiced is not that system we are told is practiced. In fact, the system practiced is the complete opposite to what we are told is being practice. *I have learned from experience* that there is no justice in the system being practiced. *I have learned from experience* the system being practiced is based on illusion, distortion, lies, and that the truth is not accepted in that system. *I have learned* that those within that system who profess to be the elected and chosen leaders are really appointed by the *Evil One* and the people elect no one. *I have learned from experience* that those who profess to be the elected and chosen leaders mock the oath they take to uphold the Constitution, ignore that same document, and deny the people their God-given Constitutionally guaranteed rights. *I have learned from experience* that trying to expose that system to the truth can and most likely will cost an individual everything. *I have learned from experience* that those within that system are not interested in learning the truth, or that they already know the truth and ignore it the same as they do the Constitutions. *I have learned from experience* the system is corrupt at the City, County, State and Federal level and no one within that system either cares or they are afraid to expose things to the light. *I have learned from experience* the system practiced is oppressive, unjust, cruel, expensive, and is based totally on greed and power, and that the system the people told is being practiced is non-existent. *I have learned from experience* the system practiced is about how much the Lawyers, Religious leaders, Bankers and Big Business can fleece from the people.

THEY are hypocrites, liars, and thieves. *THEY* are Wolves in sheep's clothing; *THEY* are Snakes disguised as humans. The people are the sheep. The wolves, the *Evil One* are in control and *THEY* devour the sheep at their pleasure and whim. That is the system truly being practiced. *All these things I have learned from experience* and the evidence is everywhere if one only looks and listens. *He who has ears, let him hear. Jesus Christ, The Bible, Matthew 13:9*

SYNONYM GAME:
MARTYR = VICTIM = PREY = TARGET = GOAL

CHAPTER 9

THE CORRUPTED OPERATING SYSTEM

"Woe to you, scribes and Pharisees, hypocrites! For you tithe mint and dill and cummin, and have neglected the weightier demands of the Law: justice, and mercy and faithfulness; But these are the things you should have done without neglecting the others. You blind guides, you strain out a gnat, and swallow a camel," Jesus Christ, The Bible, Matthew 23:23-24.

I have heard it said the only purpose a lock serves is to keep an honest person honest.

Have you wondered what happened to the person that you voted for to be your representative in the local or State government? The person that you listened to, or spoke with, believed and voted for said they held the same or near the same Constitutional concerns, values, and beliefs you held. 4-6 months after taking office, that person was totally different. It appeared they no longer held the same Constitutional concerns, values and beliefs you held. It appeared the person wanted to do nothing more than rob the people through taxes and pass more laws denying the people God-given constitutionally guaranteed rights and they were more concerned for special interest than public interest. You assume the person lied to you.

What is behind this conversion from honest person to robber and betrayer that keeps occurring over and over, and what happened to the "honest person" you voted for to hold a public office. No matter which person you voted for, if elected, the person seemed to betray the people's trust once in that public office. Over the years, it became more difficult to remove those individuals from office, and even though it appeared most people you know eventually voted against the person, they always seemed to be able stay in office. Over the years you became discouraged and no longer voted because you now believed that your vote was not counted. From lessons learned through personal experiences, I perceive that the following is going on:

A lawyer Clique is controlling the political system and governing local, county, and state governments. They are denying the people their God-given and Constitutionally guaranteed rights through the laws written and passed by individuals the lawyer Clique selects as representatives and control. These professed elected and chosen representatives only pretend to be the people's representatives. The political system is deliberately designed to *lock honest people out*, and only those that are already corrupted, or THEY are sure can be corrupted, are permitted to participate. As added insurance, the vote is fixed to prevent honest individuals that may slip through the few cracks in their system from being elected.

Honest lawyers and other honest human beings are not permitted in that political system. The initial screening process is the process used for becoming a candidate and getting on the ballot. An honest person will not submit to the unconstitutional methodology for becoming a candidate and having their name placed on the ballot, hence, the honest person is excluded from the ballot. The honest person is excluded because THEY know an honest person will not tolerate the Constitution being used as a device to rob the American people. An honest person would not permit the vote to be "fixed" and the people's vote ignored. An honest person will refuse to be *manipulated through deception* once recognizing what is being done is unconstitutional.

An honest person would not allow people to be taxed from their homes. An honest person would uphold the Constitution and what the Bill of Rights guarantees. An honest person would protect the people's vote and would ensure that vote was counted. An honest person would not tolerate the people's God-given rights being trampled with unconstitutional laws and ordinances. A truly honest person represents a threat and could initiate a process that would unravel the entire corrupt system. That is the purpose the present political system is designed to "lock out" any honest persons.

The honest person is made to think that the only way to get into the system in order to change the system is by obeying the systems rules to get on the ballot. For a person to "break into" the political system, the first thing that must be done is to have the person commit an unconstitutional act or acts to get on the ballot. That is the same as "breaking the lock" and equates to breaking the law. Once the unconstitutional act or acts is committed, then those lawyers that control the political system know they can dictate their will to that person, because that person is now a "criminal" within their political system.

The system is set up in such a manner that most people are unsuspecting and do no realize they have committed an unconstitutional act to gain access to the ballot. As another aphorism goes, "ignorance of the law is no excuse." Once the person does something unconstitutional to get on the ballot, then *that person can be manipulated through deception by being pressured, intimidated, and/or coerced into violating i.e. "compromising," other aspects in the Constitution* and that is exactly what the lawyers controlling the system want. Once selected for the position, the person takes the oath of office to uphold the constitution. But the person has already, although unknowingly, committed an unconstitutional act. Most people selected for public office have not even read the Bill of Rights, let alone the entire Constitution and are easily manipulated by the lawyers in control.

Once the honest person has "broken the lock" to gain access to the system they have become a criminal. Now that person is caught in the unconstitutional web and can be manipulated or coerced by those in control within the system. Those persons not easily manipulated or coerced are covertly or overtly threatened, or a threat against family members is hinted. Any means necessary is used to keep the person in line with what the controlling lawyer's desire. If the person selected is not intimidated and actually reads and attempts to uphold the Constitution and Bill of Rights, the lawyers controlling the system can bring it to the person's attention that the person has already violated a part or certain parts in the Constitution to get elected.

The person can be informed they have already violated the Constitution and can be tried for perjury, treachery, or treason. These are serious felonies. The person can then be given the choice to go along with the unconstitutional system, or face the consequences. Since these lawyers control that system, they can make it clear to the individual selected there is "no way out."

There is no way for a truly honest person to "break into" the system. The entire system is now set up in a manner that makes that impossible. The final step in accomplishing this was denying the people's vote. At one time, the write-in vote could overcome the honest person having to "break the lock." But now, in Oregon, the write-in votes are not even counted. I perceive the ballots are counted but the numbers provided to the public are fabricated to favor those already within the system. The people elect no one. Those controlling the system appoint the representatives. In Oregon, the Mail in Ballot along with ballot "enhancement" and the computerized vote counting machine were the final nails in the coffin for denying the people's God-given constitutionally guaranteed rights and taxing them into poverty and slavery.

Watching County Commissioners meetings, who do really think is in control, i.e., in charge? Do you think the Commissioners have the final say? How many times do you see the Commissioners look to the County Legal Counsel and the County Administrator for advice and assistance? How many times have you heard a County Commissioner, elected board member, or elected city council member say that they cannot respond to certain questions or issues because they are *legally restrained from responding*?

These are the people allegedly elected to govern your county or city, make the decisions pertaining to your County or city, vote on and pass the ordinances pertaining to your County or city, uphold your Constitutional rights, those allegedly in charge, yet they cannot "legally" respond. If they are allegedly in charge and cannot *legally* respond *then who or what is truly in charge* and can respond? And *who elected those who can respond?* How many times have you heard the Commissioners refer people to the Legal Counsel pertaining to the problems brought before the Commissioners. Who do you think is truly in charge? Did you vote for that person? Did you vote for the Legal Counsel?

Jesus Christ identified two groups as hypocrites, as a viper's brood? These groups were the scribes (writers of the law, i.e. lawyers) and Pharisees (religious and political leaders). Not much has changed. Those who profess to be the elected and chosen leaders actually follow those who are truly leading the people into a hell from which there will be no escape. Many religious leaders follow along. Today, as in Christ's day, few among the professed elected and chosen leaders appear willing to stand against the tyranny being perpetrated against the people. Few appear willing to stand for the weightier demands of the Law, those demands being justice, mercy and good faith.

Reading Matthew, Chapter 23 indicates Jesus was disgusted with, and had little respect for the scribes (lawyers) and Pharisees (leaders) in his day. I believe that same disgust and disrespect is applicable to those same groups today.

"The scribes and the Pharisees have seated themselves in the seat of Moses; therefore all that they tell you, do and observe, but do not according to their deeds; for they say things and do not do them. They tie up heavy burdens and lay them on men's shoulders, but they themselves are unwilling to move them with so much as a finger. But they do all their deeds to be noticed by men; for they broaden their phylacteries and lengthen the tassels of their garments. They love the place of honor at banquets and the chief seats

in the synagogues, and respectful greetings in the market places, and being called Rabbi by men." Jesus Christ, The Bible, Matthew 23:2-7.

Notice the do as I say and not as I do. Notice the heavy load being put on the people by the tax laws today? Notice the heavy load being put on the people by all the fines associated with all the laws one must follow today? Notice the heavy load being put on the people period by THEIR "Rule of Law," not God's commandments? Notice how the Judges and leaders like to be addressed as "Your Honor," "Commissioner," Mayor, and lawyers are titled and sign as "Esquire." Notice that many with PhDs insist they be addressed as "Doctor"? Notice the pomp that is provided for these individuals at dinners and special occasions? Notice the different standards applied when these individuals violate the law?

Nothing has really changed since Christ's day. That same *viper's brood* is *manipulating through deception* and putting a heavy load upon the people today. That same *viper's brood* is using the methodologies used in Christ's day to control and confuse the people today. That same *viper's brood* is still oppressing the people.

That same *viper's brood* makes the system look good from the outside while the system coffers are filled with robbery and corruption from the inside, self-indulgence abounds and the people can never provide them enough. That same *viper's brood* refuses to listen to the people's pleas. That same *viper's brood* swears an oath to uphold certain ideals, principles and values, then ignores that oath unless money for their coffers is involved.

The system controlling the people today is the same system that was controlling the people in Christ's day. That system is all about money and the power it can bring and keeping human beings slaves. That system has absolutely no concern for the people, for human beings. That same system is using the same *manipulation through deception* to keep human beings enslaved. *How many times must this be proven?*

If people truly want to change the system, then put honest people in the system that will not corrupt the system or become corrupted. Put people in the system that will do a clean sweep as necessary, will protect the people from those within the system that would do the people harm, will admit and correct mistakes, and that will keep the people informed about what is going on within the system. Put people in the system that will make the system work for the people, and if something is changed and the change doesn't work well, be willing to go back to and use what was working best.

Individuals will pay thousands for a computer system and then pay hundreds extra for software, expend extra time, effort and attention to protect that system to ensure that the system works well and will endure. If a software program is installed and that program corrupts the operating system or corrupts other installed software, the corrupting software program is generally removed. If a computer operating system continually has problems, such as "lock out" and is not working well for the individual, they generally look for an operating system that will do the job the way they want it to do the job. Due to the cost involved and the trouble it causes to replace a computer operating system, most people choose to hang on to the computer operating system they have as long as they can. Many replace bad components, upgrade to better components, run programs that do not harm the operating system, add more memory, make necessary adjustments, etc.

Yet that same individual pays thousands in taxes each year on a government operating system, and will not expend a little extra time, effort, or attention to ensure that system is working well for them. Human beings continually allow individuals to be "installed" and/or re-installed that they know are going to further corrupt the operating system. Human beings continue to permit those individuals to remain within the system. Human beings allow agencies to be installed that take up space and accomplish little. Human beings allow programs to be purchased that once installed bog down or "lock up" the operating system. Human beings allow many installed programs and agencies within the system to rob them, take their time, their money, accuse them for the systems wrongdoing and then punish them for things they didn't do, etc.

Our founding fathers provided "We the People" a government and an operating system called the Constitution with a Bill of Rights and a means to choose those that would manage that government and protect the operating system. That means is the vote. Everything works well if the people are willing to maintain that operating system. It is the people's responsibility to "install" good, honest people within that government to keep the operating system functioning properly. It is the people's responsibility to keep in place the necessary safe guards to ensure that the operating system is protected and stays in place to keep the government working properly. It is the people's responsibility to remove those that corrupt or try to corrupt the operating system. It appears that the "We the People" have failed in those responsibilities in Jackson County and Oregon and have allowed the operating system to be corrupted and converted to an entirely different operating system. Those that maintain the different operating system no longer permit the people's choices to be installed because that different operating system allows THEM to deny the people's vote.

AN ILLUSION CALLED YOUR VOTE COUNTS

Having once perceived that those who manage the government are good, honest, God loving people who would do the right thing, common sense dictated the system worked if people voted. Recent experiences and observations in Jackson County and Oregon shattered those perceptions. In Jackson County and Oregon, there is actually a ruling class and for this ruling class to remain in power and their system to remain the status quo, that ruling class knows it is necessary that people remain convinced they are free and that their vote counts.

Our whole Constitutional government is dependent on the vote. Without the vote it is not a government of the people, for the people, by the people, but a government ruled by a tyrant or several tyrants. Be it one tyrant, or several tyrants conspiring to rule together, the result is tyranny. The only voice is the tyrant's voice. That is exactly the system in place today. Several tyrants I call the "Clique" conspire to enhance the two party systems by making them one party with the "Clique" running the party.

In reality the system in place IS one "Clique" pretending to be two parties. The "Clique" leadership provides the people the illusion they have a choice. I perceive the leadership within the "Clique" pretend to let the people vote. It matters not who the people vote for, the results are always the same; the people end up the losers and the "Clique" the winners. People began to realize something was wrong, became disenchanted and began to disassociate themselves from the "two parties." As supporter numbers decreased, the "Clique" leadership knew their days were numbered unless they get the votes to allow them to stay in office and govern. I perceive the "Clique" leadership developed a plan to "control or eliminate the vote." Already having gained control in government the plan was easy to implement.

I perceive the Clique decided to ignore the vote. That is the same as the vote being denied. The election process has been made into an illusion, a joke, played to entertain the "Clique" and deceive the people! Considerable time, effort and money are spent to provide and perpetuate the illusion *called "Your Vote Counts."* But, there is strong evidence that indicates the people's vote is not truly counted.

The evidence indicates the numbers are fabricated and only people the "Clique" can control are actually "appointed" to public offices. Many appointed are unaware this is happening until in office and entrapped in the "Clique's" system. Those that refuse to go along with the "Clique" wishes are soon removed from office and usually in a manner as to pose no further threat to the "Clique's" conspiracy. Not only does the "Clique" mock the people by making them the butt in the election "joke," insult is added to injury by conning the people into paying for the joke's cost with tax dollars and campaign contributions. The "Clique" is laughing all the way to the bank. Are you laughing?

Issues such as Campaign Finance Reform, Term Limits, and the Mail in Ballot are presented, *as solutions, for ensuring that "better" people will be elected as representatives.* If the representatives are truly elected by the people's vote, and are not appointed as perceived, the money spent for financing the Campaign is irrelevant. *In addition, every dollar is supposedly accounted for and Campaign finance is already reformed in some ways each election.* Further, each time Campaign Finance is reformed, it excludes more and more people from the ballot by making it extremely difficult for those not already in office to raise funds for the election.

Term Limits is already designed into the Constitution. The people are supposed to be able to replace representatives at a 25%-33% rate each election by voting. *If the peoples' vote truly elects the representatives and they are not appointed, as perceived, what is the need for Term Limits? The people's desire for term limits is strong evidence the people already suspect their vote is not being counted. For what purpose would the people want term limits if undesirable representative could simply be removed by the vote? By not being able to remove undesirable representatives with the vote is strong evidence the vote is not being counted. Further, Term limits is no guarantee that better representatives will be elected.*

The Mail in Ballot is no guarantee people will vote although the "Clique" insists otherwise. But, the Mail in Ballot will ensure the Clique's (i.e. those already in office) complete control over the vote counting process.

Term Limits, Campaign Finance Reform, and the Mail in Ballot will not provide for better representation or stop the tyranny. So, what is the purpose for all the hype surrounding Term Limits, the Mail in Ballot, Campaign Finance Reform and the pretense at attempts by those who profess to be the elected and chosen leaders to change the process?

Quoting the Elite's aphorism, *Perception is the Truth*, as the paradigm, the answer is, these issues are *manipulation through deception* used to confuse and divert the people around the real truth. The real truth IS, the

Federal and State *Constitutions are being ignored, people outside the Clique are not permitted on the ballot, and the is evidence is strong that the people's vote IS actually denied, and numbers provided to the public are fabricated. If it is true the election process is fair, honest, is working the way it was designed in the Constitution, and the people's vote is actually being utilized to elect the representative, then "We the People" already have the people we asked to govern, thus deserve. If it is true the vote is being utilized to truly elect the representatives, all these changes or pretenses at changes are unnecessary. Changing or pretending to change the election rules claiming it is to ensure "better individuals will be elected," is strong evidence, and THEY are in essence admitting, that the elections are a farce, a scam, a lie, a hoax, a pretense, a big show. The evidence is strong and THEY are in essence admitting the people's vote is not really counted and is not utilized to elect the ones allegedly elected and chosen to govern. They are admitting the election process is unconstitutional.*

The Jackson County Clerk stated to me that the write-in vote is not counted unless the write-in vote exceeds the vote count for the leading candidate. I asked how do they know if the write-in votes are not counted. The reply "we can just tell." What is the purpose in not counting write-in votes? Is the write-in vote ignored in accordance with law or is the write-in vote added to the vote count for a candidate the Clique chooses? Further, if the write-in vote is not counted, what other votes are not counted? And what can they just tell? Another fabricated number? Regardless the purposes or the answers, *it is unconstitutional!*

Additionally, by controlling the vote, the "Clique" can control the court system and the Judges. Any State Constitutional Amendments wanted by the people can now be easily overturned as unconstitutional. The "Clique pretends" to "permit" popular Amendments to pass with the "people's vote," then challenges the Amendments in court to have the Amendments rescinded as unconstitutional before the amendments can possibly do the Clique any harm. This also works to their advantage as an effective smokescreen to divert attention away from the real truth that the people's vote is actually being denied. Additionally, a Constitutional amendment desired by the Clique can easily be put on the ballot by the Clique, passed, and if challenged, the Clique controlled Court finds in the Clique's favor.

The Mail in Ballot now being used in Oregon along with the computerized counting machines makes the illusion easier to achieve and extremely difficult to uncover. Having most people removed from the vote counting process eliminated nearly all threats that may have been posed by honest people working at the polls. When people voted at the polls, the ballot could have been counted and the numbers posted at each precinct. Those numbers could have been provided to the County Clerk and tallied. Enough people were involved to ensure that most polling places were not corrupted.

As the system was revised and changed, honest people were being eliminated from the process and it became easier to buy or coerce key people and "fix" elections. The "Clique" has gained total control over the vote. They can completely ignore the people's vote, put those in office who will do their bidding, pass any measures they desire, and fabricate the voting numbers provided to the public, and I am convinced that is exactly what is happening.

Our Constitution guarantees us the right to vote so the Clique pretends to allow us to vote and pretends to count that vote. I perceive they may do nothing more than count the ballots submitted. The vote may actually be counted, but in the end, that vote is not used unless it is what they want or is in their favor. There is nothing to prevent the Clique from ignoring the vote on that ballot and appointing those they want to public office. I am totally convinced OUR VOTE **IS** IGNORED. We the people assume they are using our vote to decide the elections. Remember the aphorism about the word assume:

It makes an *ass* out of *u* and *me*."

The computer chips used for counting can be programmed to provide any vote count the Clique desires. Computer chips can be programmed to add whatever desired numbered vote cast for one candidate or measure instead be added to a candidate or measure that the Elite chooses. (Example: every 5th vote that is cast for candidate X is instead added to the vote count for candidate Y). This is almost impossible to detect without a hand count and the numbers compared. The Clique has virtually eliminated that from happening because there is no longer a hand count.

What is the purpose in requiring "permission" to watch the vote count? What purpose does it serve in not allowing citizens in with video recording machines to record the count? For what purpose does it appear they do not want the counting process watched by the public?

Answer: *The Clique believes they are enhanced (better or superior) at deciding your needs and choices than you are*. In Jackson County Oregon, they now *enhance* (improve, augment, alter, change) the ballots. This was actually done in the 2000 general election in Jackson County. It is against the law to mark another individuals ballot and if done, is supposed to make that ballot invalid. If a ballot cannot be deciphered, that ballot is supposed to be set aside and not counted. For what purpose did they IGNORE the law and *enhance* the ballots at the Oregon, Jackson county office during the 2000 general election? *Could it be the votes were enhanced (added to) to match an already programmed vote count?*

Ignoring the vote is denying our human God-given and Constitutionally guaranteed right to choose. Remember the aphorism, "If you do not like something, ignore it and it will go away." The Clique does not like people having freedom, the God-given right to choose. The people in Oregon and Jackson County God-given freedoms, rights, and Constitutional government are being ignored and are "going away." I perceive the vote was being ignored and that is going away. The people just haven't been officially told because that is a secret and will not be exposed until the time is right, so I am informing you what I perceive is happening. Now, what will you do about it? I am but one voice, and it is going to take the people's voice to get the Clique's attention to stop what they are doing. How many will continue to hide their heads in the sand and permit the Clique to tyrannize the people and dictate rights/privileges?

The Clique's entire political system is based on lies, distortions, fears, and deceptions. Its root is SEMANTICS because they know that most people do not like semantics and are too busy to take the time or effort to research word meanings and synonyms.

"LEAVE US ALONE, Congress should keep hands off Oregon's vote-by-mail system" declares the Medford Mail Tribunes Editorials Clique hype. In another Medford Mail Tribune article August 10th, 2001, Oregon Clique Senators made it clear they will protect the Oregon election system at the federal level? What could threaten the Oregon election system requiring it to be protected at the federal level if that system is Constitutional? The answer, because Oregon's election system isn't Constitutional. That is proven in Jackson County Circuit Court Case No. 004001Z3. To keep secret that the Oregon Election System is unconstitutional, the Oregon Judicial System ignores/denies the demand for a jury trial by anyone filing a case against the State of Oregon related to this matter.

The assigned Judge is ordered to find in the State's favor or to dismiss the case. This further violates individual constitutional rights. Then, they have the audacity to "bill" the individual whose rights have been violated for court costs, which, in essence, is making the individual pay them for violating that individuals rights.

The most valued basic element in our government process WAS the VOTE. We all know the Parties, the Clique, the Elite, the Privileged, the *Evil One*, those who profess to be the elected and chosen ones to govern deliberately IGNORE many things including their own laws, the United States Constitution, State constitutions, local Charters, and God-given rights. I have heard some in the "Clique" comment that there needs to be a law that allows only people with certain educational qualifications to vote. Could this already be being done in secret until a law can be passed? If they will deliberately IGNORE the things already mentioned and can get away with it, what is to keep them from deliberately IGNORING (DENYING) YOUR VOTE and getting away with it?

The real answer to better representation is getting back to the Constitution as the law's foundation and using the people's vote for the true vote count.

LEAVE THEM ALONE. NO WAY! Not while the "Clique" deliberately ignores the Constitutions, the local Charter, the peoples' vote and continue to pass laws/ordinances that discriminate against and tyrannize the people. This American has not SURRENDERED, HAS NOT SOLD HIS SOUL TO THEIR TYRANNY!

Have you heard the aphorism "if you don't exercise the right to vote, you will lose it"? I perceive that is exactly what has happened. "We the people" have ignored the vote so long that the Clique is now ignoring your vote and that is the same as denying your vote, your right to choose, and that means you have lost the right to vote.

Now you know why the "bums" can't be voted from office. Now you know why people are "elected" that few voted for. Now you know why money measures suddenly pass that always failed in the past. Now you know why the Constitution is continually violated and they are allowed to get away with it. Now you know why it appears your vote is not counted (accepted). I perceive it is because YOUR VOTE IS NOT ACCEPTED. IT IS IGNORED/DENIED. THE CLIQUE PRETENDS TO LET YOU VOTE, PRETENDS TO COUNT THAT VOTE, AND YOU PAY FOR THE "ILLUSION," THE "PRETENSE," or THE "JOKE."

The incumbent in any election has the advantage due to name recognition. That was not enough insurance for the "Clique." The "Clique" then changed the election laws to favor their Major Party Candidates. That was not enough for the "Clique" so they decided to define the crucial public offices as partisan offices. As additional insurance I perceive the "Clique" can now fix the elections by denying your vote. *People within the party, the Clique, the Elite, the Privileged, those who profess to be the elected and chosen ones to govern, will claim that what is written here is just considered to be my opinion (view), which has the same meaning as perception (view). As can be seen, the evidence presented is strong to support that perception.* THE CLIQUE HAS AN APHORISM THAT STATES: "PERCEPTION IS THE TRUTH" *If that is the case, using their own aphorism as the paradigm, then what I stated here has to be the truth.*

So, BELIEVE the hypocrisy from the leadership in the Republican and Democratic Party's. Both Party's leadership spout Constitutional rights and the Law, yet the party's leadership has allowed, fully supports, and refuses to do anything about the violations occurring against the people's God-given constitutionally guaranteed rights. Party leadership mocks the U.S. and State Constitutions behind closed doors and often times openly, with the laws they institute. People cannot believe the hypocrisy displayed by the politicians. Believe it! There are reasons for the hypocrisy. The reasons are power, greed, and a conspiracy to keep all human beings enslaved and in this world.

I served twenty years in the military defending what I believed was a system based on truth, justice and the American way, i.e., God, home, country and the U.S. Constitution. When I returned home to the Rogue Valley in Jackson County, Oregon, where I was raised, I observed and experienced things from the local government that violated everything I was taught to believe in, everything I thought I served to defend against. I decided to do something about it and attempted to get into a position to stop the atrocities being perpetrated against the people.

Although having failed in those attempts, I did learn many things. I learned everything that so many have fought and died for, that so many have defended the past two hundred plus years, was a big lie, an illusion, at least in Jackson County and Oregon. What those who served, fought, and died for is non-existent in Jackson County and Oregon. Individual God-given Constitutionally guaranteed rights are denied and only a few Party members are allowed to exercise God-given and Constitutionally guaranteed rights. Those that do not belong to a Major Party, i.e., Republican or Democratic, are denied all God-given Constitutionally guaranteed rights.

Both parties are actually one party with two heads. It is one CLIQUE, a viper's brood an *Evil One* led by a few wealthy political and religious leaders dictating what happens in Jackson County and Oregon. Individual rights are denied. Laws are not applied equitably. The U.S. and State Constitutions are only used as tools for the Party convenience and to favor the Party.

And favor them it does. The Jackson County Circuit Court judges and State Appellate and State Supreme Court Judges interpret the laws and ignore the Constitutions to favor the party leadership, their friends, and their underlings. At other times these documents are twisted and distorted so they can be used to rob, cheat, and deny "We the People's" God-given Constitutionally guaranteed rights.

Most laws instituted in Jackson County and Oregon are actually unconstitutional. Those same laws are then twisted and distorted, and are not applied to those that brought about the law, their powerful friends that instituted and passed the law, or the underlings that interpret and enforce the law. The laws only apply to "We the other People."

God help an underling that attempts to enforce the law equitably and tries to make it apply to everyone, including Party members. That underling will soon be on the street looking for a job "outside" the Party, and since the Party controls the law, the law's interpretation, and the laws enforcement, most business owners will not hire that person for fear the Party will bring retribution against them and their business. In the end, that underling the Party publicly labeled a "disgruntled employee," "trouble maker," "poor worker," malcontent, etc. is forced to leave the State to seek employment. The Party considers it good riddance to a Party traitor and to someone that could not "fit-in."

Honest lawyers are afraid to speak out because they play a part in that system. That system is their livelihood, and if they do anything to upset or expose that system, those behind and controlling that system ruin their lives. Honest Judges are afraid to render just decisions because they play a part in that system. That system is their livelihood and the same consequences and punishment that applies to honest lawyers applies to honest judges. Those who profess to be the elected and chosen leaders are afraid to speak out because they play a part in that system. Their livelihood depends on that system remaining unchanged, and if they attempt to change that system they will suffer the same consequences and punishments as the lawyers and judges. Law enforcement and other underlings are afraid to speak out because they play a part in that system, it is their livelihood and fear they will suffer the same consequences and punishments they have either previously experienced or observed imposed on others that are slaves to the system.

The system and those beings controlling that system *manipulate through deception* everyone within that system. *Everyone working within that system is afraid.* That system controls their livelihood and the same consequences and punishment that applies to honest lawyers, judges, and leaders also apply to them. All those mentioned have sworn to uphold the Constitutions yet they mock or ignore those same documents. Those within the system are *manipulated through deception* into being hypocrites. "We the other people" are the losers.

What that system can and does do to a person "blowing the whistle" about wrong doings or trying to expose the system from within is to take everything the person has. The person is publicly dishonored and shunned, made to appear to be a liar, malcontent, disgruntled, trouble maker, etc., etc., etc., and their lives end up in ruin. It takes their job, their dignity, their principles, and their home, robs them, and leaves them a pauper, *and it is done deliberately as an example to others. Remember the humiliation and intimidation template?*

Consider what happens to those labeled "whistle blower." Those that have exposed wrong doing within the system in Jackson County or Oregon are now seeking employment elsewhere. Most "whistle blowers" have been "crucified" and shunned through the local media in Jackson County and Oregon by those in authority and their chances at obtaining gainful employment anywhere in the State are zero to none. Most are now broke or near broke from costs associated with doing what is right by standing against wrong doing within the system in Jackson County and Oregon. Some have become homeless or forced to leave the home where they were raised to seek another place they can call home and to earn a living in order to survive.

But, those that were exposed for their wrong doings were made out to be the victims or even "heroes." They were the system "pets." They could do no wrong. Note that most exposed in the wrong doings were in Supervisory or Management positions and made out to be the heroes. The Clique that *manipulates through deception* also controls the media and radio, and they ensure that they "protect their own." This is what is passed off as truth, justice and the American way in Jackson County and Oregon.

Be honest now, have you seen this same scenario, i.e. template, used against people where you live?

The Oregon system now appears to be the template for enslaving the other States. *According to a retired New York attorney with whom I have been in e-mail contact, New York State is looking to adopt the Oregon system and also, according to him, the Oregon system is being considered as the template for all the states.*

I was naïve enough to believe that there was a system in place in Oregon and Jackson County that could not be corrupted because I believed the people would not let that happen. I was naïve enough that I used to brag to others about Oregon, told them how upstanding Oregon was and that the people in Oregon would not tolerate the atrocities observed in other states. How wrong I was. I was naïve enough to believe that we had honest leaders concerned for our county and state and that the lawyers and judges were concerned for truth, justice and people's rights.

The Lord forgives me, but I was wrong. It is all lies, the County and State leadership lie, the court systems, lawyers, and judges lie, the Religious leaders lie, the Big business leaders lie, and the Bankers lie. The entire system in place in Jackson County and Oregon is all based on lies.

The U.S. and Oregon CONSTITUTIONS WERE "We the People's" INSURANCE POLICIES put into place to protect the people against an oppressive government. Those insurance policies have been paid for with BLOOD for over 220 years. THE VOTE, that sacred element in the U.S. and Oregon Constitutions was THE GUARANTEE that "We the People" would always have a "way out" against an oppressive government.

That GUARANTEE IS NOW DENIED and the INSURANCE POLICIES HAVE BEEN CANCELLED FOR "WE THE PEOPLE." There is strong evidence that the vote is fixed. Election Day is a BIG SHOW an ILLUSION that deceives the people into believing they have a vote and are included in the process. The entire election process in Jackson County and Oregon is one BIG LIE, one BIG ILLUSION. The only way that can be disproved is for citizens to get together after a general election and demand a hand count and compare those numbers with the computer numbers provided to the public. That will either prove or disprove what I say.

I do not believe eliminating the hand count in Oregon was a wise thing to do. It removed the people from the election process and opened the election process up for total control by an individual or group, i.e., Clique. No longer can we rely on honest individuals exposing any wrong doings. Everything is now in a programmed computer chip. Even the County Clerks may not really know if the numbers coming from the chips is a true count because they do not program the chips.

Sure, a test can be conducted but the test is run on the same computer and can be manipulated and fixed also. The chips are made and programmed by a paid private company and can be programmed to produce the results those in authority desire. The desired election results can be accomplished with the programmed computer chip that provides the necessary vote count needed to ensure the *viper's brood* appointees are "elected" and the CLIQUE, the *Evil One* appointees, remain in power and in control. I perceive the votes are not really counted. They pretend to count the votes. They only count the ballots, and when necessary, they can enhance enough ballots as necessary to match an already programmed vote count.

The whole election process is a big Party for the Clique, the *Evil One*, conducted at the people's expense, i.e., those that donate to the respective parties. The illusion with the contested vote count in Florida for the 2000 general election was a show, a *manipulation through deception* put on for the people's benefit nationally due to a book called *Votescam* and other doubts being raised about the election system. Someone please show me where in our Constitution that it states the Supreme Court will decide who shall be a President. You can't, because it is not in the Constitution. According to the Constitution, Congress is to decide in cases that a winner cannot be declared from the people's vote.

When it is stated that "your vote counts" it means that THEY consider your vote but the final decision is THEIRS TO MAKE. The Florida vote recount provided the illusion the system worked. But, Constitutionally, the Supreme Court cannot choose the President, which in essence, is what happened. It also provided the *Evil One* at the Federal level an opportunity and an excuse to further reform the system to favor THEM even more. THEY, this *Evil One*, enslave us. Thomas Jefferson tried to warn "We the People" against a Party system, Party leadership, the Clique, the *Evil One*, but few listened. Is anyone listening now? I think not.

I have learned from experience that the system being practiced today is not the system that was taught my generation by the Oregon Education system. In fact, the system being practiced is the complete opposite to what was taught my generation. Sure, we were taught about the two parties and when I questioned that as a student, I was told that was the system the people chose to put into place and to accept that. But the two party system is not constitutional. I have learned from experience that any person attempting to question or expose that system to "We the People" will be chewed up, spit out, rejected and crushed by that same *viper's brood* that crucified Jesus Christ when he exposed the same system.

That is the system truly being practiced. All these things I have learned from experience and I have evidence. Some evidence has been submitted to the ACLU (American Civil Liberties Union), ACLJ (American Center for

Law and Justice), the Oregon state court system, the new media, etc., and no one within those organizations cared, no not one! Some returned the evidence. The evidence is available to the people. The evidence is in the U. S. Constitution. The evidence is in your State Constitution. The evidence is in the laws administered. Read the sections referenced to in this book in American Jurisprudence 2nd Edition, Volume 16B, Constitutional Law. Read your newspaper; listen to the news and what is really being said. Read *The Bible*. If that is not enough evidence and you need more proof, declare yourself an Independent and attempt to get on the local ballot against a party member and demand to declare your candidacy the same as a party member. Good luck.

These organizations are controlled by the *Evil One*, the Clique, and do nothing more than help perpetuate the illusion that there is assistance within the system and that the system is working. The system being practiced has no concern for "We the People." The system being practiced has no concern for truth, justice, or the American way. God, home country and the Constitutions mean nothing in the system being practiced. Those within that system consider the Constitutions a lie and just something to be used to "sting" "We the People." The system practiced and in place has only one concern, and that is for the "Evil One," the Clique, that viper's brood. "We the People" are only welcome within that system as slaves and providers for the "viper's brood."

Many probably question what I am saying about the judges and the court system. As evidence, I was going to provide excerpts from court decisions taken from American Jurisprudence concerning constitutional challenges to the law. Because I was unable to obtain permission to "quote" from Black's Law Dictionaries I believe it fruitless to ask for permission to quote from American Jurisprudence published by the same West Group. So, I will provide my interpretations and the manner in which I understood

WHAT THE JUDGES REALLY SAID AND CALLED IT JUSTICE!

I was taught that Justice is supposed to be the fair and proper administration of laws. I was also taught that all our laws were supposed to be based on the Constitution and were to be able to withstand Constitutional scrutiny, and if there was any doubt as to the laws Constitutionality, it was to be set aside and reviewed. Recently, while I was on the Internet, I read a quote attributed to *16 Am.Jur.Sec.203 that more or less stated no person is compelled to obey an unconstitutional law and no courts are compelled to enforce that unconstitutional law.* This sounds good but is it? Something quite similar did come from *American Jurisprudence*, 16 AM Jur. 2nd, Constitutional Law, Section 203. American Jurisprudence is judicial precedents considered collectively. These are decisions made by Judges concerning regularly enacted statutes that were challenged as to their constitutionality. These decisions have set as precedence future court decisions. This has allowed our constitutional law system to be manipulated and reverted back into the *pre-Revolutionary English common law system from which our nation's founders fought a revolution to free themselves and their future generations.* According to many different court (judge) decisions made since our nation was formed, indications are that many judges are knowingly taking a part in undermining our constitutional government. The following examples are provided:

Am Jur. 16, 2nd, Constitutional Law, Sec. 166 as I understand it basically says that any complaint brought before a judge that a law is unconstitutional, the judge is to have his mind already made up that the law is constitutional. It goes on to say that *all statues are assumed rational, and are to be interpreted by the judge as constitutional* to avoid raising serious doubts or constitutional questions. Does this sound like the judge is going to make a just and impartial decision? It sounds to me like the court system is fixed to support every unconstitutional law passed and, as we all know, those are in the multitudes. According to the Oregon Constitution, one class is not supposed to be considered over another class. If the statute is rational/fair, why was it questioned? Also, I thought our Constitution ended the Class system. Guess I was wrong. But, for what reason don't they want constitutional questions raised? Because people start reading the Constitution and quickly realize what is truly going on, and write books such as this one, and start waking other people up to what is happening.

Am. Jur. 16, 2nd, Constitutional Law, Sec. 167 as I understood its meaning IS being used to promote collusion between the different branches in government to impose unconstitutional laws on the people. It indicates that there is a policy (doctrine) that prohibits one branch in state government from infringing on the power and duties in another branch government.

Excuse me, I may be wrong, but isn't our government, both Federal and State, supposed to be set up in such a manner as to allow checks and balances between the different branches in government. Would that not require one branch in that government to bring to another branches *attention* any unconstitutional improprieties in the laws they institute and *not look for ways to support them*?

Am. Jur. 16 2nd Constitutional Law, Sec 168 as I understand it says that the assumption provided that all legislation is constitutional is not absolute and it can still be challenged. But the assumption is especially strong regarding laws concerning taxation and laws being attacked by the constitution as violating the equal protection requirements in both the federal and state constitutions.

Notice *tax laws* and *equal protection requirements,* most which are unconstitutional, are the laws they do not want *attacked* and want to protect the strongest. This is saying do not even question the law concerning these issues because you will surely lose. This is the same as parents telling a child, "our rules are firm, but if you think you can talk us out of them, you have our permission to try."

Am. Jur. 16 2nd, Constitutional Law Sec. 169 as I understand it basically says that not all legislation is to be assumed as legal (Constitutional). If the legislation clearly and overtly denies, diminishes, or modifies the people a right secured under the Constitution, then that statute will be assumed unconstitutional. It goes on to say that assuming legislation is constitutional does not apply in cases involving First Amendment Rights.

If this is true, then for what purpose has legislation been enacted concerning "hate speech" and "politically correct" speech? These laws abridge the first amendment right to free speech by diminishing, denying, or modifying what people can say. Notice also, the strong hints that subtle constitutional violation via the law are appropriate, that subtle violations can be assumed constitutional, just that the violations cannot be clear and overt, i.e. explicit.

Am Jur. 16, 2nd Constitutional Law, Sec 170 as I understand it says that the ideology *that all legislation is assumed constitutional* applies to all lawmaking bodies which are legally made up and applies to administrative rules and regulations. This includes things such as military regulations, citizen initiatives, statutes adopted by state legislatures, local laws, ordinances, or regulations adopted by counties, municipalities, and administrative bodies such as zoning commissions.

In other words, ASSUMPTION of Constitutionality is to be applied to administrative laws, rules and ordinances arbitrarily passed by *hired government employees,* which laws are only supposed to be instituted by a legislative body. That is unconstitutional. Those now involved in the law making process have never read the constitution, and the laws, ordinances, rules, and regulations they institute are unconstitutional and constitute taxation without representation. Judges know this to be factual yet are allowing our Constitutional government to be destroyed from within. Just because something is legal under Rule of Law, does not make it legal under Rule of Constitutional Law.

Am. Jur. 16, 2nd, Constitutional Law, Section 172 as I understand it says the *General rule* is that every statute is to be *understood* with the Constitution in mind and that the statue involving the Constitution and the Constitutional rights will be *assumed to be the same law*. The judges when in utilizing the rules for *legislation which is under constitutional attack must* apply those rules in such a manner that the judge views the legislation in line with constitutional requirements. In other words, the *Judges should interpret the legislation in such a way that it gives it a greater chance to survive the Constitutional test.* A law is only to be held as unconstitutional as a last resort, regardless how close it is to being unconstitutional. It is only to be considered unconstitutional when it has been shown clearly and beyond a reasonable doubt that it is unconstitutional. It says the *trial judge's duty as well as the appellate judge's duty is to uphold the lawmaking power*. It goes on to say that as a general principle, the judge's duty, if possible, is to *apply particular emphasis in upholding legislation relating to exercising police power.* This is saying that legislation being questioned as to its unconstitutionality must be interpreted in such a way that it is constitutional and the duty of the courts is to *uphold legislation with a particular emphasis to police power*.

How can the legislation be under Constitutional Attack, it is the Constitution that is under legislative attack? I thought the court's duty was to uphold the Constitution, and ensure the law was within constitutional boundaries, not the Constitution within the law boundaries. Notice that particular emphasis is to be placed on upholding laws as constitutional that exercise police power. Are you listening to what is being said by these courts, i.e. judges?

As I understand *Am. Jur. 16, 2nd, Constitutional Law, Section 174* it is basically saying, be careful judges, any statute that cannot be interpreted in such a manner as to be constitutional, leave it alone and do not reword it. The legislative branch worded it in such a way that it can only be interpreted one way, do not change the wording because we will be exposed in our dishonesty and our purpose in what we are doing will be exposed. *Are you listening to what the judge is really saying?*

Am. Jur. 16, 2nd Constitutional Law Section 175 as I understand it is saying that when a statute is attacked by the Constitution, and the statute has two possible interpretations, the interpretation making the statute constitutional is the one that will be upheld. This is to be done even if the interpretation that makes it unconstitutional makes more sense and is the one usually accepted. This also applies to ordinances. In one sense, this is good because the judge is saying uphold the constitution, but in another sense he is saying it is for show because in most cases, the other interpretation is the one most accepted, except they are willing to take a loss in this one particular instance. Notice that the judge stated the *statute was under attack by the Constitution*, not that the Constitution is under attack by the statute. Do you see how things are being turned around on the people? This is saying ignore the people. *Are you listening to what the judge is really saying?*

Am. Jur. 16, 2nd, *Constitutional Law Sec. 176* as I understand it is saying that the courts duty is to interpret a challenged statute so as to save it in such a manner it appears constitutional and in such a manner as to avoid any other challenges as to its constitutionality. I always thought it was the courts sworn duty to uphold the constitution because they swear an oath to do that very thing and ensure the statue was constitutional. *It is saying the court duty is to uphold the statute and do whatever is necessary to save it from the constitution.* It must be interpreted in such a manner no one can raise another doubt that the statute is unconstitutional. Every reasonable doubt must be resolved to favor the statute in question. If at all possible, the question as to the constitutionality is to be avoided. *Are you listening to what the judge is really saying?*

Am. Jur. 16, 2nd *Constitutional Law Sec.185* as I understand it is basically saying that the spirit of the Constitution is no longer used as a valid reason for challenging any statute, although at one time this was precedence. It goes on to say that the courts are not the guardians for the people's rights except those rights secured by some constitutional provision which fall within the *legal* sense. *This court does not believe in the spirit of the Constitution. This court says its duty is not to uphold the Constitution.*

Deny the spirit and the whole Constitution is denied. It is the spirit that makes something work, makes something valuable, makes something worthwhile. Eliminate the spirit, and there is nothing but the shell. Legal does not make Constitutional, it is Constitutional that makes legal. It is obvious this court has it backward. It is also obvious that this court forget the 9th Amendment to the U.S. Constitution that states, "The enumeration in the Constitution, of certain rights, shall not be construed to deny or disparage others retained by the people." That Amendment destroys his whole argument.

Am. Jur. 16, 2nd Constitutional Law Sec. 203 the way I understand it says that until a law is declared unconstitutional, it will be enforced and the people that violate that law will be punished. Once a law is declared unconstitutional no one is bound to obey that law and no court is bound to enforce that law. Well, duh!

After reading the way I understood the few sections from American Jurisprudence 2nd Edition Volume 16, Constitutional Law, what do you think the chances are in having any unconstitutional law revoked? "When hell freezes over"? Now you know why justice is blind! Now do you believe there is a conspiracy?

There are volumes written establishing judicial precedence and I only interpreted a few from one volume containing hundreds. You do not have to take my word or my interpretations for the ones in this chapter. Look them up for yourself in your local county legal library. It is an enlightening experience.

CHAPTER 10

A FEW LIES EXPOSED

"We the People" are manipulated into being dependent on drugs, gasoline, sugar, coffee, etc. In fact, many become addicted to these things by manipulation through deception called LIES, LIES, and LIES!

Has anyone really considered the lies the system leads the people to believe? Deep down, most people already know they are lies but for reasons I cannot comprehend, people still do not demand to know the truth. Following are a few lies exposed:

Lie: There is a Gasoline Shortage.

Truth: The only gasoline shortages are those that are created to raise prices to gouge the people. Immediately after prices are raised, fuel is always plentiful. Notice that during the fuel shortages during the 1970s, fuel prices were doubled and stayed there. Smaller fuel economy cars were produced and sold like hotcakes. Larger vehicle sales came to an abrupt halt. In the 1990, that changed. The SUV push is on, and those things are gas hogs. In the 1970s I remember the people being told that within 50 years there would be no crude oil remaining. What is the purpose in producing the SUV gas hogs today? GREED! And, according to what was said in 1973-1974, there is only a 22-year oil supply remaining. But that is not the case is it?

Lie: There is a Sugar Shortage.

Truth: The only sugar shortages are those that are created to raise prices and gouge the people.

Refer to the gasoline shortage.

Lie: There is a Coffee Shortage.

Truth: The only coffee shortages are those that are created to raise prices and gouge the people.

Refer to the gasoline shortage.

Lie: By making Social Security a part in the Federal Budget will help the country by providing enough to pay the national debt and help keep the budget down and manageable.

Truth: This was a big lie. Making Social Security a part in the Federal budget in 1968 provided the opportunity to legally rob Social Security and that is exactly what THEY did. In 1968, and before it was made a part in the Federal Budget, Social security was solvent, was over *500 billion* in the black and it was said to be doing so good, there was no need to be concerned for it ever being in danger. So, THEY decided to make it a part in the Federal budget. The employer is required to match the employee 7.15% contribution to Social Security. Since its inception, Social Security has been under attack. Big business has always favored eliminating Social Security because the 7.15% they contribute matching your 7.15% Social Security contribution affect THEIR profit margins. Does anyone find it strange that the savings and loan fiasco in 1986-1987 cost the taxpayers *500 billion* dollars, the exact amount Social Security was supposed to be solvent? What happened to the savings and loan money? It did not just disappear. And, where did the money come from that replaced the missing savings and loan money? I perceive it was from Social Security. I perceive THEY had you pay back the money stolen from you in the savings and loan fiasco with your own money saved in Social Security. That money replaced THEIR 7.15% contribution. Now, THEY are claiming Social Security is the biggest drain on the budget and needs to be cut or eliminated. Do you think that if Social Security is eliminated that the Social Security Tax will be eliminated? It won't. It will be added to the already existing income tax, you will receive nothing for it in your old age because it will no longer be available, and the old will be euthanized.

Lie: ATM use will be free, will be more convenient for the customer and will free bank clerks to perform other functions thus keeping banking cost down.

Truth: That was another lie that I remember being told to the people. Notice that there are now charges for using ATMs. Notice bank clerk positions have been cut. Notice banks are making more profits. The real convenience is for the banks and thieves. How many people are robbed at ATMs?

Lie: The Arabic controlled OPEC controls crude oil prices

Truth: OPEC is a dummy organization created by the big oil companies to manipulate crude oil prices. Notice that several times each year gasoline prices rise dramatically during the peak months and holiday periods. Then they drop to a "new low" but that "new low" always seems to be a few cents higher than before the dramatic price increase. This price creep is being done intentionally to eventually raise prices to approximately $4.00 a gallon in America. How many times have you heard it said, "Americans should feel lucky, they are paying $4.00 in Europe? Yes they are and they have been paying that price in Europe for over 20 years. This is not Europe; the prices Europeans are paying for gasoline is outlandish, and the prices Americans are paying for gasoline is ridiculous. The sole reason for these high gasoline prices is GREED. There is no other reason.

Lie: Self Service gas stations will keep gas prices down.

Truth: All self-serve did was eliminate jobs and provide bigger profits for the oil companies. At self-service stations the customer does the work and then pays for doing the work in higher gas prices. The *Evil One* makes bigger profits. Notice gas prices at self-service stations are just as high if not higher as full service stations.

Lie: The lottery will lower taxes and keep them lower.

Truth: Since the lottery's inception, have taxes been reduced and kept that way? NO. But many people have become addicted to gambling thus giving their money to the state.

Lie: The budget has been cut so much that we will have to cut education, policemen, firemen and other public safety programs if taxes aren't raised or new funds found in some way.

Truth: The budget is never "cut." The supposed cuts are in the projected increases. What else explains that the overall budget is always larger each year? Public education and safety programs are always the first cut to justify larger tax increases, added fees, new taxes, etc. These programs are not really cut. The projected increases are cut, i.e., rather than a 10% budget increase; it is increased by 5%. The money goes for higher salaries, perks, and "nice to have" items and luxury equipment for the Clique.

Lie: Raising speed limits to 75MPH does not effect public safety.

Truth: Speeds above 50 miles per hour decrease the vehicles safety and driver control over the vehicle. Over 65 miles per hour a vehicle is not actually controlled, the vehicle is only "guided."

Lie: Fees are necessary to keep the government operation going.

Truth: In reality, fees are just another tax to pay for services you have already paid for with other taxes. Fees are nothing more than double and triple taxation. Would you pay a company for the same identical service three times on the same occasion or for the same item 3 times in a store? I think not. For what purpose do the people do it with the government? Could it be people are deceived into believing they are receiving something they are not. Notice the "volunteer" programs. These volunteer programs are actually functions you have already paid "your" governments to perform, but now you are performing these functions yourself. Example, the neighborhoods watch program. That is a police function. Volunteer police programs and volunteer fire departments are functions the people's taxes have paid for but are manipulated through deception into performing themselves by being told they have not been funded and were not in the budget. The government budget is 80% salaries and perks. What services do you receive for your money? Notice "experts" are always hired at $100,000 or a $1,000,000 to do a "study" on solving problems. What happened to all the salaried "experts" the government agencies have on the payroll in these areas? Do they just mysteriously disappear while still drawing a salary? A government building inspector is paid a salary and perks, yet a huge fee is required for this individual to do the job for which they are already paid? Does no one question these things?

Lie: Dealing and pushing drugs is against the law.

Truth: It is against the law for those not paying taxes on the drugs sold. Drugs are a business. The biggest drug dealer in this nation is the pharmaceutical industry, it is legal, and it is government sanctioned. Notice the increase in drug use the past 30 to 40 years. The pharmaceutical industry is using salesmen as the middleman to push the drugs to doctors. Doctors are used as pushers to push the drugs to the users, i.e. patients. The only difference between the pharmaceutical industry manufacturing and dealing drugs and anyone else doing the same is the pharmaceutical industry is government sanctioned as legal.

I will readily admit there is a difference between using drugs for healing and relieving pain and abusing drugs for profit and gain.

The pusher on the street entices an individual to try out the drug, offering it for free. The drugs are physically and psychologically addicting. Once addicted to the drug, it is suddenly no longer free. It costs a bundle. The user has to have the drug and usually turns to crime to pay for the drug. But there are side affects to the drug, such as loss of appetite frequent vomiting, headaches, tiredness, diarrhea etc., etc., etc. The drugs usually end up killing the user.

The pharmaceutical industry uses the same methodology. It entices the people to use a drug through the advertising media. In the advertising the people are told to consult their local doctor, (their dealer) for a prescription.

The doctor is provided free samples for the people to "try." If the drug works, the doctor then prescribes the drug. The drug always works, but with side effects such as diarrhea, vomiting, headaches, loss of appetite, etc., etc., etc. If you don't believe it, listen to the advertisements on television. If the user (patient) is willing to tolerate the side effects, the doctor continues to prescribe the drug. If the patient cannot tolerate the side affects, different drugs are tried until one is found that can be tolerated. Bingo, the pharmaceutical industry has a hooked user and the drug is no longer free and very costly. In many instances, the drug heals nothing and only covers up the symptoms. Eventually, the patient will die.

Drugs can and do serve a medical purpose. But the system is allowing drugs to be misused and abused and the only purpose is for greed, power and control. A drugged populace is easier to deceive and control.

Don't forget that a government sanctioned "War on Drugs" has been declared. You just weren't informed that the war was declared against the American people. It is working well isn't it? In this war on drugs, *most people* used in developing, manufacturing, selling, and pushing the drugs (the ones that work in the manufacturing plants, the salesmen, and the doctors), are totally unaware they are being used in this manner.

Lie: Law enforcement's function is to serve and protect the public at large.

Truth: At one time, that may have been true. For the past 30 years, that has not been the case. For several decades, law enforcement's primary function has been to bully, intimidate, and rob the public at large for the Clique's financial benefit, while serving and protecting the Clique from the public at large. In fact, human law enforcement officers are being trained to bully, intimidate, and rob the public at large.

If you don't believe it, read on.

There was a big article in the Medford *Mail Tribune*, May 2001, about an elitist group in the Medford Police Department calling themselves the Reservoir Dawgs. In one picture published by the *Mail Tribune* showing the entire group, these officers tried to look like the "meanest, toughest group on the block." I have seen "gangs" depicted the same way.

This group derived its' name from the 1992 movie "Reservoir Dogs. The marketing line for that film was "Four perfect killers, one perfect crime. Now all they have to fear is each other." In the movie, the Reservoir Dogs were vicious, cold-blooded killers, who in the end turned on each other due to a robbery gone sour and upon discovering an undercover police officer in their group. Below is the way I interpreted the article as read:

The Reservoir Dawgs are eight police officers working their beats along the streets of Medford from 6:30 p.m. to 6:30 a.m. every Thursday, Friday and Saturday. They are Team 5 and according to their sergeant these officers are the "best of the best."

They were described as aggressive, enthused and very motivated and it was said that *they'd stop short of nothing to get the job done right*. Their sergeant described them as the best crew that can handle anything and *that they aren't necessarily your friendly, neighborhood police officers*.

It was said that Team 5 doesn't wait for an opportunity to fall into their laps that they go out and make it happen.

Patrolling the Medford streets for the Reservoir Dawgs means taking ownership on a beat and knowing the community inside and out.

It was reported that if you are walking down the street at 3 a.m. in the morning hours a police officer is going to talk to you. It was said most people talk with the officer and tell the officer what they're doing. Some people become offended and the officers state that is when they obviously get suspicious.

One officer described the job as about taking charge, owning the streets of Medford from 6:30 p.m. to 6:30 a.m. every Thursday, Friday and Saturday, and not waiting for everything to come to them. The officers said they stayed busy and look for the bad guys. They don't wait for the bad guy to stumble onto them.

Does anyone find it disconcerting that those who are paid to serve and protect would allow an elitist group to be established within their ranks that name themselves after vicious, cold blooded killers depicted in a movie? I do, because I perceive it as an *elitist* gang with a legal license to kill.

The Reservoir Dawgs, bullies with guns and badges that look for trouble and don't wait for it to come to them. Stopping citizens on the street demanding to know where the citizens are going at 3:00 A.M. in the morning because these police officers own the streets. Getting suspicious when people get offended by being stopped and questioned for no justifiable reason. Have they ever stopped to think that it offends people to be treated like a criminal when they have done nothing?

They get suspicious if you exercise your Constitutional right to tell them it is not their business to know where you are going, anytime in the day or night. Since when did the police "own the streets" anytime, night or day. That sounds like "gang" talk to me. Good Lord, these are the people that are paid with the people's tax dollars to serve and protect!

You are over reacting some may say. Am I? Read on. The following incident happened in Central Point Oregon, a city adjacent to Medford, Oregon. Although the Reservoir Dawgs did not appear to be involved because this incident occurred on a Tuesday evening, December 28th, 1999, it is an excellent paradigm showing what appears to be the attitude by some officers on the Medford Police force:

An unarmed man was shot 23 times by Medford police officers at a State Police Station in Central Point Oregon. Central Point is not in the Medford jurisdiction. Central Point is in an adjoining town with its own police force. State, County and Central Point police officers were on the scene. The Medford Police Dispatcher had directed Medford Police Officers *not to go to the scene*, to stay away. Several Medford Police Officers took it upon themselves to go to the scene anyway. The man's wife was on the phone with the State police. She told the state police he was mentally unstable and that he would not hurt anyone. He was from another town in Oregon, and the police from that town knew he was harmless. They had similar problems with him in the past on several different occasions.

It was Medford Police Officers who shot a tear gas canister into the man's vehicle at the scene prompting the man to jump from his vehicle. The man had an object in his hand. It was Medford Police Officers who shot the man 23 times, killing him. The object in the man's hand was an empty razor case.

They are aggressive, enthused and very motivated. They'll stop short of nothing to get the job done.

I guess they are aggressive. They even go into areas they are directed not to go and are not legally supposed to go to get the job done. I guess that job also includes murder.

The team doesn't wait for an opportunity to fall into their laps. Instead, they go out and make it happen.

They sure do, they made it happen in this instance.

And these guys aren't necessarily your friendly, neighborhood police officers.

They sure proved that didn't they?

This is a job that's about taking charge, owning the streets and not waiting for everything to come to you. They stay busy. They look for the bad guys. They don't wait for the bad guys to stumble onto them.

They took charge in this situation. They owned the street that night in a jurisdiction that did not belong to them. They did not wait for anything to come to them, instead they went to a place they were instructed not to go and looked for that unarmed bad guy who was having a bad day, was mentally having problems, and the Medford police officers decided to end his misery.

Nothing happened to the officers involved. An investigation was conducted, and nothing was done to the officers. Nothing! It was determined to be *suicide* by police. It appears authorities deem any killings committed by police officers that cannot be justly explained as *suicide by police*. It appears anyone going against Medford police for any reason is committing suicide because they will shoot you for any reason.

The following incident happened in Medford April 02, 2002:

A Jackson County police Lieutenant in civilian clothes and driving an undercover vehicle on his way home for the day had a "finger waving" and verbal altercation with three Hispanic men while driving in Medford. Someone in the other vehicle gave the Lieutenant the finger and the Lieutenant returned the gesture. At a stop signal, two men dismounted from the vehicle and approached the Lieutenant's vehicle from the rear. It was reported one man was *armed* with Chinese food. One man threw a white container with the Chinese food at the Lieutenant inside the vehicle.

The Lieutenant drew and fired his weapon at the man, missing the man but hitting a nearby home. No one was injured with the round. The three Hispanic men fled and were arrested the following day. An investigation was held. The Lieutenant claimed he feared for his life, that he did not know what was in the container. It was said the Lieutenant was justified in drawing his weapon and firing at the men. *It was said the Lieutenant was only doing as he was trained to do*. The men arrested have various charges filed against them. I wonder if one charge is assault with Chinese food? According to conflicting reports, the police Lieutenant did not identify that he was a police officer to the men. The Lieutenant told the Grand Jury that he feared he was under attack because the men knew he was a police officer. Another report stated the police believed the three men did not know that the Lieutenant was a police officer. Another report stated that the one man's mother wants to know why the officer did not show his badge identifying him as being a police officer.

I thought a police officer was only supposed to draw and fire their weapon when their life or other people's lives were in imminent danger. I guess an attack with Chinese food is imminent danger in Jackson County and Medford, Oregon and justifies a police officer attempting to kill someone. This officer was said to be technically on duty although he had left work for the day and was on his way home. Police officers are citizens and civilians the same as you and I, regardless if that officer is on or off duty, and police officers are subject to the same laws as you and I.

In a news report it was indicated *the sheriff's office had never conducted an internal investigation concerning* the Lieutenant in his 23-year service. It was stated that he wouldn't have made it up through the ranks to commander, Jackson County Narcotics Enforcement Team, (JACNET), if he had been an abuser of anything in his career. I interpret that to mean they had never conducted an investigation concerning any drug abuse by him, because according to another report, there were several investigations conducted concerning his conduct.

Another news report indicated the sheriff's office had investigated four complaints against the lieutenant since his hire date 23 years previous. Two filed in 1993 claiming the Lieutenant refused to finish a criminal investigation were claimed to be invalid, and another the same year said he was rude. The fourth complaint was a tort claim filed a week prior to this latest incident alleging JACNET detectives illegally entered a rental home and tore off the doors unnecessarily to gain entrance. This incident went against the Lieutenant since he is the JACNET team commander. Yet according to the previous news report, there was never an internal investigation held against this Lieutenant as an abuser of anything, and if there had been, he probably would not be in the position he is holding today. I wonder if anyone on the Jackson County Sheriff's department has ever heard about abusing authority?

In one news report the County Sheriff admitted *it was not* the first time the sheriff's office has taken complaints about deputies exchanging obscene gestures with citizens while on duty. Some are even in marked patrol cars. He went on to say that *deputies are responding to harassment by the citizens* and are usually under some emotional strain and they get caught up in the emotion.

According to the Lieutenant's statement in the same news article, he indicated that he was not under any particular stress either personally or professionally on April 2, the day the incident occurred.

In the news report, the County Sheriff said that the Lieutenant turned and fired because he has 25 years experience and tactically, he is very good. The Sheriff went on to say that he didn't think the Lieutenant had time to get a line of sight, but fired and hoped they'd go away and it is okay if you can articulate you are in fear that you will be seriously injured. The Sheriff also indicated that to the Lieutenants credit, he was able to discern that no passer-by or residents would be in danger from the shot, although the bullet did lodge in a house.

Let me get this straight, this Lieutenant with all these years experience and tactical (planned, strategic, premeditated) know how *was unable to discern that the man had a Chinese food box in his hand. He did not have time to get a line of sight*, but fired anyway and hoped they'd go away and that was okay if one is convincing enough that one is in fear for their life or that they may have been seriously injured. *He did not have time to get a line of sight, but was able to discern that no residents or passer-by would be in danger from the shot, yet the bullet lodged in a house.* Could he see into the house? What if the bullet had gone through the house?

And the *Grand Jury deliberated for five minutes* and determined that this Lieutenant's actions were justified and not criminal under Oregon Law. Say what?

The County Sheriff went on to say that the internal investigation findings were not likely to conflict with the grand jury. Surprise, they didn't.

In another article is was indicated that a conflict of interest in the investigation is most likely more an issue in the public eyes than for police, and the investigation is more credible when more than one agency is involved. Four police departments investigated this, not the grand jury. Their finding went to the grand jury. I definitely have a conflict of interest question surrounding this case. The whole thing stinks to high heaven. Then the sheriff held an internal investigation. Is that a joke?

Something smells about this whole case, from the Grand Jury down. Someone is lying. Either the news reports, the sheriff, the Lieutenant, or the Grand Jury or some or all. My safety warning system is screaming that this whole incident calls for further investigation by a citizen review board.

I know that police officers are "technically" on duty 24 hours a day, seven days a week, but that does not give them special privileges above the law. Police officers are to be held to higher standards of conduct in the laws compared to other citizens. According to conflicting reports, the Lieutenant never identified himself as being a police officer, which is suspicious. The officer said he thought the other individuals knew he was a police officer.

As a citizen, if I drew a gun and fired at those men under the same circumstances, I would be buried under the jail. I would be charged with at least three major felony violations that I know, those being firing a weapon within the city limits (Medford ordinance), assault with a deadly weapon, and attempted murder. I know it to be true. You know it to be true. THEY know it to be true. I would be laughed at all the from the court room to the prison cell if I told a jury I feared for my life because I did not know what was in the food container being thrown at me was Chinese food. Further, the first I personally heard about this incident was reported in the morning news over radio station KCMX 880, which stated that the incident started with a confrontation in the parking lot at a Chinese restaurant. That was the first and last report that the incident started in the parking lot at a Chinese restaurant, but if that is the case, it blows holes in the officers "I didn't know what was in the box and feared for my life plea."

By no means do I want to judge the officer in this situation. I am only going by what was reported in the news, and at best the reports are scanty, and in my mind, very questionable. No one knows how one will react to any given situation, especially one in which they are confronted by at least two angry men, possibly three. If the information reported is true, then there are many questions that are left unanswered in this incident. If the information reported is true, then the officer's training leaves a lot to be desired and his conduct played a part in causing the incident. Police officers are expected to obey the same laws that you and I obey. In fact, police officers are expected to set higher standards. In this incident, the officer is a police lieutenant. He is expected to set an even higher standard for the other officers. The Lieutenant was "verbally reprimanded" for the *"finger waving"* incident which, according to the Sheriff and sheriff's office policy is a *"very minor violation."*

Once the lieutenant fired his weapon, the other individuals involved left the scene and were arrested the following day. Two were brought up on charges. The individual throwing the Chinese food is *charged for harassment stemming from the "finger waving,"* and for third degree *criminal mischief* stemming from the *Chinese food being thrown on the car's interior.* So the "finger waving" by the Lieutenant is a very "minor offense," yet the other man is being legally charged for "harassment" for the same offense. The driver is charged for reckless driving (they were behind and tailgating the Lieutenant's vehicle), and for possessing methamphetamine when arrested the following day. Do you think the methamphetamine could have possibly been planted? Take into consideration that the lieutenant is the Commander, Jackson County Narcotics Enforcement Team. And this is called justice from the system in Jackson County, Oregon.

According to a news article written August 12, 2002, the man who was charged with harassment charges for the "finger waving" and throwing the Chinese food received eight (8) traffic violations between June 2002 and

August 2002. The Medford Police Chief claims it is not harassment but the man drives in a way that he's begging to be stopped. What do you think?

The preceding story is a perfect paradigm for do as I say and not as I do, and the double standards being practiced today. This story is a perfect paradigm there are real problems with the process, the system. It further indicates that there may be something wrong in the training for our police officers, and if it is not in the training, then with the officers themselves. It was said that the Lieutenant was only doing as he was "trained." If that IS the case, then it is time to take a real close look at that training.

One expects that those hired to serve and protect aren't being trained to be bullies and hooligans, aren't being trained to escalate sensitive situations, and aren't being trained to participate in offensive "finger waving" with the people. One would expect officers be trained not to take random shots hoping the persons being shot at would "just go away." One would expect officers be trained not to act like what they are hired to serve and protect against. One expects that those hired to enforce the laws be trained to obey those laws. One expects that those hired to ensure the laws are to be obeyed be trained to set the standards for conduct, self-control, and common courtesy.

In another reported local county incident on April 10, 2002, a bloodied man that had a few minutes earlier attacked his ex-girlfriend with a steak knife was facing two officers and yelling that he was going to kill them. The man lunged at the officers while fumbling for something bulging at his waist. He ignored the officers warning to stop. They believed they were going to have to shoot the man. At the last possible instant, the man raised his hands showing that he had no weapon. One officer stated that sometimes he goes by gut instinct. He did not believe the knife wielding man really wanted to hurt him and the officer said "you don't just shoot a person for running at you." Now that is a police officer deserving respect. Also, it could have been viewed as justifiable had these officers shot the man due to the circumstances surrounding the incident involved.

I recently heard a news story about a person being arrested for assault. The person threw a pie at a politician's face. It was reported another man was arrested on a Los Angeles freeway for pointing his finger like it was a gun at FBI agent. This is evidence that those in authority are actually the ones scared and they do not need a real reason to arrest or even shoot you. They are being *manipulated through fear*. They are being trained to be fearful for their own safety, not the public safety.

Earlier, I mentioned that human police officers are also being trained to "rob" the people. Read on:

A STING is a plan put into place by crooks in which deceptions are used to swindle money from an unsuspecting person. I imagine it is called a sting because the person who loses their money is usually the only one to get hurt. It stings i.e. it hurts. There was even a movie made called The Sting.

STINGS are also used in undercover police operation in which *police pose as criminals (a deception)* to *trap law violators.* Entrap basically means to trap or ensnare by *artifice, i.e. deception.* An *artifice* is a creative plan or mechanism used in such a manner that it is consistent with trickery or fraud. It implies cunning and dishonesty, and introduces some deviation from moral and ethical principles one would not normally associate with those hired to serve and protect.

Entrapment is against the law. So when government officers *manipulate through deception* a person into committing a crime that the person would not normally commit, or plans to commit, the officers are the ones actually committing the crime for the sole purpose to influence another person into committing a criminal act. The officers *induce* the person into committing the crime in order to bring criminal prosecution against that person. A few Synonyms for induce are: bring on, persuade, make, create, construct, tempt, lure, etc.

I do not think justice is served, or is it equitable and fair, that crime is being instigated by police officers whose responsibility it is to enforce the law. The crime the police are committing is fraud. Knowingly misrepresenting the truth or concealing facts to induce someone to commit an act with the intent to cause that person harm, such as criminal prosecution is morally wrong and against the law. *And concerning entrapment, isn't it the governments responsibility to prove beyond a reasonable doubt that the defendant was not entrapped by government officers?*

Medford police set up "sting" operations to catch all the criminal drivers violating the pedestrian crosswalk laws. One police officer pretends to be a "criminal" and walks into the crosswalk so that other criminals driving cars can violate the pedestrian crosswalk laws, be apprehended by other police officers in hiding and given a ticket involving a huge fine for violating the law.

The police officer pretending to be a criminal steps into the crosswalk giving the criminals driving cars barely enough time to stop. If the criminal driving the car has his/her attention where it is not supposed to be, is distracted, or cannot react in time, bingo, the police have caught themselves a criminal and have provided the city coffers with more money.

This practice is going on throughout the state. Aren't you excited that the police are on the ball and have thought up this creative plan to catch all these "criminals"? I find it ironic that in another operation involving a radar van recently set up to trap people speeding in Medford, the first ticket issued was to an off duty police officer.

If the above is not evidence enough, that all the citizens are considered to be the criminals or potential criminals by those in authority in this city, county, or state, I do not know what it will take to convince you.

Presently, by profiling and by definition you are a terrorist and/or a criminal and you are the enemy to those in authority. You and your children are something to be used, abused, stepped on, chewed up, and thrown away. You are zilch, nada, nothing, to them and once they can trap you and get all that they can from you and are no longer useful for their purposes, you will be eliminated.

Think I am crazy? Look around you, think and wake up to what is going on. Take a trip and fly on an airline. See who is treated like the criminal. You are the one considered the "criminal" and the one truly being offended, abused, cheated, robbed and whose life is being made more difficult or taken.

Most people are not criminals and do not intend to break the law. Entrapment is not to be used to apprehend people who do not intend to break the law and the law forbids conviction is such cases. But it is obvious there are those in the system that believe they are above the law, morally and ethically, and can do as they please.

They use the system for their own benefit and rewards by inducing people to break the law so they can be issued tickets involving huge fines. *This is another example depicting what happens when the people have lost the right for their vote to be counted and used for electing representation and others to govern.* The Clique, through their appointed officials and representatives can do as they please to the people, including *"legalized robbery" called a sting.*

The real crime is the system that has been put in place to deny you your God-given and Constitutionally guaranteed rights and the real criminals are those who use that system put in place to take what belongs to others. In the above instance, the law enforcement officers are being used (duped) into committing robbery for the city coffers using public safety as a pretense. Police officers hired to "serve and protect" are being "trained" and "ordered" to virtually bully and rob honest, hard working people.

Setting up a situation where up to 60 people break the law and are issued $175 tickets each in a two-hour period is "legalized robbery." The amount to be collected by the courts in fines equates to $10,500 in two hours. Do that for 22 days a month, and the city coffers are increased by $231,000 a month or $2,772,000 a year for that one offense.

Add that to other fines for offenses such as being filmed by a camera driving through an intersection just as a light turns from yellow to red, a substantial amount can be collected.

In the first instance, there are two or three officers to "testify" the "criminal" did not stop in time to allow a pedestrian to cross although enough distance is not allowed to stop in time. It appears some police officers willingly lie on reports and in the courts when they are actually doing as ordered or as trained. The officers are "trained" to believe that the "average" person traveling the speed limit has time to stop in the distance being allowed in the sting. But do they know for sure? Most would accept this training without question because they trust they are being trained properly. But, are they?

If I were an officer and caught 50 to 60 people in a two-hour period in a "sting" operation, I would begin to question the process. I would ask about the distance and the "set up" because something is obviously wrong in the situation. But knowing the local County and State system, any officer asking such questions would probably be coerced into quitting or an excuse would be found to fire that officer. Those in authority in Jackson County and Oregon do not like to have their methods or authority questioned.

In the other instance, a person working for a contracted company looks at the film and you are issued a ticket along with pictures, although you may not have had time to stop when the light turned yellow.

Additionally, the lights are computer controlled and seem to frequently malfunction, plus the time allowed on some lights is ridiculous. I have seen lights turn from red to green to yellow back to red before one car can make it through the intersection. There are three quick lights on left turn lanes at three intersections I personally know about in Medford and cameras are being set up at two such locations. It is a certainty that numerous tickets will be issued at these lights. With a computer one can "enhance" (enhance = improve = amend = alter) digital photos to show exactly whatever one wants to show. Put in place two or three locations with "fast changing" lights and "enhance" (alter) the photos and an enormous amount in fines can be collected.

The company contracted to install the cameras and screen the photos is paid a certain percentage from each ticket collected. If this is not a get rich quick opportunity for both the city and the contracted company, someone please tell me, what is? Presently, there is one major company involved in contracting the camera systems throughout the U.S. A person can contest a ticket in court, but with the corrupt courts we have in Jackson County and Oregon what chances do you think you have in getting an unjust ticket overturned? The police officer's word will be taken over your word almost every time in the one instance, and in the other, they will have you on camera, although it *may be* an "enhanced" photo. Both "Sting" operations mentioned above are presently being used or are being put into place in cities throughout Oregon, including Medford.

If all this sounds as if I do not trust those in authority, it is because I don't. Those now in authority are being *manipulated through deception and fear and are manipulating others through deception and fear in the same manner* and have proven they cannot be trusted. Appearances are that those who are hired to "serve and protect" are actually trained to bully and rob. Every "*artifice*" they come up with for "public safety" does nothing more than put more money into their coffers and infringe on the people's God-given and Constitutionally guaranteed rights.

If it is not about money, for what purposes were the traffic fines *tripled* in the past 4 or 5 years prior to these sting operations being put into place? If it is not about money, for what purposes aren't warning citations issued for first offenders? If it is not about money, for what purposes are police officer functions turned over to cameras and police officers used as salespersons to "sell" these "artifices"?

Remember that these are the same authorities that violate their own laws and put children's safety at risk. They violate their own laws and install recap tires on school buses to save money, drive loaded school buses across wooden bridges that have not been load tested, and refuse to install seat belts on school buses due to cost. What makes people believe they are truly concerned for the public safety by putting in place all these artifices?

These artifices deny everything the American Flag represents and the Bill of Rights guarantees, that being our FREEDOM. It is all about money. I know it. Deep down you know it. They know it and they know exactly what to do to rob that money from you.

I want to make it perfectly clear that I have the utmost respect for the police officers and the filthy job they are paid to do, and I have always treated them with respect when dealing with an officer. If what is being reported about their training and personal conduct in the news is true, then there are real problems in the system that trains these officers and it is time to take a close look at that training. If what is reported about the training is not true, and the training is not at fault, then it is time to take a close look at the officers themselves.

The Clique system presently takes your children, jobs, homes, money, dignity, freedom, and I am positive THEY have taken the vote. How much longer are you willing to let them *sting* you before you are willing to stand against the Clique? It is imperative "We the People" ensure our vote is being used to choose the representatives/ leaders at all levels in our government otherwise the system will steal your soul.

Many sacrificed lives and fortunes for freedom and you receive tyranny
Your beliefs in God, country and the U.S. Constitution are mocked
You work hard for a comfortable living and only survive
You vote for representatives and get Clique appointees
You pay for an education system that does not educate
You pay for service and protection and are robbed
You expect fairness and receive insults and abuse
You trust the leadership and receive betrayal
You expect justice only to find there is none
You expect the truth and get only lies
You ask for leaders and get tyrants
Liberties bell is upside down
The system is upside down
WELCOME TO THE USSR OF JCO (UNITED SELFISH SCOUNDRELS REPUBLIC OF JACKSON COUNTY OREGON)

The Bill of Rights was the guarantee in the U.S. constitution that the people's God-given rights would not be denied and the people would be protected from the tyrants. The people's vote was the insurance policy put in place to back up that guarantee. If "We the People" continue to allow the Clique system in Jackson County and Oregon to ignore the vote then the guarantee is worthless and the Clique system in Jackson county and Oregon will continue to "sting" the people for all it can get.

Now is the time for "we the people," all human beings, to turn liberties bell and the system right side up!

Lie: Animals have rights too.

Truth: The last time I checked human beings were made the caretakers on this planet. Other animal species do not have rights. Do I think animals are to be mistreated? Definitely not! I do not think any creature deserves to be mistreated. Do I think that other species have the same rights as human beings? No, I do not? I think the other animal species were put here for human beings to use as food, pets, and to care for. When it come to reptiles, they are definitely my least favorite species, next to arachnids.

HUMAN RIGHTS VERSUS ANIMAL RIGHTS AND EXIGENT CIRCUMSTANCES

EXCERPTS FROM THE U.S. CONSTITUTION

Preamble

We the People of the United States, in Order to form a more perfect Union, establish Justice, insure domestic Tranquility, provide for the common defence, promote the general Welfare, and secure the Blessings of Liberty to ourselves and our Posterity, do ordain and establish this Constitution for the United States of America.

The 4th Amendment states: *"The right of the people to be secure in their persons, houses, papers, and effects, against unreasonable searches and seizures, shall not be violated, and no warrants shall issue, but upon probable cause, supported by Oath of affirmation and particularly describing the place to be searched, and persons or things to be seized.*

The 9th Amendment states: *"The enumeration in the Constitution, of certain rights, shall not be construed to deny or disparage others retained by the people."*

EXCERPTS FROM THE OREGON CONSTITUTION

Article 1, Section 9. Unreasonable searches or seizures. No law shall violate the right of the people to be secure in their persons, houses, papers, and effects, against unreasonable search, or seizure; and no warrant shall issue but upon probable cause, supported by oath, or affirmation, and particularly describing the place to be searched, and the person or thing to be seized.

Article 1, Section 20. Equality of privileges and immunities of citizens. No law shall be passed granting to any citizen or class of citizens privileges, or immunities, which, upon the same terms, shall not equally belong to all citizens.

Article 1, Section 33. Enumeration of rights not exclusive. This enumeration of rights, and privileges shall not be construed to impair or deny others retained by the people.

Article 4, Section 21. Acts to be plainly worded. Every act, and joint resolution shall be plainly worded, avoiding as far as practicable the use of technical terms.

The U.S. and Oregon Constitutions are to be the foundation, the guidelines for determining what can and cannot be law in Oregon and Jackson County, not a law dictionary. The law dictionaries provide the definitions for *legalese (language) lawyers have developed.* These definitions do not provide justification for passing any law. These definitions provide help in understanding what the law is stating, or what Judges have stated in past decisions. These definitions are used for defending and prosecuting cases concerning law. These definitions assist the lawyers in presenting their cases. These definitions are not intended to *justify* writing and passing laws. These definitions can be used to *assist* when writing and interpreting the laws. These are "Legal" definitions. *Legal* does not necessarily constitute what is or is not within Constitutional boundaries, i.e., Constitutional. *The Constitutions are to be the foundation for the law,* not a law dictionary.

The Jackson County Animal Control Ordinance allowing Jackson County Animal Control Officers to search for abused animals on private property and effects placed on that property without a warrant, is a huge step in taking all private property rights and completely circumventing the people's rights guaranteed by the Constitutions. These officers are to be permitted on people's property and unlocked effects to be searched without a warrant. This ordinance contradicts the 4th and 9th Amendments to the U.S. Constitution, and Article 1 Sections 9, 20, 33, and Article 4 Section 21 in the Oregon Constitution. According to the County Commissioners and county legal counsel, *exigent circumstances* are being used to justify the proposed ordinance.

Exigent circumstances means any situation that demands unusual or immediate action and that may allow people to circumvent usual procedure (law). An example would be when a neighbor breaks into someone's home to save someone that is in danger living in the home.

By legal definition, under exigent circumstances, if any neighbor or a County Animal Control officer sees an animal needing immediate attention, then their actions to immediately assist the animal can be justified to a court as necessary to circumvent laws that may prevent them from rendering assistance. For example, a neighbor is in a life-threatening situation and to save their life it became necessary to break down their door to render assistance.

If the neighbor tried to sue for breaking and entering and/or trespassing, the individual being sued could claim *exigent circumstances* to justify circumventing and breaking these particular laws. *Exigent circumstances can be used as justification for circumventing "laws" in dire emergency situations, not circumventing the Constitutions to institute law.*

Many people did not understand the term "exigent circumstances" when the Commissioners stated that was the justification for this ordinance. The County Legal Counsel stated that "exigent circumstances is legalese terminology."

Article 4, Section 21 in the Oregon Constitution states "Acts to be plainly worded. Every Act and joint resolution shall be plainly worded, avoiding as far as practicable the use of technical terms.

An *"act in the law"* is the party in authority exercising its legal power, such as a legal act, or juristic act, and in which the intentions and the effective purpose for the act/law is to transfer, create, and/or extinguish a right.

An *"act of the law"* is the laws actual enforcement which creates, transfers or eliminates a right or rights without any consent from the individuals concerned and affected by the law.

A municipal regulation such as an Ordinance or authoritative law or decree is treated the same as a legislative enactment or act that a state legislature may put into effect. Municipal governments are permitted to pass ordinances on matters that the state government allows to be regulated at the local level. Synonyms for ordinance are law and act.

In spirit and in reality, every act, every law, every ordinance takes (robs, steals) a right.

For over 140 years, Oregon had no need for an ordinance allowing any official to trespass on and search private property without a warrant. Many people will say, well times have changed and the need was never there before. That is correct, the need was never there before while time was changing for 140 years. And that need does not exist today either. *Manipulation through deception* has created an illusion that the need now exists. To what purpose has it now become an emergency to permit Animal Control officials to circumvent the Constitution? Common sense dictates that if an animal needs help, then provide help to the animal. Any neighbor can do that. Anyone can do that and it is justified.

If an animal is in trouble, assist the animal or call Jackson County animal control and inform them there is an emergency. *Under emergency conditions, anyone can take action.* If taken to court, the Animal Control Officer can claim "exigent circumstances." They have the neighbors that called as witnesses. Most neighbors would probably appreciate the assistance in having their animals saved. Considering Jackson County Animal Control was notified concerning alleged abuses and they took action in each case, for what purpose is another ordinance needed?

One Commissioner justifies the Animal Control Ordinances by stating that many animal abuses are occurring all the time throughout the county and the ordinance is needed to *prevent* further abuses. In the instances cited for justification for this ordinance, the animal abuse was reported and the Jackson County Animal Control intervened. These instances involved 500 rabbits and 45 dogs. In these instances, Animal Control warned the individuals involved in the abuse several times over as many weeks before finally taking the animals. Obviously these situations were not emergencies and in no way "justify" this ordinance. Plus, the warnings and existing laws went unheeded and did not prevent further abuse.

An emergency is something that calls for immediate action where one does not have time for all-inclusive deliberation due to unforeseen circumstances. Obviously, the situations cited for justifying this ordinance were not an emergency. Other than the rabbits and the woman with too many dogs, what other "animal" abuses have been encountered in the past 3 years?

I researched *Mail Tribune* articles the past three years concerning animal abuse cases. There was not one case that was reported and printed in the news that would warrant this ordinance. Most animal abuse cases being published in the news were abuse cases that Jackson County Animal Control would not have been able to prevent unless an officer was actually on the scene at the exact time the abuse was being committed. Cases such as a man shooting a dog, a man killing a cat, etc. In fact, no abuse can be "prevented" if someone decides to inflict the abuse when others are not around.

Are we going to hire enough Animal Control officers to implement a 24-hour a day, seven day a week watch to ensure every animal is not abused? I think not. The 500 rabbits and the 45 dogs were reported to the Jackson County Animal Control and action was taken. People reported the abuse. Action was taken. These incidents do not justify this ordinance. Another justification presented was that Jackson County Animal Control has been contacted numerous times by "neighbors" complaining that animals were left by their owners for weeks at a time without food and water, or that owners left their pets without water and chained to a tree on hot days. Another justification was that the ordinance would allow an Animal Control Officer to assist an animal it found hanging from a tree by its leash.

First, I find it difficult to believe that any animal that has not had food or water for weeks isn't already dead. Second, anyone with common sense would automatically try to assist any animal hanging from a leash and is being strangled. This is considered an emergency and warrants immediate action and can be justified in any court as *exigent circumstances*. If an animal needs water, give it water. No ordinance is needed or necessary to do the humane thing. It is an act resulting from plain old common kindness and common sense.

This ordinance being put in place is to further circumvent the Constitutions, under the animal abuse guise, to eventually allow indiscriminate private property searches at the County's whim. It is another example in *manipulation through deception*. The ordinance is denying human beings God-given Constitutionally guaranteed private property rights. It is not being instituted to prevent animals from being abused as was stated. Until someone abuses the animal, what can Jackson County Animal Control really do? There are presently animal abuse laws that have fines and punishments, including jail time as supposedly preventive measures. Obviously, if abuse is still occurring, these laws prevent nothing? Will officers eventually be permitted to come into homes and search to ensure pets are not being abused? Will THEY soon be dictating what can and cannot be fed pets? Will they soon be dictating where pets can and cannot be kept? At what point do we draw the line? This ordinance is nothing more than another unnecessary law to deny/ignore human beings God-given rights, in this case, property rights. *How many more human rights are to be sacrificed under the animal rights pretense? Someone please show me in the U.S. or Oregon Constitutions that any other animal species has rights. The only God-given and Constitutional rights mentioned are those for human beings.*

I have respect for life, especially human life. I have respect for animal life. I have owned and loved dogs as pets. It would be nice if all animals did not kill yet animals kill animals. It is in the animal nature. Human beings are in the animal kingdom. We have been endowed with the highest intelligence. Human beings have been endowed with the ability to discern right from wrong. We have been given the responsibility to be caretakers in this world. I do not believe any living thing deserves to be abused, including other human beings. I believe that all human beings have a right to their privacy, and that no one has the right to tell another human being how they can or cannot live their lives. Our Creator gave human beings 10 laws to live by. Human beings were unable to live by those 10 laws. Instead, human beings formed societies and governments and *"agreed"* to relinquish certain God-given rights to prevent harming each other.

To control human beings, whose actions demonstrate that they cannot live and let live peacefully in a civilized society, punishments have been instituted for violating the laws *the people agreed to follow*. Those who have been "chosen" to enforce those laws fairly, have now been trained to become what they were hired or chosen to defend against. Those who now profess to be the ones chosen to govern have now become those that cannot be trusted to control their own actions. The *"agreed"* has been changed to *"greed"* and those who profess to be ones chosen to govern now commit abuses against fellow human beings by denying other human beings their God-given rights through additional laws they institute. *Alleged/Pretended Animal Rights have now taken precedence over Human Rights. Manipulation through deception is at work here.*

What ordinances are being considered to help the abused "human beings" being forced to go hungry, beg, and sleep under the bridges along Bear Creek and I-5 due to the system created in Jackson County? What ordinances are being considered to help the abused "human beings" being evicted and families forced to live in cars resulting from the system created in Jackson County?

What ordinances are being considered to help the abused "human beings" in Jackson County who cannot get a job due to the system created in Jackson County? What ordinances are being considered to help the "human beings" abused by the system that has been created in Jackson County resulting from land use and planning ordinances, alleged owl rights, fish rights, cougar rights, and other alleged animal species rights? I dare say none, nada, zilch, not one. At what point do Human Rights enter into the equation and for what purpose were they ignored (denied) in the first place? *Manipulation through deception* that is what.

A NO VOTE WAS REQUIRED ON THE UNCONSTITUTIONAL Animal Control Ordinance Allowing Jackson County Animal Control Officers to search unlocked buildings, sheds, barns, etc. and their contents without a search warrant.

All the County Commissioners voted yes and passed this ordinance. Are the County Commissioners upholding the Constitution and defending human *being God-given and Constitutional guaranteed rights? You be the judge.*

The above are just a few lies, or illusions if you prefer, being practiced against human beings. Some lies are repeated over and over, just in different variations. It is said that supply and demand is the reason for price increases when there is a shortage. Notice that as soon as the price increases, the shortage disappears. Supply and demand is an illusion, a smoke screen, created to hide the reality, which is *greed.*

The Gasoline lie appears to be a favorite "price gouging" con. Every year at approximately the same times gas prices go either up or down. They always climb higher than reduced so that each year the cost is a little more overall per gallon. A penny or two extra on a gallon adds up to huge profits. Add fifty cents for a prolonged period and the profits are massive. Do you really think OPEC controls crude oil prices? What company is going to go to the trouble to set up in a foreign nation without controlling the product or what the product sells for? I will say it again. OPEC is a dummy organization set up by the oil companies to manipulate crude oil prices. Observe the evidence at your local gas stations each year.

A War on Poverty was declared over 25 years ago. Since that war was declared, the poverty rate has increased dramatically in America. That is another war declared against the American people. That war is working well wouldn't you say?

The latest war declared is a War on Terrorism. This war was declared after 9-11. The 9-11 attack was a declaration of war against the American people by some within our own government using terrorism as the tool. Since 9-11, how many more God-given Constitutionally guaranteed rights have been denied or infringed? When an American Citizen enters an airport today, every God-given, Constitutionally guaranteed right is surrendered at the airport facility doors. *The right of the people to be secure in their persons, houses, papers, and effects, against unreasonable searches and seizures, shall not be violated, and no Warrants shall issue, but upon probable cause, supported by Oath or affirmation, and particularly describing the place to be searched, and persons or things to be seized.*

...the right of the people to keep and bear Arms, shall not be infringed.

The above Constitutional guaranteed God-given rights are just a few being violated at airports today. Government officials at airports are permitted, without a warrant, to search your property, your person, your papers and your effects and take what effects they want without a warrant. The probable cause, you *might* be a terrorist in disguise because everyone now fits the terrorist profile and must be considered a terrorist. You *might* constitute a danger to everyone on board the aircraft. You *might* be someone they just plain want to harass as an example to the others. The things to be searched, anything they want. The things to be seized, anything they may deem unsafe. And there is no need for a warrant because they can completely ignore the constitution under THEIR "RULE OF LAW" for Homeland Security and get away with it. A weapon can be made from anything. You would be surprised at what can be made into a weapon that you either carry or wear on your person each day. In fact, hands and feet can be considered deadly weapons if a person is trained to use them for that purpose. Try to exercise you first amendment constitutionally guaranteed God-given right and speak out against these unconstitutional searches and you are arrested on a bogus felony charge.

The war on terrorism is another war declared against the American people and is working well. Americans are surrendering God-given rights by the score due to *manipulation through deception* using security as the excuse.

THE ENEMY CALLED "THEY"

TYRANNY'S BELL

GREED, the root for tyranny's foundation
GREED, the root problem in the county and state
GREED, the root to the hate in the county and state
GREED, the root to the conflict in the county and state
GREED, the root to homelessness in the county and state
GREED, the root to the corruption in the county and state
GREED, the root to the higher prices in the county and state
GREED, the root that keeps out GOD in the county and state
GREED, the root to high unemployment in the county and state
GREED, the root to financial enslavement in the county and state
GREED, the root that denies real freedom in this county and state
GREED, the root to high-priced health care in this county and state
GREED, the root for the declining education in the county and state
GREED, the root foundation upon which no government can survive
GREED, the root for incompetent Government in this county and state
GREED, the root for children going to bed hungry in this county and state
GREED, the same in meaning as "the love of money is the root of all evil"
GREED, ignored by those with abundance and devastating to those without means
GREED, the real Foundation for the state law upon which the county system is founded
GREED, the reason the people are denied their Constitutional rights in this County and State

GODLESS
RUTHLESS
EGOCENTRIC
EXPLOITATIVE
DECEITFUL

(Do you see the crack in the bell?)

CHAPTER 11

FOR YOUR SAFETY AND SECURITY

Daniel Webster once warned that, *"human beings will generally exercise power when they can get it, and they will exercise it most undoubtedly in popular governments under pretense of public safety."*

In the preceding chapter, I provided you my definitions for act in law and act of the law, in accordance with what I understood from the definitions read in law and standard dictionaries. Below are those definitions repeated, but modified to hopefully clarify:

An *"act in the law"* is the party in authority exercising legal power, such as a legal or juristic act that is intended to transfer, create, and deny a right and is useful in law for that purpose.

An *"act of the law"* is without any consent from the individuals concerned and is the creation, extinction, or transfer of a right through the practice in the law itself.

LAW is the system that directs human behavior and affairs through *systematically exercising force* in a politically organized society, or through societal influence *backed by force.* Generally, Law is established rules for behavior or actions put in place by those in control or in power. These laws having binding legal force. Law is something that must be followed and obeyed or legal consequences will be brought to bear against the citizens. Those in authority say that *Law is a solemn expression of the will of the supreme power of the State.*

The Constitution says different. The Constitution says the law is the will of the people.

Many are calling the recent 9-11 attack on the United States a "cowardly act." I disagree with that assessment. This was far from a cowardly act. People willing to do a kamikaze dive with airplanes into buildings knowing they are going to die is far from a cowardly act. They have a purpose and have delivered a message that war has been declared against the American people.

THE ENEMY CALLED "THEY"

To better understand what this war is about, it is necessary to understand the enemy.

This attack was planned and that constitutes a conspiracy. Some synonyms for the word conspiracy are plot, scheme, plan, system, etc. Humans have been trained to consider any connection to the word conspiracy as something to be avoided, and anyone using the word is considered to be a "crackpot pot" or "conspiracy nut."

An agreement between two or more persons to play a joke, trick, or illusion on others is a conspiracy. An agreement between two or more persons to do anything to anyone is a conspiracy.

Legally, an agreement between two or more persons to commit a criminal action or actions for illegal purposes is a *Conspiracy*.

Seditious conspiracy

A plan (system, method, or scheme) to forcibly overthrow or destroy the U.S. government, or oppose its authority, or prevent its laws from being carried out or to seize or possess its property is a seditious conspiracy. There is a Seditious conspiracy (conspiracy=scheme=system=plan) to undermine this nation's Constitution (authority). There is a conspiracy (system) to overthrow and destroy our government. There is a conspiracy (system) to seize our property. Those involved in the conspiracy (system) are ignoring the Constitutional laws. The 9-11 attack played a part in the conspiracy and this American wants to know those truly responsible. The underlings, the scapegoats, and those sacrificed to commit the atrocities will no longer satisfy this American. This American wants those who authorized the atrocities, those behind the scenes. These are the murderous, treasonous, treacherous, *Evil One* really in hiding behind the scenes and this American's demand is that they be found, exposed to the light and brought to justice. In order to find and expose them it will be necessary to follow the money. Money is their god, greed is their creed, terror their tool, and tyranny over all human beings in the world their ultimate goal.

The methodology used to declare this war was also a message. Americans are being told we are not secure in our own land, that THEY can hit Americans anytime, anywhere and that *all our security measures will not stop them*. THEY are telling Americans THEY will use our all own resources against us, including our own planes, our own fuel, our own people, and our own training. THEY are telling Americans they do not need guns to instill fear and to control Americans, that any weapon will do, even a box knife. THEY have trained Americans into being cowards and now use our own fears against us. THEY have proven that Americans have been indoctrinated (synonyms: educated, trained) to be cowards (easily intimidated) and that those who profess to be chosen to govern are weak-willed (synonyms: pathetic, gutless, cowardly, boneless, spiritless, sad). THEY want Americans to panic, over react, and put more restrictions on themselves. THEY *want Americans to believe they have to surrender GOD given freedoms and rights for security* so THEY can more easily accomplish THEIR ultimate goal to totally enslave America and then the world.

Americans stating "we will have to *give up* some rights for security" are saying exactly what those who planned these atrocious (extremely wicked or cruel, appalling, horrifying, revolting) acts wanted to hear. These Americans are saying we will have to surrender.

Surrender means to yield to another's power or control, i.e. giving up rights and becoming slaves.

Saying we have to give up some rights for security, is a giant step toward Americans *complete and total surrender* and total domination over Americans.

Terror is extreme or intense fear. Terror is being used to intimidate human Christian Americans into that surrender.

Terrorism is the doctrine designed to use threats or violence to intimidate and cause panic in order to change or influence *political conduct and* is the tool that is being used to get Americans to surrender.

Terrorists are those who commit the actual acts and are the tools used by *Tyrants* to acquire and maintain control over a people or nation.

Tyrants manipulate others through deception into committing terrorist acts and practice terrorism.

Tyranny is government abusing its power to oppress the populace. Oppressive, unjust, arbitrary behavior or control is what characterizes Tyrannical.

Tyrant is a ruler that uses terrorism by *manipulating others into committing terrorist acts through deception* in order to acquire and maintain political control and power, then exercises that power unjustly and arbitrarily to oppress the nations populace.

There are many tyrants in this world, in this nation, and THEY have formed a *conspiracy* (plan, scheme, or system) to take this nation and the world from within. Tyrants are behind these atrocious acts. THEY are using terrorism (*the use of threat or violence to intimidate or cause panic, especially as a means for affecting political conduct*) to overthrow our

THE ENEMY CALLED "THEY"

Constitutional form of Government.

THEY have infiltrated our government at all level and some even govern. THEY have used *manipulation through deception* including loud threats, intimidation, our own doubts and fears, lies, distortions, and every other devious methodology available to scare Americans and turn Americans into a weak and terrified people.

THEY have used issues such as political parties, race, gender, sexual preference, religion, environment, and even smoking as a means to fragment (divide) Americans and overcome (conquer) Americans. In order to divert attention away from themselves for the atrocities they conspire and authorize, they manipulate and use people from other nations into committing the atrocities. THEY use Flag waving Patriotism to *manipulate through deception* the American people into a revengeful fury against the scapegoat's nation, and into giving up more rights for security.

These tyrants are *manipulating the American people though deception*, and are rapidly moving toward completing and implementing their agenda to dominate the Americans and the world. While our keepers, (those actually chosen to govern, our guardians) have been asleep at our own gates, these tyrants infiltrated all aspects in this nation, our government, our corporations, small business, our schools and universities, our media, those chosen to govern, and even our churches. They have used our own gullibility and naivetes against us and have slowly *re-indoctrinated (re-educated)* our populace against all the morals and values Americans used to treasure.

Recent and past attacks were tests, planned, perpetrated, and financed by tyrants within our own borders and within our own hierarchy in our government. We have been infiltrated. We are being taken from within. It is not only important to continue to maintain vigilance outside our borders, but is has become critical to maintain vigilance within our own house. It is crucial that we *do not surrender more freedoms* and imperative we *get back to the U. S. Constitution* to regain the freedoms already *surrendered*.

That enemy is here with us, among us, and has become us. The enemy does not want to be recognized until they are ready to expose themselves. By then it will be too late to stop them. It may already be too late because *too many human Christian Americans* are asleep and *refuse to* wake up, listen, *stand and fight*. Hopefully there are enough human Christian Americans still awake in our nation and within our government to seek out those truly responsible for this latest atrocity and other treasonous acts, expose them, and hold them accountable, be they outside or within our own borders.

Cowardly act, I think not. Cowards for not revealing who they truly are and their real purpose, I think so. *To truly reveal what THEY are would expose that they are not human.*

Has anyone noticed our nation's "enemies" have all been trained, educated, supplied and armed by our own government agencies such as the CIA, FBI, and DEA, etc, or has had previous ties to those agencies? Does anyone find this odd or extremely coincidental? Does anyone realize it is treason to materially support our enemies? Does anyone find it strange we have experts <u>on</u> terrorism in our government and not experts against terrorism? That there is a war <u>on</u> terrorism and not a war against terrorism, a war on drugs and not a war against drugs, a war *on* poverty and not against poverty? For what purposes are the wars *on* these things and not against (in opposition to) these things? This appears to be somewhat peculiar. Did you know a synonym for *on* is *supported*?

ON can be *used* as a function word to indicate a position over and in contact with or indicated as being a part in something and supports that something from underneath. Does *on* sound like these things are being opposed, or does it sound like they are being supported. Did you know synonyms for war are movement, campaign and pressure group?

A campaign is a military operation in a war. The war itself can be considered a campaign. The word Campaign is also used in connection with a plan to bring about a particular result such as in an election (election campaign). How many times have you heard war terminology used in election campaigns? The Wars on Terrorism, Poverty, and Drugs can be worded: CAMPAIGN SUPPORTED TERRORISM, CAMPAIGN SUPPORTED POVERTY, AND CAMPAIGN SUPPORTED DRUGS! *CAMPAIGN CONTRIBUTION ANYONE?* There are those in our governments who are "over" (above, on top of) and are specialists in these things? Hmm?

Through experiences, observations, and lessons learned the past several years, semantics is an art form for those who have infiltrated and wish to conquer our nation, our world. This art form allows them to twist and distort the truth to hide their real intentions. Americans have always taken pride in the fact they say what they mean and mean what they say, tell it like it is, are up front, etc. Those who are now attempting to overthrow the American government use semantics against Americans by twisting and distorting what human Christian Americans mean and say to obtain THEIR goals.

Many that govern do the same with the laws that they write in order *to manipulate others through deception* into voting for those laws to have them passed. Have you noticed that many laws passed have the complete opposite effect from what the American people are told they will accomplish? The reason this occurs is semantics and the fact that the American people have been taught not to take things literally.

Do you know there has never been a true "tax cut"? THEY only cut the projected (estimated) increase. Did you know there has never been a "budget cut." THEY only cut the projected (estimated) increase. Did you know they have designed the system to "punish" good supervisors who actually cut costs and save money? The money that a supervisor saves one year will be cut from that supervisor's budget the following year. Would you try to save if you knew it would be taken from you the following year?

Have you noticed that individuals who expose wrongdoings are the ones who are punished? Have you noticed that safety (security) has become a fall back position for justifying the American people giving up their rights, rather it be on the job, in the dentist's or doctor's office, in school, at airports, restaurants, etc? Have you noticed how conveniently placed the cameras were in filming the planes flying into the World Trade Center buildings? Did you notice? This American noticed! Was this a coincidence? Did you hear the news report within minutes after the buildings in New York and Washington D.C. were hit that a plane involved was missing? Did this strike anyone as peculiar? How did they know what planes were involved? How did they know a missing plane was involved? How did they know? Was it a coincidence? Have you noticed or heard anything peculiar? Did anything that you hear sound scripted? This American did. Have you noticed that security measures being implemented at the airports have nothing to do with what supposedly occurred on the aircraft? This American has. Have you noticed that now "everyone" is being treated as a terrorist at the airport facilities?

"They that can give up essential liberty to obtain a little temporary safety deserve neither liberty nor safety."—Attributed to Benjamin Franklin

"Never could an increase of comfort or security be a sufficient good to be bought at the price of liberty."—Attributed to Hillaire Belloc

If it sounds as if I am repeating myself, you are right. Some how, some way, human Christian Americans have to wake up. What God-given rights and freedoms will you surrender (give up) for a false security (safety)? Those that say Americans must surrender their rights for safety/security, and ignore the sacrifices made by so many for our FREEDOM are either involved in taking our nation from within or are being manipulated by those who are involved. These tyrants do not want Americans to have freedom. Tyrants do not want any human being free.

THEY ignore the Constitutions, the laws, and human being God-given rights. These tyrants, these *other beings* are **G**odless, **R**uthless, **E**gocentric, **E**xploitative, **D**eceitful and their only god is money and their **GREED** has no limits. These attacks on the World Trade Center and the Pentagon aren't the first and by no means are they the last. They have even told Americans there will be more terrorist attacks. Did you listen? What God-given rights will you surrender the next time?

THEY do not care how many thousands they kill to acquire their goals. All human beings, including Americans, are in a battle (fight) about good and evil. The enemy isn't overseas, isn't on our flanks, behind us, nor does the enemy have us surrounded. The enemy has overrun America, the world, and is among us. All human beings including Americans are in a knock down, no holds bared, all out fight (battle) for our lives, souls and everything in which we profess to believe. There are no civilians in this battle. It is crucial that all human beings, including Americans, fight back to drive this enemy from America, from the world. It is time for true human beings, including Americans, to stop hiding, take a stand, seek out and discover those beings truly behind the atrocities, expose them to the light, hold them accountable, and have THEM pay a price THEY and THEIR ancestors will regret for the next thousand years.

Who has the most to gain from a war between the Americans and the Arab nations? Perhaps big oil, big business, big government, who? As the old aphorism goes, "follow the money." Over 2000 years ago, Jesus Christ told us that the *love of money is the root of all evil.* Where are those who profess to believing his teachings and what are they doing? Are they looking for the root in this evil that has been committed, or are they just knocking off a few expendable leaves and branches on the tyranny tree to make appearances and look good? Are they really looking for the *Evil One* involved in this, the masterminds, the planners, the ones who hide behind the scenes while manipulating others to do their dirty work?

Those who doubt what I say, remember men like Hitler, Stalin, Saddam Hussein, Idi Amin, etc., the methodologies used to conquer their nations from within, and the thousands and or millions butchered to acquire and keep power and wealth.

THE TRUTH ABOUT 9-11

"Beware the leader who bangs the drums of war in order to whip the citizenry into a patriotic fervor, for patriotism is indeed a double-edged sword. It both emboldens the blood, just as it narrows the mind. And when the drums of war have reached a fever pitch and the blood boils with hate and the mind has closed, the leader will have no need in seizing the rights of the citizenry. Rather, the citizenry, infused with fear and blinded by patriotism, will offer up all of their rights unto the leader and gladly so. How do I know? For this is what I have done. And I am Caesar."—Attributed to Shakespeare's *Julius Caesar*, although the real author is apparently unknown

As explained in a previous chapter, every American Citizen meets the terrorist profile and is considered a terrorist or potential terrorist. It is recommended that everyone read *USA PATRIOT ACT HR3162-PL107-56 2001*. If nothing else, look at the Act and judge for yourself about what I say. After reviewing the Patriot Act, if anyone can tell me that this was written in a 6 week period and passed by both Congressional Houses *with full knowledge* concerning its contents, then every Congressional Representative that voted for the Act should be tried for treason against the United States. This one Act defies everything our Constitution and Bill of Rights guarantees, everything the U.S. Flag represents, and everything millions have died preserving the past 220 years.

The Acts very complexity and length leads me to believe that this Act was worked on well before the 9-11 attacks. There is no way that anyone in government could have completed this Act in such detail in the 6 weeks following the 9-11 attacks. Looking at the Patriot Act's length, its contents, and the rush to get it passed indicates that the 9-11 attacks were planned by some within our own government and this act was already written well before the 9-11 attacks occurred. My perception is that the attacks were planned by some within our government to provide an excuse to send more troops to the Middle East to guarantee access to Middle Eastern oil *and force the "Patriot Act" through Congress* to further trample the American people's Constitutionally guaranteed God-given rights.

One can't help but notice the great patriotic movement since 9-11? Notice all the flags flying from buildings, cars, homes, etc. War on terrorism is now the "battle cry." Avenge 911, get the bastards, kill the terrorists are the cliché's. Has any one noticed the terrorists that allegedly committed the acts are actually already dead? They allegedly died in the plane crashes. Has anyone noticed that those who allegedly "planned" and financed the 9-11 Acts of War are still free while billions have been spent in overthrowing a puppet government that some within our government set up in the first place in the 1980s? Has anyone noticed that all the "war on terrorism" has accomplished is that the American people have had their God-given constitutionally guaranteed rights trampled? Just look at what is going on under the illusion called Airport Security. Every American citizen entering a domestic Airport is expected to surrender all rights at the airport's terminal doors because they will be denied those rights inside the airport terminal. Try to exercise "any" rights and you will be arrested as a terrorist. And it is claimed you are living in a "free" country and you have the freedom to do as you choose?

Soon the War on Terrorism (declared against Americans) will be called a War Against Terrorism in America because is will be out in the open that they now consider every American citizen as a potential terrorist to be caught in their net.

The local Jackson County prosecutor made a statement on a local talk radio program to the effect "we want to catch every citizen we can in our criminal net." Notice that what was said was "citizen" and not criminal. THEY have devised a *law network* (system, conspiracy) *in which every human Christian American citizen is a criminal*. What is done with criminals? They are incarcerated and become virtual slaves till released. Think about what I am saying. Please, listen.

Has anyone noticed that the "War on Terrorism" declared by our President is exactly like the "War on Poverty" and the "War on Drugs." Notice how many more Americans are at the poverty level and how many more Americans are using drugs. Americans are losing all these wars. In reality, these wars were not only declared against the American people these are wars declared on all human beings worldwide and the human beings are losing.

Osama Bin Ladin and his group were *created* by some within our government, *trained* by some within our government and *used* by some within our government to fight against the Communists in Afghanistan. Now that same group is being *used* to commit terrorist acts against the American people, the Capitalist. The terrorist acts are committed in order that the American people will surrender their God-given rights to the terrorist within the government.

Doesn't it amaze you that with the technology, money, and intelligence network at this nations disposal that every allegedly terrorist "rat" is being caught or killed *except the allegedly major leader*? In the process, we have overthrown a government and plans are being put into place to attack other nations and overthrow their governments. Doesn't this appear the least bit suspicious to anyone? Everyone wants to wave the flag, but no one wants to uphold what that flag represents, what our nations Constitution with the Bill of Rights guarantees, our nations moral and ethical values, and the freedom these things represent and provide.

Our nation has been infiltrated at all levels including government, business, education, religious organizations, etc. The real "terrorist" plan is to overthrow our nation from within by destroying what our flag represents, what our Constitution with its Bill of Rights guarantees, and the moral and ethical values on which this nation was founded.

Our nation is under siege from within and no one that professes to be chosen to govern seems to care or willing to stand against the terrorist within. Those that profess to be chosen to govern continually compromise with the terrorist within and now Americans are either on the run, in a panic, in a full retreat or have already surrendered. Terrorists within the governing ranks in our government do everything within their power to undermine the American way, the U.S. Constitution and deny the American people freedom. Human Christian Patriotic Americans are trying to wake up other Americans but are being shouted down by the terrorist cronies and are being labeled hate mongers, racist, trouble makers, politically incorrect, etc. Calling oneself a Christian in what was once considered a Christian Nation has become dangerous.

So, I ask all those waving the flag, do you really believe what that flag represents? Do you really believe what the Constitution with the Bill of Rights guarantees? Do you really want to regain your freedom? If so, when was the last time you read the Constitution, or even the Bill of Rights? When was the last time you read your state constitution and compared it with the laws in your city, county, or state? If you have read these documents and did the comparison, are you mad as hell and doing something about it? For what purposes are the schools allowed to pass students who cannot read, write, or do basic math? For what reasons are college athletes given college degrees when they cannot even read or write?

The major reason our young people are sent into battle is to fight wars for a Clique's wealth and power? For what purposes are those in that same Clique allowed to betray those same young people and deny them medical care for their injuries and renege on their promises concerning the future benefits those people were promised they would receive?

Those that profess to be chosen to govern betrayed the veterans from WWI, WWII, Korea, Vietnam, and Desert Storm. That same governing power (*Clique*) has been betraying the American people, ignoring the Constitution, American people's freedom, and has allowed the tyrants to infiltrate and rule. For what purposes is that *Clique* allowed to tax Americans at a rate that people lose their homes and property to the "tax collector"? For what purposes is that *Clique* permitted to rob the elderly? For what purposes is that *Clique* permitted to deny people their God-given and Constitutionally guaranteed rights and who provided THEM that authority?

Previously I explained Act in the Law and Act of the Law. *An Act in the law is intended to create, transfer or extinguish (deny) a right*. Rights are God-given and are guaranteed under the Constitution and therefore an Act in the Law cannot provide a right. God-given rights cannot be transferred because they already belong to every human being. *Extinguishing a right is the only thing an Act in the Law can truthfully accomplish.*

An "*act in the law*" is the party exercising legal power to create a law for the purpose to make it legal to extinguish a right.

In reality, it cannot even do that. What is God-given cannot be extinguished. Just as God created energy cannot be destroyed, neither can a God-given right be extinguished. A right can only be denied. An Act in the law *denies* an individual or a certain group a right. *And that intent, is exactly what every law, every ordinance, every act instituted is designed to accomplish.*

When an act in the law is signed into existence and put into practice or implemented it is then is called

"*Act of the law*." When enforced, the law is intended to deny a right without consent from the individuals involved.

That intent to deny "We the People" a right without the "We the People's" consent is the very thing being accomplished and it is being done by *manipulation through deception* using *Legal Definitions and the Law*. And the whole process is unconstitutional unless the people consent or the people's representative consent. *With the Party, the Evil One, dictating who the candidates for representatives will be, dictating through laws those that are allowed on the ballot, making those candidates pay to get on the ballot, making you pay for a stamp to mail in your ballot, makes the whole process unconstitutional. I know it, you now know it, and THEY knew it when THEY instituted it.* That makes it a government of the party, for the party, by the party. THEY have given themselves the authority to deny your God-given, constitutionally guaranteed right with THEIR Rule of Law.

"EVERY LAW IS AN INFRACTION OF LIBERTY"—Jeremy Bentham

By legal definition, the *law is the expression of the will of the Supreme power of the State. According to the Constitution, the law is the will of "We the People."* Those who profess to be the ones elected and chosen to govern were supposedly elected to protect and uphold the Constitution and the people's rights, or WERE THEY? ARE THEY?

Although "We the People" may say a law is unconstitutional, *every law is Constitutional if those who make, institute, interpret, and enforce the law say it is Constitutional.* Hence, those now in authority are rewriting the Constitution, and if **THEY** so desire, **THEY** will rewrite that Constitution to oppress the people, which in practice, is exactly what **THEY** are doing and intend continuing to do.

COMING SOON TO AN AIRPORT, BANK, STORE, NEWS MEDIA, HIGHWAY OR GOVERNMENT FACILITY NEAR YOU:

For everyone's safety and national security it will be necessary to strip search everyone entering the airport terminal that airport security personnel may deem a terrorist threat.

For everyone's safety and national security against terrorist threats, it will be necessary for everyone to have an identification chip in their hand or forehead. This chip will also be an advantage in that it can also be used for all banking, buying and selling.

For everyone's safety, national security against terrorism, and due to the time taken for proper searches, domestic and international flights will be limited to 3 flights a day for all major airlines conducting international flights, and 5 flights a day for domestic flights.

For everyone's safety and national security against possible terrorist activities, all rest areas on all major interstates and state highways will be converted to check points to search all vehicles traveling between states and cities.

For all Americans' safety and national security, all illegal aliens discovered will be executed on the spot.

For everyone's safety, due to court case overload, and for everyone's convenience, all traffic violators will be required to pay the officer upon being stopped by the officer. Only serious felony offenses will be referred to the courts.

Due to the court case overload, the court will no longer handle civil cases. No longer will jury trials be convened in such cases. Such cases are to be referred to an impartial mediator selected by the Court Clerk. This mediator must be a practicing lawyer or sitting judge.

To save government printing costs, paper, minerals, and for other environmental reasons, paper and coin monies will no longer be produced or used. All books and printed material are banned and all monies and books will be used electronically.

For everyone's convenience, the banks and stores will no longer use plastic credit cards since everyone will have the implant chip. This will also help the environment and save on oil since all plastic products are made from oil products.

For everyone's health, resource conservation, and convenience, the State will decide everyone's food intake and other personal needs. Each person will be allotted a certain amount in products each month.

For water conservation, drinking water will be rationed at one quart per person per day. Everyone will be permitted to take one shower a week for 5 minutes or one bath. Clothing may be washed once a week and cars once a month with a 10-minute time limit for the cars.

Think I am crazy. You will learn. The *Evil One* can and will do whatever THEY want, when THEY want, because THEY have "trained" the American people to be "afraid" and obedient like sheep being led to the slaughter. By the time you learn you have nothing to fear, that the *Evil One* are all bluff and are actually the ones afraid, it may be too late.

All human beings are not equal (alike, the same), but all human beings are equal in right. Mankind is created equal in that all humans are born with a freewill, the same spirit. That does not make them equal in all other aspects, for we all have "natural" abilities and are better at certain things than others. In *The Bible*, these natural abilities are referred to as "spiritual gifts." Not all humans are born equal physically. Not all are born equal mentally. We are all equal in Spirit. The gifts may vary, but we all derive or draw from the same spirit. How we use what we draw from that spirit can be used for evil or good purposes.

We are all born with the same freewill and equal in right. We are born into a world where a struggle (game, contest) between good and evil "systems" is being waged. When the game first started several thousand years ago, 10 basic ground rules governing human beings conduct in the game between good and evil were provided. Human beings were deceived into refusing to follow those 10 rules and were manipulated into making the rules as the game is played. This is what I refer to *as manipulation through deception.* It is the same with the U.S. Constitution and the first 10 Amendments called the Bill of Rights. There are those who profess to be human beings and Americans that refuse to live up to that Bill of Rights. THEY have taken it upon themselves to "make up the rules as they go along," as things occur, as time progresses. These same beings have also taken it upon themselves to "re-define" word meaning as the game is played in order to favor themselves. Many who now profess to be our elected and chosen leaders have a law degree and it is by obtaining this degree that many believe allows them the authority to change the rules as the game is played.

Only it is not a game, it is a fight, and it is for human beings lives, their souls. These rule changes affect each and every human beings day to day lives. As the rules and word meanings are changed, human beings God-given rights are denied to suit the needs for those instituting and enforcing the laws, i.e.; those professing to be the ones elected and chosen to govern. This will continue until humans become aware that what is happening is enslaving them and they revolt, or until it is too late and they are completely enslaved. The ultimate goal is enslavement for all human beings and world domination by those who profess to be the elected and chosen ones to govern. Soon, the war will be over for all human beings. Except for a few human Christian Americans still standing and fighting the fight that is required, it appears Americans in the silent majority are not interested in the fight results and have already surrendered their God-given rights to the oppressors. They have already surrendered to the evil system, that system which is the Antichrist. They have become Insulated Zombie Enslaved Demons.

Human Christian Americans are waiting for an individual to appear on the scene as the Antichrist. In reality, the Antichrist has been among us all along. The Antichrist is the *Evil One's* system that has been governing mankind since man first rebelled against God. Someday, someone or something will be put into position and will have complete control over that system. When that occurs, the Antichrist, the system, will have complete control over human beings throughout the world.

This does not have to happen. God gave us a freewill to keep this from happening. We have been forewarned. Those who have willingly surrendered to the *Evil One* system will live in a hell. Hell can either be a physical place or state in one's mind in which torment or evil prevails. Hell is a place or state of mind where constant turmoil and destruction prevail. Hell is the sovereignty belonging to the Evil One and the criminals where the damned (hopeless, ruined, lost, done for, etc.) submit themselves to everlasting (endless, perpetual) punishment (chastisement, reprimand, penalty, criticism, rebuke, etc.). Looking around you, would you describe what is going on here on earth as "hell"? I will.

Christian people are led to believe they should not be involved in the political system in this world, yet it is that very system that can be good or evil, the Christian way to live life, or the antichrist way to live life. Christianity is not a religion, but is a way to live life. Christ taught men this, but most did not listen. Most are not listening today. The only power evil has is the power we, as God's children, as human beings permit in the system. That system can either be good or the Antichrist. Without human acceptance, evil cannot survive. Our choice is between Christ's system or Antichrist's system, i.e., good or evil. Choose.

The following definitions are my interpretations as derived from definitions found in Black's Law Dictionaries 6th and 7th additions:

TYRANNY can be legally interpreted as an unfair or dictatorial government; the cruel and dictatorial implementation in ultimate authority, whether that authority be provided constitutionally in one ruler or seized by one ruler by violating the separation and sharing in governmental powers. It is government abusing its power to oppress the populace and oppressive, unjust, arbitrary behavior or control that characterizes Tyrannical.

TYRANT can be legally interpreted as a Party (sovereign) or a leader, *legitimate or not*, who exercises power unjustly and on a whim to oppress the citizenry. A tyrant is a ruler who exercises power unjustly and arbitrarily to oppress the nations populace by using terrorism and terrorists *manipulating others through deception into committing terrorist acts* in order to acquire and maintain control and political conduct through terror.

A Tyrant can be a bully, dictator, oppressor, *Party*, group, etc.

SOVEREIGN is a person, body, or state provided with, and given as a right, *inaccessible* and supreme authority. Sovereign can also be considered the ruler in an independent state.

SOVEREIGN PEOPLE *is a political party made up from the citizens qualified as voting members who cling to the powers to control and exercise those powers through THEIR chosen representatives.*

WHAT DOES FREE, FREEDOM, LIBERTY, EQUAL AND JUSTICE

LEGALLY MEAN as can be interpreted from *Black's Law Dictionaries 6th edition*:

FREE means not being subjected to *legal constraints* (limitations, safety checks, control, etc.) put into place by another.

FREEDOM is a condition in ones mind that one is free, has liberty, and can choose for oneself, i.e. self-determination; Freedom is having no restraints and is the opposite too slavery. Freedom is conducting oneself according to ones moral conscience and according to what one's will may dictate, without others examination, interference, or prevention except those that *may be imposed by just and necessary laws* and the responsibilities required for social order. The government and the constitutions put into place in such a system is to ensure liberty to the individual citizen.

CONSTITUTIONAL RIGHTS, according to the constitution are natural, civil, political, and personal.

POLITICAL RIGHTS is to participate, directly or indirectly, in establishing and administrating government, and as a citizen to vote, hold public office and to petition.

LIBERTY is freedom from all restraints except those that are fairly and impartially (justly) required by law. It is essential that this freedom from restraint be under the condition that others are allowed to enjoy in this same freedom that is regulated by law. This freedom is to be absent from ridiculous limitations, yet is not exempted from sensible regulations and prohibitions essential to a community.

EQUAL, put simply, is what is good for the goose is good for the gander. Whatever applies to one person applies to everyone within that community. Laws are to be applied to everyone in the same manner. Fines are to be the same for everyone. Everyone is expected to adhere to the same rules. The same punishments are to apply to the same law for everyone.

EQUAL PROTECTION OF THE LAW under the Constitution means that as a citizen in the United States, no person, party, group, or class, shall be denied the same protection under the law that is enjoyed by others persons in like circumstances. Like circumstances include their lives, liberty, property, and in their pursuit for happiness. 14th Amendment simply means that similarly situated persons must receive similar treatment under the law, i.e. the law is to be applied to everyone equally.

JUSTICE is the acceptable administration in laws to ensure that every man is rendered his due at all times in legal matters? It is also simply a title given to judges.

JUST. In compliance to or in agreement with what is legal or lawful. Legally right or reasonably right according to the law and the judge.

FREE AND EQUAL. No definition found.

WHAT DOES FREE, FREEDOM, LIBERTY, EQUAL AND JUSTICE LEGALLY MEAN as can be interpreted from *Black's Law Dictionaries 7th edition*:

FREE is having legal and political rights, enjoying political and civil liberty as a free citizen, a free populace and not being subject to the restraint or power of another; enjoying personal freedom; liberated. Free is Characterized by choice, rather than by force or limitations such as free will. Free is to take somebody's place such as land was free of any encumbrances. Free is not restricted by force or restraint such as being free from prison. Free is unconstrained and indulgent free trade. Free is costing nothing, free of charge.

FREE means to liberate or to remove a person or animal from self-control or responsibility.

FREEDOM is a political right to be free or liberated.

POLITICAL RIGHT is a right, such as the right to vote, to participate in the establishment or administration of government or cling to public office.

EQUAL. No definition found for the word equal

EQUALITY a condition that equal is an illusion in power or political status.

EQUAL PROTECTION. The 14th Amendment guarantees that under the same circumstances, the government must treat a person or class the same as it treats other persons or classes. As the constitution is practiced under today's jurisprudence, equal protection means that legislation can discriminate but must have a rational basis for doing so. If the legislation that discriminates does affect a fundamental right (such as the right to vote), and it can withstand a strict scrutiny, it will not be considered unconstitutional. This is what is meant by equal protection of the laws and equal protection under the law. The law is to be protected at all costs from the constitution, and that law will be protected under the law umbrella.

JUSTICE is administering the laws according to the judge and what is proper.

JUST is what is legally right, legally lawful, and legally equitable

EQUITABLE. Is what is legally right, legally lawful and legally equitable, and conforms to what the judge deems is right and his principles.

FREE AND EQUAL Pertains only to an election which is conducted so that the electorate has a reasonable opportunity to vote, with each vote given the same outcome.

Every human being knows within themselves what their God-given rights are and when those rights are being denied. Human beings are born knowing this. The *Evil One* using *manipulation through deception* is denying Human being God-given rights with semantics, changes in word meanings, and laws instituted that circumvent the U.S. Constitution.

Notice the differences in the definitions. Notice that the term *free and equal* was not in the 6th edition, but was put into and defined in the 7th edition and notice that it applies only to the vote. Notice there was no definition for the term *free and equal* in the 6th edition, only for the separate words *free* and *equal*. Notice in the 7th edition, the words *free* and *equal* when applied together as in the term "free and equal" have nothing to do with the separate word definitions "free" and "equal." Notice that according to the definitions free and freedom in the seventh addition are "political rights." Notice the way that I interpreted the Equal Protection under the law definition in the 7th edition. That is not exactly what the definition for Equal Protection under the law said, but it definitely can be interpreted that way, if one so desires. And from what is happening today, I would say that is the way it is being interpreted.

The point in all this is to demonstrate that those beings holding the power make the rules and can change those rules as THEY wish. If a legal definition for a word works in THEIR favor, it stays the same. If a legal definition for a word works against them, it is changed to favor THEM. If THEY decide that THEY need a new legal definition, they make one up as they wish to suit their purposes.

The one important point for you to remember concerning what is happening is THEY have subtly changed the legal definitions to make it appear THEY provide you your God-given rights. And THEY want to make it appear that all your God-given rights are politically created, politically transferred, politically controlled, and can be taken through the political legal process, by THEM. *It is a lie. It is an illusion. The Declaration of Independence, the U.S. Constitution, and the Oregon Constitution is my evidence to that fact.* Governments do not provide human beings rights. God provided human beings their rights. Government is not God.

<u>Basic law</u> throughout the world was founded on the 10 Commandments. No longer is this so. The Constitution was provided by this nation's founding fathers to be the foundation for our law in America. No longer is this so. One

way to circumvent and change the Constitutions without the people being aware, is to change the Constitutions word definitions in the legal dictionaries to suit those in authority. This legalese circumvents the original intent in the U.S. Constitution and the State Constitutions. And, without the vote, the people can do absolutely nothing about it.

Every law is a *legal constraint* against freedom and infringes upon a right. *"Every law is an infraction of liberty" Jeremy Bentham.* It is imperative that laws are necessary, just and applied equitably. That was the purpose *our founding fathers put in place "Rule of Constitutional Law."* That is not what we have today. The *Evil One* controlled system is fixed" so the people's vote is ignored. The result today is the "Rule of Law." In Oregon and Jackson County the *Evil One* controls the vote thus the law. It was through Christian silence that the *Evil One* was empowered to circumvent the U.S. and Oregon Constitutions and that same silence now permits the *Evil One* to ignore the people's vote. *But don't forget it is for your safety that this is being done.*

"They that can give up essential liberty to obtain a little temporary safety deserve neither liberty nor safety." Benjamin Franklin, Historical Review of Pennsylvania, 1759.

MORONS VERSUS THE EVIL ONE
"You have heard the ancients were told, You shall not commit murder and whoever commits murder shall be liable to the court. But I say to you that everyone who is angry with his brother shall be guilty before the court; and whoever says to his brother, you good-for nothing, shall be guilty before the supreme court; and whoever says, you fool, shall be guilty enough to go into the fiery hell," Jesus Christ, The Bible, Matthew 5:21-22.

Are you a moron? According to the Clique, the *Evil One*, human beings are morons. According to some *Evil One* members, all human beings are morons. Obviously the *Evil One* are not human, or THEY would also be morons.

A MORON is considered to be a feebleminded or mentally defective person whose mental potential is limited to the ages between 8 and 12 years old. It is said a moron is only capable to perform routine work under supervision. A moron is also considered to be a very stupid person or a FOOL.

A FOOL is considered to be a person lacking in Judgement (reasoning) or prudence (good sense). A fool was said to be a retainer (servant) formerly kept in great households to provide casual entertainment and was commonly dressed in motley with cap, bells, and bauble. A fool can be someone that is victimized or made to appear foolish such as the butt in a joke, or the DUPE. A fool can also be considered a harmless disturbed person lacking in common ability and understanding with a noticeable tendency or aptitude for a certain activity. Synonyms IDIOT, IMBECILE, MORON, SIMPLETON, The shared meaning for these synonyms is one who is mentally defective

On local radio station KCMX 880, Medford, Oregon, one talk show host obviously closely associated with and *manipulated through deception* (aren't we all?) by the Clique, the *Evil One*, made the comment over the airways that people are morons. This comment is a perfect example demonstrating how the Clique, the *Evil One* running the news and entertainment media and those in power truly perceive "We the People." Notice that those controlling government, education, business, the news and entertainment media treat all human beings like morons.

Considering that those in control in your local and state government think that you are a feebleminded person, a moron, do you really believe THEY are going to let you choose your elected representatives by counting your vote?

THEY do not think you have the common sense, the brainpower, the smarts, the knowledge, or the capability to vote the right way. What is the right way to vote you may ask? The right way to vote is to vote for their party candidate, i.e. those THEY choose and permit on the ballot, those THEY continually praise and tell you to vote for. As added insurance, the voting numbers are fabricated to ensure those THEY choose are selected. The Clique, the *Evil One* believes the people are morons and cannot choose for themselves. THEY believe the people are morons and are to be treated as children. THEY believe the people are morons and need to be told how to live their lives. THEY believe the people are morons and cannot think for themselves. THEY believe the people are morons and cannot perform the tasks the Clique, the *Evil Ones* performs. THEY believe the people are morons and cannot make rational choices. THEY believe the people are morons because THEY train (educate) the people to be morons.

Two synonyms for educate are brainwash and indoctrinate. We think the education system is teaching our children to learn and to think for themselves. In our education system today, telling a child to think is taboo. The entire education system has been convoluted into a brainwashing/indoctrination system. Anyone within the education system caught telling a student to think will most likely face serious repercussions. THEY do not want human beings to think. THEY want human beings to be like mindless robots and that is exactly what is happening. Human beings are being educated, trained, indoctrinated, brainwashed, or whatever synonym you prefer, to be like and act like mindless robots.

A few minutes later on that same local radio station, Paul Harvey News announced that a gang was breaking into homes, robbing and raping the women in those homes. The perpetrator's ages were said to be between 12 years and 8 years. It was put that in that manner, ages between 12 and 8 years? That may have been a misprint being read. The point is, these kids are behaving, as they were educated (indoctrinated) to behave. Sex education is being taught in school, so that is what the kids expect, want and will use whatever means necessary to get. Talk about something long enough, and it puts ideas into peoples minds, especially the young who are easily susceptible to suggestion. There is a difference between sex education and teaching kids to have sex. Teaching the reproductive processes in biology is one thing. Teaching kids how to put on and use condoms to have safe sex is another and is harmful to their spiritual well being.

Treat someone in a certain manner and expect that someone to act in a certain manner and eventually, that individual will become that in which the manner expected and treated. Children are being educated, treated, and expected to be like morons by the Public Education System, hence, are being educated as morons, and are beginning to act like morons. Notice that the children are not learning reading, writing, and arithmetic but are learning about sex, condoms, abortion, etc. Treat human beings as criminals, and many become criminals. Treat human beings as drug addicts, supply the drugs, and many become drug addicts. Train human beings to kill each other in war, supply them the weapons, and that is exactly what they do, kill each other in war. Train human beings to hate other human beings that look, talk, or act different and that is exactly what they do, hate each other.

The Clique, the *Evil One* is *manipulating the people through deception*, to do the *Evil One's* will. God gave human beings a free will, to choose between right and wrong, good and evil, but the *Evil One* do not want human beings to decide, so The *Evil One manipulates human beings through deception* into disobeying God and make the choice for you. The *Evil One* has been *manipulating human beings though deception* since the Garden in Eden. THEY have *manipulated human beings through deception* into believing there is no right or wrong, no good or evil. THEY have *manipulated human beings through deception* into believing there is no God. THEY have *manipulated human beings through deception* into being the *Evil One's* slaves, working for THEM, providing for THEM, entertaining THEM and doing THEIR will. THEY have manipulated human beings into being mindless robots.

It is amazing that people will believe, with absolutely no proof or evidence, except evidence that *the Evil One* fabricates through false science and out right lies, things that supposedly occurred millions or billions of years in the past. There are no eyewitness, no written testimony, no evidence or proof. Only a *false science* that makes up the information as it goes along.

Yet people will readily believe there is no GOD, when there is evidence to the contrary everywhere one looks and the real science is ignored. The evidence is in the order in things about us such as an atom's structure, the four seasons in a year and the way they always come around, the planets and their orbits. The evidence is in the natural laws such as the law of gravity; watching a baby being born, planting a seed and watching it grow into a strong healthy fruit bearing plant. There is evidence in the stars, the wind and rain, the animals and the order among their species. There is an order to everything. That order had to come from something or someone. It did not just happen from a "big bang" as people are led to believe by *manipulation through deception.* And there is eyewitness evidence, people who have put it in writing and passed it from generation to generation. That evidence is in *The Bible*, and documents discovered to validate its validity. But the greatest evidence is within you. You know deep within there is a GOD.

Among the military personnel, there is a saying "there are no atheists in a foxhole." That is very true. Even the most primitive tribes, that have never seen or read a Bible, worship a God. God's spirit is in every human being from birth. Every human being is born knowing the difference between good and evil, right and wrong.

How can I say that you ask? How does a child react when that child is wronged? He/she lets you know it. Human beings can be "trained" to hate and do evil because we have those evil tendencies in us the same as we have the good tendencies within us. Human beings can be "trained" to behave in a good way. The one thing human beings cannot be trained to do is love. Love comes from the God spirit within. Human beings are not born with a heart filled with evil and hate. Human beings are born with a heart filled with the spirit. In their youth, human beings are taught to fill their hearts with hate, greed, and jealousy. I know this, because GOD does not create anything that is evil. Evil comes from another force, another power, another kingdom and that is where humans hearts are manipulated through deception into being filled with hate, greed and jealousy. Human beings are not born wrong doers, but are born in to a world filled with wrong doers, humans that are doing wrong because they are being manipulated through deception. Human beings are trained from birth to be wrongdoers.

People are not born morons regardless any physical or mental defects one may have at birth. But, people are being trained to behave and act like morons. People for the most part are trusting. That is what gets people into trouble. Eve believed The Snake in Eden and got into real trouble. Eve was trusting. Adam trusted both Eve and The Snake and he got into trouble. Both Adam and Eve were sent (expelled) from Eden to their rooms (earth) for punishment (allowed doing as The Snakes wished). Human *beings continue to trust the Snakes*, the *Evil One,* and are led astray. The Snakes wants human beings to be their servants, not servants to God. God sent Jesus to provide people a way to free themselves from The Snakes, but the people did not listen and they still aren't listening. God's Son, Jesus Christ died that human beings might be saved from the Snake's hell.

As long as human beings listen to and follow the *Evil One*, the people will *be manipulated through deception* and led down a path that leads nowhere but into an abyss, with no way out. The Snakes (*Evil One*) will always consider human beings that are *manipulated though deception* as morons. Once a person realizes what the *Evil One* is doing, that person becomes expendable and is no longer permitted to "serve" in The Snakes (*Evil One*) system (thank God). The Snakes (*Evil One*) entire system is illusions, deceit and lies and is based on semantics.

The Snake's (*Evil One*) manipulate the people into providing the Snake's (*Evil One*) with a royal life style while the people are provided the scraps. The Snake's (*Evil One*) system unmercifully taxes those who work and attempt to live a simple yet comfortable life as God originally planned. The Snake's (*Evil One*) want human beings to have barely enough to survive while providing for The Snake's (*Evil One*) creature comforts.

The entire political, religious, and business system is established for The Snake's (*Evil One)* comfort and well being, not the people. Could this be the reason for the big animal rights and environmental movements going on today? Notice how we are told to learn about and understand the reptiles and the many TV shows about these animals. Makes one wonder.

Genesis, Chapter 3 verses 1-5. "Now the serpent was more crafty than any beast of the field which the Lord God had made. And he said to the woman 'Indeed, has God said you shall not eat from any tree of the Garden?' The *woman said to the serpent, 'from the fruit of the trees of the garden we may eat; but from the fruit of the tree which is in the middle of the garden, God has said you shall not eat from it or touch it or you will die.' The serpent said to the woman 'you surely will not die! For God knows that in the day you eat from it your eyes will be opened, and you will be like God, knowing good and evil."*

Definitions to words as interpreted and understood from Webster's dictionary.

CRAFTY means to be skillful, clever and adept at subtlety, cunning and guile. Synonyms are cunning, sneaky, devious, sly, shrewd, deceitful, tricky, scheming, etc.

SUBTLE means to be elusive, difficult to understand or distinguish. It is something put into practice that is meant to confuse and be vague.

Synonyms for the word elusive are indefinable, hard to pin down, hazy, etc.

SERPENT is a noxious (harmful, poisonous) creature that creeps, hisses or stings such as a snake. The Devil and a treacherous person have been defined as a serpent by some.

SNAKE is a limbless, scaled, reptile with a long tapering body and salivary glands often modified to produce venom that is injected through grooved or tubular fangs. A treacherous person is another definition for a snake.

Many are probably offended that I refer to the self-proclaimed illustrious local, state, and federal leaders as The Snakes. By their actions and by definition, that is what THEY are. THEY like to "profile" people, and using their own profiling system THEY fit the snake profile perfectly. THEY *manipulate through deception* that which is *harmful* to human being livelihood. THEY are very *skillful and cunning* in the way they manage to con or rob human beings' earnings and property. THEY are very *adept at the subtle* methods in which THEY *manipulate human beings through deception* and convince people that the people voted for laws and State Constitutional Amendments that deny human beings their God-given rights in Jackson County and Oregon. THEY are *difficult to understand*, are *hard to pin down*, and THEY are extremely *vague* in their answers to questions, if THEY answer the question at all. THEY *spread venom* (hatred) everywhere between (democrat & republican, liberal & conservative, black & white, Christian & Islamic, Communist and Capitalist, etc), and *poison the people* with their venom (hatred). THEY use templates to spread their hate. THEY set up operations to "STING" the people in order to take people's money and possessions. THEIR *treachery* has no bounds in order to betray the Constitutions THEY have sworn an oath to support.

If this does not describe the crafty serpent called a snake, what does? If The Snakes are permitted to refer to human beings as morons, then I reserve the same right to refer to those in the Clique, the *Evil One*, as the Snakes.

Jesus Christ stated that "whoever says you fool is guilty enough to go into the fiery hell." In Matthew, Chapter 23 Jesus describes those who are in the "viper's brood." He is speaking about the Lawyers (scribes) and Leaders (Pharisees) (religious and political) throughout the chapter. In verse 33 Jesus states "You serpents, you brood of vipers, how will you escape the sentence of hell?" Nothing has changed. Even today, the leaders (religious and political) and the lawyers are still committing the same atrocities that were committed against the people 2000 years ago.

Snakes are interesting to watch. They are the most ruthless, cold-blooded creatures God created. Snakes will devour their prey alive. Snakes have no loyalties, and cannot be trusted. They do have patience. A snake will wait patiently for hours, even days for its prey to come within striking distance, and then strike without mercy. Much like those who profess to be the elected and chosen leaders. While there are many honest lawyers, many also belong to the viper's brood, The Snakes. The honest lawyers are excluded, while the Snakes belonging to the inner circle are those that truly control the system. The Snakes control the government, education, business, news and entertainment media, etc.

THEY are presently controlling human beings lives. THEY control human beings with their poison, they smother human beings by not letting them breathe freely, then they eat the human beings. The Snake's poison is hate and the methodology used to turn human against human. They smother humans with legalize, taxes, and fines to keep humans bound and trapped with no breathing room. They eat humans alive by taking everything humans have and your human soul.

If a snake threatens someone, the snake is generally eliminated. What puzzles me is that we have all these Snakes within our local, state, and federal government, taking human children, homes, property and money, threatening and stinging humans in every way possible and humans do nothing. The Snakes remain in public office and people accept The Snakes abuse and allow The Snakes to train children to be morons. Humans allow The Snakes to treat the humans as morons. Humans are trained to act like morons in order to satisfy and entertain The Snakes.

I do not believe human beings are morons, but I do believe The Snakes make humans afraid. The Snakes feed off this fear and use it to hide what they do. Humans fear for their jobs, fear they won't be able to pay their bills, fear for medical care, fear terrorists will attack them in some obscure way in their home towns, fear nuclear attack, biological attack, etc., etc., etc. It is this fear that gives The Snakes the power over the human beings. I am here to tell you, do not be afraid.

The Snakes are cowards and if the humans unite and stand against them, they cannot harm you. For what other purposes do they hide what they do and make their plans behind closed doors and in secret, if not afraid? The Snakes fear the truth and what the human beings will do if the humans learn the truth. The Snakes cannot handle the truth. The Snakes indoctrinate humans to be afraid so humans will not question what THEY do. People have nothing to fear if people treat others the way they themselves want to be treated. If human beings refuse to harm each other, and treat each other respectfully, there is absolutely nothing to fear. Once that fear is gone, The Snakes will be exposed for what they are and humans will truly be free.

God created the plant earth and it is here for all human beings to live on and enjoy. There is nothing on this planet that cannot be shared by all. God set up governments among humans for all humans to share, enjoy and to protect them, not abuse them. That is not happening. An enemy that has an agenda to enslave humans, and in order to do so, has infiltrated the governments and manipulates government against government, human being against human being. The time has arrived for human Christians to accept their responsibility, seek out and destroy that enemy and reinstate God established governments.

All human beings are God's people, God's children. He created us all. Human beings are not the enemy. The enemy has been identified for us in The Bible, only the enemy, utilizing manipulation through deception has human beings warring against other human beings as the enemy. The real enemy is sitting back comfortably in its easy chair, laughing and having a good time, entertaining themselves watching human beings bicker, fight, and kill each other for the scraps THEY leave us.

As stated before, the Snakes consider people (human beings) morons, so the Snakes are obviously not human beings or THEY would also be morons. So if they are not human beings, what are THEY? That will be revealed in a following chapter. I say it is time "We the People" remove The Snakes from government, chase them back to the hell from which they came and take back our homes, our government and reinstate our Constitution. Then and only then do I believe we have the right to ask, GOD BLESS AMERICA, and "We the People" better hope he does, because that is the only real Safety and Security.

BY REMAINING SILENT THE SILENT MAJORITY
Surrendered freedom of the press for smut
Surrendered the Constitution to oppressors
Surrendered the "Bill of Rights" to tyranny
Surrendered Oregon and America to tyrants
Surrendered freedom of religion to persecution
Surrendered human witnesses for a video camera
Surrendered human rights to animal species rights
Surrendered freedom of speech for permitted speech
Surrendered the right to petition for the right to plead
Surrendered its defense and weapons to the oppressors
Surrendered the right to vote for the right to be ignored
Surrendered their children to indoctrination and sex abuse
Surrendered property to thieves masquerading as bureaucrats
Surrendered the right to an impartial jury trial to a trial by a persecutor
Surrendered just, equitable, and humane for excessive, cruel and unusual
Surrendered to a system that enslaves
Surrendered to a self created hell
Surrendered to the Antichrist

(Do you see the crack in the bell?)

CHAPTER 12

THE "PARTISAN SYSTEM" EXPOSED

In previous chapters I explained the *Evil One* methodology, the tools used, the templates, provided examples, exposed the Evil One's system for what it is and what I believe has resulted from the Christian silent majority remaining silent and uninvolved concerning the *Evil One's* system. I even provided oral arguments in an actual court case. I have also provided evidence about what I maintain using interpretations in THEIR own law and standard dictionaries, and using *The Bible*.

I will provide more evidence about the *Evil One's* political system about which I have written and what it practices in order to enslave human beings. Since what I learned was from the Oregon and Jackson County political system, again, that is what I will use. A book called *Votescam* attempted to reveal the same about the Florida political system over 20 years ago. Compare these things with what is going on nation wide, I believe you will find the same unconstitutional system being practiced everywhere. I definitely recommend everyone reading the book *Votescam*. I wish I had read it before going through the experiences encountered the past several years.

ARTICLES FROM THE OREGON CONSTITUTION
Article 1, Section 1. Natural rights inherent in people. We declare that all men, when they form a social compact are equal in right: that all power is inherent in the people, and all free governments are founded on their authority, and instituted for their peace, safety, and happiness; and they have at all times a right to alter, reform or abolish the government in such manner as they may think proper.

Article 1, Section 33. Enumeration of rights not exclusive. This enumeration of rights, and privileges shall not be construed to impair or deny others retained by the people.

Article 1, Section 20. Equality of privileges and immunities of citizens. No law shall be passed granting to any citizen or class of citizens privileges, or immunities, which, upon the same terms, shall not equally belong to all citizens.

Article II, Section 1. Elections free. All elections shall be free and equal.

Article II, Section 7. Bribery at elections. Every person shall be disqualified from holding office, during the term for which he may have been elected, who shall have given or offered a bribe, threat, or reward to procure his election.

HOME RULE CHARTER OF JACKSON COUNTY, OREGON

Chapter III Section 9. Board of County Commissioner. The governing body of the County is the Board of three County Commissioners, *who shall be nominated and elected from the County at large.*

Chapter V, Section 20 (1). The elective administrative officers of the County shall include, in addition to the County Commissioners, the Sheriff, the Assessor, the Clerk, and the Surveyor.

Chapter VI, Section 21. Qualifications (1) An elective officer of the County: (a) Shall be a legal voter of the State, and (b) Shall have resided in the County one year immediately before assuming office.

Chapter VII, Section 26. Nomination and election of County Officers. The nomination and election of candidates for *elective County offices* shall be in the manner now or hereafter prescribed by the laws of the State for *nominating and electing county officers in general.*

FROM OREGON ELECTION LAW

Oregon Revised Statute 249.056 Filing fees. (1) At the time of filing a declaration of candidacy a candidate for the following offices shall pay to the officer with whom the declaration is filed the following fee:

(a) United States Senator $150.

(b) Governor, Secretary of State, State Treasurer, Attorney General, Commissioner of the Bureau of Labor and Industries, Superintendent of Public Instruction, Representative in Congress, judge of the Supreme Court, Court of Appeals, or Oregon Tax Court, or executive officer or auditor of a metropolitan service district, $100.

(c) County office, district attorney or circuit court judge, $50.

(d) State Senator or Representative or councilor of a metropolitan service district under ORS chapter 268. $25

(2) No filing fee shall be required of person filing a declaration of

candidacy for precinct committee person or justice of the peace.

In the County Candidates Manual, there are different filing requirements for different candidates. Major Party Candidates may declare their candidacy and get on the ballot by filing two forms. All other candidates must gather signatures. At least that is what they are told when filing. These other candidates are told to fill out different forms and provide different information. They are told to jump through hoops more difficult than Major Party Candidates and are told they cannot declare their candidacy the same as major party candidates.

Legal definitions as interpreted from definitions provided in Black's Law dictionaries.

OFFICE is a *privilege or immunity* and *financial legal obligation* to make use of a public *charitable trust* that has been created to benefit a specific charity or the general public.

PUBLIC means it is *open to all* in a state, nation or whole community and is common among many and open to common use. *Belonging to the people in general* and *not limited or restricted to any particular class in the community.*

PUBLIC OFFICE—the *right authority*; and *duty* created and bestowed by law, that for a time either fixed by law or *lasting at the preference by the creating power*, an individual is endowed with some part in the governments ruling functions *for the public benefit*.

COUNTY OFFICE—*Public office* to be filled by the people entitled to vote in the entire county.

STATE OFFICE—*Public office* to be filled by the people entitled to vote in the entire state.

PARTISAN is a supporter in a specific party or cause and is *opposed to the public interest at large*.

PARTISAN OFFICE—No definition found.

Using the definitions for partisan and office, observing those placed in partisan offices and their actions, the following is how I interpret a Partisan office:

Partisan Office is a supporter in a specific party or cause and a member in a light troop detachment or guerrilla band. The supporter is placed in a public *charitable trust* that has been created to benefit or aid the members organization operating within enemy lines, and to finance attacks harassing the enemy and is opposed to the public interest at large.

NON-PARTISAN—No definition found

The way I interpret non-partisan is the general public which are those that are considered the opposition (enemy) by the partisans.

NON-PARTISAN OFFICE—No definition found

Deciphering the definitions for the words partisan, office, and non, the following definition is provided for non-partisan office:

Non-partisan office is a person from the general public that may or may not be a partisan member, although closely associated with and *manipulated through deception* by the partisans, and placed in a less influential charitable trust position to benefit the partisan's cause financially and provide aid.

PRIVILEGE—An individual and special benefit or advantage enjoyed by a person, company, or class beyond the common advantage granted other citizens and is considered an exceptional or extraordinary power or exemption. It provides the ability to take steps opposite another individual's legal right and prevents that individual from having legal redress resulting from the consequences that act creates.

Recall that earlier FREE meant not being subjected to *legal constraints* (limitations, safety checks, control, etc.) put into place by another. Note, this gives the impression that THEY provide the freedom and can subject that freedom to legal constraints if they wish hence, *manipulation through deception*. Freedom is God-given and it is HE that makes human beings free.

PUBLIC RIGHT is a *right belonging to all citizens* and is usually *implemented by a public office or a political group*. If you notice a public office or political group implements a public right, which subtly gives the illusion again that THEY create rights. It is *manipulation through deception*.

POLITICAL RIGHT is to participate, directly or indirectly, in establishing and administrating government, and as a citizen to vote, hold public office and to petition. These are not political rights, these are God-given rights guaranteed in the Constitution and according to Christian teachings, God sets up governments among men. Interpreting legal definitions, THEY, *the Evil One* want to provide the illusion that THEY provide the rights and that THEY set up the governments not God. More *manipulation through deception*.

EQUAL defined legally means everything is the same, i.e., same rules, same basic uniforms, same playing field, same privileges and rights, *for those with like experience, importance, price, degree, or privileges*. The words "equal" used in laws is a duality and using one thing as the measure for another, and not individual character. For example, political offices are only for those who have gone through the *same or similar process politically*, that being from or associated with a family involved in politics. They must be important to some degree either through their own merit or a family member's merit which will determine the office they are allowed to hold and the price they are paid. They will be entitled to the same privileges/rights as the others that hold that same or like offices. According to the *legal* definition, equal has nothing to do with identity, i.e. a person's character or individuality, such as everyone one being born with the same God-given rights. More *manipulation through deception*.

OREGON ELECTION LAW DEFINITIONS ORS 249.002

(7) "Non-partisan office" means the office of judge, Superintendent of Public Instruction, Commissioner of the Bureau of Labor and Industries, any elected office of a metropolitan service district under ORS Chapter 268, justice of the peace, county clerk, county assessor, county surveyor, county treasurer, sheriff, district attorney or any office designated nonpartisan by a home rule charter.

(9) "Public office" means any national state, county, city or district office or position, except a political party office, filled by the electors.

OREGON COUNTY CANDIDATE'S MANUAL DEFINITIONS

COUNTY OFFICES- The *elected public offices* of an area of land which has been designated by the state as a county and which may be voted on only by the registered voters of the office's electoral district. *County offices generally include County Commissioners, a County Assessor, a County Clerk, a County Sheriff, a County Surveyor and a County Treasurer.*

NON-PARTISAN OFFICE—An office for which the candidate does not run under the name of any political party. Non partisan offices include: Judge (Supreme Court, Court of Appeals, Tax Court and Circuit Court), Superintendent of Public Instruction, Commissioner of the Bureau of Labor and Industries, any elected office of a metropolitan service district under ORS chapter 268, Justice of the Peace, Sheriff, County Clerk, County Treasurer, County Assessor, County Surveyor, District Attorney and all city district offices. (The nonpartisan offices may vary depending upon a county or city charter and ordinance requirements or a districts statutory requirements. Contact the appropriate elections official for further clarification.

PARTISAN OFFICE—An office for which the candidate runs under a political party affiliation.

Following are 10 questions pertaining to the Oregon Election Process.

Using the information provided, you decide if the election process in Oregon and Jackson County is Constitutional, free, and equal, as you understand the terms. Feel free to look up the definitions in any dictionary. Please remember to compare what you read with what is really going on and

YOU BE THE JUDGE

Comparing the legal definitions in Black's Law Dictionary, or any other dictionary, as you interpret the definitions, and the U.S. and Oregon Constitutions and the County Charter information, do you believe:

(1) Any *public office* can truthfully be considered a *partisan office*?

(2) Did you know that in Jackson County, any public office that is not listed as "non-partisan" in ORS 249.002 (7) is *"assumed"* to be a partisan office?

(3) Did you notice that the *"partisan office" and "non-partisan office" definitions* in the County Candidates manual and the Oregon revised statutes *are fabricated and do nothing more than dictate which offices are "non partisan."*

(4) With the information you have been provided, do you think it Constitutional that any *elected public office* is to be considered a *partisan office or non-partisan office?*

(5) With the information you have been provided do you believe the candidate filing fees are constitutional?

(6) According to the information that was provided from the Jackson County Charter do you think that the County Commissioners offices in Jackson County are "partisan offices?

(7) Can anyone recall voting on a measure that designated any Jackson County elected office as being "partisan"? The answer to the question is no. It was never put up for a vote. When I challenged the County Clerk's office to provide information proving that the people voted on this, the information could not be provided.

(8) If the people did not vote on this, then for what purpose is this being allowed in the Election process in Jackson County and Oregon?

(9) Considering the facts presented, do you believe the Oregon Election Law to be Constitutional?

(10) For what purposes do you believe that all "public offices" in Jackson County and Oregon have been designated either "partisan" or "non partisan" by the legislature in the Oregon Election Law?

If you answered the same as I did, you now realize why there is not a better candidate selection from which to choose during elections. You now realize why you must always choose between the lesser of two evils. People are being prevented equal access to the ballot. The ballot is controlled by the *Evil One's* party system claiming to be two parties and they make it as difficult as they can for other candidates to get on the ballot. Some candidates are told they have to gather signatures for "permission" to be a candidate. The candidate must even obtain "permission" to gather the signatures from the County Clerk. Major Party candidates are not required to gather signatures, the signatures are supposedly "guaranteed" by the Major party.

Constitutionally, people do not need permission to offer themselves for service in a public office. The permission comes from the people's vote, if that vote was counted. The election process in Jackson County and Oregon is nothing more than schoolyard bullies using intimidation, lies, and fear to control the other kids in the schoolyard. They will continue to bully, take people's money and win any games played because they make the rules and change the rules as the games are played.

Persons that do not belong to a Major Political Party and do not meet the criteria for the *legal definition for the word "equal"* are prevented from having their name placed on the election ballot for "public offices." Such offices include President, Governor, State Senator, State Representative, U.S. Representative, U.S. Senator, Secretary of State, County Commissioner, etc. Those who try are told to go through a different filing process and requirements that are more difficult than the Major Party candidates who simply declare their candidacy, file two forms, and pay a filing fee (very small bribe). The non-party candidates that may be permitted on the ballot will certainly lose, because the vote is also fixed. If the major parties do not want you on the ballot, you will not be on the ballot. If by chance you are permitted on the ballot, they will fix the vote so you will lose. If you win, you will never know it because the major parties control the vote count. There is an aphorism *"those who rule make the rules, and those who make the rules, rule."* That is exactly the system in place today, and "We the People" are not permitted to participate.

When choosing between the lesser of two evils, you are still choosing evil. Catch 22 anyone.

It is readily apparent the "fix is in." The entire election process is an illusion, a trick, a joke, a con, a scam, a show put on to entertain the *Evil One* and to dupe ""We the People" into believing "We the People" have a voice in government. "We the People" have a voice in NOTHING AND ARE A SLAVE TO THE SCHOOLYARD BULLY CALLED:

CLIQUSYSOREPUBOCRAT (Clique system of Republicans and Democrats) which is actually controlled by the *Evil One*. The irony is, we pay for it in more ways than you can imagine.

THE OATH OF OFFICE

In Oregon election law, for what purpose is any public office defined as a partisan office if not for the purpose to keep those in the general public from becoming a candidate for that office?

My answer: It is for that purpose and other purposes which are to be revealed. Read on.

Did the general public in Jackson County or Oregon vote on making elected public offices partisan offices in Jackson County or Oregon?

My answer: No!

Do you think that it constitutional that public offices be considered partisan offices by those in authority?

My Answer: No!

By doing these things, those in the general public are prevented from becoming candidates for public office unless they join "The Clique Party" because there are no public offices, according to state election law definitions.

So, by definition, if the elected offices are partisan offices, whom do you think the elected representatives will be concerned about representing?

My answer: The Clique *(Evil One)*

A Candidate may be a partisan when offering himself/herself for public service in a public office. Constitutionally, the public office cannot be considered a partisan office and still be a public office.

The most valued, precious, basic element in our entire government system was the vote. The vote WAS "guaranteed" and protected" under our Constitution. Most people are convinced our vote is no longer utilized to elect our representatives, but that the representatives are "appointed" by a Clique. For what purpose then is it required the elected representatives take the following oath:

I, (name), do solemnly swear, or affirm, that I will support the Constitution of the United States, and the Constitution of the State of Oregon, and that I will faithfully discharge the duties of (office name) according to the best of my ability.

It is obvious from the actions by most "representatives" they have no intentions to support the Constitutions. How can anyone support that which they either do not understand or blatantly ignore? Most representatives uphold the "Rule of Law," or pretend to uphold the law. Law makes legal. *As interpreted and understood from the definitions provided in* Blacks's Law Dictionary 6th Edition:

PARTISAN is an activist in a specific party or cause and is *opposed to the public interest at large.*

PUBLIC means it is common among many and *open to all* in a state, nation or whole community and open to common use. *Belonging to the people in general* and *not limited or restricted to any particular class in the community.*

CONSTITUTION *is the written* or unwritten natural and most important law in a nation or state that establishes the moral fiber and design for its government and arranging the basic principles to which its internal soul is to conform. It is to be used for organizing the government, regulating, distributing, and limiting the functions for its different departments, and prescribing the extent and manner to implement the powers necessary to accomplish lawful ends and purposes for government.

CONSTITUTIONAL is in harmony with the constitution, allowed by the constitution and is not in opposition to any condition in the constitution or fundamental law in the nation allowed under the constitution.

DISCHARGE in a generic or literal sense means to free, to let go, cancel, relieve or ease, disencumber; release, remove the load from a person or a duty and to extinguish the persons obligation to that duty.

SWEAR is to take an oath and that you are bound live up to that oath.

OATH is a pledge or promise made by a person in other's presence and is made under an immediate or direct sense as being *a responsibility to God.*

SUPPORT means to provide for financial resources or income in order to preserve and defend the nation so that nation can survive and provide a process by which to continue defending and preserving and to provide the people in the nation help through representation.

LEGAL means according to or conforming to the law *as opposed to equity.*

Flexible Constitution is a constitution that is not clear or in a written document and cannot be distinguished from any other law in the way its terms can be legislatively changed, enhanced, or altered. The British constitution is of this type.

Rigid Constitution is *a written instrument representing the fundamental law in a nation and is a living document which provisions (conditions) cannot be changed, altered or enhanced by ordinary legislative process, and can only be altered, enhanced or changed with special and separate approval. The U.S. Constitution, which cannot be changed without the consent from three-fourths majority in the state legislatures or through a constitutional convention, is this type.*

OATH OF OFFICE is a pledge or promise made by a person in other's presence and is made under a direct sense as being a *responsibility to God* by persons who are about to enter upon the duties of a public office and concerning their performance while in that office.

Look at the definitions for legal and partisan. Synonyms for equity are: fairness, justice, fairplay, impartiality, etc. Legal is opposed to these things, by definition. Partisan is opposed to the public interest at large, by definition. Need I say more?

As can be interpreted from the definitions for legal and constitutional, *legal does not necessarily characterize CONSTITUTIONAL. There is a huge difference between "Rule of Law" and "Rule of Constitutional Law."*

Our "elected" (and I use the term elected with much skepticism) representatives are allegedly in office to ensure that the people's Constitutional rights are not denied or violated with the laws passed and that any laws passed are within Constitutional boundaries. The Oath of Office is the promise to do that.

When the duties of an office become such that these duties cause an unnecessary government imposition or burden on the people and violate the Constitution, the person holding the office is sworn to do everything within their ability to *discharge (ease or cancel) the duties that office implements*. They are sworn to bring the duties performed by that office back under the constitutional umbrella, i.e. in line with the constitution. And it matters not if the burden is financial such as taxes, or unjust, arbitrary law.

It is imperative that representatives have the ability to read, understand, and interpret the constitutions to which they have sworn an oath to support. Our founding fathers wrote the documents as a guideline for self-government. Our founding fathers freed themselves from a corrupt, unjust system in which those who ruled were tyrants and in which nepotism and favoritism throughout the system were the norm. The founders wrote a Constitution that made it clear the powers the government has and the restrictions put on that government. The Bill of Rights restricts what the government can or cannot do, restricts what laws can or cannot be passed and put other restrictions on the government to keep the government from abusing and oppressing the people. The Bill of Rights states certain rights that the government shall not pass any laws with regards to denying the people. It protects the people.

Yet, each day, on the City, County, State, and Federal level, these representatives "of the people" pass laws that trample the people's God-given rights guaranteed in the constitutions they have sworn an oath to support. Each day, these representatives ignore the Bill of Rights and pass laws that deny or take the rights that are "guaranteed" in the Constitutions as untouchable. Each day the Bill of Rights comes under attack from the very representatives that are "sworn" to support those rights, and each day the representatives' yield rights belonging to all the people to the Rule of Law.

A written law makes something legal, but legal does not necessarily embody constitutional. It is clear from the laws and ordinances regularly passed that the County and State Representatives sworn oath to support the Constitutions is a false promise. Oregon lawmakers redefined what were once "public offices" as "partisan offices." How can any public office be considered a partisan office and for what purposes was this done in Oregon election law? ANSWER: *Redefining most public offices as partisan offices in State election law provided the means to circumvent the constitution intent, i.e., a representative government of the people. It is also legality, by law and by definition, that releases those who take the Oath of Office from all responsibility to live up to the oath.*

An Oath of Office is Constitutionally required for those entering *public office*. Redefining public offices as partisan offices in State election law circumvented the Constitutions intent and made the elections under the Rule of Law, *legally* unconstitutional, easier to dominate and made the Oath of Office a mockery. Legally, in Oregon, according to the "Rule of Law" it is no longer required for the "representatives" to live up to the Oath of Office or support the Constitutions. Legally, under the Rule of Law, their "promise made under a direct sense of responsibility to God," does not mean to the public, only to the *Evil One*.

By redefining public offices as partisan offices, the *Evil One* made it easy to deprive people their God-given and Constitutional protect rights. Since the office is now "defined" as partisan, it cannot be a public office. The Oath taken is for a *public office*. The office the *appointee* is accepting is a *partisan office*. Now you know why they do not live up to the sworn oath and continue to ignore the Constitutions. Do you understand? Do you see the *manipulation through deception*?

The *Evil One* controls the elections and *appoints the "elected representatives" and "judges."* The *Evil One* appointed representatives pass unconstitutional laws, and the *Evil One* appointed Judges uphold those unconstitutional laws. This is known as the "Rule of Law." The people that do realize what is happening and attempt exercising their Constitutional rights soon discover it is too late. Suing for those rights in the courts is useless because the Judges ignore the Constitutions and make decisions based on the laws the *Evil One* instituted and not the Constitutions. It was designed in the U.S. Constitution that all laws instituted in this nation are to be Constitutional yet this is not being accomplished. Considering that the representatives are appointed and not elected, are not responsible to the people, and these appointed individuals pass tax laws and "authorize" hired employees to institute taxes disguised as fees, we now have TAXATION WITHOUT REPRESENTATION. *The system in Oregon has reverted to the old British common law and resulting tyranny; the very system our founding fathers fought a revolution against in order to be free. I will almost guarantee the same has happened in every state.*

Government's purpose is to govern with justice, protect and serve? I have seen no justice and little protection for our GOD given and Constitutional guaranteed rights. We pay extra fees (taxes) for services that we have already paid for with property, income, and other hidden taxes. If you want a copy, pay a fee (tax). Want to file a complaint, pay a fee (tax). Want to build a home, pay a fee (tax). Want to start a business, pay a fee (tax), want an education for your children, pay a fee (tax), want to vote, buy a stamp. I notice any service a business, group, or individual wants from our city, county, or state government a "fee" (tax) is collected for that service. Exactly what do the tax dollars taken as property taxes, income taxes, etc. pay for and to what use are these additional tax (fee) dollars used? From what I have experienced and observed, the people are not being served. Those "allegedly" elected to represent actually dictate people's lives, and "We the People" are paying THEM to accomplish that feat.

The first ten Amendments to the Constitution, known as the Bill of Rights, were ratified on December 15, 1791, 8 years after the Revolutionary war ended. The Bill of Rights is the insurance policy, the guarantee that government cannot and will not oppress the people. The oath sworn by the "elected" representatives is their promise they will support (defend, uphold) that guarantee. Those who will swear an oath then knowingly refuse to live up to that oath obviously feel no responsibility to those they are supposed to represent, have no respect for the constitutions they swore the oath to support, have no honor, are treacherous, treasonous, perjurers, and are traitors. *But these traitors are protected by the unconstitutional "Rule of Law." And most do not even know that they are doing these things because the Evil One manipulates all human beings through deception.*

You have been informed the evidence IS your vote is being ignored/denied and that the representatives are appointed and are not elected. As you listen to the candidates and their false promises during elections, ask yourself which candidates will truly support the Constitutions with their Bill of Rights. Question them about the Bill of Rights and have them explain what it means and see if they interpret it the same as you. Ask them to explain the 9th Amendment. Ask them if they think it Constitutional under the 7th, 8th, or 9th Amendments that a disabled man be removed from his home by force, his property sold for back taxes, and the money above what was owed in taxes be kept by the government as a "windfall." Ask them if they think it Constitutional under the 5th or 9th Amendments that a person's property is taken by the government for any reason without just compensation. Ask them if they think it Constitutional under the 4th and 9th Amendments that any government official be permitted to search private property, locked or unlocked, without a search warrant. Ask them if they think it Constitutional under the 7th Amendment for a person to be denied a jury trial in a civil case involving 10 billion, 240 million dollars and in which a trial by jury was demanded. Ask them if they think it Constitutional under the 4th and 9th Amendments that School District bus drivers be used to report to county officials private properties on school bus routes that have sheds, buildings, trailers etc, that might house persons unknown to the county. Ask them if they think the excessive traffic fines now being imposed in Oregon are Constitutional under the 8th and 9th Amendments.

Ask them if they think an unarmed man's 5th and 9th Amendment rights were violated when he was shot 23 times and killed on December 28, 1999, by Medford police officers. Medford Police Officers who were directed by their dispatcher not to go to the scene at the Central Point, Oregon, State Police station. Ask them if they think it Constitutional under the 1st and 9th Amendments the local ordinances passed restricting petitioners from gathering signatures in public places such as malls, shopping centers, etc. Ask them if they think it Constitutional under the 1st and 9th Amendments that ridiculous time restrictions (3 minutes) be placed on individuals speaking at public meetings. Ask them if they think it Constitutional under the 1st Amendment the restrictions put on the people in the county to petition. Ask them if they think it Constitutional under the 14th Amendment that different standards are required for candidates that are not major party candidates, standards that favor major party candidates. Ask them when was the last time they read the Bill of Rights in the U.S. and state Constitution. Ask them what the Oath of Office means.

How many tried to evade, side step, or ignore the questions with ramblings or explanations that said or meant absolutely nothing and did not address the questions? How many fell back to the "Rule of Law" safety position?

Most candidates have not read the Bill of Rights, let alone the Constitutions. How can one support that which one has not read, blatantly ignores, and let others do the interpretation for them? By permitting your vote to be denied, you are surrendering to the tyrants? Are you going to continue to go along with the illusion, the ruse, the scams being passed off as elections? Or are you going to make sure that for this election, and future elections, the people's vote is truly counted and utilized to choose those who will represent the people? That choice is yours. Without the vote, "We the People" truly have no choices, have no voice in the government and its actions, have taxation without representation, and will be ruled through tyranny. Those are facts that cannot be refuted.

CHAPTER 13

THE REVEALING!
CHRISTIAN, DO YOU TRULY BELIEVE?

Over 200 years ago, Goethe said, "None are more hopelessly enslaved than those who falsely believe they are free."

FREEDOM is GOD given and the price for that freedom was for paid in blood, on a cross. To KEEP that freedom from being denied, there is also a price, and that price has been, and will always be, paid in blood.

How many times have you heard "THEY" do this, or "THEY" do that, "THEY" etc., etc., etc.? I have even used "THEY" throughout this book. "Who are THEY"? When asked to identify THEY, all one can do is say, those in control and running things, "You know, THEY"? Who is this *Evil One* that is so elusive and cannot readily be identified. I am going to reveal who "THEY" are, and most will not believe. Many will call me insane. The choice to believe or not believe is yours. Whatever label you decide to put on me is also your choice. I reveal only what I have discovered. What you do with the information is entirely up to you.

Three years ago, I would not have believed what has already been revealed in the previous chapters. Three years ago, I definitely would not have believed what is about to be revealed to you in this chapter. In fact I would have labeled anyone telling me what I have told you and what I am about to tell you, crazy, nuts, weird, insane, etc. Yet, all one has to do is look, listen, and see what is going on around them and the entire world appears insane and that the inmates are running the asylum. *But those truly running the asylum use the three templates and the tools already presented to manipulate the inmates into doing insane acts.*

Many Christian people (human beings) profess to literally believe *The Bible*. Many do not. Human beings interpret *The Bible* differently. Christians are also told to believe that there is symbolism (imaginary, representation) throughout *The Bible* and that it is saying something other than what it is saying. I believed that same way for over 55 years. Today, I believe somewhat differently. Today, I am convinced that *The Bible* means exactly what it says, literally. There is no symbolism in *The Bible*. The people who wrote the books in *The Bible* over several thousand years were revealing exactly what they experienced and observed. They passed that information from generation to generation. So, which is it? Are Christian human beings to accept the literal meaning or the symbolized/represented meaning that we are taught and are supposed to accept? A college professor that teaches law and that I was in email contact with for approximately 18 months kept telling me not to take the literal meaning about everything I read, especially *The Bible*.

How many times have you been told "do not take things so literally"? For what purpose are we told, "do not take everything so literally"? Do you say what you mean and mean what you say? Do you write what you mean, or do you write with hidden meanings? Do you write in code so that those with whom you are trying to communicate do not understand what you are really saying? Do you talk in a code so that others cannot understand what you say unless they know the code, or do you write and say what you mean? I don't communicate in code. I say and write what I mean. Do you?

People can interpret differently what one may say or write than what was actually intended. That may be deliberate or may be misinterpretation. In a case where one is misinterpreted, an explanation for clarification can be provided, if the person doing the misinterpretation is really interested in the truth and will accept that explanation. Those that believe what they want to believe will not accept an explanation.

Only those with something to hide create secret organizations. Only those with something to hide write in code. Only those with something to hide speak in code. Only those with something to hide use symbolism to communicate and to hide what they really represent. Only those with something to hide meet and discuss things in secret. *What do THEY hide?*

That will be revealed to you in this chapter if you truly believe that God's Word is to be taken literally. If you do not truly believe that Gods Word is to be taken literally, then you will in all likelihood label me a completely insane person. You will not believe. You will continue to be a slave in THEIR system. That choice is entirely up to you.

Sometimes we can say and write things that are "perceived" incorrectly by others, and those perceptions are in total disagreement with what was intended by our remarks. That is because human beings are *taught to think critically and to be judgmental* and to look for faults in what others say, write and do. Take a college course in "Public Speaking" and you will find this to be true. The first thing students are instructed to do is to evaluate others when everyone gives their first 2 minute speech. Students are instructed to look for several "faults" with the persons speaking and their mannerisms and several things they do properly (as taught in the book or by the professor).

We *are taught Perception is the Truth.* We *are taught to distrust* each other and to twist and distort what is said. We *are taught to keep our mouths shut* in fear that what we say may offend someone and be twisted and distorted into something we did not say. We *are taught not to write about what we really think* because it might offend someone and be twisted and distorted to mean something other than what we truly meant. *We are taught to gossip* behind people's back so they won't know how we really feel about them because we might offend them. *We are taught to take offense* at certain things people may say to us. *We are taught to be intimidated and afraid*, and soon everything can frighten us. We are taught to be skeptical about each other and to be offended by the truth. *We are taught these things so we will learn not to question* what is going on around us, what is truly happening, and not to take things literally.

There are those among us who do write in code, who do talk in code, and everything THEY say and write accomplishes the complete opposite what THEY *claim is intended*. Human beings are taught not to take things literally in order to deceive and fool them, and *manipulate them through deception*. Human beings are taught these things because *the Evil One* do not want human beings to take things literally and know that the *Evil One's* intentions are to do exactly as they write, which is to keep human beings enslaved. Confusing, you bet it is.

That is what these other beings intend to do, confuse and deceive human beings, in order to *manipulate human being through that deception*, the same as they did at the beginning in the Garden of Eden. It is the greatest con (sting) going.

For example, a Legislature writes a law. The Law reads that it will deny a right and oppress the people, but those writing the law say that is not so, that is not the laws intent. Because human beings have been *taught* and have been *manipulated through deception* into believing that things do not really mean what they state, people are convinced the law as written does not say what it says and will not do what the law states. People are told the law will not deny a right or oppress the people. After the law is passed, it is administered exactly as it is written and accomplishes exactly what the law states. It denies a right and oppresses the people.

But, people say, that was not the law's intent. It was intended to do something else. Was it? People were *told* that was not the intent. People were *told* it would not deny a right and oppress the people. People were *manipulated through deception* into believing it said something other than what it was saying. People were *told* the law would not do as it stated, just like the serpent in Eden told Eve that God's law did not mean what it said concerning eating the fruit from a certain tree. What was it God told Adam and Eve according to Genesis 3:3? *"But from the fruit of the tree which is in the middle of the garden, God has said, 'You shall not eat from it or touch it, or you will die.'"* Do people die? Yes they do. Eve was *manipulated through deception* because the serpent told her she wouldn't die, that the law would not do as it said. People are *manipulated through deception* with a bombardment from the news media, talk radio and TV, letters to the editor, editorials, news article and releases, etc. People are confused and in shock by the time it rolls around to vote or for the legislature to vote on a law. The message is in people's head, this law will not do what it says.

But people learned differently after the law passed because, as administered, the law did exactly as it stated. Now, for the real kicker, these other beings that write, interpret and administer the law have written it so it can be twisted and distorted in such a way that it does or does not apply to them as the need may arise. These other beings control the system at all levels and in the courts, and now do as THEY please while interpreting the law in their favor and against human beings. The human beings really have no say, no choice. Or do we? We know the truth because we are born with it in us and is gut instinct. What we have to do is listen. We let ourselves be *manipulated through deception* because *we want to believe what we are being told*, although we know what we are being told is not the truth.

In *The Bible* it states exactly what it means, what has happened, what is happening, and tells us what is going to happen if we will only accept what it is saying. There is no code, there is no hidden meaning, there is no symbolism in *The Bible*, but people are *manipulated through deception* into believing it has another intent, that there is a hidden meaning, that there is symbolism, that there is a code. People spend time, effort and money into seeking a code in *The Bible* that does not exist. *The Bible* is a book that provides mankind's (human beings) history, past, present and future. Yet, it is important to ask God for guidance in determining what is truth and what is deception within its pages. Remember that earlier I stated that I believe the

Evil One has been allowed to "enhance" *The Bible*. God's word, His spirit, His meanings in the law stays the same, but it is important to ask for guidance to learn the TRUTH from the illusions/deceptions implanted throughout the millenniums about *The Bible* by the Evil One.

Some will say this is blasphemy, that God's Word cannot be changed. *The Bible* is published and written by humans. Each version is different than the others. Books have been added and deleted by humans. The Evil one *manipulates all human beings through deception*. Remember that the Evil One is skilled in using semantics to deceive. Gods Word, His promise, His spirit, His Law has not changed. Do not confuse the term God's Word with the term God's Words. *The Bible* is not *God's Words* because the words in *The Bible* are changed all the time. Compare the different Bible versions if you do not believe me and see the evidence for yourself. God's promise, His spirit and His meanings in the law in *The Bible* cannot be changed. Do not let the Evil One deceive you. Ask God for guidance when reading *The Bible* to discern the truth from the deceptions, and it will be revealed.

There are among us *other beings* that are determined to conquer mankind and possess mankind's souls. I have heard it said, *"behind every myth there is a truth"* or *"inside every myth there is a hidden truth?"* Well how about this for a new aphorism, *" the myth is actually the truth disguised to make it appear a myth."* How can this be you ask? Another aphorism I have heard explains it. *"Sometimes the best disguise is no disguise at all."*

There is a battle going on in this world between good and evil. These other beings, the Clique, the *Evil One* is tyrannical and the goal is to keep mankind (human beings) enslaved and posses mankind's souls. Since the *Evil One leadership* likes to develop profiles to identify human "criminals" I developed the following profile so that the people can identify the *Evil One leadership*. I encourage everyone to accept its literal meaning as written and *do not read between the lines or, look for symbolism, nor give it a different interpretation*. It says exactly what I want it to say:

EVIL ONE LEADERSHIP PROFILE

They meet and hide in secret places throughout the world where they make their diabolical plans to cause hate and destruction throughout the world.

They have set themselves up as world leaders.

They allow only those within their bloodlines or those human beings they can control as leaders.

They have created such things as Banking, Stock Markets, Real Estate

Markets, Marketing, Loan Institutions, Credit Card Institutions, and other institutions to financially enslave the people.

They are pushing for the New World Order, the one world government, one world bank, one world currency, one world religion, one world everything.

They established a special education system for their children and created the public education system to indoctrinate you and your children.

They set up a completely different medical system for themselves and their children.

They allow only their children and a few specially selected human children they can control into their institutions for "higher learning." (Yale, Harvard, Princeton, Oxford, and other "Elite" universities)

They form secret organizations and societies among themselves and allow only off spring or those that they can control into those secret organizations and societies.

They establish organizations such as the United Nations, NATO, SEATO, etc., to control nations.

They create wars among nations.

They create weapons for mass destruction such as nuclear weapons, biological weapons such as anthrax, and chemical weapons such as nerve gas.

They control the news media and manipulate the people with their propaganda.

They will turn on and devour their own kind.

THEY are Godless, Ruthless, Egocentric, Exploitative, Deceitful, vipers, snakes in the grass, lizards hiding in their holes and their GREED knows no limits. They try to devour all with which they come into contact.

These beings posing as *human leaders* are *ian*, as in Reptilian. The suffix ian is one that is or relating to something. Example: A lizard is having or resembling reptile characteristics and is related to reptiles.

What! You are probably asking yourself at this point. Are you nuts, you are probably asking about me? Well, I am not crazy. If you literally believe *The Bible*, then literally, *THEY are identified as Reptilian in The Bible:*

In *Matthew, Chapter 12:34* Jesus Christ identified them as Reptilian when he said, *"You brood of vipers, how can you, being evil, speak what is good?*

In *Matthew, Chapter 23*: 33-36 Jesus Christ again identified them as Reptilian when he said *"You serpents, you brood of vipers, how will you* escape the sentence of hell? Therefore, behold, I am sending you prophets and wise men and scribes; some of them you will kill and crucify, and some of them you will scourge in your synagogues, and persecute from city to city, so that upon you may fall the guilt of all the righteous blood shed on earth, from the blood of righteous Abel to the blood of Zechariah, the son of Berechiah, whom you murdered between the temple and the alter. Truly I say to you, all these things will come upon this generation."

In Matthew, Chapter 3:7 concerning John the Baptist, *"But when he saw many of the Pharisees and Sadducees coming for baptism he said to them: 'You brood of vipers, who warned you to flee from the wrath to come? Therefore bear fruit in keeping with repentance; "*

In Isaiah 14:29, it is written, *"Do not rejoice, O Philistia, all of you, Because the rod that struck you is broken' For from the serpent's root a viper will come out, And its fruit will be a flying serpent."*

In Jeremiah 8:17 it is written, *"For Behold, I am sending serpents against you, Adders, for which there is no charm, And they will bite you"* declares the Lord."

In Deuteronomy 32:33 it is written, *"Their wine is the venom of serpents, And the deadly poison of cobras."*

In Psalms 58:3-5 it is written, *"The wicked are estranged from the womb; These who speak lies go astray from birth. They have venom like the venom of a serpent; Like a deaf cobra that stops up its ear, So that it does not hear the voice of charmers, Or a skillful caster of spells."*

In Isaiah 27:1 it is written, *"In that day the Lord will punish Leviathan the fleeing serpent, With His fierce and great and mighty sword, Even Leviathan the twisted serpent; And He will kill the dragon who lives in the sea.*

In Job 26:13 it is written, *"By His breath the heavens are cleared; His hand has pierced the fleeing serpent."*

In Luke 10:18-19 it is written, *"And he said to them, 'I was watching Satan fall from heaven like lightning. Behold, I have given you authority to tread on serpents and scorpions, and over all the power of the enemy and nothing will injure you'."*

In Genesis Chapter 3, it is the serpent that manipulated Eve through deception to sin against GOD. Adam *chose* to sin against God with Eve.

In Revelation 20:1-3 it is written, *"Then I saw an angel coming down from heaven, holding the key of the abyss and a great chain in his hands. And he laid hold of the dragon, the serpent of old, who is the Devil and Satan, and bound him for a thousand years; and he threw him into the abyss, and shut it and sealed it over him, so that he would not deceive the nations any longer, until the thousand years were completed; after these things he must be released for a short time.*

It is written in at least 8 different books in *The Bible*, written in as many different time periods, by different people, and THEY are identified as reptilian. THEY are also identified as reptilian in legends, fairy tales, and myths. THEY are identified as reptilian in American Indian historical writings found on the walls in caves, pyramids, etc. THEY have been identified over and over, yet human beings still do not believe THEY exist. Why? Because human beings are *manipulated through deception* into believing THEY exist only in childhood fairy tales. The truth has been hidden in fairy tales. Anyone believing such a thing is "labeled" crazy, a nut case, paranoid, freak, weird, etc., by those doing the manipulating. Anyone believing such a thing has to be crazy, right? Think about this, how many time have you heard it asked, "who are *THEY*," or "identify *THEY*"? How many times have you heard people say that *The Bible* is not true, that it is symbolism, or religious fairy tales?

We are *manipulated through deception* into believing there is no *THEY*, but we all know *THEY* exist. We all know within ourselves that THEY must be monsters, because no human being in their right mind would commit the atrocities that *THEY* perpetrate. We assume *THEY* are human beings who are behind those who profess to be the elected and chosen leaders, but when asked to identify "who *THEY* are," no one can really explain, because we do not know the real *THEY*. Now you do. Only *THEY* are not truly human, *THEY* only look human. *THEY* are the ones that have created this evil system, the ones behind all the atrocities, and are the ones *manipulating human being through deception, just like in the beginning, in the Garden in Eden.*

THEIR leader has many names such as Lucifer, Satan, Devil, the Great Pretender, etc. He is real, he exists, and it is his system that is presently in place. *THEY* have the ability to change into human form and walk among us although they come from a different place, a different dimension. *THEY* come from the abyss.

REPTILIAN is having or resembling reptile characteristics and being related to reptiles.

REPTILE is from the Latin word reptus, to creep, and is an animal that crawls or moves on its belly (as a snake) or on small short legs (as a lizard).

SERPENT is a poisonous creature that moves stealthily, hisses or stings such as a snake. A treacherous person is considered to be a serpent, a snake.

It is written the Devil is a serpent.

VIPER is a venomous snake. A vicious or treacherous person is called a viper.

BROOD is a group (class, family) having a common nature or origin.

ABYSS is a bottomless gulf (pit) somewhere in the cosmos (universe). I like to describe it as the "arm pit" of the universe.

TYRANT is derived from the Greek word *tyrannnos*.

LIZARD is derived from the Greek word *sauros*.

TYRANNOSAUR is derived from Greek *tyrannos* tyrant+ *sauros* lizard.

Looking at what *The Bible* said, THEY are not human. THEY are a viper's brood. They are reptiles. *I repeat Jeremiah 8:17, "For behold, I am sending serpents against you, Adders for which there is no charm, And They will bite you, declares the Lord."* Jeremiah definitely identifies them as serpents, which separates them from human beings. *Human being* is defined as mankind, the human race, (homo sapiens), primate mammal, people, etc.

THEY are further identified separately from man in Genesis 3:1 where it states *"Now the serpent was more crafty than any beast of the field which the Lord God had made."* By defining a serpent or a viper as one that can be a treacherous person, human beings are provided the illusion that those perpetrating the atrocities are actually just treacherous human beings. It is made to appear that these creatures are actually human beings so "We the People" *assume* that THEY are human. THEY are treacherous, and THEY do disguise themselves as human, but THEY are not human beings. And THEY are making *ass*es out of y*ou* and *me* utilizing *manipulation through deception*

The scientific name for these other beings, these creatures is REPTILIS TYRANNOSAUR (Reptilian Tyrant Lizard). *THEY* exist, they are real, can change to appear as human beings and *THEY* are among us, AND THEY PROFESS TO BE OUR ELECTED AND CHOSEN WORLD LEADERS. This is not science fiction, a myth, nor a fairy tale. This is as real as it gets and human beings are in a battle for our lives, our very souls. We are taught that things are not always as they appear, that we are only to believe half the things that we see, and nothing that we hear. Then we are bombarded with "Perception is the Truth."

So which is it. Which statement reflects the real truth? Are things not as they appear, or is Perception the Truth. It cannot be both.

LITERAL means according with the letter of the law and/or sticking to the facts. When one takes things literally, there is little if any exaggeration or *enhancement*.

EXAGGERATE means to extend outside the boundaries or the facts, i.e., to make a mountain out of a molehill.

EMBELLISH means to ENHANCE something to make it appear something it is not. By enhancing something it can be made to appear prettier than it actually is, such as decorating a Christmas tree and making it beautiful with decorations, rather than relying on its natural beauty. Some men and women are also notorious for this by attempting to make themselves beautiful with make up or clothes that they wear.

ENHANCE means to increase, improve, augment, add to, alter, or change.

TRUTH means sticking to the facts without lies, distortion, enhancement, embellishment, etc.

Those who do not believe in the literal meaning do not believe in the facts, do not believe in the truth and believe Perception is the Truth. The truth is made into the myth by enhancing (exaggerating or embellishing) it to the point it can no longer be believed and it becomes a myth. Disguise the truth in an unbelievable form, and bingo, the truth is a myth and won't be believed.

I stated earlier that The Bible did not contain any symbolism. I will now clarify that. *God's Word, His Truth* does not contain any symbolism or hidden meaning. *The Bible*, as written, contains symbolism through the semantics game created by the REPTILIS TYRANNOSAUR to deceive and confuse human beings from learning the truth. *God promised his Word, His Truth would not change.* Go to any bookstore and compare several *Bible*s by different publishers and they all do not have the same word use. There are many different versions and each one is worded a little different. If this is God's words, and cannot be changed, then where did all the different *Bibles* come from and which *Bible* does one choose to believe?

TRUTH = Certainty = Assurance = Pledge = PROMISE. God's Word, His Truth, *His Promise* has not changed, but is has been enhanced to disguise it and make it appear like something it is not. It has been embellished to make it appear impossible.

As an example, many question the virgin birth and claim that a virgin birth is impossible. IS the virgin birth impossible? If a woman can be impregnated today through artificial insemination, what would prevent our Creator from doing the same thing to a virgin woman He had chosen? Inseminate is defined as sow. How many times have you seen that word sow in *The Bible*?

Does a virgin woman who has been artificially inseminated remain a virgin? According to the definition for a virgin, yes. A VIRGIN is a person (man or woman) who has not had sexual intercourse. Artificial insemination is not sexual intercourse. So, why is the virgin birth so difficult for people to comprehend? Because human beings are *manipulated through deception* into believing such a thing IS impossible. If mankind can do it today, what is to prevent the Creator from doing the same?

This expanded paradigm is presented to provide human beings with the literal truth concerning *the real enemy* that human beings are combating. This enemy has formed a conspiracy (methodology, system, plan) to keep all human beings enslaved. *This enemy is not human and is identified throughout The Bible as reptilian. Using the enemy's own profiling methodology THEY are identified as reptilian. This enemy has been identified in Greek myth as reptilian, Medusas being one. This enemy has been identified in Chinese folklore with the one headed and two headed dragons, and European fairy tales with the Knights fighting the dragons, etc.* How much evidence, how much proof do human beings require?

The enemy has confused, deceived, and convinced human beings into believing it doesn't and never did exist. Then, we are *manipulated through deception* into believing such creatures existed, only THEY *tell us* it was millions and billions of years ago and that they actually ruled on the earth and were called dinosaurs. Human beings are *manipulated through deception* into believing that humans evolved from a lower life form that crawled from the ocean, developed lungs, legs, stood upright, and walked. Human beings are taught that the universe and the earth were created from nothing when a big bang occurred billions of years ago. WHERE IS THE PROOF, THE EVIDENCE? All we have is *THEIR WORD, THEIR FALSE SCIENCE, and THEY have proven themselves to be liars over and over and over, yet "We the People" still continue to believe THEIR LIES.*

Someone, anyone, please explain how anything can be created from nothing. I defy anyone to create anything from nothing. I remember in Vietnam, our team had a motto that went "We have done so much with so little for so long, that we can now do anything with nothing." I have no idea where that aphorism actually originated, but I have heard it many times. " In reality and literally, i.e. in all honesty, we all know that something cannot be created from nothing. That goes against every law in physics.

Human beings are taught to despise semantics and the reason is, semantics is the very tool that REPTILIS TYRANNOUSAUR uses in the conspiracy to enslave human beings and THEY do not want that known. Remember the aphorism, "the pen is mightier than the sword." Could this be the reason God set the ground rule that His Word, His Truth, His Promise would not be changed. In order to combat this, the enemy devised semantics to exaggerate and embellish *The Bible* in order to hide Gods Word, His Truth, i.e. His Promise?

Welcome one and all to the REPTILIAN TYRANNIES world, a world presently controlled by REPTILIS TYRANNOSAUR which is referred to in *The Bible* as Satan, Devil, wicked one, lord of death, ruler of demons, the great pretender, tempter, and the great dragon (Revelation 12:9). NOW I ASK AGAIN, CHRISTIAN, DO YOU REALLY BELIEVE?

CHAPTER 14

THE TRUTH

AWE has two entirely different meanings. Awe can mean fear or it can mean wonderment. It is the only word I know that has opposite meaning for the same word.

FEAR is a strong emotion that warns a person or animal about imminent danger. This emotion can be unpleasant and difficult to deal with. If a person learns to control their fear, it is very useful and plays a big part in their safety warning system. Unchecked, fear can cause panic and be used to control an individual or animal. Synonyms for awe: fear: terror, dread, fright, horror

REVERENCE is holding someone in such a high regard it borders on worship. Such a person is said to be *awesome*, or looked upon with *awe*. Many people in clergy and leadership positions wish to be viewed in this manner, yet very few reach that goal. Synonyms: Respect, admiration, worship, and awe. Synonyms for awe: wonder, admiration, respect, amazement.

RESPECT is considering someone in a praiseworthy manner and holding them in high esteem. Respect is earned and is not something that can be demanded. One can respect a person's position, yet abhor the person holding that position.

HATE is extreme hostility and dislike usually resulting from fear, anger, or a sense of injury, such as hypocrisy. The root cause for hate is fear.

Synonyms for hate: abhorrence, detestation, revulsion, disgust, extreme dislike, abomination, offense

Humans are taught by religion to fear God. Hate is derived from fear. Fear leads to hate.

The first commandment from God in Exodus 20:3 is *"You shall have no other gods before Me."*

In Exodus 20:5 it states, *"You shall not worship them or serve them; for I, the Lord your God, am a jealous God, visiting the iniquity of the fathers on* the children, on the third and fourth generation of those who hate Me, but showing loving kindness to thousands, to those who love Me and keep My commandments."

In Matthew 22:34-40 it states, *"But when the Pharisees heard that Jesus had silenced the Sadducees, they gathered themselves together. One of them a lawyer asked Him a question, testing Him, "Teacher, which is the greatest commandment in the Law?" And He said to him " 'You shall love the Lord your God with all your heart, and with all your soul, and with all your mind.' This is the great and foremost commandment. The second is like it, 'You shall love your neighbor as yourself.' On these two commandments depend the whole Law and the Prophets."*

Jesus is saying that there is nothing in the Law that says people are to fear God, but they are to Love God. Since fear leads to hate, then why would God want us to fear him? This appears contradictory and it is, because this is what religion teaches and not what God instructed. Satan has attempted to "change" Gods Word, through translations, rewrites, books removed from *The Bible*, and every other devious, deceitful means possible. Satan has tried to change God's commandments with religion and God will not allow that to happen. Religion is the viper's brood doctrine, not God's doctrine.

In Matthew 15:6-9 Jesus states, *"And by this you invalidated the word of God for the sake of your tradition. You hypocrites, rightly did Isaiah prophesy of you: THIS PEOPLE HONORS ME WITH THEIR LIPS, BUT THEIR HEART IS FAR AWAY FROM ME. BUT IN VAIN DO THEY WORSHIP ME, TEACHING AS DOCTRINES THE PRECEPTS OF MEN."* (Emphasis are mine)

Satan and his *Evil One*, through semantics tries to change God's Law, but cannot succeed because Gods' law is Love, and Satan cannot change love. The *Evil One* can change man's words, but God's Love cannot be removed from what God has created. That cannot be changed.

So God tells us to love him, yet religion teaches mankind to fear God. Religion is used by the Evil One to deceive mankind. Fear leads to hate. One cannot love that which one fears. God does not want mankind to come to him from fear, but from love. Love is a strong, warm feeling or affection for someone or something. Love is derived from Latin *Lub re, Lib re* which means "to please"

God created mankind in his own image and we are His children. God wants His children to please Him. Do you want your children to fear you? I don't. I want my children to love, trust, and respect me. I want my children to please me. God loves his children, so for what purpose would He want His children to fear Him? *Wanting someone to fear you results in the ability to exercise authority through tyranny.* The God I worship is not a tyrant, a REPTILIS TYRANNOSAUR, Satan.

Awe (Hate) can be gained through fear, but fear eventually leads to hate. Awe can come about from being unfair in the law's application and playing favoritism.

Awe (Love) can also come about through fair and impartial application in the law. Satan wants people to worship him because they fear him. Hate is what Satan feeds on. God wants people to worship Him because they love Him. Love is what God gives and wants to receive.

Which "AWE" do you prefer in control?

Trust and respect are earned by treating other with the same trust and respect you expect, enforcing the law firmly and fairly so that the law applies to everyone equally, and treating others the way you want to be treated. Love eventually develops from this trust and respect.

There are those who do not want you to trust and respect each other or the laws to be applied firmly and fairly. THEY have written their own laws and imposed them on mankind, on human beings (people) to replace God's law, so that their law can be twisted and distorted to favor them and their kind. THEY do not want humans to love and worship God, THEY want us to hate God and worship the REPTILIS TYRANNOSAUR, Satan. THEY teach mankind that we must fear God, which leads man to hate God. Deceiving mankind into fearing and hating God and each other is accomplished through word semantics administered through a template methodology and claiming that only by fearing God can we learn to love God. That is false, yet it is taught in almost every religion.

Hate and Love are complete opposites and cannot be derived from the same root. So if hate is derived from fear, how can love also be derived from that same root (fear)? It can't. So, which is it, does God want mankind to look upon him with the AWE such as fear and hate him, or does God want mankind to look upon him with the AWE such as respect, admiration and love and trust Him.

I believe that God wants mankind, all human beings, to trust, respect and love Him. That is what God said he wanted, that IS what Jesus Christ taught, and that IS our purpose for being. The choice IS yours. Love God and each other and end the insanity, or hate God and each other and continue allowing yourselves to be slaves to the templates that hold you on the insane path to destruction. *The choice is yours.*

MORE ACRONYMS

S SNAKES	E EVERYTHING	D DECREE
A AGAINST	V VEILED	E EVERYTHING
T THE	I IN	V VEILED
A ALMIGHTIES	L LIES	I IN
N NATION		L LIES
G GUARDIAN	G GUARDIAN	C COMMON
O OVER	O OVER	H HUMANS
D DECEIVED	O OPPRESSED	R REFUSING
	D DECEIVED	I ISOLATION
		S SHOCK
		T THERAPY

God's Promise: *"For God so loved the world that He gave His only begotten Son. That whoever believes in Him shall not perish, but have eternal life." John 3:16.*

God Promised to send His Son to *save mankind* from Satan, the Devil, the wicked one, lord of death, ruler of demons, the great pretender, tempter, *Evil One*, the great dragon, the antichrist. His Son was sent the first time to give man a chance and to provide a way for mankind to be free from *the Evil One*. Man refused to accept and the *Evil One* crucified His Son. God promised He is sending His Son one more time, and it will be as a warrior to destroy the system and the Evil One. It is going to be a time for kicking butt and taking names, not a time for teaching and preaching. That time is near, the Reptilians know it and are gathering human beings to be their cannon fodder in the upcoming battle. Now is the time to choose which side you want to be with for eternity. These reptilian entities control the system THEY created and THEY are hypocrites and liars.

THEY "control" the political system, the city, county, state and federal government in all nations except one. That one is the Christian nation. THEY institute laws that apply only to human beings, make human beings criminals or terrorists, laws that allow them to "legally" rob you, permits their underlings to "legally" search and confiscate human possessions at their whim and take human property, jobs, lives, and enslave humans. This is the system PRACTICED today, even in America, which professes to be a free Christian nation. America is not the Christian nation. That ceased to be when America first turned its back on God and left God out. The Christian nation is all the human beings who believe in God, His son, and the Spirit. The system practiced is not the system that human beings are led to believe is practiced. Millions have sacrificed or died defending one system while an entirely different system is in place and practiced. "We the People" have been and are being deceived by the VIPER'S BROOD whose only goals is to keep human beings enslaved with *manipulation through deception* for THEIR GREED and POWER regardless the cost in human life.

The evidence is everywhere and it is not circumstantial. What will it take to get human beings to believe? What makes human beings believe the ILLUSIONS, the distortions, deceptions, and the lies time and time again, while refusing to accept the reality, the truth from "eye witnesses" that experienced the atrocities time and time again? The masses are willing to convict a man when the glove didn't fit. The masses are willing to convict a man on evidence that was hearsay. The masses are willing to convict a man with no eyewitnesses to the crime he was accused to have committed. One prime prosecution witness, a police officer was discovered to have been lying. A jury found the accused man innocent.

The masses still believe him guilty due to manipulation through deception. The man had a jealous temper and in the past had angrily confronted his wife and hit her when he found she had been with other men. That is politically incorrect. He was tried again in another court, for the same crime, and found guilty for the sole purpose to take his property and belonging. THEY claim he was not tried for the same crime in the second trial in a civil court, but regardless the spin or semantics you put on it, it boils down to the man was tried twice for the same crime. Ask O.J. if you do not believe me. Is he guilty? I have no idea, but God knows, and it is God's judgement that will eventually prevail.

Yet the masses will not accept the evidence that is all around them. Everywhere one looks the evidence is unmistakable about what I say. If you do not believe *The Bible* and do not believe THEY are reptilians disguised as humans, then using their own profiling system, explain the reptilian profile that fits them like a glove? THEY lie to, cheat and "sting" the people. THEY poison the people with hate. THEY crush the people with laws, then devour all the people possess. THEY are sneaky, devious, and patient and lie in wait for people to make a mistake so they can strike. THEY hide in dark, secret places and are hard to find. THEY are cold blooded. The profile fits a reptile, a snake, like a glove. They look like human beings and act like reptiles. I personally do not know any human beings that fit this profile.

Things that are good THEY believe to be bad, and things that are an abomination THEY believe to be good. THEY believe there is a devil when they say the devil made them do things, but then say there is no God. THEY believe there is wrong when THEY are wronged but THEY do not believe there is such a thing as right or wrong. THEY believe abusing animals is wrong, but commit worse atrocities against human beings and do not even bat an eye. THEY say THEY do not believe in murder, yet *manipulate human beings through deception* into killing each other for THEIR entertainment and profit. THEY do not believe God's 10 Commandments, yet have libraries that contain volumes filled with THEIR laws. THEY do not believe in Christ, yet use the season human beings celebrate as CHRIST'S birthday to plunder the people with the cheap products THEY produce then complain if THEY do not get enough plunder. THEY have the audacity to complain when human beings spell CHRISTMAS and not XMAS to celebrate CHRIST'S birth. What will it take to get you to see the light? The Viper's Brood, it's system and laws, are the problem! The choice to whether you do or do not believe is yours.

Most human beings I know are warm-blooded, believe in live and let live, and will only hurt others to defend themselves and loved ones. Human beings want to be left alone to live their life the way they see fit without doing any harm to anyone else. Human beings only want what they work for, do not like to cheat or be cheated, do not like to lie or be lied to, and do not want to devour anyone.

Which profile do you believe fits those who profess to be the elected and chosen leaders and the system that has been created? You decide!

"THE TRUTH! YOU WANT THE TRUTH? YOU CAN'T HANDLE THE TRUTH!" (Jack Nicholson from the movie *A Few Good Men*)

THE TRUTH IS:
"WE THE PEOPLE" ARE
SLAVES TO A REPTILIAN LIFE FORM CALLED:
"THEY"
"THE ELITE"
"THE CLIQUE"
"THE BULLIES"

"THE DEMONS"
"THE SNAKES"
"THE EVIL ONE"
"THE VIPER'S BROOD"

ON
SLAVE SHIP
PLANET EARTH
(SS REPTILIS TYRANNOS)

THE CAPTAIN IS CALLED:
"THE GREAT PRETENDER"
"THE LORD OF DEATH"
"THE GREAT DRAGON"
"LEVIATHAN"
"THE DEVIL"
"SATAN"

The system Satan and his followers created IS the "Antichrist" and that system enslaves human beings to do evil. Satan uses hypocrisy, fear, semantics, aphorisms, profiling, competitiveness, safety, greed, stress and frustration as tools within the three templates to *manipulate human beings through deception* into hating each other and God. They manipulate human beings into committing revolting sexual acts to each other and to human children for self-gratification. Human beings filled with hate pitted against other human beings filled with hate ARE what the *Evil One* needs to survive. Without the hate, the *Evil One's* system cannot survive.

"And let us reflect that, having banished from our land that religious intolerance under which mankind so long bled and suffered, we have yet gained little if we countenance a political intolerance as despotic, as wicked, and capable of as bitter and bloody persecutions." Thomas Jefferson, First Inaugural Address, March 4, 1801.

From each according to his ability, to each according to his need. Attributed to Karl Marks

Acts 2: 42-47 states: They were continually devoting themselves to the apostles' teaching and to fellowship to the breaking of bread and to prayer. Everyone kept feeling a sense of awe; and many wonders and signs were taking place through the apostles. And all those who had believed were

together and had all things in common; and they began selling their property and possessions and were sharing them all, as anyone might have need. Day by day continuing with one mind in the temple, and breaking bread from house to house, they were taking their meals together with gladness and sincerity of heart, praising God and having favor with all the people. And the Lord was adding to their number day by day those who were being saved.

Acts 4: 32-37 states: And the congregation of those who believed were of one heart and soul; and not one of them claimed that anything belonging to him was his own, but all things were common property to them. And with great power the apostles were giving testimony to the resurrection of the Lord Jesus, and abundant grace was upon them all. For there was not a needy person among them, for all who were owners of land or houses would sell them and bring the proceeds of the sales and lay them at the apostles' feet, and they would be distributed to each as any had need. Now Joseph, a Levite of Cyprian birth, who was also called Barnabas by the apostles (which translated means Son of Encouragement), and who owned a tract of land, sold it and brought the money and laid it at the apostles' feet.

Matthew 19: 20–26 states: The young man said to Him, "All these things I have kept; what am I still lacking?" Jesus said to him, "If you wish to be complete, go and sell your possessions, and give to the poor, and you will have treasure in heaven; and come follow me." But when the young man heard this statement, he went away grieving, for he was one who owned much property. And Jesus said to his disciples, 'Truly I say to you, it is hard for a rich man to enter the kingdom of heaven. Again I say to you, it is easier for a camel to go through the eye of a needle, than a rich man to enter the kingdom of God." When the disciples heard this, they were very astonished and said, "Then who can be saved?" And Looking at them Jesus said to them, "With people this is impossible, but with God all things are possible."

WHO DECIDES EACH INDIVIDUAL'S NEEDS?

Matthew 6: 30-34 states: You of little faith! Do not worry then, saying, 'What will we eat?' 'What will we drink?' 'What will we wear for clothing?' For the Gentiles eagerly seek all these things; for your heavenly Father knows that you need all these things. But seek first His kingdom and His righteousness, and all the things will be added to you. So do not worry about tomorrow; for tomorrow will care for itself. Each day has enough trouble of its own.

The idea that is called the "fair share" maxim, i.e., "From each according to their ability, to each according to their need!" did not originate with the

Karl Marx Communist Manifesto as taught. As seen from the above quotes it actually originates from *The Bible* and is called "sharing."

A synonym for Communist is common. A person can be a Capitalist and still believe in the common good. A person can be rich and still share with others. A person can own land and still share for the common good. There is nothing wrong with human beings working together for the common good.

The problems occur when God is eliminated from the equation. In the Soviet Union, the first thing that the *Communist Party* eliminated from the system was God. God was replaced with the *Party* and man made laws and power. Greed became the norm in the Soviet Union when humans let the *Evil One* dictate the peoples needs. It then became the powerful whose greed and needs came first. It was because the Soviet Union leadership denied there was a God and left God out that the nation and ideology was doomed to failure from the start. The Soviet Union only lasted approximately 73 years.

In America, the U.S. Constitution was put in place to guarantee God-given individual freedom, including religious freedom. Our nation was founded on the principle that God would always be at the nation's helm and would decide the nation's needs. Everyone was to stay united for the common good. A nation that prays together stays together.

Everyone was granted the freedom to excel and do their best to contribute to the society in the best way they could, and would reap rewards for their efforts. Everything was there for everyone to share. But soon, the leadership were *manipulated through deception* by the *Evil One* into leaving God out, greed became the norm among the leadership, and we now have a nation being oppressed by that greedy leadership. In the early 1960s, our leadership was *manipulated though deception* into leaving God out in our schools. Notice the evil that now permeates our nation. Now God is being excluded in every aspect in our Government. June 26, 2002, the 9th Circuit Court of Appeals said the Pledge of Allegiance was unconstitutional because it contained the words "under God." Our nation has turned its back on God and that is the worst mistaking this nation will ever make. That mistake started the process for this nation's demise. Look how far we have fallen since making that mistake in the early 1960s.

It matters not if *those in power* call themselves Republicans or Democrats, Liberal or Conservative, Socialist, Communist, Marxists, Fascist, Nazi, or whatever, they are all from the same mold, and that mold turns out those that are after wealth and power and they are the *Evil One*. The *Evil One* is now in control in this nation because the Christian silent majority surrendered.

Missionaries are sent to other nations from Christian churches while this nation wallows in evil, children are starving, people are without work, greed abounds and hypocrisy runs rampant in America. God's law and commandments are made a mockery. *"Woe to you scribes and Pharisees, hypocrites, because you travel around on sea and land to make one proselyte; and he becomes one, you make him twice as much a son of hell as yourselves."—Matthew 23:15*

What did the Christian people do to combat the *Evil One* in their own home? The Christian human beings let the *Evil One* replace the Constitutional system passed to them from the founding fathers with the very system the founding fathers fought a revolution to free themselves from living under. *The Christian human beings surrendered and did not even put up the good fight.* They made it easy for the *Evil One* and went along with the *Evil One* system, which is the Antichrist that is leading human beings into eternal slavery.

The *Evil One* are trained from birth to take over the power structures put in place and they pass the power and wealth from *THEIR* family generation to family generation. The world is one big game to the *Evil One*. Human beings are their pawns, the play pieces. War is their chess game, economics their monopoly game, politics their controls game, religion their divide and conquer game, semantics their deception game and the law their oppressor game. The *Evil One* play these games with human lives and *manipulates human beings through deception* into fighting and killing each other for the *Evil One's* pleasure and gain. The *Evil One* competes for control among its own members using human being against human being to implement their schemes.

The *Evil One* selects leaders from among the human beings and *manipulates these human leaders through deception* into abusing, deceiving and betraying the people they are to serve and protect. These human leaders do this for wealth and power. These human leaders are then *manipulated through deception* into *manipulating other humans through deceptions* into fighting and killing each other. The human young are sent to war against each other, and each war fought is gain for the *Evil One*. The *Evil One* feeds off the hate created among humans. The humans are the losers. The human leaders even end up betraying those they send into battle. This same scenario keeps recurring over, and over, and over, and over, as can be attested to in recorded history. Human beings are *manipulated through deception* into fighting among themselves for the same causes, just under different names.

Human beings are letting themselves be divided by the *Evil One* and it has been going on since the beginning, since Lucifer's fall from grace and mankind's expulsion from the Garden in Eden. Remember that Lucifer's fall was due to his quest for power. Lucifer wanted to become as God and for God's creation to worship Lucifer, not God.

Jesus, God's only begotten Son, came as a common human being to show human beings that they could resist and be free from Satan and his *Evil One*. Christ showed the way. All one has to do is believe. The way to break Satan's bond is through love for your fellow human beings, love and trust God, and *make a stand against the Evil One and its system*, the antichrist. The antichrist does not believe in Christ. The system in place today does not believe in or recognize Christ. Christians are refusing to stand and fight the good fight. Think about that.

John 3:16 "For God so loved the world he gave his only begotten Son, that whoever believes in Him shall not perish but have eternal life."

God said he wants mankind's unconditional love, the same as a parent wants a child's love. Human beings demonstrate love by their actions. Our children demonstrate their love to us as parents by their actions. By our actions as children belonging to God, our Creator, do you think we are demonstrating love? Remember that we reap what we sow.

Irrefutable evidence has been presented in this book that there is a conspiracy. Evidence has been presented that the conspiracy is to keep human being enslaved in a system designed to deny every human being their God-given rights. Evidence has been presented the system is designed to pit human being against human being through a methodology using templates. Evidence has been provided that human beings are provided an illusion that a system providing freedom is being practiced when in reality an evil system that enslaves is actually being practiced. Evidence has been provided that the system being practiced in what is called Christian Free America has been corrupted and has been replaced by the *Evil One's* system. Evidence has been provided that the system being practiced is controlled by beings that are not human but are identified as being Reptilian. Whether or not you accept that evidence is entirely your choice. You are the jury. Make your choice based on the evidence.

In this book, you have been told the truth. That truth has been repeated several times in different ways, as different examples.

Mark 8: 36-38: "For what does it profit a man to gain the whole world and forfeit his soul? For what will a man give in exchange for his soul? For whoever is ashamed of Me and My words in this adulterous and sinful generation, the Son of Man will also be ashamed of him when he comes in the glory of His Father with the holy angels."

Matthew 10: 32-38: "Therefore everyone who confesses Me before men, I will also confess him before My Father who is in heaven. But whoever denies Me before men, I will also deny him before My Father who is in heaven. Do not think that I came to bring peace on the earth; I did not come to bring peace, but a sword. For I came to set a man against his father, and a daughter against her mother, and a daughter-in-law against her mother-in-law; and a man's enemies will be the members of his household. He who loves father or mother more than Me is not worthy of Me; and he who loves son or daughter more than Me is not worthy of Me. And he who does not take his cross and follow after Me is not worthy of Me. He who has found his life will lose it, and he who has lost his life for My sake will find it.

A <u>cross</u> in Christ's day was an execution device. The cross was not made into a religious icon until quite sometime after Christ was crucified. In fact, the fish was the first symbol used by early Christians to identify themselves to other Christians.

When Christ said to take up the cross and follow him, it was not in the context that many are led to believe. The cross was not yet a symbol representing his crucifixion, death and resurrection. It couldn't be because he was still living when he told the people to take up the cross and follow him. He was living then as he is *living with us in spirit today*. Christ was saying, take up your execution device and follow after me. *I did not come to bring peace, but a sword.* He was saying we are going to do away with this viper's brood. All one need do is read what Christ was saying. God loved his people. His people had allowed themselves and their hearts to be hardened against Him by the *Evil One*, the viper's brood. Christ attempted to explain, teach, and educate the people, yet the people did not listen, refused to hear, could not hear, did not want to hear. The people were afraid and Christ was the one that ended up being executed by the *Evil One*. Even today, when people stand against the *Evil One*, on other people's behalf, they are generally left standing alone. For God so loved his people, His spirit manifest itself into flesh and came His only begotten son. God sacrificed his Son to show His people the "real enemy," and to inform human beings that the enemy is not their fellow human beings, but the same Reptilian viper's brood that has *manipulated human beings through deception* since the Garden in Eden. Christ ended up a "blood sacrifice" for breaking no laws except to stand up to the viper's brood on the people's behalf. God will not forget that. His blood is on the viper's brood head.

When a father loses a child to anyone through wrong doing, that father holds the ones committing the wrong doing responsible for that child's pain, suffering and death. That father will spend a lifetime looking for those that caused his child's pain, suffering and death. That child's blood is on their hands and those responsible will pay. The father does not hold those who were not involved responsible, only those involved. That is the same with Christ. The viper's brood is the one's responsible, and for them there is no forgiveness. But, it was human beings that allowed it to happen, stood by and did nothing to prevent it from happening. For that there is forgiveness, if one just asks. Christ died showing mankind the right way to live life and to stop the wrong doings *human beings are manipulated through deception* into committing against each other. In that mankind did nothing to prevent those responsible for crucifying Christ, it is up to each individual human being to ask for His forgiveness. It costs nothing, and it is free, because it is your apology for doing nothing to help stop the tyranny against a fellow human being while allowing Him to sacrifice everything to gain your freedom.

Even today, many human beings let other brothers and sisters sacrifice jobs, homes, life, limb, property, friends and family fighting against an *Evil One* for freedom while standing by and doing nothing to help because they fear the cost, do not want to make the sacrifices. Instead they stand by and watch in horror as they continue to let themselves be *manipulated through deception* into hating those that are fighting the *Evil One*. Hating the very ones who love them and are standing and fighting the battle for their freedom.

The "battle" has been going on since mankind's fall, his surrender to the *Evil One* in the Garden in Eden. Since those times it has been one continuing battle after another. These battles being waged are called "wars" by the Evil One to deceive mankind into believing that their always will be wars among human beings. Actually, each war fought for freedom throughout history has been a major battle against what human beings believed to be *the Evil One*, only the *Evil One* is not participating. The *Evil One* is *manipulating human beings through deception* into fighting the Evil One's battles. And, by human beings fighting the *Evil One's* battle's against fellow human beings, the *Evil One* has invented a self perpetuating, self fulfilling, prophesy that mankind is destined to continually fight wars. Each war human beings fight against each other is a battle won for the *Evil One* because we are fighting each other and *not the Evil One*. The *Evil One* has taken God's people, human beings and turned them into armies against themselves with *manipulation through deception*. While we fight each other and grow weaker and weaker in our resolve, the real enemy has been preparing for the final battle in the real war against all human beings. *The only true war is the war against the Evil One and its tyranny.* As the war continues, those *manipulated through deception* and used by the *Evil One* to do the evil deeds against their fellow human beings do not realize the real cost, for it is their soul. It is destined to stay enslaved forever. Those human beings that continue to allow this to happen continue to be enslaved by the *Evil One*. The real war is not against fellow human beings, it is against the *Evil One*, and they are disguised to look like us.

If you sent your child to lead those children to freedom, to safety, that are too cowardly to fight for themselves, and while these same children stood by and watched the tyrants crucify your son and his life taken and sacrificed wouldn't you want them to apologize to your child. Wouldn't you want punishment for those actually committing the atrocity? God does want those children to ask for that forgiveness, and God will punish those committing the atrocity.

A few words from Onward Christian Soldier explains much:

> Words: Sabine Baring Gould 1865
> Onward, Christians soldiers, marching as to war,
> With the cross of Jesus going on before.
> Christ, the royal Master, leads against the foe;
> Forward into battle see His banners go!

The Bible is human kinds story repeated over and over and over and over. God sent his spirit once as his only begotten Son, as a child. Although God created us, we are his "adopted" children. Only by going through what His Son went through can we really understand what His Son sacrificed for human beings freedom. Only then can we began to fathom His love for us, and His Son's love for us. He suffered so that humankind did not have to suffer if mankind only believed and would stand against the tyrants themselves. But mankind refuses to accept and believe and mankind continues to suffer. As long as humankind refuses to accept and believe, and chooses to be slaves to the *Evil One, the viper's brood* and its system, humankind will continue to suffer. How many times must the price be paid to get the people to come to their senses? God's Son was the ultimate sacrifice, the ultimate price and that will not be forgotten, and his suffering will not be forgiven until forgiveness for that wrong doing is asked, by you from Him.

The biggest illusion, the greatest deception, the greatest show the *Evil One* perpetrates is the illusion that Christian people are not to get involved in politics. The *Evil One* has manipulated Christian human beings into believing that someday, everything will be made right. That Christ will come and make everything okay, someday. God's spirit, is the Christ spirit, and the Spirit has been with us since the fall in the Garden. The Father, Son and Holy Ghost are the same Spirit and are one. That spirit never left us and has been with us all along. Human beings are being deceived into not listening to that Spirit by *manipulation through deception.* Human beings are manipulated into criticizing each other and telling each other that we cannot do certain things because we have not been "trained" in that area, we should listen to the experts, we should, we must, we have to, we need to, etc. etc. etc. These words, you should not, you need not, you must not, you cannot, are subtle doubt inspirations. These words *dictate* your needs, your wants, your desires, and what you can and cannot do. You can do anything the Spirit leads you to do, even if you do not have the "proper education" or training. The Spirit is within each human being and it lets human beings know their capabilities. It is human beings own doubt about what the Spirit can do through them that makes human beings doubt their own abilities/capabilities and that causes humankind's grief. It is the *Evil One* that instills these doubts and human beings listens to THEM and not God's spirit. THEY tell human beings that they do not have the proper training, knowledge, ability, know how, intelligence, etc, etc, etc., in order to put those doubts within humans. Then humans go to THEIR schools and training facilities where the indoctrination continues. Am I against learning? No! Am I against education? No, provided that education teaches human beings to think, and not to be robots.

God set down in the 10 Commandments what we must, should not, cannot, and shall not do. It is written he wants us to love him. It is written He does not want us to worship any deity, idol, icon, spirit i.e. God but Him. It is written He does not want us to worship idols that we create or build and turn them into our god, such as money or possessions. It is written He does not want us to use His name in vain, i.e. in a useless, unproductive, conceited, self important, ineffective way. It is written He wants humans to keep one day a week holy, a Sabbath, a day for rest, contemplation, a spiritual day for you. It is written He wants us to respect, admire, and hold in reverence, i.e. honor our father and mother. It is written He does not want us to devastate, murder, injure, harm, tear down i.e. kill other human beings. It is written He does not want us to obligate ourselves to unfaithfulness, infidelity, disloyalty, treachery, or to commit adultery. It is written He does not want us to cheat, embezzle, con, rob, take, capture i.e. steal. It is written He does not tolerate untrue, false perceptions, nor want humans to lie, or gossip i.e. bears false witness about other human beings. It is written He does not want us to desire, want, crave i.e. covet things that belong to other human beings. It is written he does not want humans to resist an evil person.

Christ came to show us the law could be obeyed, could be accomplished, can be fulfilled. Until God loving (Christian) Human beings accomplishes that, the Law will remain in effect as long as there is a heaven and earth. And sitting around waiting for it to happen, one had better bring a huge lunch, because it is going to be a real long wait, because you have to make it happen.

What is a Christian? Earlier I said that Christianity is not a religion, but a way to live life. There is a Christian Religion. I do not belong to that religion. I am a Christian. What is a Christian you may ask? Christian is an acronym for Common Humans Resisting Intensely Satan's Trap In All Nations. Christians are those that believe in God and that He sent His spirit in the flesh as His son to show human beings the way to stand in the Evil One's way. Christians belong to every nation in the world, belong to every religion in the world, are every color, gender, and are in every profession in the world, EXCEPT one profession. That is Politics. Christians are those who are standing in the *Evil One* and its political systems way that has been put into place on planet earth. Christians are not knowingly permitted in the political system, and if found, are expelled from the political system by whatever means necessary such as fear, intimidation, and if necessary, murder.

I am sure there are some that are going to say that I am contradicting myself. First I say humans are to resist Satan's evil methodology, then say that it is written not to resist the evil person. Every human being is being manipulated by the methodology and that makes every human do evil to some degree. Christ did not say human beings were not to resist evil. Human begins are not to harm each other when resisting evil. When human beings resist each other as being evil, then human beings get hurt. Humans are to resist the methodology, the templates, i.e. the system, the Evil One, the antichrist. These things are the evil humans are in a battle against. It is the evil system Christian human beings are to resist. Human Christians are now in subjection to an evil authority. This has resulted due to *manipulation through deception*.

Since God sets up all governments and the governing authorities, it then makes sense Human Christians are to be involved in those governments and Human Christians are to be in subjection to the governing authorities. It is also that same God that gives Christian human beings the responsibility and authority to change an oppressive government. It is the Christian human beings duty to recognize the chosen authority and put that authority into place. God gave Christian humans the duty to accomplish that, our founding fathers knew this and provided this nation the Constitutional means. From the evil that permeates Jackson County, Oregon, and our nation today, and from what I hear from human Christians that they are not to get involved in government, it is obvious that human Christians have failed in that duty. Human Christians have allowed evil to infiltrate and replace the system God and the founding fathers intended. The governing authority is not the governing authority God put into place. *God does not set up evil governments over His people.* He gave the people the free will to choose, and by choosing to succumb to the Evil One, the people choose evil. Each election the people say that all they have to choose from is the lesser of two evils. *I will say it again, choosing between the lesser of two evils is still choosing evil.* If human Christian become involved in the government, God will provide. God will deliver the people from that oppressive authority and provide the people new authority from which to choose as he did when Moses led the people from Egypt. Do nothing, and nothing will be done.

    Matthew 7:7: *"Ask, and it will be given to you; seek, and you will find; knock and it will be opened to you."*

CHAPTER 15

FREEDOM FROM THE CLIQUE

There comes a time in human beings' lives it is necessary for the People to do away with the Political Bonds which have joined them with others, and to take for themselves the earthly Powers, the separate and equal Position that God and the Natural Laws entitle them. For respect due those from whom they cut the ties, it is necessary for those individuals to explain the reasons that push them to that separation, which have connected them with others.

We know it to be certain that all humans are created equal and are gifted by the Creator with certain inherent Rights and that among these Rights are Life, Liberty and the Pursuit of Happiness. To ensure these Rights are not violated, Governments are instituted among the people. The Governed gives the permission for the Powers granted to these governments. Whenever any Government becomes destructive to the gifts provided humans by the Creator, it is in the People's Rights to change or to throw out that Government. It is in the People's Rights to put in place a new Government, laying its Foundation on such Principles, and giving the power to govern to the new Government to safe guard their Safety and Happiness. Caution dictates that Governments long established should not be changed for frivolous and fleeting reason; and it has been shown throughout history, that Humans are more likely to suffer, while Evils are bearable, than to change that to which they become familiar. When the Abuses and Atrocities continue to occur, progressively get worse, and it appears to be a plan to lead people into absolute Tyranny and Oppression, then it is their Right, it is their Duty, to eliminate such Governments to provide new Safe Guards for their future Security.

Such has been the patient Suffering by the people in Jackson County, Oregon. It has become Necessary to change or alter that Government which causes that suffering. The present Jackson County Government has a History that entails repeated Injuries and Injustices against the people in Jackson

County. These Injuries and Injustices have appearances that there is being Established in Jackson County a government that intends to ultimately exercise absolute Tyrannical Rule over the People.

To prove this, let the following Facts be submitted to all the people:

The Jackson County Government has refused to Agree to GOD'S Laws that are most wholesome and necessary for the public Good.

The Jackson County Government has forbidden teaching GODS laws and refuses to pass laws that are Constitutional. The Government allows hired Agencies to pass rules and laws to govern the people. These Agencies are answerable to no one but themselves. The Government fails to control the Agencies it creates and neglects to control these Agencies Actions.

The Jackson County Government is in reality, one party pretending to be two parties with two heads. The people have no voice in who is allowed to participate in the Government although the ruling elite deceives the people and it is pretended the people elect the leaders. These two heads are composed from an elite group that further deceive the people by pretending to fight for control over the one body Government in order to oppress the people in the fashion the controlling elite determines. This government by the Elite hereafter shall be referred to in this document as the Clique.

The Clique supports and participates in an elections system that excludes individuals from getting elected to any public office that the Clique dictates and allows special privileges to the Clique Candidates during elections. The Clique has also declared that most elected Public Offices are Partisan Offices. The people can no longer participate in the government process except by the vote, and now the Clique is either altering or denying that vote.

The Clique passes special laws for special interest groups, providing those groups with special privileges not allowed other people. The Clique accepts tax dollars from the State Clique that relinquishes County rights, and the County willingly relinquishes the people's rights.

The Clique keeps secrets from the governed claiming it is for Security reasons, and refuses to provide the people the right to know what the Clique is doing. The Clique now appears designed for intimidating, frustrating, and coercing the people into compliance with its measures.

Supervisors hired by the Clique officials are allowed to unjustly punish, harass, ostracize, and coerce employees into quitting.

The Clique has passed laws allowing the individual property owners lands to be taken without just cause and compensation.

The Clique continues to allow slavery within Jackson County Borders, refuses to stop the illegal drug flow into the County, and refuses to regulate tobacco and other products that endanger the people's health.

The Clique officials have obstructed the Administration of Justice by refusing to prosecute law breakers within the Clique and by refusing to make the Clique Agencies and people working within the Clique Agencies obey the laws they themselves institute. These officials further allow these agencies and individuals within those agencies to ignore Federal and State laws.

The Clique has made Judges dependent on the Clique's will alone, for the Tenure of their Offices, and the Amount and Payment of their Salaries. One such Jackson County Circuit Court Judge has acknowledged that the U.S. and Oregon Constitutions are not worth the paper they are written on. That those documents are a lie, the "left out" people have no rights and the County and State has his courts permission to continue governing by tyranny, that they are the RULING classes and will continue to RULE. (Case # 004001Z3)

The Clique has created numerous Agencies, and sent Officers in swarms to harass the People, and take their monies, property, and belongings in the form of taxes and special taxes disguised as fees. Some Agencies are allowed to confiscate people's Property who are suspect in dealing in drugs. These Agencies are not required to provide any Proof there is any wrong doing by the people they accuse.

The Clique has combined as one to subject the people to a Jurisdiction foreign to our Constitution, and unacknowledged by our Laws; giving its agreement to their Acts of pretended Legislation:

The Clique protects it own, by mock Trials, from Punishment for any Murders that they commit on the Inhabitants in the County.

The Clique Agencies are allowed to impose Taxes disguised as Fees on the people without the people's Consent

The Clique deprives the people, in many Cases, a Trial by Jury:

The Clique tries people for pretended Offences

The Clique is abolishing the free Constitutional founded Laws, establishing instead absolute arbitrary administrative laws.

The Clique is denying the people their Christian beliefs, abolishing the people's most valuable Laws, and altering the values on which our Constitutional Government was formed.

The Clique is violating our Constitutions, abolishing our most valuable Laws, and altering the fundamental foundation for our Government and laws.

The Clique claims we are not under its Protection and now wages War against the people.

The Clique's officers have entered homes and killed residents.

The Clique has turned its back on the military by closing and/or cutting back on veteran facilities and benefits and denying retired veterans jobs and unemployment benefits.

The Clique, at this Time, transports large Armies of our young people to accomplish the jobs that should be done by the County and benefits the Clique. This is totally unworthy for a civilized Nation.

The Clique hires our fellow humans as Police Officers to bear Arms against their own, to become the Executioners of their Friends and Brethren.

The Clique has ignored the GOD given right to life and is permitting murdering babies, our future generations, in the womb through abortions and murdering the elderly generations through euthanasia.

The government has become a Government of the Clique, for the Clique, by the Clique, it ignores the pleas and cries from the People, and has become a Clique Oppressing the People

In every stage during these Oppressions people have Requested Redress in the most humble Terms: The people's repeated Requests have been answered only by repeated Injury. Any Government, whose Character is thus marked by every act which may define a Tyrant, is unfit to be the Government for a people who assert themselves a FREE People.

NOR have we been wanting in Consideration to our Clique Brothers. We have warned them from Time to Time about the Attempts by their Legislature to extend an unwarrantable Jurisdiction over us. We have reminded them about the Circumstances that invade our rights. We have appealed to their native Justice and Fairness, and we have encouraged them by the Ties to our common Kindred to renounce these Injustices and Atrocities, which would inevitably interrupt the American Spirit of Liberty and Justice for all. They too have been deaf to the Voice of Justice and of Conscience. We must, therefore, agree to announce our Severance, and hold them, as we hold the rest, Enemies in War, in Peace, Friends.

WE, therefore, the People in Jackson County, in GENERAL, appeal to the Supreme Judge over the World (Our Heavenly Father) for the Righteousness about our Intentions. We do, in the Name, and by the Authority vested in a Free People, solemnly Publish and Affirm, That the People in Jackson County are, and of Right ought to be, FREE AND INDEPENDENT; that they are absolved from all Allegiance to the Jackson County Clique, and that all political Connection between them and the Jackson County Clique, is and ought to be totally dissolved; and that as FREE AND INDEPENDENT People, they have full Power to do all Acts and Things which INDEPENDENT PEOPLE have the GOD given right to do. And in support for this Affirmation, with a firm Reliance on the Protection of heavenly Providence, we mutually pledge to each other our Lives, our Fortunes, and our sacred Honor.

The above is actually the *Declaration of Independence*, modified semantically to fit the circumstances in Jackson County today. How much longer must God's people endure before everyone wakes up to the truth? Our system is in trouble. Regardless who is in power, that power is abused. Man cannot and will not administer the power given him fairly unless he has a superior power to answer too.

That power was at one time our Creator, that which we call God. Our system has excluded God and now our system is not working, people are still being oppressed in what is supposedly a free nation. It is only free to the Clique, their relatives, and their friends within the Clique. One party within the Clique declares God is dead, there is no God, the other party within the Clique claims to be God. The parties are wrong. There is a God and Human beings are made in Gods image, all creatures and vegetation his creations. Human beings are answerable to that God, and will answer to that God. I implore those in power, free the people you have enslaved and do what is just and equitable. Most people want the laws simple and applied equitably. Most people want liberty and justice for all, not just the Clique. Most people want God back in control in our county. Most people do not have this from the government that exists in Jackson County and that government has provided no indication that they have any intentions to listen to the people's pleas.

RIGHT REASONS RECALL
TREACHERY? PERJURY? TREASON?

"Our government...teaches the whole people by its example. If the government becomes the lawbreaker, it breeds contempt for law; it invites every man to become a law unto himself; it invites anarchy." –Attributed to Justice Louis Dembitz Brandeis

The State calls it own violence 'law', but that of the individual 'crime'- Attributed to Max Stirner

Oregon Constitution, Article II, Section 18. Recall; meaning of words "the legislative assembly shall provide."

(1) Every public officer in Oregon is subject, as herein provided, to recall by the electors of the state or of the electoral district from which the officer

is elected.
(3) They shall set forth in the petition the reasons for the demand.
U.S. Constitution, Amendment I
Congress shall make no law respecting an establishment of religion, or prohibiting the free exercise thereof; or abridging the freedom of speech, or of the press, or the right of the people peaceably to assemble, and to petition the Government for a redress of grievances.

In a Medford *Mail Tribune* editorial 18 November 2001, the editors disparaged people in Shady Cove for exercising their 1st Amendment right to petition. In September 2002, the *Mail Tribune* Editors again were in agreement with the State abridging the peoples Constitutionally guaranteed 1st Amendment right to petition. How can someone from the press advocate such a stance you may ask? Doesn't the first Amendment guarantee free speech and freedom of the press? Yes it does and at the same time, the 1st Amendment also guarantees the people's freedom to exercise religious beliefs, the right to assemble and the *right to petition*. It appears that the *Mail Tribune* editors do not believe in people exercising their guaranteed rights. The editors want to put restrictions on some people constitutionally exercising their rights.

In Jackson County and Oregon, people are being deprived their rights, and when anyone attempts to exercise a right are criticized publicly by the media, as the *Mail Tribune* editors criticized the people in Shady Cove for exercising their right to initiate a recall petition. September 4, 2002, the *Mail Tribune* editors claimed the wrong people they called, "cynical interest groups bent on dismantling the government" were using the petition process. The editors claimed the recall petition in Shady Cove was for the wrong reasons. What are the right reasons for a recall? That is supposed to be up to the voters in Shady Cove to decide? Perhaps the people have been unsuccessful in attempts at speaking to the elected City Council members about the issues

Or perhaps the people know that these allegedly elected officials are making decisions based on what is best for a certain interest group, while ignoring other peoples' God-given Constitutional rights. Perhaps the people were ignored, decided they have taken enough abuse caused by decisions these allegedly elected officials make and due to their frustration and as a last resort made a decision to do what they believed to be right for the city and attempt a recall.

People in Shady Cove have the U.S. Constitutional 1st Amendment right and Oregon constitutional right to initiate a recall. *Article 1, Section 1 and*

Article II Section 18 in the Oregon Constitution states that fact and states that the reasons for the demand will be set forth in the petition.

It was frustration with a tyrant king and tyrannical government officials that resulted in the Declaration of Independence being written and signed. The Declaration of Independence can be considered a signed petition. It was telling King George that many people in the colonies did not believe he was fit to govern due to his tyranny and the terror inflicted on some people by his officials. Perhaps some people in Shady Cove are initiating a petition that is telling the City Council they are not fit to govern due to the tyranny and the terror they are inflicting on some people in Shady Cove.

Some people may have resigned due to attempted recalls but I can't remember any recall election actually being successful in recent years in Jackson County. In the past 2 decades, few if any have been removed from office due to a recall election. I perceive it is due to the vote being "fixed" by the *Evil One* (Clique) that is governing the local and state government. Let someone within the *Evil One* (Clique) initiate a recall petition against someone trying to do the right thing, and the Tribune editors are for the recall 100%.

The *Mail Tribune* editors went on to say, "either vote for the person's opponent during the next election or run for the seat yourself." Surely they jest. How much more damage will the individuals cause if left in the seat until the next election? If you do vote for the opponent, that opponent is the same if not worse than the one already in office because that opponent is also a member in or controlled by the *Evil One* (Clique). Further, if it is as perceived and the people's vote is being ignored, it doesn't matter who the people vote for.

Telling people to run for the seat themselves is a "dare." Most people just want to be left alone. Most people do not want to govern. The *Evil One* (Clique) knows this and taunts those who challenge THEIR authority. Most people back down from the taunting. The *Evil One* (Clique) relies on this. For those that do not back down and do try to get on the ballot, the *Evil One* (Clique) has instituted inequitable rules to hinder individuals that the *Evil One* (Clique) does not want on the ballot. The *Evil One* (Clique) controls the whole election process. Have you noticed that people are "interviewed" before they can run for a seat on a city council?

Elected public offices are not a job, but people representing people and the people vote is to decide who gets elected. Where in our constitutions does it state that any person putting himself or herself forth as a candidate for any *public office or seat* has to be interviewed by the *Evil One* (Clique) first?

An *Evil One* (Clique) is running the county and state government and that violates the U.S. and Oregon Constitutions. Mentioning God-given Constitutionally guaranteed rights to people in or controlled by the *Evil One* (Clique) guarantees being listed as an "undesirable." The *Evil One* (Clique) interviews people to decide whom they will accept for a *public office or seat* and only those individuals are permitted on the ballot. The *Evil One* (Clique) wants people the *Evil One* (Clique) can control. It is the same for all the *public offices* in the city, county and state. The people's choices are restricted to only individuals acceptable to the *Evil One* (Clique). As added insurance, the *Evil One* (Clique) has instituted special "laws" making it more difficult for "outsiders" to get on the ballot.

These special "Laws" only apply to those individuals outside the *Evil One*. *As a last resort, I perceive the vote is fixed to ensure the Evil One's choices are the only ones "elected."*

I believe that people beginning to exercise their rights in Oregon and Jackson County is making it more difficult for the *Evil One*. People are starting to question what is going on in the process and are awakening to the fact that the people outside the *Evil One* have no say in the local and state government.

The more that the people exercise their rights, the more the system is exposed and people begin to discover the truth that the system has been manipulated to exclude those outside the *Evil One*. People are beginning to discover that the *Evil One* has taken a government system that was supposed to belong to all the people, manipulated the law, and made it into a system of the *Evil One*, for the *Evil One*, by the *Evil One*.

People that were once loyal to the *Evil One* have been separating themselves from the *Evil One's* control in droves because they do not agree with what the *Evil One* is doing to many people. The *Evil One* feels especially threatened whenever people exercise the right to serve in a *public office*. *Public offices* are considered power seats by the *Evil One*, which they cannot afford to lose to *outsiders*. If that happens, their scheme in manipulating the system falls apart and the people are again in control the way our Constitutional founders intended. That is why most public offices have been redefined as partisan offices. That is why the *Evil One* has manipulated the election laws so that only those they want to be elected to any *public office or seat* can be put on the ballot as candidates.

The *Evil One* knows that they will be able to control anyone that does not question their rules and adheres to their policies for getting on the ballot. Anyone who realizes that what the *Evil One* is doing is unconstitutional and brings that fact to their attention is told to sue if they do not like it. Since the *Evil One* controls the government in Oregon and Jackson County, including the judicial system, suing is useless. All it does is allow the *Evil One* to financially break those standing up for the U.S. and Oregon Constitutions.

The *Evil One* has covered the bases at all levels in the election process to keep many people out. This can only be discovered when those people outside the *Evil One* start exercising their God-given and Constitutional rights. Rights such as putting oneself before the people as a candidate for a *public office*, exercising free speech, freedom of religion, freedom of the press, *right to petition*, right to bear arms, right to a jury trial, etc. My perception is most Oregon Editors are either privy to denying peoples' rights or are being *manipulated through deception* along with many others by the *Evil One*.

Elected public servants have a sworn duty to uphold the Constitutions and to *discharge* the duties of the office held. While in office, and after having it brought to their attention, these public servants continue to permit people's constitutional rights to be violated with the decisions made and permit paid government employee to deny people's constitutionally guaranteed rights, then they are violating their oath, the Constitution, and the people's trust.

Violating the people's trust is treachery and violating an oath is perjury, and punishable as a crime. Violating people's Constitutional rights is Tyranny. Tyranny against a people by its government is terrorism. The United States has declared a War against Terrorism and violating constitutional rights is supporting terrorism. *Attempting to overthrow the government to which ones owes allegiance, either by making war against the state or by materially supporting its enemies is treason.* That is a crime and so is perjury. Officials knowingly violating "We the People's" constitutional rights are deliberate attempts at overthrowing our Constitutional government for the tyrants they serve. That is treason. When this occurs, the people have every right to initiate a recall petition and have it put before the voters to decide. In Jackson County and Oregon, that right to petition is being hindered by every means possible and is being *denied* by the *Evil One* and its vote fixing process.

The *Evil One* is making it extremely difficult for the people to petition. No longer can petitioners' stand outside public places such as grocery stores, malls, shopping centers and other business establishments and petition. The

Evil One is using intimidation to influence businesses and is using the news media to *manipulate people through deception* into believing petitions and petitioners are harmful. If petitions are so harmful, for what purpose did the founders list it along with other fundamental 1st Amendment guaranteed rights and God-given freedoms in the Bill of Rights?

Rights that the *Congress shall make no law with regard to abridging* including "*FREEDOM TO PETITION*" which the Oregon and *Mail Tribune* editors seem to forget? If restrictions were put in place that prevented newspapers from being sold in or outside businesses such as grocery stores, mini marts, hotels, restaurants, etc., or were told what they should or should not write where would the editors stand?

For what purpose did the founding fathers *petition* King George with a document called the Declaration of Independence? Do you think the founding fathers were serious about the Bill of Rights? Do you think the founding fathers fought a revolution almost a decade for fun against forces that outnumbered them and had better weapons? Do you think they were joking when they sacrificed everything they owned, their lives, and their families lives for your FREEDOM?

Expecting these same officials to change the system is ridiculous for they are controlled by the *Evil One* to do the *Evil Ones'* bidding, and are not going to hurt themselves. Hired government officials' are permitted to murder unarmed people in the street or in the home and nothing is done to those officials. These officials are permitted to rob or steal people's property and nothing is done. Officials are permitted to lie to or about the people and nothing is done. Elected(?) officials permit hired officials to institute excessive taxes disguised as fees against the people and nothing is done. The list goes on. The local and state government system is tyrannical and using terror tactics against the people and it is *LEGAL*, because in Oregon and Jackson County the Constitutions have been render powerless by "defining" public offices as partisan offices and non-partisan offices in Oregon statutes. No longer are the Constitutions or the Oath of Office applicable under Oregon's "Rule of Law." Rule of Constitutional law does not apply. Only Rule of Law is applicable.

I ask the *Mail Tribune* editors, are treachery, perjury, and/or treason against the people according to Constitutional law good enough reasons for a recall? Or, do the Editors advocate these things as being LEGAL for the Clique to do against the people according to the tyrant's Partisan control under the old English "Rule of Law"? We are in a battle against terrorism in this nation. Where are all the Patriotic Christian Americans standing against the tyrants and the terrorist enemy within?

A LETTER OF APOLOGY
Dear Tom,

I write this letter with deep regret, sorrow, and shame. No one else appears willing to write, so I take that duty upon myself. A great loss has come upon Americans. After the sacrifices you, Ben, George, Pat and the others made to gain those things that were supposed to be shared by all, I am ashamed to pass on to you that it was all for nothing. It seems that those individuals for which you and the others sacrificed so much have allowed themselves to become apathetic and complacent and are again willing to let a small Clique dictate how human beings, how Americans should live their lives.

The courts have decided it is right for the government to kill people in multitudes in order to bring one to justice. Just recently, people belonging to a religious group in a place called Waco, Texas were massacred because the Bureau of Alcohol, Tobacco, and Firearms was unable to arrest a man who went to town 3 or 4 times a week. This man was the group religious leader and he lived in a compound with others possessing the same beliefs. Although the individuals in the compound had not broken any laws, government troops were sent in to wipe this nest of "offenders" out and arrest any survivors. Over 80 men, women and children were slaughtered Tom. Another man, who had committed no crime except to speak his mind and was entrapped into selling an illegal weapon to a government agent, had his wife and son killed by other government agents at a place called Ruby Ridge. Do these incidents emulate the Boston Massacre Tom? I think it much worse.

Another group in government, called the Drug Enforcement Agency, can now confiscate your money and property if they "suspect" you may be dealing in illegal drugs. This government agency can keep all the money it takes and any money from the sales of the goods it confiscates and use it in its efforts to further "confiscate" more money and goods. A government agency, called the Internal Revenue Service, can more or less do the same but puts the money it collects in the government coffers. Remember what you boys did at Lexington and Concord when the government attempted to confiscate the power and ball belonging to the people. It is still called the" shot heard around the world." That incident started a revolution. Today, people sit back and do absolutely nothing.

THE ENEMY CALLED "THEY"

In the county in which I live, 20 armed county officers physically removed a disabled man in a wheel chair from his home for taxes he owed. His home had been taxed at a rate he thought absurd and was contesting the assessed taxes. This had been going on for several years and the county grew tired and decided to take the property. The house was sold to a realtor and a lawyer at approximately 1/2 the assessed value at which the home was taxed. After the taxes were paid, the county kept the remaining money as a "windfall" to fill their coffers. When this incident occurred, no one stood against the tyrants to help the man Tom. And you boys dumped tea into a harbor over a few taxes on tea.

Another confused and depressed unarmed man was shot 23 times by local police officers. Those who actually did the shooting were not even supposed to be at the scene. The dispatcher instructed those officers to stay away from the scene yet the officers disobeyed and went on their own accord. What is even more astounding is that Christian Americans remain silent while these atrocities occur. Does all this sound familiar?

Tom, did you know there are places where you cannot smoke your pipes, cigars and cigarettes? You cannot smoke in any government building, most public buildings, some cities do not allow smoking in public and now there are those who want a law passed making it illegal to smoke in your own home. Sound familiar Tom? American are told that smoking tobacco is harmful to their health, and if that truly be the case, then tobacco needs to be declared a dangerous substance and banned from being sold. As long as the government allows tobacco to be grown, processed, and sold on the open market, then people have the right to smoke it when and where they want.

I really need to tell you about the Congress and Senate. No longer are we getting men with character, wisdom, and common sense into office. Would you believe that Money is the major factor in deciding who holds a public office or that most public offices are now considered partisan offices and non-partisan offices? The more money that can be collected, the more likely you are to get elected. The Clique has made it virtually impossible for those that do not belong to the Clique to get on the ballot as a candidate. It appears those allegedly elected now "sell" their votes to the highest bidder (contributor). The common man has been forgotten for big business interests and for greed. Graft and corruption have replaced principles, values, and moral responsibilities in representatives. Does this sound familiar Tom?

Remember the values you boys wanted in a leader Tom. Firm, fair, honest, hard as nails when needed, yet tempered with compassion. Well, guess what the people are getting as leaders today. Individuals who refused to serve in the Armed Forces, individuals that have been caught in numerous lies to the people, have been unfaithful to their wives, and have moral and ethical values that would put an alley cat to shame.

I realize there are no provisions in the Constitution that states an individual must serve in the Armed Forces or have certain moral or ethical values in order to serve in a political office. But, it sure raises questions in my mind about voting for someone to govern that refused to serve in the national defense or has little moral or ethical principles. I guess that is really a mute point, as I will explain.

You remember how important the vote was to your people Tom? Well, it means nothing to the people today. Where I live, people don't even go to the polling place to vote. A ballot is "mailed" to the people at home. Now get this, on money issues, if you don't vote, it counts as a "no" vote. The people have become so apathetic in shirking their responsibility by not voting it is automatically a no vote. Can you believe it?

If things are worded just right, the people can easily be fooled and laws passed denying their rights. In fact, I believe that has already happened. There are real strong indications the vote is being ignored/denied and the numbers being provided to the public may be fabricated. The vote counting process has been turned over to a machine that can be programmed to provide whatever numbers someone may decide. The public is being removed from the voting process Tom. You won't believe this but they now "enhance" the ballot at the county office. You and I both know that no one is supposed to mark another individuals ballot. In reality, no one is elected, only those appointed by the Clique are allowed to serve now Tom

Remember how the building blocks and foundation for the nation was based on God and Christian beliefs, and that some school lesson were taught from The Bible? Well, today your children can be suspended from attending school for praying or even talking about God. Freedom of Religion only applies to atheist. Get this "Tom," there are those who believe we evolved from a monkey. In fact, the smarter we become, the more we try to make monkeys out of ourselves. (Just a bit of humor Tom)

A theory or theology called evolution has become a new "religion" that is being taught in the public school system, but no other religions are permitted in or around public schools. The people that believe this theology are called evolutionist. They believe that everything has evolved from nothing and that every species including plant, animal and mineral needs to be protected from extinction and that they are gods. Another religious group supported by government and related to the evolutionist theories is environmentalist. Environmentalists worship the earth and believe the earth is god. The Federal government has passed special laws to protect these people and their theology and has instituted a government agency called the Environmental Protection Agency. How about that for violating Constitutional 1st Amendment rights?

It seems, in their great wisdom, our courts have decided it is reasonable to destroy human life while it is still in the mother's womb. Baby fetuses by the millions are murdered each year, yet we have laws protecting fish, whales, snakes, rats, and other animals. Can you believe we now have animal "rights"? Human beings in the millions are being denied the right to "Life," Liberty, and the pursuit of Happiness, yet the law instituted under the Environmental Protection Act protects animal species, their eggs, and unborn. Yet, it is legal to kill human babies in the mother's womb. Do you think that insane and does this sound familiar Tom? We even have laws protecting trees and other plant life!

What I am about to say now will convince you what is occurring is insanity. Where I live a law has been enacted, and supposedly voted into law by the people, that permits a physician to assist a person in committing suicide. Hard to believe, but it is true. Perhaps the Hippocratic oath that doctors take to preserve life and do no harm should be changed to the hypocritical oath, what do you think Tom? As a human Christian American, I have no explanation for this insanity that has allowed plant life and lower animal life to become more meaningful than human life.

I want to mention one more thing before closing. Remember how all you boys believed we should always have the means to stop tyranny in government. Well, there are Americans today that believe those means are no longer necessary for the people. I believe you can tell from what little I have written here the need is just as great today as it was in your day for the people to have the right to free speech, religious freedoms, right to vote, posses and bear firearms, etc. There are many Americans today that believe that time is past and that the Constitution and the Bill of Rights are no longer applicable. You and I know different don't we Tom?

Americans today do not understand what freedom is really about and are giving or letting it slip away. I guess it gets back to the old adage that people only appreciate what they earn. It appears that the gift so graciously given to Americans by your generation Tom, the sacrifices made and the costs to so many to acquire and keep that gift, have become mute points. It appears it has now become a tarnished gift to most Americans, they no longer want it, and act as if they are ashamed to have it. Those that did not have to make any sacrifices to obtain or keep that gift can never understand its true value. They can't seem to understand that it can be polished and repaired to regain its luster and beauty. They just do not want to take the time or put forth the effort to repair and polish that gift, they would rather throw it away. And that is a shame for that is a decision you and I know they will live to regret.

Well, I will close now. Again, I want to extend my deepest apologies to all the men and women for wasting all your time, money, efforts, and lives to give Americans the gift of Freedom and a Constitution to live by. Much like spoiled children, Americans today have decided to throw a great gift away.

Sincerely,
Randall C. Hale

This letter is what I would say to Thomas Jefferson, George Washington, Ben Franklin, Patrick Henry, John Hancock, John Adams, and the other millions who have sacrificed so much in the past 220 years to earn and keep what human Christian Americans today are so willingly giving away. That precious gift is human beings and America's:

FREEDOM

F
R
E
E
D
O
M

EPILOGUE

America, once the land of the Free and home of the Brave, once a land with open arms to all the oppressed masses throughout the world. A land that was a refuge to all seeking freedom.

The eagle, America's national bird, represents strength, a free spirit that fears nothing and goes where it wants, when it wants.

The American flag represents truth, courage, honesty, love, sacrifice, unity, justice, and freedom. The American flag represents a Nation with GOD at its vanguard and a nation indivisible. The American flag represents a signal to the world this is a moral and just nation where the oppressed have a place to seek refuge, a place to be safe from tyranny and be FREE from oppression. The American flag represents a system with the concept that INDIVIDUAL RIGHTS are as important as MAJORITY RIGHTS, a system in which every individual vote is counted and every individual can endeavor to be elected and have a voice in its government. The American flag represents a system in which there is EQUAL JUSTICE for all, with laws that have a Constitution as their foundation and those laws are enforced and apply to everyone equally and are administered through a fair and impartial court system. The American flag represents a system of LIFE, LIBERTY, & PURSUIT of HAPPINESS. The American flag represents a system rooted in FREEDOM!

I was born and raised in America and have always considered America my home. I served twenty years in America's military defending against tyranny from other nations. The past decade, I have seen tyranny in the system in America no different than the tyranny I was sent to defend against in other nations. I have seen a system here that does not believe in GOD. I have learned through personal experience there is a system here in which the INDIVIDUAL HAS NO GOD GIVEN RIGHTS, only PARTY RIGHTS. I have learned through personal experience there is a system here that is corrupted by FAVORITISM AND NEPOTISM with laws that are enforced according to ones' whim and who happens to be in charge and in control at the time. I have learned through personal experience there is a system here that ignores its own Constitutions, and with the Courts help, twists and distorts those Constitutions and the laws to deceive people into believing they are being treated fairly, while serving injustice. I have learned through personal experience things that lead me to perceive there is a system here in which the elections and the voting numbers are fabricated and/or fixed so only the party Elite, the Clique, can be elected. I have learned through personal experience there is a system here that utilizes FEAR, INTIMIDATION and COERSION for control. I see a system in America that mocks the people, and keeps the people separated though hate while manipulating the people through deception, and lies. I have learned through personal experience the system actually being practiced in America is about OPPRESSION, ENSLAVEMENT, HOPELESSNESS and GREED. I have learned through personal experience the system being practiced in America is the same system I was taught as a youngster that the Nazi and the Soviet Flags represented. I have learned through personal experience, observation and listening that the Republican Party represents fascism and the Democratic Party represents communism. Those are "We the human Christian American People" only two Party choices to which we are permitted to belong. "We the human Christian American People" that refuse to "join" a party become "outsiders" and are not permitted to participate in the government, or in jobs, and are no longer considered Americans.

It is shameful what is occurring in America today. All the things that the Eagle and the American flag represent are no longer in America. We have holidays celebrating the system that one flag represents; yet allow, practice, support, and perpetuate a system that other flags represent. For what purpose do "We the human Christian American People" allow the flag representing one system to be flown, yet allow an entirely different system to be practiced? For what purpose do "We the human Christian American People pledge allegiance to one flag and the system it represents yet allow another system other flags represent to be practiced? In doing so, we DISGRACE the very flag to which we pledge allegiance and display. By allowing, practicing, supporting, and perpetuating a system that our founding fathers fought against, we DISHONOR the very individuals we claim to honor. WE make their sacrifices a mockery. Tyranny is tyranny, regardless how subtle it may appear.

Every person that claims to be a human Christian American can hang their heads in shame for what is being allowed in this once great nation. "We, the Human Christian American People" have allowed America to become the very oppressive nation that once stood against such tyranny and oppression. Our government has been allowed to adopt the very same tactics used by the Nazi and Communist governments that "We the People" claim to abhor. What hypocrites "We the human Christian American People" have become. Our founding fathers are looking upon their posterity in this generation with shame.

"We the human Christian American People" in this generation have surrendered, without even a fight, what so many in past generations sacrificed so much to acquire. "We the human Christian American People" in this generation have failed to uphold the standards the American Flag represents. "We the human Christian American People" in this generation have failed in our duty to keep our government in check. "We the human Christian American People" in this generation have failed to vote and now permit the vote to be denied by not ensuring that the vote is even counted. "We the human Christian American People" in this generation have failed to hold the representatives and bureaucrats in government accountable for their actions. "We the human Christian American People" in this generation have failed to ensure justice is served through our court systems. "We the human Christian American People" in this generation have failed in ensuring that no individual can be enslaved in America. "We the human Christian American People" in this generation have instead allowed ourselves to become enslaved. "We the human Christian American People" in this generation have become apathetic, complacent, defeated, frightened, weak, enslaved CHICKENS and that is exactly what THEY wanted. "We the People" in this generation strut around like banty roosters, and at the first sign of trouble in the hen house go running about clucking and screaming like the chickens we have become.

And now that enemy, the bullies, the Clique, the Elite, the Evil One speak and "We the human Christian American People" jump to their every whim. THEY have won. "We the human, Christian, American People have become enslaved, frightened, sniveling cowards whining "What can we do?

What I did was write this book informing you about what is really happening. I ask you, what did your founding fathers do? I will tell you if you do not know. They stood against and fought their oppressors. Our ancestors, our founding fathers would rather die than live enslaved. They fought a revolution which YOU celebrate every July 4th. This generation does not have that same courage because this generation, by saying, "What can I do," is asking for permission.

Do you think your oppressors are going to tell you what you can do to stop them? Do you think they are going to give you permission to fight them? Oh, sure, THEY will tell you to fight them in THEIR FIXED COURT SYSTEM, or in THEIR FIXED ELECTIONS, or complain to THEIR APPOINTED REPRESENTATIVES. But do you really think they are going to tell you to stand against them and actually fight an honest fight, in which THEY do not make the rules. Do you think they are going to give you permission to ensure that the vote is counted in elections? Do you think they are going to give permission for those who are not THEIR bought and trained lawyers to run as Judges or those without THEIR police training to run as a Sheriff, or those without THEIR lawyer training to run as representatives. THEY are the ones that invented what THEY call the necessary QUALIFICATIONS and TRAINING to get on the ballot. THEY ignored the Constitutions in doing this. THEY made up the rules for the elections. THEY ignored the Constitutions when THEY made these rules. THEY are afraid to compete with "We the human Christian American People" in an honest election because "We the human Christian American people" outnumber them. "We the human Christian American people's" primary insurance policy against the tyrants was the vote. The gun was the secondary or back-up insurance policy. THEY have cancelled the primary insurance policy by denying and refusing to count the people's vote and are now trying to cancel the secondary or back-up insurance policy by taking your guns. "We the human Christian American People" will always be destined to lose competing against THEM, in THEIR system, using THEIR rules while following the constitution. How do I know? Because I tried to compete against THEM in THEIR system, using THEIR rules while trying to follow the constitution and that is how I learned the truth. THEIR system and rules are hypocrisy. THEIR system and rules contradict the Constitutions. To that I have provided the evidence.

It is imperative that the voting insurance policy be renewed, i.e. reinstated according to the Constitutions. Without the vote, and without the Constitution in place, "We the human Christian American People" have no alternative but to resort to the backup insurance policy, i.e., the people's guns. But the time is real short. THEY have already developed the process by which to take your guns, thus taking the people's means to defend themselves against THEIR forces.

THEY are small in number and only constitute approximately 10-20% of the population. In a fight, THEY would lose and THEY know it, so THEY rule "We the human Christian American People" through fear, intimidation, coercion, lies, hatred, deceit, manipulation and force. THEY are doing everything they can to take away our means to defend ourselves against THEIR forces, and "We the human Christian American People" are allowing it to happen. THEY pit human against human.

I have spent much time writing about God-given constitutionally guaranteed rights in this book and how those in authority are violating those rights by being *manipulated through* deception and manipulating others through that same deception. I want to make it perfectly clear, along with God-given rights come responsibilities. The 10 Commandments are the "Safety" rules governing those rights. God said there were certain things he wanted and did not want human beings to do. We can choose not to obey those commandments, but we will be punished for so choosing. Those 10 Commandments are set up as our safety net against the "Evil One" and those that allow themselves to *be manipulated through deception*. Jesus Christ boiled it down to two basic concepts, one is to love God and the second is to love your neighbor as you love yourself. If people do these two simple things, everything else will automatically fall into place. Loving your neighbor as yourself basically means to treat others the way you want to be treated. By doing these two things, loving God, and treating others the way you want to be treated, you will have accepted the responsibility that comes with God-given rights.

I can safely say this because no one wants to be treated badly and everyone wants the rules and regulations to apply to everyone equally. No one wants to be murdered, cheated, robbed, lied too, have lies told about him or her or have their mate commit adultery. No one wants to have their nation attacked by another nation or have nuclear, biological or chemical weapons dumped on them, and I think if most people think about it, they do not like being mistreated in any manner. It will surprise most people how far an "I am sorry" or a helping hand will go when we hurt someone else. It is important to remember every other human being has the same God-given rights and that by having that individual's rights denied opens the door to having your rights denied. Look around you and think about what human beings are doing to other human beings due to *manipulation through deception*.

As human Christian Americans, we have a responsibility to our neighbors everywhere. I do not think that responsibility is to take what belongs to others, to attack others, to bomb others or to interfere in others national affairs. If help or advice is asked for, or the subject is brought up and indicated that advice or help is wanted, then I think it appropriate to lend a helping hand or provide the advice. If that help or advice is not wanted, then all that is needed is to say so and as human Christian Americans, we back off and tend to our own affairs.

Christian, Muslim, Buddhist, or what ever religion you are, the commandment is to love each other, not to point fingers at each other, not to kill each other, not to hate each other, and not to commit atrocities against each other. Human beings are not to kill each other or harm each other. Human beings are to do as Christ taught. Playing THEIR game THEIR way does nothing but lead to trouble. I know. I have allowed them to play THEIR game in my yard for 58 years, but no more. I want the rules to change, the game to be eliminated and to live life the way our founding fathers intended and that is in accordance with our Constitution and the Christian way to live that life. That is another responsibility that we, as human Christian American have, to ensure that very thing. Life is not a game. Games are for children to play in school playgrounds, video arcades and parks. Human lives and souls are the stakes in real life and yet THEY have made it into one big game for their entertainment and benefit.

Our government is not something that is to be taken lightly, and those that have allegedly been elected and chosen to govern haven't the authority to take that responsibility lightly. When those allegedly elected and chosen to govern allow themselves to be *manipulated through deception* into ignoring human being God-given rights and pass laws that favor one group over another group, then they are failing in that responsibility. Those people are abusing the authority provided them by God to govern the people.

When will human Christian Americans accept the responsibility and exercise the authority that it will take to get those allegedly elected and chosen to govern to stop their actions against human beings? What will it take to get human Christian Americans involved in their own nation's government? What is it going to take and how many more atrocities have to be committed before human Christian Americans accept the responsibility and exercise enough authority to put a stop to the politics game that is leading people into an enslaved hell?

Human Christian Americans teach that God sets up governments among men. Since that is the case then doesn't it make sense that He wants His people involved in operating those governments? So what makes human Christian Americans say that they are not to get involved in government? The answer to that question is manipulation through deception. The state teaches human Christians are not to get involved in government and then the religions teach it. I say this one more time, Christianity is not a religion it is a way to life.

America has become the land of the oppressed, depressed, apathetic, and complacent. America has become the home of the human Christian American Chicken. America has become a land that is allowing it's arms to be closed to all the other oppressed masses throughout the world and has grown selfish in its wealth. America has become the oppressor to the masses. "We the human Christian American People" have allowed ourselves to become the *manipulated through deception.* "We the human Christian American People" have allowed ourselves to become SLAVES.

THEY train us in the way THEY want us to interpret what we read, say and think. THEY train us in our religious believes and train us in what THEY want us to believe *The Bible* says, what the Constitutions say. THEY train us to believe the unbelievable, train us to believe false science, and then THEY train us not to believe the truth. THEY train us to kill each other. THEY train us to commit atrocities. THEY train us to hate. THEY train us to act like morons then frustrate us into doing moronic things, so they can punish us for doing as we were trained.

"What can I do?" you may ask. Look within yourself for the answer. Only, have the courage to follow what your heart tells you. The least that can happen is that you will learn the truth. I did. Using the Constitution as the evidence against THEIR "Rule of Law," I fought THEM within THEIR system in THEIR courts, using THEIR rules and laws, and the only way THEY won was by having the case dismissed. But at least I learned the truth. The Constitutions were the evidence, and THEY did not want that evidence presented before the people in a jury trial, which means the Constitutions, are more than enough evidence refuting THEIR "Rule of Law." THEY know this is factual, and THEY know THEY would have lost in a jury trial of my peers. THEY would or could not even present oral arguments supporting THEIR "Rule of Law" before THEIR own judge that what they are doing is Constitutional, because THEY know that THEIR "Rule of Law" IS unconstitutional.

Freedom: is a gift from God, and the price He paid for that freedom is His son. To keep that freedom there is also a price and that price has always been paid in blood. So that everyone can keep that precious gift called freedom, others may be required to make sacrifices and shed blood. Are you willing to make the sacrifices? Are you willing to put it all on the line when it counts? Are you as a human being, an American, a Christian ready to walk the walk?

Either you are for freedom or you are against freedom. If you are against freedom then that means you are for slavery and will continue to sleep with your heads hidden in the sand against seeing the real enemy. If you are for freedom you will take up that cross, your execution device, your weapon, and seek out the Reptiles truly causing the atrocities and chase that enemy back into the abyss from which they came.

The real enemy is not human but actually Reptilian disguised in human form. According to what others have written, even today, a few have actually seen the enemy and he looks like us, talks like us, and is among us. The enemy has a problem in that it cannot stay like us. If you do not believe *The Bible* or me perhaps you will believe other authors. After discovering what I discovered, a friend referred me to several books written by David Icke (pronounced Ike). Three such books are *The Children of the Matrix, And the Truth Shall Set You Free* and *The Biggest Secret*. I read *The Children of the Matrix*, and Mr. Icke names several people who have actually seen these beings change from human to reptilian. It seems the enemy has a difficult time maintaining the illusion that it is human and it is becoming more difficult as time progresses. The enemy's time is short and so is the time for human beings to act.

Now, how do we expose the enemy to the light? Perhaps by testing the spirits. 1 John chapter 4: 2-3 tells us how to test the spirits. *"By this you know the Spirit of God: every spirit that confesses that Jesus Christ has come in the flesh is from God; and every spirit that does not confess Jesus is not from God; this is the spirit of the antichrist, of which you have heard that is coming, and now it is already in the world.*

Perhaps another way is by blood tests. Do you notice that world leaders are treated in special medical facilities by special doctors? For what purpose is this done? Since all doctors go through the same training or specialty, aren't all doctors equally qualified in their specialty? THEY claim that many things can be determined today from blood, including DNA. I wonder how many world leaders actually have reptilian DNA?

Many that profess to believe in God's word, *The Bible*, and profess to be Christian will not believe what is written here in this book and will deny "THEY" exist. If *The Bible* is to be believed, and is not a fairy tale, then "THEY" do exist because *The Bible* says they exist. So, either one believes *The Bible* and believes THEY exist or *The Bible* is a fairy tale and cannot be believed. It cannot be both ways.

In his writings, Mr. Icke has indicated that there is a certain earth "frequency" that permits these beings to stay in human form, and that the frequency is changing making it extremely difficult for "THEM" to remain in human form. That is the reason for the big push to get a one-world government in place. If this is the situation, then it is imperative that human beings work together to find a way to disrupt that frequency to expose these beings for what they are so that they can be stopped and/or destroyed before they can complete their conspiracy to totally enslave mankind.

I am positive there are others that know the truth and the only thing that keeps those individuals from coming forward and speaking out is fear that other human beings will label them insane, weird, a nut case, conspiracy theorist, etc. Silence is exactly what THEY rely on because the more people speaking about the truth, the more THEY are exposed. Perhaps that is the "frequency" that will truly expose THEM.

The only real choices "We the Human Beings" have on this slave ship called planet earth is between slavery and freedom, Christ and the antichrist, a good system or an evil system, a system rooted in hate or a system rooted in love.

SYNONYM GAME:
HUMAN BEING = HUMAN KIND = HUMAN RACE = PEOPLE

You now have the truth. You have been provided evidence and now know human beings are slaves. You have been shown the methodology, the tools and the templates used to keep human beings in that condition. You have been provided evidence through the atrocities being committed against your fellow human beings. The real enemy has been revealed and you have been provided *Biblical* evidence THEY exist. Now do with that truth, as you will. Your time is short. Choose.

There is no real ending to this book because each day the atrocities abound. It will be up to those who profess to be human Christians to decide what they want to do with the truth about the *Evil One* and the system that has been created in this nation, in this world. Legend has it that St. Patrick drove The Snakes (*Evil One*) from Ireland. Who will drive The Snakes (*Evil One*) from America and from the earth? Who will drive *the Evil One*, the viper's brood, from this world back into the abyss from which they came? *The Bible* says it will be Jesus Christ. Until that time, human Christians have a responsibility to stand against the Evil One and its system here on this earth.

I personally challenge any within the viper's brood and/or within the system about which I speak to come forward and deny that about which I have written in this book.

"Beware the leader who bangs the drums of war in order to whip the citizenry into a patriotic fervor, for patriotism is indeed a double-edged sword. It both emboldens the blood, just as it narrows the mind. And when the drums of war have reached a fever pitch and the blood boils with hate and the mind has closed, the leader will have no need in seizing the rights of the citizenry. Rather, the citizenry, infused with fear and blinded by patriotism, will offer up all of their rights unto the leader and gladly so. How do I know? For this is what I have done. And I am Caesar."—Attributed to Shakespeare's Julius Caesar, although the real author is apparently unkown
   Amen.

References used or quoted in writing this book include:

Declaration of Independence, signed 1776
U.S. Constitution
Oregon Constitution
Oregon Revised Statues
Oregon 1999-2000 Election Law
Oregon 2000 County Candidates Manual
Jackson County Circuit Court Case # 004001Z3
Home Rule Charter of Jackson County Oregon
Life's Personal Experiences and observations
Other human being's experiences
Famous quotes obtained from Internet correspondence
Associated press article written by Tom Hays Reprinted with permission of the Associated Press
Scripture taken from the NEW AMERICAN STANDARD BIBLE®, Copyright © 1960, 1962, 1963, 1968, 1971, 1972, 1973, 1975, 1977, 1995 by the Lockman Foundation. Used by permission.
Definitions provided are composites created from the legal and standard definitions.
Information for writing this manual was also gathered from the following references although exact quotes were not used due to copyright:
Webster's New Collegiate Dictionary (1977 Edition), Copyright ©1977 by G. & C Merriam Co.
Black's Law Dictionary Abridged Sixth Edition, West Publishing Company, Copyright ©1991 Permission to quote not granted.
Blacks Law Dictionary Seventh Edition, West Group, Copyright ©1999 Permission to quote not granted.
Roget's 21st Century Thesaurus, Second Edition, Copyright, ©1999 by the Philip Lief Group, Inc.
American Jurisprudence 2nd Edition, Volume 16 Constitutional Law. Copyright © 1998. Permission to quote was not requested due to being denied permission to quote legal definitions.
Medford *Mail Tribune*, Medford, Oregon permission to quote requested but was not received.
Paul Harvey News
KCMX 880 talk radio shows, Medford, Oregon
Fox News and every news and information source heard daily by the people.

Printed in the United States
1266600003B/106